Praise for

Beach House
for Rent

"Reading this novel feels like a long, luxurious trip to the beach. Mary Alice Monroe writes gorgeously, with authority and tenderness, about the natural world and its power to inspire, transport, and to heal. Readers will love this story of two unforgettable women—one reeling from an unexpected tragedy, the other drawn into a daring and passionate new love."

—#1 *New York Times* bestselling author Susan Wiggs

"Mary Alice Monroe understands that a house is never just a house. As we revisit the Beach House, we are immersed in the heartbeat and pulse of her South Carolina Lowcountry as never before. Monroe's singular ability to blend the natural world with the emotional world allows for a gorgeous novel, wondrously both bittersweet and also life-affirming. The story reveals its secrets with shorebirds and human hearts at the center of its graceful axis. No one else tells an insightful and powerful story quite like Mary Alice Monroe—and in *Beach House for Rent*, you won't be able to stop reading—for even that glass of sweet tea."

—*New York Times* bestselling author Patti Callahan Henry

"Monroe's newest installation in her Beach House series also serves as stand-alone novel, but faithful readers will recognize her ability to blend uniquely human stories with pressing environmental issues. Fans of Mary Kay Andrews and Mary Simses will adore this novel of simple pleasures, shifting priorities, and the power of self-discovery. Tender and inspiring with a touch of romance, it's just the thing to fill an empty beach bag."

—*Booklist*

". . . a charming and poignant story ideal for summer reading."

—*PopSugar*

". . . a skilled storyteller who never lets her readers down . . . [Mary Alice Monroe] makes Isle of Palms come enticingly alive, calling all readers to this garden of paradise which is just ripe for a visit. Mary Alice Monroe creates characters that you wish/hope could be real people so that they could become your friends. And you feel if you could visit the Lowcountry they would be there waiting."

—*Huffington Post*

"[Mary Alice Monroe's] hallmark knack for plumbing the inner depths of her characters and connecting them with one another in ways that feel perfectly organic—all the while weaving in those environmental issues near and dear to her heart—is a winning formula that's made Monroe one of the most beloved authors in the nation and a well-known champion of conservation causes."

—*SCNow*

"[Readers] will delight in this latest novel featuring women who need the healing power of nature."

—*Library Journal*, starred review

"*Beach House for Rent* is choice property."

—*Star News*

Mary Alice Monroe

Beach House *for* Rent

GALLERY BOOKS

New York   London   Toronto   Sydney   New Delhi

G

Gallery Books
An Imprint of Simon & Schuster, Inc.
1230 Avenue of the Americas
New York, NY 10020

First Gallery Books paperback edition March 2018

GALLERY BOOKS and colophon are registered trademarks of Simon & Schuster, Inc.

For information about special discounts for bulk purchases, please contact Simon & Schuster Special Sales at 1-866-506-1949 or business@simonandschuster.com.

The Simon & Schuster Speakers Bureau can bring authors to your live event. For more information or to book an event contact the Simon & Schuster Speakers Bureau at 1-866-248-3049 or visit our website at www.simonspeakers.com.

Interior design by Davina Mock-Maniscalco

Manufactured in the United States of America

20   19   18   17   16   15   14   13   12   11

Library of Congress Cataloging-in-Publication Data is available.

ISBN 978-1-5011-2546-1
ISBN 978-1-5011-2552-2 (pbk)
ISBN 978-1-5011-2551-5 (ebook)

For Louise Burke and Jennifer Bergstrom
With great love and deep appreciation

Dear Reader,

If you are like me, you love to walk the beach and see flocks of shorebirds and seabirds gathered at the water's edge . . . pelicans gliding gracefully over the sea in formation . . . peeps playing tag with the waves. Shorebirds are some of the world's most amazing migrants. Many species journey thousands of miles each year. During their travels, they stop to rest and fuel at important way stations, which is critical for their survival. Disturbances force them to use vital energy. For nesting birds, the parents must leave their nest exposing eggs and/or young to predation. Surveys of migrant shorebirds in the last three decades indicate most shorebirds are in serious decline.

Many of my readers ask, *What can I do to help?*

There are simple but crucially important steps you can take to make a difference.

- Do not let dogs or children chase or scatter shorebirds. Leash dogs when shorebirds are near. Honestly, if we just do this we will have made a difference!
- Keep away from posted nesting and feeding areas. You can unknowingly step on nests.
- Be aware of birds calling loudly nearby, which indicates that you are too close to nests or chicks.
- Avoid the ends of barrier islands, inlets, and remote stretches of beach where birds cluster. Again, don't let your dogs run free in these areas.
- Take your trash with you.

- Avoid landing boats on small islands where birds (i.e. pelicans) nest.
- Make certain all fishing line and hooks are cleared away after use and not left in the water.
- Teach your children and grandchildren to appreciate shorebirds and seabirds. They are tomorrow's stewards!

With your help, our beloved shorebirds will be here for future generations to enjoy.

Mary Alice Monroe

Part One

ARRIVAL

Barbara J. Bergwerf

RED KNOT

One of the largest sandpipers, red knots are bulky with a medium-size bill and ruddy-colored plumage in the breeding season. A large portion of the species travel thousands of miles to spend the winter in the southern part of South America, while another portion of the species spends the winter on the southeastern coast of the United States. Knots nest each year in high arctic regions. Overall, the number of red knots has declined nearly 75 percent over the last fifteen years.

Conservation status: *Greatest Concern*

Chapter One

T HE BEACH HOUSE sat perched on a dune overlooking the Atlantic Ocean. Small and yellow, it blended in with the waves of sweetgrass and sea oats and the delicate yellow primroses for which the cottage was named. For eighty-five years it had endured the fury of hurricanes, the rush of tidal surges, and the ravages of the salt-tinged air. It had withstood the test of time.

The beach house was a survivor.

As was she, Cara Rutledge thought, staring up at the house. She held a paintbrush in one hand and, shading her eyes from the gentle rays of the sun with the other, surveyed the fresh coat of gleaming white paint she'd just finished applying to the front porch and railings. How many times had she painted these porches? she wondered. Or repaired the pergola, fixed the plumbing, trimmed the shrubs and trees? Living by the sea was a constant exercise in the art of nip and tuck, especially for an old cottage like Primrose. But she didn't mind the time or expense. She would repair and paint it every year she could still lift a paintbrush or afford a plumber.

Because even more than the historic house on Tradd Street in Charleston, or the treasured, centuries-old family antiques that filled the Rutledge family's home, this modest 1930s beach house held the real memories of her family.

Only the good memories, she corrected herself with a wistful smile as her thoughts floated back to the halcyon days of her childhood.

When she was growing up, summer meant leaving the bustle and noise of Charleston and coming out to Primrose Cottage on the Isle of Palms with her mother, Olivia, and older brother, Palmer. It might have been only a trip across the Grace Bridge, some twenty miles, but back in the day, the change was so significant they might as well have journeyed to another country. Many of the girls she knew from school spent summers at family cottages on Sullivan's Island. But her mother claimed she preferred the relative isolation and the maritime forest on Isle of Palms. Cara, too, had preferred the Huck Finn lifestyle of Isle of Palms, where her mother would open the screen door and let her children run wild till the dinner bell at 5 p.m.

Cara sighed, slipping into the vortex of memories. Her gaze scanned the quaint cottage under the brilliant azure sky. She had achieved many lifetime firsts here. She'd learned to swim on the beach just beyond the house, kissed her first boyfriend on the back porch, confided secrets with her best friend, Emmi, over cookies and sweet tea in the kitchen, broken her first bone falling from the live oak tree that thrived until Hurricane Hugo blew it down. She'd caught her first fish from Hamlin Creek on the back of the island, and made love with Brett amid the clicking sea oats on the dunes. Of all her memories, those of the man she'd fallen in love with late in life, married, and forged a new life with here on Isle of Palms were the sweetest.

Cara closed her eyes and took a deep breath, inhaling the sweet sea air. She heard the sounds of the island—the soft humming of bees, the purr of the ocean. She felt the caress of a breeze ruffle her hair. Whenever she had memories of the beach house, the image of her mother formed in her mind. Olivia Rutledge, affectionately known as Lovie—slight, ageless, her blond hair pulled back into a stylish chignon, her blue eyes shining with warmth. Opening her eyes, Cara almost expected to see her mother walking around the corner carrying the red turtle team bucket.

Primrose Cottage had been her mother's beach house. No, Cara thought on reflection. More than her house. The cottage had been her mother's sanctuary. Her place of refuge. Her source of inspiration. Lovie had come here to escape the burdens of her social obligations in Charleston. On the island she was free to pursue her passion—sea turtles. Lovie had been the Isle of Palms's first "sea turtle lady." She'd formed the first turtle team. She'd even named her only daughter Caretta, after the Latin name for the loggerhead, much to Cara's lifelong chagrin.

They'd been close when she was young, but as Cara grew tall and statuesque, her opinions matured as well. She'd found herself growing increasingly distant from her mother—in fact, from both her parents.

Especially her father.

When Cara was eighteen, to her traditional father Stratton Rutledge's disappointment, she had refused to become the southern belle she was expected to be. Her hair was too dark, her feet too big. She was too tall, too bookish, and far too independent-minded. After graduating high school with honors, Cara had informed her parents, in a tone of voice that implied she was well aware they would not approve, that she wasn't going to the local college they'd selected for her but would instead attend a northeastern college. Perhaps Boston University. Maybe even Harvard. She was proud she'd been accepted. Her father, however, wasn't accustomed to back talk, especially from his daughter.

"Who the hell do you think you are, little girl?" he'd roared, his voice echoing in the large dining room of their grand home. Her mother had sat quietly at the other end of the table, her eyes meekly downcast. "You'll do as I say. And if you step one foot outside this town—out of this house—that'll tear it between us, you hear? You leave and you'll not get one dollar, not one stick of furniture, not so much as a nod of the head when you pass me or your mother on the street, hear?"

But Cara was more like her father than he'd realized. She'd turned heel and run as far away from her parents, that house, Charleston, and all the expectations and demands of a southern woman from South of Broad as she could get, heading to points north to seek her freedom, fame, and fortune. Her father was as good as his word. He'd cut her off and never looked back. He refused to pay her tuition, so she'd never gone to a prestigious Boston college. Instead she'd nailed an interview for an entry-level position at an advertising firm in Chicago, and had gone to night school for seven years while working full-time, finally earning her degree in communications. She'd climbed the corporate ladder and, though she wasn't wealthy, she'd achieved success on her own merit. Cara had come home only once, for her brother's wedding, and sent a handful of Christmas and birthday cards over the years. There was the occasional phone call with her mother. Her relationship with her family was polite at best.

When her father died, Cara returned home for his funeral. Like the man he'd been throughout his lifetime, his will was cold and vindictive. As Stratton had sworn all those years ago, he didn't leave her as much as a stick of furniture. Cara had neither expected nor wanted anything from him. But the silence from her mother upon finding out that he'd made good on his pledge had hurt.

Then, on Cara's fortieth birthday, her mother had written asking her to come home for a visit. And she'd obliged. A weekend at the beach house had turned into a summer of reconciliation.

"Oh, Mama," she whispered so softly that her voice was carried off by the breeze. Cara had lost Lovie again to cancer right after they'd found each other once more. Even after ten years, Cara's heart yearned for her.

Her father had left everything to Palmer. But the beach house was her mother's, and when Lovie died she'd left it to Cara, knowing she would care for Primrose Cottage—and all the secrets associated with it—with the love and attention to detail that Lovie herself had exhibited. And Cara had fulfilled that promise.

Studying the beach house in the softening light of day's end, Cara shook her head ruefully. If someone had told her when she was eighteen that decades later she'd be back on the Isle of Palms as mistress of Primrose Cottage, she would have laughed out loud with disbelief.

But here she was, turning fifty, living on the Isle of Palms again, married to the love of her life and giving Primrose Cottage yet another coat of paint. "What goes around comes around," her mother used to say. Cara chortled and shook her head. As usual, her mother was right.

Cara rolled her stiff shoulders, then traipsed across the sand and wildflowers to the waiting bucket of soapy water. She set her brush to soak, then put her hands on her back and once again stretched her aching muscles. Fifty certainly wasn't the new forty, not in Cara's opinion anyway.

No more daydreaming, she told herself as her usual practical, no-nonsense attitude kicked in. Rental season was around the corner and there was a lot left to do—and she couldn't afford to hire anyone else. She was committed to keeping the beach house up to the standards set by her mother. Still, she'd miscalculated the strength of the early spring sun and she could feel the pinpricks of sunburn on her arms.

The sound of a car pulling up the gravel driveway distracted her. She stopped studying her arm and looked over her shoulder to see her brother's gleaming white Mercedes sedan easing to a stop. He gave a gentle toot of the horn to herald his arrival. She chuckled, thinking Palmer always arrived with fanfare. She removed the man's denim shirt irretrievably splattered with paint, one of Brett's rejects, from over her black T-shirt and tossed it on a nearby wheelbarrow. The front car door swung open and one polished slip-on tasseled loafer peeked out from the car, then Palmer Rutledge hoisted himself out with a muffled grunt.

At fifty-two, Palmer was two years older than Cara, but he looked a good decade older, thanks to the bloated, florid face and the paunch at his waist from his lifestyle as a businessman and successful real estate maven. While his habits had led to a less-than-healthy physique, Cara couldn't deny that Palmer had an enviable sense of style. Even as a boy he'd always been an impeccable dresser, a sharp contrast to Cara's tattered, beachy sartorial choices. Today he wore a tan golf jacket over a polo shirt and pressed khakis. Cara wiped the flecks of paint from her hands onto her torn jeans and took a step toward him, a smile of welcome spread across her tanned face.

"Palmer!" she exclaimed with an exuberant wave. "Come to see how the other half lives?"

Her brother held out his arms and she walked into them for a bear hug, highlighting the physical ease and sense of closeness that they shared as children remained. Cara believed their mother's death had made them not simply orphans, but all too aware of their own mortality.

"That's enough of that," Palmer said with a low laugh, gently disentangling himself. "You smell ripe, sister mine."

"Thanks," Cara replied breezily, not in the least embarrassed. "Comes from decent hard work."

"Mama never lifted a paintbrush in her delicate hands."

"Mama had more money than me. And, brother mine, I believe you do, too. So if the sight of my chipped nails and paint-splattered clothes offends you, kindly offer me the funds to hire out."

"I'd love to, honey, but we both know Julia spends every penny I earn faster than sand through fingers." Palmer rolled his eyes as he so often did when speaking of his socially conscious, designer-driven wife. His gaze shifted to the cottage. "Nice job," he said. Then he slanted her a look. "Do *you* hire out?"

Cara slapped his arm teasingly. "Don't get me started."

"Seriously," Palmer said, crossing his arms over his belly, "the place looks good. Real good."

"It's a pretty place," she said, looking again at the beach house. And it was true. With its mullioned windows and broad porch filled with baskets of ferns and white rockers, she'd always thought that it was a picturesque image of a lowcountry cottage. "Say what you will about all these mansions," she said with another wave of her hand, indicating the enormous newer houses. "You can't buy that old-world charm."

"You ever been in those big houses?" Palmer teased. He looked around, searching. "So where's your better half?"

"Brett is out back building a new pergola over the enclosed back porch. He's worked so hard on it. It's almost done, and I have to say it turned out so well."

"Wait," Palmer said, holding up his hand. "What enclosed porch?"

"You haven't seen it yet, have you?" Cara asked in surprise. Though Palmer and Julia lived just over the bridge in Charleston with their two children, Linnea and Cooper, she and they didn't spend time together outside of family events and holidays. Cara doted on her niece and nephew, but with school and social schedules it seemed everyone was always too busy. "Come on 'round. Brett will want to show it off. He did all the work himself."

"That man sure is handy," Palmer said as he followed her.

Cara knew he meant it as a compliment. Palmer had tried for years to get Brett involved in flipping houses, especially on the islands. But Brett was as stubborn as he was talented. He truly loved working with wood. He was as much a craftsman as a builder. Like so much else in his life, he did things his own way and wouldn't be hurried.

She led the way around the cottage, her shoes crunching in the dry sand and shells. Cara kept the property wild, as nature had intended. Only palm trees, wild grasses, and flowers sprouted on her property, especially in the spring, when the island was practically bursting with life. Wildflowers colored the dunes with soft yellows, vibrant blues, and fiery oranges. In the trees birds sang out mating calls, while overhead migrating birds soared, returning home from southern climes.

This side of the beach house faced the long stretch of dunes that reached out to the Atlantic Ocean. The mighty sea reflected the mood of the sky—sometimes dark, turbulent, and gloomy, other times a soft, introspective gray-blue. Today the water was the color of unbridled joy and hope, a blue so vivid the horizon line disappeared where sea met sky, creating an infinite stretch of blue. Sunlight danced on the ocean, making it appear a living, breathing thing. Cara paused to stare out in awe. The dazzling sea always had the power to take her breath away.

"Beautiful day," Palmer said with gusto, rocking back on his heels and echoing her thoughts.

"It is," she replied softly, sharing the moment with her brother.

"And a stunning view. I've always said that," he added, then gestured toward the ocean. "No houses standing in the way. You've got a straight shot to the sea with that vacant lot in front of you."

His words broke through her quiet reverie as she realized

Palmer wasn't appreciating the spiritual quality of the view, but rather the commercial value. He spoke as if she didn't realize all these fine points of her own home. Going for the hard sell, as always. She turned her head to scrutinize him.

Her brother was, in fact, wearing business attire, she suddenly realized, not the sporty shorts and Tommy Bahama shirts he wore for leisure. His gold signet ring caught the sunlight and drew her attention to the papers he was carrying in his doughy hand. Cara sighed inwardly, even as she steeled her resolve.

This wasn't a social call. Palmer had come on business. Without speaking, she turned the corner of the house toward the back.

"Whoa," Palmer exclaimed. He paused, hands on hips, to take in the new sunroom attached to the back of the house, the new deck spreading the entire width of the sunroom, with stairs leading out to the dunes. "What have you and Brett been up to?"

"This is what I wanted to show you," she replied, excited to show off the project that had dominated their lives the past several months. "We enclosed the old porch and gained so much more space, all facing the ocean. We just love it. And then, of course, we will finish the deck. You can see the outline," she said, pointing to the wooden frame. "It will spread the entire width of the sunroom with stairs leading out to the dunes. Mama would roll over in her grave if we didn't have a proper deck overlooking the ocean. And if you recall, Brett repaired Mama's pergola every time the wind blew it down."

"I do recall."

"So after we enclosed the porch, Brett built this pergola in her honor."

Palmer's face softened. "Did he really?"

She nodded as she surveyed the thick, treated wood of the pergola. Once it was sun-cured, she'd paint it a glistening white.

"When Brett's done with the pergola, we'll put out the rocking chairs." She smiled at the memory of sitting with her mother on the back porch in companionable silence night after night that final summer. "Mama would be so pleased."

The sound of hammering drew her gaze upward. Brett was perched on top of a paint-splattered ladder, hammering nails into the pergola with focus. Brett was a big man, broad-shouldered and fit. He wore ragged tan shorts, a faded plaid shirt with rolled-up sleeves, and scuffed work boots, revealing the leathery, tawny skin of a seaman. Her mind flashed back to when she'd returned home that fateful summer and had seen him hanging on the nets of a shrimp boat, every bit as dashing as Errol Flynn. Brett Beauchamps was the love of her life, and even after ten years of marriage, bits of gray hair notwithstanding, the sight of him could still make her swoon.

She tented her hand over her eyes as she looked up at him in the fierce sunlight. "Brett!" she called. "Honey!"

The hammering stopped and he turned her way. She couldn't see his eyes behind his Ray-Ban sunglasses.

"Palmer's here! Come on down."

Brett lifted his hand in acknowledgment. "Be down in a minute," he called back. "Almost done."

One of Brett's strengths was his work ethic. He was tireless, pushing himself without pause. She knew he wouldn't stop until the job was done, and done right.

Cara chuckled. "That means he'll be a while. Let's go inside," she told Palmer. "I'll show you the inside of the sunroom."

Palmer followed her as they crossed the work zone, his gait slow and measured. Cara watched as Palmer walked around the sunroom, his head swinging from left to right to take in the new glass doors, swung wide open to admit the balmy breeze of the mercurial spring weather, the Mexican tile on the floor, the tall green plants and white wicker chairs with cushy, bright blue cushions. She'd decorated the space in clean lines to allow the undistracted eye to seek out the ocean beyond. This view was what the tourists came for, she knew. Twenty years as a successful advertising executive in Chicago had taught her a few lessons.

"Very nice," Palmer said after several moments of silence. He crossed his arms and faced her. "Must've set you back a few pennies."

Cara was disappointed by his lackluster response. "More than pennies," she replied soberly. "We found some termite damage on the porch and figured why not bite the bullet and build the sunroom we'd wanted to all these years, instead of making do with more repairs? Look how much more space we've added. And that's a sleeper sofa. So we can raise the rent a bit. We figure it'll all equal out in time." She shrugged. "Unless we get hit with another hurricane."

"Always a possibility."

"I know," she acknowledged ruefully. "With climate change

and the sea levels rising, I've seen for myself how much beach we lose every year. Of course, that's the job of the dunes, to protect the inland property. But we've never seen the dunes just swept clear away. It's becoming the new norm."

Palmer rolled his eyes and put his hands up in an arresting motion. "Now, let's not start talking climate change. We always lose some beach, and it always comes back."

Cara couldn't stand his patronizing tone, but didn't want to get into another round of debate on the reality of climate change with her older brother. It wasn't worth it, and she only ended up infuriating herself. He'd say the moon was a wheel of cheese if it sold a house. She allowed him the final word.

"How about some sweet tea? I made a fresh batch for Brett. Put a sprig of mint in it, too. My herbs are up. God, I love spring."

She led Palmer from the sunroom into the main house. Here nothing had changed since their youth, save perhaps for there being fewer of the knickknacks, family photographs, and books that her mother had cluttered the house with. Like many women of her generation, the older Lovie had got, the more reluctant she became to throw anything away. Every photo had to be saved, every memento ensconced on a shelf. When Cara inherited the house she'd promptly cleared away the clutter, painted the rooms a soft ocean blue trimmed neatly with clean white, replaced the family oriental rugs with ones made of grass, and selected only a few pieces from her mother's vast art collection to remain on the walls. But she'd kept the timeless chintz chairs and sofa with their Palm Beachy flowered pattern. The result was a house still filled with her mother's furniture, art, and most prized possessions, but with a younger, fresher feel.

"The place looks good, Sister," Palmer said.

"Why thanks," she said, striding with her long legs to the small galley kitchen.

Here changes had been made as well from when the house had been under Lovie's purview. Even while her mama was still alive, Cara had repainted the old white wooden cabinets, but over the past few years she'd replaced all the old appliances with gleaming stainless steel ones. She opened the fridge and pulled out the pitcher of tea. Although she'd provided a new set of white dishes for the rentals, she still kept her mother's old china locked in an out-of-the way cabinet for her own use on the few nights she came here to sleep in her mother's bed. Cara retrieved a key from the back of a drawer and unlocked the cabinet. Smiling at seeing the mismatched china and crystal her mother had enjoyed using at the beach house, Cara reached for two of the old Waterford cut-crystal tall glasses. She quickly added ice, poured two glasses of tea, and handed one to Palmer. She watched, pleased, as he drank thirstily. When he finished, he released a long, satisfied sigh.

"Sister mine, you make some good sweet tea. You ought to give the recipe to Julia."

"She should already have it. It's Mama's recipe. It's making the syrup first that's the secret."

"Ah," he said with a sigh of understanding, adding with a sorry shake of his head, "she won't do it. She's always adding that fake sweetener to my drinks, telling me I've got to lose weight." He patted his belly. "I don't need to lose weight. Hell," he said proudly, "this paunch is a symbol of my prosperity."

He laughed, a low, throaty chortle that prompted her to join in even as she inwardly agreed with Julia. Her brother had gained at least fifteen pounds in the last decade, but Cara wasn't going to be the one to tell him. She suspected Julia told him often enough as it was.

He took another long swallow from his drink, then smacked his lips, his gaze sweeping the rooms again. "This house isn't worth putting any more money into." Palmer turned to face her. His blue eyes shone under brows gathered in concern. "I've told you time and time again, the value of this place is in the land."

Cara groaned loudly, shaking her head. *Here we go*, she thought. Their mama had once told her that Palmer was the sort of person who was always hungry for more, in both a literal and a figurative sense. He was never satisfied. Palmer was like their father this way. Palmer had been angry when he'd learned that Mama was leaving Cara the beach house, even though he'd already inherited the big house on Tradd Street and all its expensive contents. But Palmer wanted the beach house, too. Not because he loved it, but because he'd always had big plans for developing the property.

"Hell, one of these days you're going to listen. Look at that empty lot out there. It's a gold mine."

"And one of these days you'll accept that lot can't be touched," she fired back. "Russell Bennett left that land in conservation."

"We might could get around that," he said with a dismissive wave. Whenever her brother slipped into the vernacular, she knew he was deep in thought. Palmer looked out at the empty lot in front of them the way Cara looked at the ocean. Where she saw beauty and felt a near-spiritual sense of awakening, he saw dollar signs.

"It's got to be the only waterfront lot left on this entire island. Even if you don't build on it, you've got this house with guaranteed views. His eyes were brightening as he got deeper into his sales pitch. "The real estate market has bounced back, and strong. The demand is high. Now's the time to act."

Cara didn't grace him with a reply. She picked up her glass and turned her head away to look out the window as she sipped her tea.

Palmer sighed and put his hands on the table. "Okay, okay. I'll give up the hard sell. But listen to me, Sister. The reason I'm trying to get you to sell the beach house now—aside from the fact that it's a good idea—is because I'm involved with a new business venture that should reap big profits."

He paused and waited for her to look back at him. His eyes gleamed.

"I'm talking really big. This one investment could put you in high cotton. For life. Now," he drawled and lifted his palms. "What kind of a brother would I be if I didn't share the opportunity with my beloved sister?"

Cara looked at him with thinly veiled interest. "What business venture is this?"

Palmer leaned in and talked in a lower, more urgent voice as though in secret. "It's a new housing development."

"I thought you just flipped the occasional house. This sounds risky."

He shook his head. "No, ma'am. The location is going to explode. It's all hush-hush until word of the new highway extension is announced. But the inside scoop is that it's a done deal. I know this town and I'm telling you, I'm all in."

Cara listened, chewing her lip. She'd love nothing more than to get in early on a deal like this. Palmer had good contacts that went deep in the city's politics. The kind that were forged in school days. God knew, she and Brett needed the money. But their financial situation wasn't such that they could consider big investments.

"We don't have any money to invest," she said. "Frankly, we're strapped."

Palmer leaned back, clearly disappointed. "I'd loan you some. That's how much I believe in this project. But all my money is already tied up in this deal."

"Doesn't matter," she said with a hint of annoyance at her situation. "We couldn't pay you back. Our money's completely tied up in the business."

Palmer turned his head to spear her with a no-nonsense gaze. "So I'm left to wonder . . . why are you wasting good money fixing up this old cottage, when you could make a fortune tearing it down and selling the land."

When her brother talked like this, his tone and body language eerily reminded her of their father's. And a more pugnacious, proud, callous man she'd never met.

"Palmer, just stop," she shot back in a tone that brooked no argument.

A voice broke the sudden, awkward silence. "Palmer, are you still trying to convince Cara to sell this house?"

Brett stood at the sunroom entrance, a lazy grin on his handsome face. His long arms stretched out as he leaned against the doorframe. The man filled the doorway with his size. His face was flushed from exertion, but Cara immediately recognized the relaxed manner that always came from having finished a tough job to his satisfaction.

Palmer walked toward his brother-in-law with his hand extended and the two men shook hands warmly. Friends since they'd been surfing buddies in their youth, they'd followed diverging paths as adults when Palmer assumed his role in old Charleston society and Brett, indifferent to the social hierarchy, followed his passion as a boat captain on the sea.

"Brother, don't you have any control over your wife?" Palmer asked jovially.

"Brother," Brett replied with a slap on Palmer's back, "don't you know your sister yet? Nobody has control over her."

"At least over her pocketbook."

Cara was practically seething, but Brett just laughed. The guy was unflappable, just one of the many reasons she loved him. "She runs the books, did you forget?" Brett stepped to Cara's side and slipped his arm around her waist, as though sensing she needed the extra comfort. "So what's up?"

"I'm trying to convince the little lady that she needs to sell this place before dumping any more money into it."

Cara knew he was prodding her, using phrases like "little

lady," knowing they'd find their mark. "It's our money. Don't worry about it."

"If you get off your high horse and sell the beach house and invest in this deal, you can make a fortune," Palmer urged. "Hell, even if you don't do the deal, you'd make a small fortune just selling the house."

Brett dropped his arm from Cara and put his hand on his hip and looked at Palmer more attentively.

"Seriously?"

"I'm telling you . . ."

"The market's that good?" Brett rocked on his heels. "How much could we get for this place? Just a ballpark figure."

"Brett," Cara interjected testily, trying to ward him off the topic.

"No harm in asking," Brett said.

Palmer was like any fisherman who feels the first tug on the line. He rubbed his jaw and took a step closer to Brett. When he spoke, it was in that man-to-man tone that set Cara's teeth on edge. Palmer didn't even realize he'd turned his back on Cara.

Or, more likely, he absolutely did.

"Hard to be exact. Depends on whether you want to build a house yourself—and you could, you know," he added in an encouraging tone. "The land alone is worth over a million dollars. The house . . ." He gave the rooms a cursory glance, then sighed. "It'd be considered a teardown."

"That's it," Cara said sharply. "Don't even suggest that."

"Stop being so sentimental," Palmer said, and this time his voice wasn't teasing but more persuasive. "You're just going to turn down all that money? And for what? You don't even live in the house! You spend year after year patching the old place up. What for? The measly rent? What are you hanging on to? Mama is dead, God rest her soul. No one misses her more than me. But she isn't coming back to this house, Cara. She's never going to see everything you've done and tell you she's proud of you for it. Mama's gone. You've got to face that."

Cara swallowed hard. These rooms signified more than a house to her. This house was not just her mother's touchstone, she realized. It was hers as well. If she sold the beach house, she'd be selling a part of herself. The best part.

If Palmer had left it at that, peace would have prevailed.

"Besides, Cara, who are you saving this old beach house for?"

The pain came so quick and sharp Cara sucked in her breath. She felt Brett's arm settle on her shoulder with a reassuring squeeze. Palmer was unaware of the dagger he'd thrown. The father of two children, he couldn't understand her and Brett's sense of loss. Not having children was their single greatest regret.

Cara couldn't stop the anger that sparked from the comment. She stepped out of Brett's hold toward her brother. At five feet ten inches, Cara was eye-to-eye with her brother. Cara had moved on from her corporate life. Even though in the past ten years she had adopted Brett's more laid-back low-country lifestyle, vestiges of her former ball-busting self still emerged when pushed. Cara stared Palmer down with an icy glare that would have sent shivers through her former colleagues in the boardroom at Leo Burnett.

"Let me make myself perfectly clear," Cara said, her voice more strident than she'd intended. She pointed a digit near his face. "This house is not now, nor ever will be, for sale. Got it?" Her rising emotion brought her to a shout. "The beach house is for rent!"

Chapter Two

THE SKY WAS deepening from periwinkle to purple by the time Cara and Brett locked up the beach house that evening and headed home. Overhead the birds were silent as a great hush settled over the lowcountry; in the cab of Brett's pickup truck, things were just as silent.

The rumbling truck made its way north on Palm Boulevard to the back of the island. It was a short journey that felt like many miles amid the pensive, heavy mood that permeated the cab. Yes, they were both exhausted from the day's work. But Cara suspected their prolonged silence had more to do with Palmer's visit and less with fatigue.

Brett turned off before a small stucco house partially hidden from the street by an enormous live oak that spread its thick, twisting boughs like a fan. The house on the creek had been Brett's home back when they were dating. The first time Cara had seen it, she'd laughed out loud at the cotton-candy-pink façade. Only someone as confident in his manhood as Brett could have a pink house, she'd remarked, giggling. After they'd married, they'd decided to live there and rent Cara's beach house. The income was greater for a place with an ocean view. But more, Cara wasn't ready to live in a house she'd always felt truly belonged to her mother.

The slamming of the truck doors echoed in the quiet night. They made their way up the tabby walkway to their front door. The house was painted a soft gray now, at Cara's urging, and trimmed in white to create a clean, tranquil aesthetic. Black shutters bordered the windows, and azalea bushes along the front porch held buds that would soon burst into color. Cara had painted the front door a bold cherry red. She was comfortable here and it felt like home. Brett unlocked the door and held it open for her. They both were moving slowly after the long day of physical labor and emotional gymnastics at the hands of Palmer.

"I'll make a salad," Cara offered automatically, setting her bundles of painting equipment and purse on the chair by the front door.

"I'll start the grill."

Brett followed her into the kitchen to grab a beer from the fridge. She heard the soft pop of the cap flipping off. Husband and wife fell into their pattern: he grilled, and she made the sides. So much of their life had slipped into a comfortable routine, she thought, from what time they awoke and went to bed to who slept on which side of the bed. Who did the grocery shopping and who went to the hardware store. Who took out the garbage, who got the mail. It was all unspoken. Comfortable. Predictable. As she approached fifty, Cara wondered if this was what it meant to grow old.

After washing her hands, Cara carried dishes to the dining table. It wasn't so much a dining room as an eating area outside the kitchen. In the ten years they'd lived together, Cara had turned Brett's bachelor pad into their home. They'd opened up the walls and created a lovely, light-filled area in which to eat and look out over Hamlin Creek. Brett's scant, mismatched furniture had been replaced with contemporary pieces in clean lines that suited them both. Cara had redone the kitchen using stainless steel appliances, but she'd opted for brown and white tile for Brett's sake instead of the all-white tile she'd installed in the beach house. The three-bedroom house wasn't large, but big enough to afford them each an office. They'd never needed a nursery.

"Want a glass of wine?" Brett asked, already uncorking the bottle. The question at the end of a long day was more a polite formality.

"Love one."

As he poured the rich red liquid, she foraged through the fridge looking for salad ingredients, locating the omnipresent kale and leftover greens. All the vegetables looked as tired as she was. Brett drew near to hand her a glass. She immediately took a sip, enjoying the full, robust, fruity flavor of her favorite Malbec.

"You know what, let's order out," she said. "I'm not in the mood to cook and I can't face another piece of grilled chicken."

"Fine with me. I'm pretty tired myself."

Over the rim of her glass she watched Brett move to the drawer where they kept a folder filled with take-out menus. His large hands were tanned and crisscrossed with scratches from the day of construction and a lifetime on the tour boat he captained. She'd put her life into those big, capable hands. Her decision to marry Brett had meant giving up her executive corporate position in Chicago to settle on Isle of Palms. But if she was being honest, she'd wanted to come home. Even needed to.

For ten years she'd managed his ecotour business. Together they'd watched the business grow along with the local tourism. They were not rich. But they lived a good life.

She turned and carried her wineglass to the back of the house. While Brett phoned in an order for pizza, Cara stood at the French doors and looked out over Hamlin Creek. The world was all purple-and-gray shadows streaked by the brilliant crimson color of the sunset. Squinting, she could barely make out their dock that stretched out over the deep water. Brett's johnboat was tied to the dock, bobbing as it strained against the strong current.

She was feeling introspective, a mood brought on by Palmer's comments. As well as by the inescapable fact that her fiftieth birthday was around the corner. Tonight Cara felt like that little boat, struggling to launch into the strong current, yet held tight to terra firma by an unbreakable bond.

"Pizza on the way," Brett announced.

When she didn't answer, she heard his heavy footfalls on the wood floor as he drew near. He put his hand on her shoulder and pulled her gently into his chest. She acquiesced and leaned into him, felt his strength, the warmth of his body. She caught the scent of beer on his breath when he spoke.

"You're quiet. What are you thinking about?" Brett asked.

Cara continued to stare out the window and said in a low voice, "If the rope on the johnboat broke, where would it end up?"

Brett thought for a moment, then said, "Who knows how

far the current would carry it? Maybe out to the ocean. Maybe to the harbor. Maybe a few feet before it got stuck by the dock next door." She felt him move as he looked down at her. "That's an odd question. What's up?"

She took another sip of her wine, not knowing how to answer. Being at the beach house today—cleaning, tending—had stirred up a lot of memories. Especially of her coming home from Chicago for a weekend that ended up lasting the rest of her life.

She'd always been what her mother called a "solitary swimmer," like the loggerhead sea turtle for which she'd been named. But tonight she wondered if the solitary swimmer was not adventurous but rather merely swimming in a pattern, following the great current, stroking one flipper after another, as generations had before her. Was this all there was left in her life?

"Maybe Palmer's right," she said in a despondent tone. "Holding on to the beach house, I'm just holding on to a memory."

"So that's what's wrong," Brett said with understanding. "Don't listen to Palmer. You've never done so before. Why start now?"

Cara swirled the wine in her glass. "Because my birthday is coming up. That's why."

Brett scoffed. "I'm fifty already. So what?"

Cara slipped out of his hold and turned to look up and meet his gaze. She studied the sharp contours of his handsome face, coursed with new lines that only added to his appeal. Brett was a naturalist, born and educated. Though they'd both grown up in the lowcountry, Cara, the daughter of a privileged Charleston family, had gone to private schools. Brett was the son of a harbor pilot and had attended local public schools. In high school, Brett's reputation as a football star was well known in every school in Charleston County and beyond. He'd been a popular jock as well as a good student. Cara, by contrast, was an academic who eschewed the popular boys. They might have had friends in common, but they definitely didn't hang out in the same circles.

So when Cara had returned to Charleston ten years earlier at the ripe age of forty, she was surprised—even stunned—that Brett was not only still single, but also that he'd known who she was. Theirs was an unlikely courtship that seemed destined from the start. Brett, always a romantic, claimed he'd been waiting for her to return.

In the past decade she'd seen all sides of the man she'd married in haste. The man who repaired and rebuilt her mother's beach house out of kindness, the man who never said no to a friend in need. He'd helped Cara to appreciate a simpler life than the fast-paced, high-style one she'd lived in Chicago. Being a naturalist, he'd also guided her to appreciate the beauty of what was wild not by preaching but by taking her fishing and baiting her line, helping her cast a shrimp net so it unfolded like a blossom over the water, pulling up crab pots full of snapping claws, and cuddling together under a blanket on the dark beach watching the Perseid meteor shower. She thought of how many times he'd gone shopping unasked, brought flowers home for no particular reason, woken her up with a cup of coffee in hand. How Brett had waited on her hand and foot when she was bedridden through each of her five miscarriages, never complaining, always supportive, even while his heart was breaking. He was a good man. Her best friend.

And on top of all that, the man was plain gorgeous. His brown hair that caught glints of red was now also streaked with the first strands of gray. His brilliant blue eyes were sometimes covered with eyeglasses now, which she thought only added to his attractiveness, making him appear clever. It was brutally unfair of God to allow men to improve with age while women suffered the indignities of gravity. They were an unlikely couple. Brett was the man she'd never looked for when she was young, which was why it had taken her so long to find him. But she had at last. Thank God.

"I don't like getting old," she said with a slight whine.

"Fifty is still young. And you're still beautiful."

She made a face. "I'm not talking about my looks. Lord knows that's a losing battle. I'm talking about *me*. Who I am, what I have yet to offer. I'm beginning to feel like my best years are behind me."

"Cara, we have a lot of years left. Some twenty, thirty years. Or more! A lifetime. Spent with me. Does that sound so bad?"

Cara stared at him, vaguely shocked at the concept of so many years. "When you put it like that, it sounds like a long time. Another lifetime. You're right." She tilted her head looking at the situation differently. "In that case, the question I have to ask myself is—how do I want to spend the next twenty, thirty years of my life?"

Brett whistled softly. "It's kind of . . . freeing."

"Exactly," she said with heart, glad he understood. "If I sold the beach house . . ."

"But you just said you'd never sell it."

"I know. Mostly I wanted Palmer off my back. But ever since we left the beach house, I've been thinking of the possibilities that money would open up to us. I mean, we're relatively free. We could move anywhere. Travel. No responsibilities. We have nothing to hold us here. No . . ." She paused before entering into tender territory, then pushed on. "We have no children."

Brett pursed his lips. "There's my business."

"Well, yes," she acknowledged. She rested her hand on his arm. "But we could sell it."

"Sell it?" Brett's face appeared thunderstruck. "I'm not ready to sell. Not yet anyway."

Cara felt a crushing disappointment and slowly removed her hand. "When would you be ready?"

Brett shifted his weight. "I don't know," he ventured, caught off guard. "Ten years, maybe?"

Ten years sounded like one hundred to her tonight. "So *long?*"

"As you pointed out, I'm fifty." His smile was wry. "No matter what you're thinking, fifty is not old. I'm not ready to retire. Besides, I love my job." He added carefully, "Cara, I'm content with our lives just the way they are."

Cara looked at him sharply. "You're content," she repeated, and set down her wineglass. She gazed down at her hand. Her wedding band was the only jewelry she wore. She felt a crack in her composure as an old hurt resurfaced. She crossed her arms. "And me?" She shrugged. "Not so much."

Brett's brows gathered as he suddenly understood the

conversation had taken a dangerous turn. "What? You're not content?"

She looked away and brusquely shook her head.

Brett pushed out a plume of air. "Well." He put his hands on his hips in thought. "That's news to me."

Cara turned to face him. The silence lay thick between them. Outside a dog began barking.

"I thought we were pretty happy," he said at length.

"*You're* happy," Cara said. "I know that. You've always loved working for yourself. You have your own business that you love. You're out on the water all the time, doing what you trained to do. What thrills you. Why wouldn't you be happy?" It came out like an accusation, which she didn't mean. But she couldn't take the words back.

Cara stepped closer and cupped his face in her palm. "I love you. You know that." She let her hand slip with a slight shrug. "I'm just feeling a bit unmoored about the direction my life is taking."

"It's your business, too," he said as though trying to convince her. "If it weren't for you, it never would have grown the way it has. It was entirely your advertising plan. Your PR ideas. Your business sense." He ventured a half smile. "Did you forget my accounting system?"

She laughed shortly and shook her head. Brett's idea of accounting before Cara came along had been shoving records, bills, and receipts written on yellow sticky notes into a file drawer.

"It's still *your* business. Your dream. I just helped. You could have hired anyone to do my job."

"I hired you."

Cara smirked. "You married me."

Brett smiled smugly and kissed her lightly on the lips. "Call me lucky."

Cara wanted to smile as she kissed him back, wished she could cast off the heaviness in her heart—but she couldn't. Her feelings went deeper than just the fact that she worked for Brett's company. Far deeper.

Cara reached for her wineglass and took a long swallow. She felt the liquid slide down her throat, reviving her. "The ecotour business was never *my* dream," she began. "It was something I could do while raising our children. That was the plan." She paused and looked up at him, gauging his reaction. "But that plan didn't pan out, did it?"

Brett's eyes reflected his sorrow as he took a long drag from the beer bottle.

She turned away and walked toward the bottle of wine on the side table, needing to create a distance between them. She didn't want to hurt him. Didn't want to fight. They both knew that the subject of children was their trigger point. Bad feelings quickly ignited after years of heated arguments and shouting matches that left them drained and desperately sad. Though it had been years since they'd stopped trying, the hurt and frustration still bubbled under the surface like hot lava ready to spew out.

She poured a second, generous serving of wine into her glass, spilling some in her haste.

Brett released a long sigh, then pulled out a chair from the table and lowered into it, stretching his long legs out. Catching her eye, he held out his hand, indicating a chair across from him. Cara hesitated. She really wanted to take a shower before the pizza arrived, ached for the swell of warm, soothing water to wash away the sweat and dirt from the day's exertions. But she saw the vulnerable look in his eyes—and the determination—so she obliged and slid into the chair.

"Okay," Brett said in that tone that told her he was being serious and wanted to get to the heart of the matter. "You're not happy."

It sounded horrible when he put it like that. "I'm happy with *you*," Cara amended. "Let's say I'm not content with my career."

"Okay," Brett said, accepting her clarification. "You're not content with your career path. So, you're considering selling the beach house. Right?"

Cara nodded.

"What would we gain by selling it? Aside from money, of course."

Cara took heart that he was open to discussing it. She often found that if she could air out her thoughts, it released tension and frustration, allowing her to think more clearly.

"Well," she began, leaning forward against the table. She set her wineglass down and let her fingers tap against the surface. "For starters, I'd quit Coastal Ecotour. It's a great company and I'm mad about the boss." She gave him a little wink, and Brett allowed a small smile in response. "But I want to do something that *I* am passionate about. If I'm going to choose what I want to do for the next twenty years, I figure I damn well better love it."

To his credit, Brett nodded in understanding. "Agreed. Okay. So . . . what would that passion be?"

"That's the problem," she said hesitantly. "I don't know. I—"

The doorbell rang.

Cara's mouth snapped tight.

"That's the pizza," Brett said, and pushed back from the table to amble toward the door, pulling out his wallet en route.

Cara leaned back against the hard chair, oddly relieved at the interruption. She had no clue what her passion was. None whatsoever.

The aroma of hot cheese, oregano, and sausage sparked a sudden ravenous hunger after the day's physical labor. The red wine flowed while they ate, and as the evening darkness deepened, the candle she'd lit at the center of the table glowed brighter. Cara felt the tension of her worries lessen as her stomach filled and the wine swirled through her bloodstream, and decided to put the conversation on hold for the time being. Maybe this new feeling of being unmoored, of lacking purpose, would right itself after a hot supper and a good night's rest. Going around and around in her head—or with Brett—would just make her crazy.

Instead, she tilted her head and listened as Brett talked about two young boys on the ecotour that week. Brett was a natural storyteller. He related in colorful detail how he'd taken a family from Ohio out to Capers Island and taught the two little boys how to fish for crabs using nothing but a string and a chicken neck. The older brother, ten years old, attracted the first crab. When he pulled the chicken neck out of the water, however, the boy freaked at seeing a crab clinging to it with a claw and let go of the string. But his six-year-old brother was fearless. With Brett's guidance, he caught four crabs and was proud as a peacock.

"A born fisherman," Brett concluded with a soft smile.

Cara saw the pride in Brett's face that he'd taught the boy how to catch his first crab. Brett's ability to instruct was almost as innate to him as his storytelling gift. It was that passion thing again, she realized. He truly loved his work as a naturalist. For him, heaven meant being out on the water with his boat filled with tourists who hailed from all over the world, including those from South Carolina who'd simply never been out on the ocean. He loved to reveal the secrets of the sea, bringing people up close to crabs and shrimp, to sharks and dolphins. To reveal the majesty of the tides, the mysteries of the mudflats, and to impress upon adults and children alike a reverence for the natural world, believing that if his students experienced the wonder of the wild, they would carry that revelation in their hearts and fight to protect it.

She thought again what a wonderful father Brett would have made. Cara took a deep, slow breath, then leaned back and watched while Brett ate the last of the pizza. She glanced at the wine bottle and noted that they'd finished it off. They were both tired. Cara knew if she lingered any longer, they'd slip back into the conversation that they'd both assiduously avoided during dinner. She loved Brett, but she wanted time to herself to figure things out. Maybe she'd skip the shower and instead soak in a hot, scented tub, letting the aches of a day spent painting ease away.

"Thanks for ordering the pizza, hon. Did the trick," she said, and began gathering the dishes.

But when she reached for Brett's plate, his hand rose to clasp her arm.

"Feeling better?" he asked earnestly.

She forced a short smile. The truth was she'd been feeling better over the cheesy pizza and easy conversation, but now the worries over her future were creeping back in, making her stomach turn. "A bit."

He nodded, accepting her answer. "Hold on a minute, Cara."

Cara sighed. "Let's table this until tomorrow. I'm really tired and I want to take a bath."

"But we never finished our conversation. You brought up a couple of important subjects and we didn't give them their full due."

Cara hesitated, but set the plates back on the table. Brett could be like a dog with a bone about unfinished business, work or personal.

"Cara, I don't care if you sell the beach house," he told her. "Or keep it. I support whatever you decide."

"Thank you."

"Now . . . the other subject." He pursed his lips as he folded his hands on the table. "If you're unhappy working with me at Coastal Ecotour, don't wait. Quit now."

Cara looked at him, startled. "I can't just—"

"Yes, you can. We'll manage. And I can always ask you to help out if we run into trouble." His laugh was good-naturedly self-deprecating. "And you know I will."

She looked at her hands, pensive. "But I haven't a clue what I'd do."

"Then take the time to figure it out." Brett's smile was full of compassion. "I want you to be happy, Cara. I don't want you to feel stuck. Or tethered."

She blanched when she saw the hurt spark in his blue eyes and realized he'd caught her meaning earlier. "I don't feel tethered to you," she said, grasping his hand. Then, looking at their joined hands, she laughed. "Well, I guess I am. We're married. . . . I'd never feel stuck with you." She squeezed his hand. "I love you."

He returned the squeeze, his hand so large it engulfed hers. "And I love you." He pushed his chair back to stand, tugging at her arm to guide her to her feet. His ruddy, tanned face eased into a seductive smile. "Come on," he said. "Let's take that bath."

The pizza carton, the plates, and the wine bottle lay forgotten on the table as they made their way across the living room, still hand-in-hand. They'd just reached their bedroom when the front doorbell rang.

Brett cursed under his breath. "Now, who the hell could that be at this time of night?"

Cara fought the urge to duck into the bedroom. She wasn't up to talking to anyone. But curiosity won out. She followed Brett to the front door and arrived just as he swung it open. Standing at the door was her brother.

"Palmer!" Brett called out in a somewhat forced cheery tone of welcome. "Can't get enough of us?"

Cara peeked around Brett's shoulder. "What are you doing here? Is everything all right?"

Palmer had the faint sheen of too much alcohol on his face, and under the harsh light of the porch lamp she could see where his blond hair was thinning on his scalp. Palmer grabbed his handkerchief from his pocket and waved it in the air. "I'm waving the white flag," he said. Chuckling, he tucked the handkerchief back in his breast pocket. He was smiling wide, bursting with news. "I had to come over and tell you in person. I've got news."

"Well, come in," Brett said, and opened wide the door.

As he entered, Palmer was shaking his head with disbelief. He stopped in front of Cara.

"This afternoon you shouted so loud that the beach house was for rent I swear God must've heard it. What was that thing Mama always used to say? Something about God closing a door?"

Cara looked at her brother, amused. "When God closes a door, He opens a window."

"That's the one. Well, sister mine, God opened a window."

"Sit down and tell us all about it," Brett said, slapping his hand on Palmer's shoulder. "Want a beer?"

Cara shot him a warning glance. It seemed Palmer had already had enough to drink.

"Nah, thanks. I just came from a dinner meeting." Palmer walked to the brown leather chair near the fireplace and unceremoniously plopped down into it. He looked up at Cara expectantly.

She went to the leather sofa beside him and slid onto the cushions. Brett sat beside her.

"So what's up?" she prodded.

Palmer spoke with intent. "First, answer me this. Is the beach house already rented out for the summer?"

Cara shook her head. "Actually, no. I kept it off the rental market until we finished the renovations. You never know if there are going to be delays. I was about to put it back on."

"Well, don't."

Cara glanced at Brett.

Palmer had the look of the cat that had just swallowed the canary. "Not long after I left the beach house today—after you shouted at me the house was for rent and not for sale—I got a call from Devlin Cassell."

"As in Cassell real estate?" Cara asked.

"The very one." Palmer grinned with amusement and singsonged the firm's slogan: *"Your house is your castle."* He chortled. "Nice guy. You remember him?" he asked Brett. "Old surfing buddy from way back."

"Sure. Know him well. He flips an occasional house, and sometimes he contracts me for the odd job here or there."

That interested Palmer. "Does he, now? Well, hell, Brother, remind me to talk to you about that later. I have a few ideas I want to toss around. But for now . . . after I left you, I returned Devlin's call." He steepled his fingers and leaned forward. "It seems he's got this banker from Charlotte looking to rent a small beach house *for the entire summer.*"

Cara's eyes widened. "For the summer?" Normally she had to schedule renters week by week, the usual summer routine. The relief—the luxury—of a single renter for the whole summer seemed too good to be true. "Does he have any idea how much a house rents for by the week?"

"He does. Apparently money is no object. The problem is finding a place that's available. This late in the season, most everything is booked for large chunks of time. Dev called me to ask if I knew of anything, and voilà!" He spread open his palms. "I thought of you. Destiny, don't you think?"

Cara leaned back against the cushions. "I'm stunned."

"Well, I'm relieved," Brett said. "I confess I was worried we were entering the rental market late. After all the work we did, we could sure use the income."

"He's willing to pay the going rate?" she asked.

"He is," Palmer assured her. "Dev says he's as rich as God. So when that proverbial window opened, he got the word direct." Palmer pointed to the heavens.

Cara laughed and said, "Mama would say you're being blasphemous."

"Hell she would. Mama would be dancing right now with this news."

"This is so unexpected," Cara said, still in disbelief. "A whole summer rented to one person." She paused as an unwelcome thought broke through her relief. "There's got to be a catch. Is he weird or something?"

Palmer shook his head. "It's not for him. It's for his daughter. The scoop from Devlin is that the daughter is in her twenties. Some kind of artist. Professional, not hobby, that much I got. I gather she needs a place to paint this summer for a project she's working on."

"She must be doing well to be able to rent the house for a whole summer to paint."

"Who knows?" Palmer made a face. "She still lives at home with Daddy. But the father is getting married again. So . . ."

Brett finished the sentence: ". . . he's looking to boot his daughter out of the house."

"Could be."

Cara didn't think that was unreasonable for the father. A woman in her twenties should be able to take care of herself. After all, Cara had left home at eighteen without a dime of support. Her father sure hadn't rented a place for her. But none of this speculation mattered. The salient point was that the father was renting the beach house for his daughter for the entire summer.

"When does she want to arrive?" asked Cara. "I still have finishing touches to do on the beach house."

"The wedding is in early May, so I'm guessing as soon as possible."

"That doesn't leave us much time," said Brett.

"We don't have much left to do." Cara shook her head in wonder at the whims of fate. Here she'd been considering selling the beach house, and suddenly a regular renter appeared out of nowhere. Maybe it was fate giving her a postponement on dealing with what she'd need to do to change her status quo. Cara was good at making snap decisions, and this one was easy. She'd do all the preliminary background checks, of course, but one renter for the entire summer likely meant less wear and tear on the house, fewer loud parties, and less worry about people squeezing in extra guests under the radar.

"Oh," Palmer interjected, "there is one thing."

Cara groaned softly. "I knew it was too good to be true."

"No," Palmer replied with a light laugh, "it's no big deal. She has canaries. She wants to bring them."

Brett guffawed. "That's a new one."

"I guess a canary is okay," Cara said.

"More than one. I believe he said three or four."

"As long as she keeps them in cages and the seed swept up. We don't want bugs. Shouldn't be a problem."

"So I should say yes?" Palmer confirmed.

Cara glanced at Brett, and he nodded. She turned to her brother. "Yes."

Palmer clapped his hands together in finality. "I guess that's it, then. The beach house is officially rented out for the season."

"Wait. Who is this new tenant? What's her name?" Cara wanted to know.

Palmer lifted his phone and, after a few minutes of scrolling, said, "Name is Heather." He looked up. "Heather Wyatt."

Chapter Three

May 2016

HEATHER WYATT SAT upright in the passenger seat of her father's luxury black Cadillac SUV. She breathed deep, doing her best to contain the growing panic inside of her. Her hands were white-knuckled in her lap; her knees pressed together tightly so she wouldn't visibly shake. Her mouth was set in a straight line, but inside she was cringing with fear, curled up in a ball as her mind screamed *No, no, no!*

She could barely look out the window at the trees and billboards and countless exit signs on the highway as they whizzed by. It was May, and already the South was blanketed in a thick, lush green, especially the vines of kudzu that climbed the telephone poles and trees on the edges of the roads. They rode with the windows up and the air-conditioning on, as the humid, sultry heat that defined a coastal summer had already descended. She closed her eyes and tried to distract herself by singing along to the playlist she'd created titled "Journey to Isle of Palms." Before leaving Charlotte, North Carolina, she'd packed her computer, books, art supplies, and work files into neatly organized plastic bins. She'd moved her three treasured canaries into special travel cages. Finally she'd notified anyone of importance of her change of address—*even if it was only for the summer*. This was the salient point. The one that gave her the strength to persevere. At weak moments she told herself she was returning to Charlotte at summer's end to resume the comfortable, productive, safe life she'd enjoyed before her father had taken the bold step of renting her a beach house all the way over in South Carolina.

This, in fact, marked the first time she'd left home alone. At twenty-six, Heather was well aware that it was long overdue. She was an adult. An accomplished illustrator. She'd been awarded a commission to paint shorebirds of the Atlantic Coast for the United States Postal Service. A heady accomplishment. She still couldn't believe that her art would someday become stamps that people—millions of them— would affix to their envelopes. The award was hard-won and presented a tremendous challenge. Her pride in the achievement boosted her lagging self-confidence enough that she agreed to her father's offer to rent her a beach house. But of course, moving to the beach house meant leaving the safety of home.

Heather brought her fingers to her mouth and began chewing her nails. She didn't like to think of herself as agoraphobic. She preferred to describe herself as shy. That's what her mother had said whenever she had to push her young daughter forward to greet a stranger: "Heather's a bit shy." Yet she'd never outgrown her shyness, and as an adult Heather was well aware that her anxiety levels went far beyond normal. She wasn't completely housebound, a classic sign of the disorder. She functioned pretty well, considering that her anxiety sometimes spiked through the roof. She was proud of how she'd managed, all in all.

As an illustrator she was able to do most of her work at home. But she ran errands in town and visited shopping malls, and she and the FedEx woman were on a first-name basis. She regularly saw a therapist, took her medication religiously, and was encouraged that her last panic attack had been well over a month ago. Heather chewed another nail. Stressful situations, however, could still bring on a full-blown attack. And moving to a new house in a new city—a new state—certainly qualified as a high-stress situation.

Her father wasn't booting her out, he'd assured her. Heather snorted. *Right.* . . . She got that he wanted some time alone with his bride. To be fair, she couldn't deny his argument that she needed to go to the shore for her work. But he was still firmly, albeit lovingly and generously, forcing Heather to leave the family home. She glanced over at her father.

David Wyatt's considerable frame filled the driver's seat. He was a big man in stature but had a gentle spirit. He slouched comfortably, one long arm extended over the wheel, idly moving his fingers in time to the country ballad on the CD. His salt-and-pepper hair was expertly trimmed—short enough to befit his position as a bank executive and long enough to still be attractive to women. By any standard, David Wyatt was a handsome man, and as a widower, he'd been the most desired bachelor in Charlotte.

Until his recent marriage to Natalie Sanders.

Heather shifted in the seat to wrap her arms tightly around herself. Whenever she thought of her father's marriage, she felt an acute sense of betrayal. Not only because her father was allowing some stranger to take her mother's place as Mrs. Wyatt, but because her new stepmother was twenty years younger than her father. That made the woman more a contemporary, and it made Heather feel downright strange to think of Natalie as her mother—even her stepmother. She shuddered at the word.

Her father pressed on the accelerator and shifted to the left lane, passing several cars as the big engine roared.

"Daddy, don't speed," Heather said through clenched teeth, her hands immediately dropping, bracing herself against the seat. "Please."

David swung his head around to glance at his daughter. She couldn't see his eyes behind the dark aviator shades. "I'm only doing seven miles per hour over the speed limit," he said reasonably.

"Seven over the speed limit is still speeding," she insisted plaintively, hating that she sounded like such a baby but powerless to stop. She was already wired after hours of holding herself together. "You know how much I hate speeding."

"Honey, I'll slow down, okay?" he said reassuringly. "Try to relax. Look"—he pointed out the windshield—"there's the first sign for Charleston we've seen. Shouldn't be too much longer now." He craned his neck to get a peek at the sky. "Want to beat that rain."

Heather looked up as a sudden barrage of fat raindrops splattered the windshield. She sucked in a breath.

"Now, come on, Heather," her father said soothingly, noting her instantaneous reaction as he flicked on the windshield wipers. "We could use some rain, baby. It is spring, after all."

His tone was cajoling, and he turned his head and smiled in an attempt to calm her.

It wasn't working. Lightning splintered the gray sky, followed by the guttural roar of thunder. Heather trembled as a rush of memories flooded her mind, as electrifying as the sky. Her heart beat in time to the accelerated metronome clicking of the wipers. Far ahead there appeared to be a veil of rain, and they were heading right for it. Traffic slowed and a line of brake lights went on for as far as she could see. She searched through the gray mist to read the road sign.

"The next exit is Orangeburg. Maybe we should take it. Get off the road," she said in a shaky voice.

"We're okay," her father replied in a placating tone. "It's just a cloudburst. It'll pass."

Sure enough, they drove straight into the downpour. It rained with such force, thundering on the car roof with a deafening roar, that they couldn't see more than ten feet ahead. The wipers clicked to their fastest gear, whipping back and forth in a frenzy. Heather startled as another clap of thunder burst seemingly overhead. Her father's smile was gone now. He slowed to a crawl and turned on the emergency blinker. Heather saw his fingers tighten on the steering wheel as he leaned forward, peering into the road ahead.

"Can't see a damn thing."

Wide-eyed with fear, Heather curled her legs up onto the seat while her mind flashed back to the horrible car accident with her mother. . . .

She'd been riding in the passenger seat that night, too. A similar cloudburst. The highway growing foggy and slick. It was the night of her high school graduation party. Her mother had come to pick her up because Heather had had too much to drink, but she'd been cool about it. She wasn't a mother who lectured.

"Do you feel tipsy?" her mother had asked. When Heather had replied a nervous yes, her mother took it in stride. "Remember what that feels like, so next time you know when to stop." Then with a smile she added, "Okay?"

"Okay," Heather replied, grateful her mother was being so reasonable. It was her first offense, after all, and likely her last, the way her stomach was roiling. But she'd actually had a good time at the party—danced, laughed, felt like one of the crowd for once. "But to be honest, I kind of liked tipsy Heather. She's a lot more fun. I mean, I actually talked to guys."

Her mother turned her gaze from the road for an instant and smiled. "I happen to love Heather just the way she is."

Well, that made one of them. Heather didn't much care for the excruciatingly shy girl who usually clammed up around boys, especially those she liked. Who couldn't get two words out without blushing. Most of the time she was standing alone in some corner, the classic wallflower. Heather preferred to be at home in her room with a good book. She'd successfully avoided parties throughout high school, but she had gone to this final hurrah for Mother's sake. The fact that she wasn't invited to many didn't matter to Heather, but her vivacious, popular mother took it as a personal affront.

On that fateful night, the windshield wipers were clicking in a steady rhythm as they talked. Heather was so wrapped up in relating the highlights of the party she didn't notice how heavily the rain was coming down until her mother hushed her.

"Hold that thought just a minute, honey," her mother said, leaning forward over the steering wheel and peering out. "I need to concentrate." She tsked with frustration. "I can't see a thing."

Heather sat up straighter in her seat at the tone of worry, and silently peered into the narrow cone of vision provided by the yellow beams of light. Her mother slowed the car to a crawl on the highway, the wipers now whipping back and forth at a frenzied speed.

"Only one exit more and we'll be off the highway," she said encouragingly.

Suddenly, out of the fog, a car was coming right for them, hydroplaning at an angle across the traffic lanes. Heather stiffened involuntarily, bracing for a hit. She pressed far back against her seat, her mouth opened in a silent scream as time seemed to slow down. The SUV was white and huge. Her mother swerved to get out of its way.

The last thing Heather remembered was her mother's arm pressed against her chest, protecting her. . . .

The memory of the crash hit Heather hard. She saw again the glare of headlights in her eyes and everything in her mind went white. Heather sucked in air and tugged at the seat belt pressed against her chest. Smells, sounds, screams of the accident replayed in her mind. The terrible, deafening thud of metal hitting metal . . . and then nothing. Heather covered her face with her hands as soft, whimpering sounds escaped from her lips.

Her father looked her way, worry etched on his face. "It's all right, baby," he told her, and reached over, trying to grab her hand. She held herself too tightly. Grimly he set his jaw and, peering out his window, flicked on his turn signal and guided the car across the slick highway to the exit. Every foot advanced was a victory in the torrential downpour.

At last the car came to a stop. Heather felt her father's hand on her shoulder, big and comforting. "Heather?"

Heather dropped her hands and, looking around, knew where she was. She still had control. She saw her father's face near her own. His sunglasses were off, and she stared into blue eyes soft with concern and sadness.

"I thought it was a good time to take a break," he said gently. He stroked a hunk of hair from her face. "You okay?"

Heather chased away the images from her mind. Very slowly she moved to lower her legs and straighten in her seat. As she did she felt her mind uncoil as well, releasing the nightmare that clung to her like a second skin in the light of reality. She was angry with herself for still having the flashbacks. She'd worked so hard with her therapist, taken her medications, but she felt powerless against them.

Taking a deep, calming breath, she peered out the windshield. It was still raining steadily, but no longer the desperate downpour. She could see they'd parked at a rest stop. They were off the road. Several other cars were idling there, waiting for the storm to pass. From the backseat came the sounds of her birds chirping in their covered cages. She felt some comfort at the sound.

Heather nodded and ventured a wobbly smile. "I'm okay. I just need a minute."

Her father reached into the back to retrieve a paper bag of bottled water and snacks. He offered her a bottle, then pulled out some granola bars. "Natalie packed us a few things. Might as well enjoy them while we wait out the storm. What do you want?" He looked between two of the bars and made a soft grunt of disapproval. "It's those damn healthy things you like. See? She's got you in mind." Then he mumbled, "Certainly not me." He held out both bars. "Lemon or coconut?"

"Just water, thanks," she said softly. Her stomach was in knots. She couldn't eat. She reached to the floor of the car and grabbed her purse. Her hands were still shaking, but she managed to pull out her medicine bottle and shake out one pink tablet. Popping it into her mouth, she swallowed water, hoping the tiny pill would do its job.

David watched her helplessly, then tore into a health bar and began chewing. "These things taste like shit. No wonder you don't want one."

Heather tried to smile. Her father was making an effort to improve her mood, distract her.

David finished his bar, complaining about it the whole way through, and crumpled the paper in his big hand. Heather noticed the gold wedding band, shiny and new, on his ring finger. Around them the rain pattered steadily, streaking the windows as the engine rumbled beneath them. David drank from his water bottle, then spoke as he screwed the top back on.

"I know driving in a car is hard for you," he began haltingly. "And this rain didn't help."

Heather looked away. She couldn't begin to help him understand the torture inflicted upon her by her memories. He couldn't comprehend how on that evening her life had been broken, never to be fully repaired. "I-I'm sorry," she stammered. "I didn't mean to overreact."

"Baby, you don't need to apologize. You've been doing so well. You have to remind yourself of that. You've driven in cars countless times since then. You even got your license."

"Yes," she replied, frustrated at herself for sliding back. "The rain, the highway . . . it was too close to that night. The memories . . . I can't control when I get the flashbacks."

"It's been eight years since the accident. Your therapist said you were ready for this change."

Heather didn't want to talk about what her therapist had said.

"Honey, sometimes we just have to overcome our fears and move forward in life."

"I know that, Dad," she replied testily. She didn't want to be treated like a child. She'd been working very hard for those eight years to overcome the blowup of fears and anxiety brought on by the accident. She'd made great strides. She'd managed a successful career and had agreed to take this big step in her life. But the anxiety was still there, a beast lurking inside of her, waiting to emerge at any new situation or trigger.

"I am moving on." She looked at her hands. "Clearly you've moved on." Her voice rang out with accusation.

His face drew in. "Yes, I have."

Heather turned her head to look out the window in a rebuke-filled silence.

"When are you going to stop this grudge against my marrying Natalie?" he said. "It's childish. And, frankly, beneath you. It's not Natalie's fault your mother died."

Heather swung her head back around, shocked he would say such a thing.

"And it's not your fault, either," he continued. "It was a

horrible, terrible accident. We all suffered. But it was nothing short of a miracle that you survived. No one who saw that crumpled car would believe anything else. Heather, you lost your mother. I lost the love of my life. But it happened. And I thank God every day that He spared you."

Heather fought the tears that filled her eyes. It wasn't often they spoke about the accident. Yet it was always hovering nearby, the elephant in the room.

"Wasn't I enough for you?" she cried, finally asking the question that had been niggling in her brain since he'd gotten engaged and then married to a woman twenty years his junior. "I thought we were doing pretty well. We were happy. I did my best to take care of you."

"No, Heather," he said, suddenly sounding weary. "It wasn't enough. I was lonely."

"How could you have been lonely? You dated every woman within a fifty-mile radius of Charlotte."

He didn't rise to the bait, merely releasing a sardonic smile. "It sure felt like it. But dating can be lonely, too. You're not the only one who had a hard time letting go of your mother. You'll never understand the depth of that kind of loss until it happens to you. And I pray it never does. It took me a long while to be ready to let someone else in. And when I was, I met Natalie. She's a wonderful woman. I wish you'd give her a chance. She's my wife now. You can't change that. And your stepmother."

"She'll never be my mother!" Heather shot back. "Or any other kind of mother to me. I'm twenty-six years old. I don't need a mother."

"Then not a mother," he replied, still in that calm voice

that was beginning to irritate her. "How about you start out as friends?"

"Then why did *my friend* demand that you get me out of the house?" Her voice was querulous, to show she was no fool.

"She didn't. *I* asked you to leave."

"Wha—" Heather was stunned. Then hurt. She'd never imagined it was *him*.

"For the summer," David hurried to explain. Then he added, in a tone that implied she should know all this already, "Natalie and I need some time alone together. We need to get to know one another better. Settle in. And"—he paused—"you need time on your own, too. You need time by the sea for your art. And, as you said, you're not a child anymore. Frankly, honey, in bird terms"—he jerked his head toward the backseat where the cages of birds were nestled in boxes—"it's time for you to leave the nest."

Heather's eyes flashed with anger mixed with embarrassment at the truth in her father's statement. "It's more like I'm getting kicked out of the nest."

"Hardly. You're going to a luxury barrier island for the summer to complete your art commission. To a charming house that you picked out and I've paid for. I wouldn't exactly call that a hard landing."

Heather's cheeks burned. What he said was true. She knew she was behaving churlishly. Like a spoiled child. She knew she wasn't a child any longer, nor did she want to behave like one. Since the trauma of the accident, her childhood shyness had grown into a case of full-blown social anxiety. She'd attended a local college rather than the prestigious art school she'd been accepted to because she wouldn't consider leaving home. She rarely dated. When she did, it was usually a favor set up by an acquaintance, or the son of one of the women her father was dating. It wasn't Heather's looks—in the least self-aggrandizing way possible, she knew she was an attractive woman. But her shyness hung over the coffee/dinner/drinks and ultimately doomed the relationship, no matter how promising it seemed.

She wasn't unhappy. In fact, Heather was quite content with her life. When people sometimes raised their eyebrows at her isolation, she blithely referred to herself as the Belle of Charlotte, a nod to her favorite poet, Emily Dickinson. Who, Heather believed, had suffered from social anxiety as well. Emily Dickinson had retired from society in her twenties and had still lived a fruitful, productive life. Heather believed she could, too.

She knew this day had to come. Her father had dated so many women, and Heather hadn't found any of them suitable for him, for them, for the quiet but relatively satisfied life they'd led together after her mother's passing. She'd been critical of them all, assuming they were all calculating how to get their hands on his wealth. She'd never considered that someone might actually truly fall in love with her father, and he with her.

What hurt the most was that she felt she was losing her best friend. Again. Once her mother had been her confidante. After her mother's death, her father had taken her place as Heather's best friend.

She felt his hand pat her back gently in the same rhythmic beat with which he'd consoled her for as long as she could remember. She relaxed into the familiar scent, the sound of his heartbeat. He was a good father. A good man. She had to love him enough to let him live his own life.

Heather pulled back and wiped her damp cheeks with her palms. She looked down at her crumpled clothing and stroked away the wrinkles. Slim camel-colored pants, a thin white boat-neck sweater, and an Hermès scarf that had been her mother's. On her feet were strappy sandals that showed off her new cherry-red pedicure, a bold color she'd chosen hoping it would make her brave. She wanted to appear mature and confident when she met her new landlady.

Heather pulled back and ventured a forced smile. "Looks like the rain has slowed down. I guess it's time to get back on the road."

～～～

HEATHER DIDN'T KNOW when she fell asleep. Somewhere after Orangeburg, she supposed. She awoke when her father nudged her shoulder.

"You won't want to miss this," he told her, smiling with anticipation. "Welcome to Charleston. No city like her anywhere in the world. Take a look."

Heather straightened, blinking the sleep out of her eyes, disoriented in the bright sunshine. Outside her window she could see they were approaching a great bridge that spanned the harbor. She gazed with wonder at the shining, towering, diamond-shaped structures that held the suspension design. From a distance they looked like two sailing masts.

"That's the great Cooper River," her father informed her. "We're leaving Charleston, now heading to the islands."

Already? she thought. But she remained silent, peering

over the guardrails to take in the scope of the busy harbor as they sped by. The storm clouds had not reached this far south. The sky shone blue, dotted with white cumulus clouds that cast shadows on the sparkling water below. Here and there she spotted small sailboats cruising the harbor between the Charleston peninsula and Mount Pleasant. But the enormous cargo ships dominated the scene. The behemoths lined the docks like sleeping beasts, while beside them equally giant cranes loaded colored containers into the ships' holds as if they were Lego pieces. The stacks were so high it was hard to believe the ships wouldn't topple over.

Heather studied the miles of shops that lined the four-lane road as they journeyed through the town of Mount Pleasant. Which would be her grocery store, her gas station, her butcher? At last they reached the long, curved, arched road that took them away from the mainland to the small barrier island called Isle of Palms. She leaned closer to the window, amazed at the sharp contrast to Charleston Harbor the vista of wetlands offered. Vast acres of sea grass stretched out seemingly forever, dotted here and there by tiny islands that held a few palm trees. This truly was going someplace far away, she thought with a mixture of wonder and trepidation. The car climbed higher up the arched span of road, and at the top, in a breath, she was staring at the great expanse of the Atlantic Ocean. The suddenness caught her by surprise and elicited a soft gasp. The mighty ocean was so huge, so vast, it seemed to stretch out into infinity. In light of such power, Heather felt her own smallness and relative weakness.

"We're here, baby," her father said with relief. "Not bad, huh?" He turned her way, searching for her approval.

She smiled, trying to be upbeat. "It's beautiful," she said. "And it's not raining!"

They began their descent past the Intracoastal Waterway where speedboats raced full-throttle and the narrower Hamlin Creek, lined with long docks with boats at moor. Without further fanfare they were on the Isle of Palms.

Heather's head turned from side to side. She'd visited other barrier islands along the southeastern coast—Hilton Head, Tybee, the Outer Banks. This one wasn't so different. Long and narrow, it held a grocery store, a few shops, a gas station, and hotels. That would make her life here much easier. Mostly, however, there were private homes owned by those lucky enough to live on the island full-time, those who came here for part of the year, and those who rented by the week, eager to escape the heat and spend precious vacation time on the beach. She couldn't imagine what it would be like to be able to live here all summer.

When her father turned off Palm Boulevard onto a narrow street, Heather sat straighter in her seat. He drove slowly a few blocks till they reached Ocean Boulevard. On the ocean side a row of mansions, one after another, lined the sea, blocking the water from view. Across the street more houses filled every lot, but here there remained some of the smaller, historical cottages that had once been oceanfront before the dunes were paved over. They drove a few blocks south and she kept her eyes on the smaller cottages, seeking out the one she'd seen online. She'd taken one look at the quaint house and something inside of her had pinged. It had spoken to her of the quieter, nostalgic island living she not only wanted . . . but needed.

"There it is!" she exclaimed, leaning forward and pointing.

Primrose Cottage was perched on a dune between wispy clumps of greening sweetgrass and leggy stalks of sea oats that grew wild, a sharp contrast to the meticulously landscaped properties of the mansions beside it. The house was as pale a yellow as the blossoms of wild primroses that crisscrossed the dunes among the brilliantly colored gaillardia and purple morning glories, creating a riot of color. For all the reticence she'd felt as she began this journey, Heather suddenly couldn't wait to get inside. All along she'd known they were lucky that her father had found any house available for a summer rental at such a late date. Yet now, seeing the beach house, she felt that the small cottage had been waiting just for her.

At last they pulled into the narrow gravel driveway beside the house. The car came to a shuddering stop when the ignition turned off. Heather and her father sat quietly in the resulting hush. Neither of them spoke or moved, simply looked out at the house in a companionable curiosity flavored with relief. Heather felt the miles still racing in her veins as she stared at the cottage, devouring the details. The front yard also had the slightly unkempt appearance that she preferred. A broad, freshly painted front porch was lined with hanging pots of trailing asparagus ferns, and at the foot of the steps sat two large pots filled with cheery red geraniums.

As lovely as everything appeared, inside she was feeling a great deal of dread at meeting her new landlady. She wished her father could just get the key and let this Mrs. Rutledge leave.

As though reading her thoughts, her father called out, "Ready?"

Heather darted a quick glance at her father. His face was an open book. Clearly he hoped she could be brave and not turn heel and run screaming. As filled with apprehension as she was, Heather couldn't do that to him. Or to herself. *This is it*, she told herself. There was no turning back. She had arrived at her destination, and today she was moving into this sweet beach house for the summer. She turned again to the yellow cottage. It was some consolation that the house did, in fact, resemble the photographs. If the inside was anything like the outside, she felt she would be able to manage.

Heather lifted her chin. "Ready."

Chapter Four

HEATHER PUSHED OPEN her car door and, to her surprise, felt a delightful breeze sweep over her. Cool and refreshing. She caught the scent of something floral floating through the air. Not at all the press of heat and humidity she'd been expecting. The air was as balmy as a spring afternoon should be, she thought. Stretching in the sunlight, she held her arms out, embracing the breeze more fully. After hours confined in a car, it felt heavenly.

The chirping of her canaries caught her attention.

"Lend me a hand with the birdcages, Dad?"

David was by the trunk hoisting out her large suitcases. Every square inch of the car was tightly packed with boxes crammed full of possessions Heather couldn't live without, from clothing to her computer and books to the special health foods that helped her anxiety.

Heather carefully lifted a small travel birdcage from the car and handed it to her father. It was covered with an old pillowcase. From beneath she heard the strident, curious call of the bird. David took the cage and began his trek through the scrubby grass to the front stairs. Heather murmured reassurances as she retrieved the two other cages, then slammed the door with her hip. Once on the porch, she set the birdcages at her feet and waited for someone to open the wooden door. It was freshly painted a brilliant blue and had a weathered door knocker in the shape of a mermaid. She wiped her hands on her pants. She was habitually nervous when meeting new people, and her palms were already sweating.

The door swung open. Standing in front of her was a beautiful woman, tall, slender, and so striking it caught Heather by surprise. She'd been expecting someone middle-aged, soft and sweet with blond hair, not this chic woman of indeterminate age with full dark hair pulled back into a high ponytail. She was casually dressed in tight jeans and a crisp white cotton blouse, rolled up at the sleeves. The woman's gaze shifted to the birdcages at their feet with uncertainty—perhaps even amusement—before a wide grin of welcome spread across her face.

"You must be the Wyatts!" she exclaimed.

Heather felt like shrinking into her shoes, confronted with such poise and confidence, but her father displayed no such reluctance. He'd always been his most comfortable and charming among comely women. He stepped forward, an amiable grin on his face.

"We are indeed. And you must be Cara Rutledge?"

"Guilty." Her dark eyes shifted. "And these are the birds I'd heard about?"

Heather nodded mutely.

"Well, come in, please!" Cara exclaimed, stepping back to allow them to pass.

Heather bent to pick up a birdcage in either hand and, careful to avoid eye contact with Cara Rutledge, hurried into the house. Inside, she was struck by the welcoming scent of fresh paint and polished wood. Someone had worked hard to prepare the house for her arrival. The walls were painted a pale ocean blue, and the floors were covered with large grass rugs, giving it a coastal feel. The foyer was very small, just an entry-way to the large, open living room. Looking in, she saw two plump upholstered chintz chairs on either side of a coffee table topped with a tray holding fresh flowers. It looked like an old English cottage with a beach spin. Old-world yet fresh. On the right she caught a glimpse into a small galley kitchen and a bedroom beyond. To the left, a narrow hall led to more rooms.

"Welcome to Primrose Cottage," Cara said as she closed the door behind them. She spoke with the authority of the mistress of the house. "It's a small house, but it's cozy. It used to belong to my mother and she passed it on to me. Much of the furniture and artwork is original to the house, though I've updated it some for rental." Cara paused and looked around the house, and her face softened with a wistful expression. "But it's still very much the same place."

Heather's first impression was that the little beach house was perfect. Not big, shiny, and new. Rather the cottage was filled with the charms of a vintage house—moldings, built-ins, and old-world quality. She felt right at home the moment she stepped into the house.

"You probably want to find a place to put your birds," Cara offered, noting the birdcages weighing down Heather's arms.

"Please," Heather said.

"Maybe the sunporch?" Cara lifted her arm, directing their attention to the back of the house.

Heather felt a surge of delight. The possibilities fluttered in her mind as she hurried across the living room, lugging her cages, David and Cara trailing in her wake.

"I didn't know there was a four-season room!" she exclaimed.

"We just built it," Cara explained, pushing the French doors open wider so they could fit the cages through. "I didn't have time to update the website photos before you rented. It all happened so fast," she added with a light laugh.

Heather set her two cages on the white wrought-iron, glass-topped table. Her father deposited the final cage beside the others. That done, she looked at the wall of windows bringing in great shafts of sunlight. It had a pretty effect on the room, but she worried it was too much light for her birds.

As though reading Heather's mind, Cara walked to a window and pulled on the string that lowered a sunshade. "These shades will control the sunshine and heat in here. You can lower the shades and still see through them. You'll appreciate that on days when you want to cut the glare but not feel cooped inside."

Heather met her father's gaze and knew they were both thinking the same thing. Cara could not have known how important it was that Heather not feel cooped up inside the house.

"There's a ceiling fan, too," Cara added, pointing overhead. "I recommend that during the nights and early mornings you turn off the air-conditioning and let the ocean breezes cool you. The ocean sounds are like a lullaby. I live on the creek side of the island, and though I love looking at the wetlands, I miss the sound of the ocean while I sleep. On super-hot days, though, keep those doors to the house closed and turn on the AC."

She turned toward the ocean and her voice softened. "But you will love this view. We wanted to offer maximum opportunity to enjoy it year-round." She pointed. "That ocean lot in front was left to conservation and will never be built on, so the view is guaranteed."

David whistled softly. "That's a lucky break." He stood at the open window, hands on hips, taking in the wide expanse of ocean view.

"More than luck. It was determined by a friend of my mother's. Mr. Bennett was a sea turtle expert and hoped to set a precedent for conservation. As it turned out, no one else followed suit. This is the only lot that's been left to conservation that I know of, which makes it all the more precious."

"It certainly adds to the value of your property." His eyes gleamed with appreciation. "Yes, sir, it's a very special spot."

"The deck isn't quite finished," Cara said, assuming again the role of landlady. "We still have to add some more decking and finish the stairs and railings. You'd better not go out there until it's done. Someone will come by tomorrow to work on it. I hope it'll be finished this week. I do hope that's not an inconvenience."

"That's no problem at all," David assured her. He looked at

Heather. "I know Heather is happy with the sunroom. Aren't you, honey?"

She nodded and smiled briefly. In her mind, she was working out where to put the cages.

"You'll love the deck when it's done," Cara assured Heather. She turned to look out again through the glass. "We have several white rockers that will go out on the deck after it's stained. Brett, my husband, is painting them even as we speak. You'll be able to sit out there and enjoy the sunsets like a proper islander." She paused. "My mother and I used to sit out every night, just the two of us, and watch the sun go down, before she . . . passed away."

Cara's voice trailed off and she quickly turned her head from the view and looked at Heather, catching her gaze. Though surprised, Heather shyly smiled in return. She felt a sudden, unexpected bond with this fellow motherless woman.

"My sympathy. When did your mother pass?" David asked.

"Ten years ago this summer," Cara replied, turning back to face David with a perfunctory smile. "Her name was Olivia Rutledge, but everyone called her Lovie. You'll likely hear stories about her from some of the islanders. Everyone knew her and, I daresay, loved her. She was kind of an institution on Isle of Palms. She was the island's first turtle lady."

Heather brightened. "Has . . . has turtle season begun?"

"We're just starting to walk the beaches this week. We don't have any nests yet." Cara wiggled her brows. "But soon!"

"Maybe you could paint one," David suggested to Heather. "I could try."

"That's right," Cara said with interest. "You're an artist."

Heather looked at her hands, feeling that choking sensation she always experienced when put on the spot. "I-I'm not in galleries or anything like that. I do illustrations for textbooks."

"Don't be modest," David said, his chest expanding with pride for his daughter's accomplishments. He extended his arm her way. "Heather was just awarded the task of painting shorebirds of the southern Atlantic Coast by the United States Postal Service. They're going to make stamps from her work. She had to beat out several other contenders to win the commission. It's a great honor to be selected."

Heather felt a bit embarrassed by her father's boasting. She explained in a soft voice, "That's what I'll be working on this summer."

"Really?" Cara said, obviously impressed. "I've never met someone who paints stamps. Do you paint very, very small?" She lifted her fingers to indicate the inch size of a postage stamp. "I would think that's very hard on the eyes."

A laugh escaped from Heather. She shook her head, knowing full well Cara was joking. "Thankfully, no."

"And you're doing shorebirds. I'm glad they're getting the attention they deserve. Pelicans especially. They're my favorite. I think everyone's," Cara added.

Heather felt encouraged by Cara's enthusiasm. She walked over and began lifting the covers from the birdcages. Immediately the canaries began jumping from one perch to another, chirping, obviously excited to be back in natural light. Heather watched them like a mother hen, checking for any trouble wrought by the long journey. She was pleased that they appeared to have done just fine. They were sprightly, tight-feathered, and healthy-looking. Their chirping was melodious and sweet-sounding to her ears.

"So those are canaries?" asked Cara.

"Yes. They're the sons of champions," Heather said proudly. Her beloved canaries were the one subject she could open up about without feeling anxious or forced.

Cara drew near the cages, making smacking noises with her lips. It was a common mistake people made with caged birds. Heather knew that in a moment Cara would be sticking her finger into the cage. She wanted to tell Cara not to stand too close to the cages. Most people didn't realize canaries were not like the ever-popular parakeets. The most she could muster was "Canaries don't like to be touched." Her voice was so soft she wasn't sure Cara heard her.

"Oh," Cara said, and immediately stepped back. "They're charming birds. So pretty. I hope I'll get to hear them sing someday."

"You won't be able to *not* hear them," David said with a laugh. "Those birds sing all day. And I mean *all* day."

Heather was grateful to him for smoothing over the awkwardness created by her shyness.

"I remember my grandmother had a canary in her front room on East Bay Street," Cara said, reminiscing. "It had the prettiest pagoda cage. She adored that bird. But I don't see many canaries anymore. Not any, really." Cara again addressed Heather. She seemed determined to draw her out. "You're quite young. How did you get interested in canaries?"

"My mother always had a canary," Heather said simply. She caught her father's eye and he returned a sad smile of understanding.

Heather didn't remember ever *not* having a canary. After her mother died, she'd taken care of Hanzie, her mother's Belgian Waterslager. The little yellow bird's song lifted her spirits during the desperate days of her mourning. She'd missed her mother terribly. Heather had talked to Hanzie, pouring out her grief-stricken heart to the bird as though she were talking to her mother. In some ways, that little bird had saved her. Not long afterward she got a second canary, this time the popular American Singer. She quickly fell in love with Pavarotti's robust song. When Hanzie died, she spent weeks researching breeders and at last found and bought another rare Waterslager. Then, as happens, a neighbor who was moving had asked if Heather would please adopt her American Singer, bringing her collection of canaries to three.

Each bird was a pet with his own personality and quirks. Heather spent hours studying the small birds—their behavior, the way they moved, how they expressed their personalities through cocking of the head, tweets and chirps, positioning of their bodies. They were her first bird models and taught her how to pay attention to the telling details. Her work with the birds prompted her focus on art and led to her career illustrating birds and small animals for textbooks. They were, in short, her muses.

"Well, if the birds are settled," Cara said, indicating the living room. She was clearly ready to move on to business. "Let's take a brief tour of the house. I'll try to answer all your questions. But don't worry," she said, offering Heather a quick smile. "You'll have my home number and you can call me anytime."

Heather returned the smile politely but doubted she'd ever call. She found her poised, self-assured, striking landlady quite intimidating.

~~~~~~

TWO HOURS LATER Cara had provided her new tenants with a thorough tour of the beach house, taking the time to make sure Heather knew how to work all the appliances. She also provided a thick portfolio that included not only household information but also emergency numbers, groceries, restaurants, local shops, and assorted other services. Heather watched Cara drive away in a gold VW convertible bug, not quite the car she would have imagined the stylish woman driving. As much as she liked Cara Rutledge, Heather felt a great relief that she was gone and at last she could truly relax.

"That woman is a wonder," her father proclaimed as they closed the door.

"Yes. A force of nature."

"She was very thorough. The folder of information is jam-packed. I thought she was very thoughtful, didn't you?"

"I do," Heather replied hesitatingly. "But a bit reserved."

"That's class," he said with authority. "She's from an old Charleston family. One of the originals. Probably a DAR. I'm surprised she's not wearing pearls. Count your blessings—you probably won't see much of her. Some landladies like to get in your business." Her father turned to face her and placed both hands on her shoulders. "My dear. How are *you*? Do you like it here?"

Heather cast a sweeping glance around the front rooms. "I

do," she replied, and was pleased to find she meant it. "I feel comfortable here. Not quite at home yet, but I suspect that will come."

"Well, I think you're all set. Everything is out of the car. I double-checked." He shifted his weight, a frown of worry creasing his brow. "Are you sure you don't want your car delivered?"

Heather shook her head. "We'd just have to have it driven back to Charlotte at the end of summer and that'd be a hassle. I don't need a car. I can always call a cab or have food delivered. And I can get a bicycle. Or walk. There's a grocery store on the island. I'll be fine."

Her father didn't look convinced.

"Besides, you brought enough food to feed an army. I wonder if they have Uber out here?"

"I doubt it. But it's quite a hike to the grocer's. That reminds me—Natalie and I have a housewarming gift coming for you. Delivery is scheduled for next week. I tried to get it here sooner, but—"

"What is it? A Crock-Pot? Please don't let it be a Crock-Pot. I will never use it."

He laughed. "No, not a Crock-Pot. And don't bother guessing. I won't tell you. You'll just have to wait. But I think you'll like it. You'll certainly use it. At least, I hope you will."

"Then thank you in advance, Daddy." She stepped closer to deliver a kiss to his cheek.

Standing at the front door, he gave the house a final look around. "I guess that's that. You're settled in."

"I am." She sensed his reticence to leave. But the hour was

growing late and her father had a four-hour trip back to Charlotte. "Are you sure you can make the drive back? You can spend the night if you'd like."

He waved his hand. "Nah, I'll be fine. You know me. I like to drive."

Heather realized then that she'd misread him. He was, in fact, eager to leave. To get back on the road to his new wife who was, undoubtedly, waiting for him with a cocktail and dinner. David lifted his wrist to look at his watch. It was the gold Patek Philippe that her mother had given him on their twentieth anniversary. He never wore another, not even now that he'd remarried. Heather was glad to see it. It reminded her that, even as things changed, some things remained the same.

David stepped forward and wrapped his long arms around Heather, dwarfing her. "You're going to do wonderful work here. I know you will."

"Thanks, Dad. I have to admit it's the perfect place for me to do my work on shorebirds. If I can't do it here, I can't do it anywhere. You know"—she hesitated—"I haven't properly thanked you for finding this beach house for me." She laughed. "And renting it."

"No thanks necessary."

"I think they are. I was so caught up in my fear over leaving home that I didn't tell you how grateful I am. My work is important to me, so I appreciate your support. I'll do my best. I promise you."

"That's enough thanks for me. I have confidence in your talent. And in you." He paused. "I'll miss you."

Heather offered a tremulous smile, holding back tears. "I'll miss you, too."

"We'll come for a visit soon."

"Don't wait too long."

Her father straightened and took a step back. She was stunned to see his eyes were misty.

"Call or text me when you get back," she told him. "No matter how late."

"Who sounds like the parent now?"

She looked into her father's eyes and was overcome with a sudden rush of love for this man who was still raising her, caring for her, worrying about her, even though she was well past grown. It was about time he found some peace, she reflected. Impulsively, she offered him the kindest farewell gift she could think of.

"Send Natalie my love."

~~~~~

AFTER HER FATHER left, Heather closed the door and leaned against the wood. In the resulting quiet she slowly let her gaze sweep the softly lit beach house.

She was, Heather fully realized, truly alone. She paused, expecting to feel some tremor of anxiety. But to her surprise, she felt none. Just a slight sense of unease at being in a strange place. Perfectly normal, she told herself. Just new smells, not knowing where everything was. Everything unfamiliar. She pushed away from the door, eager to get busy.

She went first to the kitchen to take stock of the groceries her father had brought with them from Charlotte. Her heart softened at imagining him pushing a cart through the grocery store, something he wasn't accustomed to. Heather and her mother had always done the housework in their traditional home. That he had offered to "pick up a few essentials" for the trip had meant the world to her. David had been a single father for eight years and they'd regularly cooked and shared meals during that time. No one knew her tastes better than he did, and her stringent scrutiny for organic products.

She pulled out a can of vegetable soup and, rummaging through the wooden cabinets, found a dented pot and dumped the soup into it. After a few tries, the gas stove lit. A good start, she told herself. The fridge was sparkling clean, always a relief. From it she pulled out a bag of prewashed organic lettuce and kale. While she waited for the soup to heat, she found the corkscrew and uncorked a very nice bottle of Cabernet that her father had selected. Mentally thanking him for his generosity, she found where Cara kept the wineglasses and poured herself a liberal amount. Good wine, salad, and the heated soup—an adequate dinner for a first night in one's new home, she thought. She put everything on a tray and carried it out to the sunporch.

The sun began its slow descent, drenching the sunroom in magenta. The birds were restless at the light change of a day's end, hopping back and forth on their perches. The sound of their evening song was comforting, like whispered good nights from dear friends. She didn't feel so alone with their persistent chatter. She went from cage to cage offering them small bits of kale after the long trip. Like her birds, Heather picked at her food, too restless to eat. As the sky slowly shifted from lilac to purple to indigo she grew increasingly aware that she was alone in a big, dangerous world. Looking out, she hadn't anticipated that at night the ocean was one vast, unbroken blackness. She rose and one by one she closed all the shades. Then she went from room to room turning on lights. The soft yellow light immediately warmed the living room and made it feel cozier, not so empty. Glancing at the clock on the wall, she saw it was already nearly 9 p.m. Not that late, but it had been a very long day. Tired, she covered her birds with cloths and bid them good night, then went into her room.

The master bedroom was connected to the sunroom by French doors and decorated in crisp white and mahogany wood, like an old Jamaican inn she'd once stayed at with her parents. A tall mahogany four-poster bed dominated the room. It was luxuriously outfitted in crisp white cotton sheets, a fluffy white down blanket, and several pillows. A large painting of a beach scene with two children—a dark-haired girl and a blond boy playing with a shovel and bucket in the sand—hung over the bed. During the house tour, Cara had mentioned that her mother had commissioned the painting when she and her brother, Palmer, were children. Long white lace curtains fluttered in the evening breezes.

Yet as charming as the bedroom was, after Heather had changed into her nightgown, washed her face, and crawled into the spacious bed, sleep eluded her. She'd tried to follow Cara's suggestion to leave all the windows open and enjoy the sounds of the ocean, but she only startled at every noise, shivering at every foreign murmur and echo. A feral cat was courting. A few cars drove past. Her imagination became a terrible thing, conjuring up burglars and worse. With a huff of frustration, Heather flung back the duvet and went from window to window in the house, closing each tight and locking it. Climbing back into her bed, she felt safer, more secure, even if the air grew stifling. She propped up a few pillows and began to read the book she'd placed on the bedside table, a love story. The night dragged on. Gradually, in the wee hours, her eyelids grew heavy and, too tired to fight against it, Heather relinquished her fears to a deep sleep.

She awoke from her sleep once, sometime before dawn, calling out for her mother. Sitting upright in bed, she remembered her dream. There was a mother—not her mother, she realized now, but someone like her mother with golden hair. And kind. Even loving. The air was filled with the scent of jasmine. This woman she didn't know had smoothed back the hair from her face, then placed a tender kiss on her forehead. It was one of those dreams that had felt so real. She wasn't frightened by it. On the contrary, she felt comforted, soothed. Even welcomed. She sighed, feeling the need for sleep overcoming her once again.

Part Two

GROWTH

Barbara J. Bergwerf

AMERICAN OYSTERCATCHER

Oystercatchers are large, boldly patterned birds common to seacoasts in temperate to tropical parts of the world. Their heads and necks are black, and the wings and backs are dark brown, and have white breasts and bellies. Their distinctive, bright red, long bills are used for feeding on oysters, clams, and mussels.

Conservation status: *Greatest Concern*

Chapter Five

THE NEXT MORNING Heather felt refreshed, despite the sheen of sweat forming on her brow. The house was muggy and hot shafts of sunlight pushed through the slim cracks in the plantation shutters. She rose to sit at the edge of the mattress, then slowly yawned and stretched her arms over her head, blinking in the light. From the brightness, she could tell the sun was high. She reached over to grab her watch from the bedside table and was shocked to see it was almost 9 a.m. She couldn't remember the last time she'd slept so late.

A burst of birdsong from the porch brought a smile to her face. Her birds! *The poor things,* she thought, whipping back her blanket. *They're still under their covers. And they're singing! What good sports.* She slid off the mattress and hurried out her bedroom door that led to the sunporch. Part of her joy in having canaries was their cheery disposition early in the morning. It was as though they started her days off on the right note. Despite the drawn shades, she was surprised that there was quite a bit of sunlight filtering into the room. It was no wonder the birds were awake and singing.

"Coming, sweet friends," she sang out as she rushed to the cages. One by one she lifted the white cotton covers. The canaries were bright-eyed, jumping from perch to perch in the tiny travel cages. Their cheerfulness was contagious.

Heather hurried to the windows and sliding doors of the sunroom and opened them wide. Feeling the cooler air blow in she breathed in and knew she had to overcome her fears and leave the windows open at night as Cara had recommended. She paused to stare out at her first morning on the beach.

The sun was high in the sky and the great ocean glistened blue in reflection. It had rained during the night, no doubt the same fast-moving storm that she'd driven through, but it was far out to sea now, leaving in its wake a crisp morning sans humidity. She docked her phone in her speaker. In another moment she heard the rich baritone of Johnny Cash.

Heather stretched out her arms and began dancing to the beat. Music had the power to scatter her inhibitions and allow her to feel free. It filled the empty spaces of her life as a shut-in. She shared this love of music with her birds who sang exuberantly in the background. For her, music was better than medicine. It never failed to lift her mood and boost her energy. The strong backbeat had her feet moving and she laughed out loud with the joy of it.

—————

MUSIC POURED OUT from the open doors and windows of the beach house when he arrived. Bo dropped his heavy bag of tools on the ground and rolled back his shoulders. His heavy work boots made imprints on the sandy soil as he walked around the frame of the deck, assessing what had to be done.

Brett had explained the job thoroughly; a deck wasn't rocket science. Still, Bo took pride in his work and wanted to build the best deck he could. Brett was his mentor and his friend. He'd expect no less from him.

Bo surveyed where the dunes ended and how much room he had to play with for his steps. As he walked, the shape of the deck formed in his mind. At least he'd be out on the island near the surf as he worked this job, he thought with pleasure. As with Brett, the ocean called to him. Whenever the waves were forming in the early hours of morning he grabbed his board and headed for the beach to surf.

He walked up to the deck to get started. The voice of Johnny Cash floated out from the house and he smiled, grateful for the choice of music. Then he laughed, hearing the song punctuated by the high trill of birdsong. Brett had told him he had a new tenant. A young woman with birds. He laughed again at the notion. She had to be weird. . . . Looking toward the house a movement inside caught his eyes. It was his custom to knock on the door and make his presence known. He didn't want some freaked-out homeowner to call the police on him. He walked carefully along the narrow strips of wood toward the screen door. Then he stopped short, arrested by the vision of movement waltzing across the floor.

The young woman was beautiful. Damn gorgeous, in fact. Her arms were stretched out as her feet moved in time to the music, her long white nightgown twirling around her ankles, her blond hair loose down her back. She hummed as she danced and it took him a minute to realize she was talking to those birds, moving from cage to cage as she fed them. He wasn't a voyeur. It wasn't his style to peek inside windows at pretty ladies. But something in her movement, so uninhibited, told him this was meant to be private. He didn't want to interrupt, or worse, embarrass her.

Without knocking he stealthily moved back and climbed down off the deck. He stood a moment, flummoxed. There was something about this girl . . . a spirit of innocence and joy . . . that he felt drawn to. Like a moth to the flame, he thought ruefully. This girl was here for the summer, Brett had told him. Then she'd be off again, back to Charlotte. He shook his head of fanciful thoughts and looked at the pile of lumber waiting to be installed. *Mister, you have your work cut out for you and best get started,* he told himself. He could make his presence known in a little while, after the lady of the house got settled.

The music changed. Now Bob Dylan was singing "Girl from the North Country." One of his favorites. Bo took one last glance at the house then turned and began working, singing along with the song.

~~~~~~

HEATHER PUT FRESH water and seed into the small glass containers. The morning routine of moving from cage to cage was akin to a dance with smooth movements that she'd perfected over time. As she fed the birds, she sang and called them by name, and they responded to her calls.

That done, Heather went into the kitchen and started the coffee. She was very particular about the way her coffee was brewed. She used only organic, free-trade coffee beans and ground them fresh for every pot. She filled the kettle and turned on the gas, ground the beans and lined the drip filter.

While waiting for the water to boil she opened the window over the sink. This one overlooked the neighbor's yard and the large 1920s Victorian-style house trimmed with gingerbread and painted a soft blue. A white picket fence corralled the property that, like hers, rolled down to Ocean Boulevard. A woman stood trimming the hedge with large, unwieldy clippers. She was tall with short white hair under a broad straw hat. She appeared to be rather old—in her eighties, perhaps—but vigorous. She was really going after those shrubs. Heather watched her for a moment, debating whether to go introduce herself, but then another woman stepped from the house and called the gardener in for breakfast. Heather thought she'd heard the red-haired woman address her as Flo.

The teakettle boiled, demanding her attention. She poured the steaming water in the filter and, humming again, cut up organic kale for the birds. They loved their daily greens and would greedily gobble them up in no time. When all was ready, she carried a tray with her cup of coffee and the birds' kale back to the sunroom.

Three large boxes filled with metal birdcages took up much of the floor space, waiting for her to assemble them. It wasn't easy removing the folded metal cages from the boxes. They weighed a ton and clattered noisily as she spread them out on the floor. They took up the entire room. The task suddenly loomed larger than she'd anticipated. She'd never been handy and didn't know a screwdriver from a wrench.

An hour later, she sat in front of a partially assembled birdcage staring at the directions with utter dismay. They didn't make any sense. She felt sure the maker had mistranslated something. Heather had no natural talent for building, and this mishmash of directions would take a master builder. In a fit of pique, she crumpled the offending pages and threw them across the room with a growl of frustration. She would have given up, except she couldn't leave her birds in travel cages for the entire summer.

"Don't you worry, boys," she said out loud to the birds, more to encourage herself. "I'll figure something out."

A gentle knocking sounded on the sliding doors of the sunroom. Heather startled and jerked her head toward the door. A man was standing at the screen door. His hair was a shaggy blond, which gave him a youthful appearance, but even through the dark screen she saw that his physique was too formed, his stance too confident for him to be a boy.

Heather rushed clumsily to her feet, clutching the neckline of her nightgown, poised to run. What an idiot she was to unlock all the screen doors! There was nothing to stop him from coming inside.

"Hello?" The man called out in a friendly tone.

Heather paused at her bedroom door and cautiously turned toward him. He hadn't moved from his place outside the screen door; he might even have taken a respectful step back. He was young, about her own age, she figured. He was casually attired in jeans and a black T-shirt; she couldn't see his eyes behind the dark sunglasses he wore. She might have scurried off but for the aura of sweetness that rose up with his smile. It changed his face, like the dawn breaking the darkness.

"Ma'am?" he called out, lifting his hand in a quick wave. "Didn't mean to startle you. I just wanted to let you know I'll be starting work out on the deck. My name's Bo."

Heather's breathing returned to normal with the dawning

of understanding. Right—Cara had told her that someone was coming to finish the deck this morning. She relaxed slightly but still clutched her nightgown close to the neckline. She was embarrassed to be seen by a man who'd come to work while she was still in her relatively revealing, flimsy nightie.

She suddenly realized that he was patiently standing there, waiting for her to respond. Her cheeks flamed as she raised her hand in a small wave. "Okay," she called back, still half hidden by the door.

He smiled again, and this time he seemed amused by her reaction.

"Yes, ma'am," he replied, then turned and departed.

Yes, ma'am? she thought indignantly. She was too young to be called "ma'am" by someone the same age as her. Was he teasing her? Or, she wondered with chagrin, was she behaving like an old woman? Her cheeks flamed; it was likely both. She retreated behind the doorframe, then peered from behind the slanted shutter to watch as he walked back to the edge of the deck and jumped with athletic ease down to the sand below.

When she was convinced his attention was otherwise occupied, Heather slipped back out to the sunroom and locked the screen doors. A woman living alone couldn't be too careful, she told herself. Then she hurried to her bedroom to dress. She locked that door, too. The bathroom was small, but Cara had done a nice job renovating it all in white tile and upscale fixtures. The compact shower had a luxurious rain showerhead. As she scrubbed her long blond hair, Heather felt the miles she'd traveled swirl away down the drain. After drying off, she wiped the large mirror clean of condensation, and her large blue eyes stared back at her.

"Not a good start to your first day," she told herself reproachfully as she pulled her hair up into a loose topknot and wrapped an elastic around it. "First you can't figure out how to put together the cages, and then you freak out when some guy comes to work on the deck. Get a grip, girl." She dropped her arms and gave herself a scolding look. "You're the mistress of Primrose Cottage now."

Filled with resolve, she began to plan a strict routine for her summer. *Time to get rolling,* she admonished herself. She might even create schedules she could affix to the fridge with magnets. She secretly loved making charts and to-do lists. They made her feel organized and boosted her confidence. Plus, just because she was living alone now didn't mean she could laze around all day. She began working out what she'd need to put on the chart, things like what day to shop, exercise—and, of course, a large chunk of each day would be set aside for her art. Mulling all these possibilities, she pulled clothing from one of the suitcases that lay on the bedroom floor. She slipped into wrinkled navy shorts and a navy-and-white-striped nautical T-shirt. Flip-flops for the feet.

Eager to start working, Heather headed toward the sunroom. She'd decided it would serve as her art room. The light was excellent, she could get fresh air pouring in when needed, and it afforded her a fabulous view of the beach. The problem was that there was a strange man working out there, too. Certainly a distraction.

She peeked out the slats of the plantation shutters on the bedroom door to the sunroom. Yes, there he was, working farther out on the grounds. Curious, she opened the slats a bit more so she could watch him work. He was handsome, she couldn't deny that. He began hoisting long pieces of lumber as if they weighed nothing and carried them up onto the deck. She was aware of the strength that took. Each time he dropped the heavy slat of wood, it banged loudly, startling her.

When he'd moved all of the slats to the deck he stopped, hands on his hips, to catch his breath. It was a hot morning and he was dripping sweat. In a swift movement, he reached down and lifted his T-shirt over his head, then used it like a rag to wipe his forehead and the back of his neck. He tossed the shirt on the deck and turned to stare out at the ocean. From her hiding spot, Heather couldn't help but stare at him. She couldn't take her eyes off his body. She wasn't a voyeur. But as a woman—as an artist—she was struck by its tan, smooth, stark beauty.

His was a young man's fit body, all lean, sinewy muscle, flat abdomen, and broad shoulders. There wasn't any of the bulk that she found unattractive, or the thickness that might come later in life. This was a body in its prime.

At first she simply stared unabashedly. Then the artist in her picked up the details. Following a sudden urge, she hurried from the bedroom out to the sunroom and dug through her boxes until she found her sketchbook and pencil. She slid onto a wicker chair, flipped open her notebook, and began to sketch. She worked quickly, catching how different movements changed the muscle. He picked up a hammer and bent low, a few nails in his mouth. When he lifted his arm, the muscles changed. Soon the rhythmic pounding of hammer against wood filled the air, a backbeat to the scratching sound of her pencil on paper.

The pencil flew over the paper in short, quick strokes, capturing the taut muscle, the protruding vein, the droplet of sweat trickling down his taut abdomen. She sighed, thinking it was no wonder Michelangelo so often drew and sculpted a man's body. Around her the birds chirped, but she didn't hear them. She was completely focused on her work. So much so, she didn't notice when her model stopped working.

"Hello!" he called out.

Heather gasped and swung her head around to again find the young man standing at the door. He was wearing once more the now-sweat-drenched black T-shirt and he held one hand cupped over his eyes as he peered in. She flipped her sketchbook closed and slammed her hand over it, blushing furiously and wildly wondering if he'd seen her gawking.

"Sorry," he said, removing his sunglasses. "I seem to be making a habit of scaring you. I knocked, but you must've been too busy working there. And those birds sure sing loud."

"Oh. Yes. Sorry." She put the sketchbook on the table and stood up. "Can I help you?"

"It's getting hot out there. Could I trouble you for some ice?"

"Of course. Come on in."

The screen door jiggled, and he looked up with resignation. "It's locked."

"Oh." Heather rushed across the room to unlock the screen door. He slid it open, and suddenly she was face-to-face with the most stunning blue eyes she'd ever seen. It felt like she was looking into the ocean when the sun made the water sparkle. She stood staring into them, mesmerized.

"Uh, excuse me," he said politely.

Flustered, Heather stepped back, cheeks aflame, muttering apologies, cringing inwardly at acting like a silly schoolgirl.

He walked past her into the house. He was at least six feet tall and deeply tanned, even so early in the season. Probably from working in the sun. His tanned skin was a sharp contrast to his almost-white blond hair and made his brilliant blue eyes shine out like beacons.

As he passed, Heather felt a sharp zing of attraction, unexpected and thus all the more powerful. Whenever she was attracted to someone, it made her even more embarrassingly awkward and tongue-tied. She clutched her hands together, holding herself erect in what she hoped appeared a poised stance similar to Cara Rutledge's.

By contrast, he didn't seem the least bothered by the awkwardness. His manner was easy and friendly without seeming overly forward. He stopped a few feet into the room.

"I don't want to track sand into your house. If you could just put some ice into this here glass, I'd be grateful." He held out a Tervis tumbler.

His hand was deeply tanned with long fingers and short nails. She clutched the tumbler, careful not to touch his fingers. "D-do you want some water, too?"

"Don't trouble yourself. I've got water outside. I just need the ice. Thanks." He sniffed the air and looked at her with charming appeal in his eyes. "Is that coffee I smell?"

"Yes."

He looked at her.

"Oh," she sputtered, realizing he was hoping she'd offer him some. She could be so dense. "Would you like a cup?"

"I wouldn't say no. It sure smells good."

Heather felt a fluttering in her stomach as she hurried to the kitchen and completed this simple task, returning a few minutes later with the tumbler filled with ice water and a mug of coffee. The man was standing near the birds, bent at the knees and making soft whistling noises. He straightened when she entered the room. Once again she was struck by how gorgeous a blue his eyes were. They drew her attention, sucking her in.

"What kind of birds are these?" he asked, gesturing. "Canaries?"

"Yes," she replied softly, and handed him the tumbler. "I, uh, put water in, too. It's nice and cold. And the coffee's hot." *Could she be more inane?* her inner voice asked. *Of course the coffee was hot.*

"Thanks," he replied, and almost as a gift offered her a dazzling smile that carved deep dimples into his cheeks before he took a long sip.

"That's good coffee."

She nervously tucked her hair behind her ear and took a few steps back.

"They all the same kind of canary?" he asked, turning back to the birds.

"Uh, no," she replied, surprised he'd asked. Most people thought all canaries were the same diminutive yellow bird. She walked over to the travel cages sitting on the table. She pointed awkwardly, not meeting his gaze. "The two yellow ones are American Singers. That white one is a Belgian Waterslager." She paused, then added, "One of the few white ones in this country."

His brows rose. "So I'm in the presence of a celebrity."

She laughed.

"They sure can sing," he said, his tone impressed.

Her face softened as she looked at her birds. There was so much she'd like to tell him about the birds—their history, how a canary was prized for its singing, how they could brighten even the gloomiest day.

He bent to look at them again. "Is it true only the boy canary sings?"

"Yes."

He cocked his head toward her. "Sort of like those famous choirboys from England."

"The Westminster choirboys?" Heather released a short laugh, delighted with the comparison. "Yes, I suppose they are."

"Do they have names?"

She took a step closer to the cages and pointed quickly to each bird. "The white one is Poseidon," she began, deliberately keeping her eyes on the birds. "Because he's a Waterslager. He sings the most beautiful water notes. The yellow one is called Moutarde because he's not only yellow but he has a spicy personality." She laughed briefly at the description, pleased to hear him chuckle, too. "And the variegated one is Pavarotti."

"The fat one's called Pavarotti?" He laughed, straightening. "That's funny."

She blinked. He'd surprised her again by knowing the name of the great opera tenor. She felt sheepish that she'd fallen into the stereotype of assuming that a man who worked with his hands wouldn't know opera.

He took a long sip of his water and lowered his hand, nonchalantly scoping out the room with unabashed curiosity.

"What you got going on here?" he asked, indicating the pile of white metal cage parts scattered on the floor. "Armageddon?"

"That," she said on a dramatic sigh, "is my futile attempt at putting together the birdcages." She shook her head with resignation. "I'm afraid I'm hopeless. As are these directions." She looked accusatorily toward the balled-up wad of paper she'd angrily tossed in the corner earlier. "They're impossible. They don't make any sense."

"They rarely do anymore. All that stuff is made in China. The translations are the pits. Do you want me to take a look?"

She was struck with hope of rescue. On the one hand, it would mean this strange man with the brilliant blue eyes would be in her space, maybe even wanting to talk, for a significant chunk of time. On the other hand, her poor birds needed *their* space even more than Heather did.

Heather's love for her birds won out. "Would you?"

"Honey, a lowcountry man never leaves a damsel in distress."

Heather didn't know how to respond. She didn't know modern men could still be so chivalrous. She looked at her hands and asked. "I'm, uh, sorry, but . . . what did you say your name was?"

"Bo. Bo Stanton. Not spelled B-e-a-u. Just B-o." He seemed intent that she got that point. "My father's name is Robert and Bob. When I came along I was called Robert, after him. I could've been Bobby or Little Bob or Bobbie Lee, but my grandmother declared I'd just be called Bo. And it stuck."

Heather looked quickly up at him. "Well, thank you . . . Bo. I'd be grateful for your help. I surely need it."

He cocked his head and his eyes sparkled with curiosity. "And what's your name?"

"Oh," she replied, flushing slightly at the oversight. "Heather. I'm Heather Wyatt."

"Heather," he repeated. "That's a right pretty name. Suits you." He stretched out his hand. "Nice to meet you, Heather."

She stared at his hand for a nanosecond, then tentatively placed her smaller palm in his large, roughened one. Every neuron in her skin came alive at his touch. She felt herself blushing again and discreetly pulled her hand back. Was he flirting? It had been a long time since she'd felt this kind of attraction to a man. But it seemed somehow improper. The last thing she wanted was to give the impression she was one of those seductive women coming on to the workman.

As though sensing her shift in mood, he turned to look at the birdcage parts scattered on the tile, all business.

"Where are the directions?" he asked, glancing around the room.

"I, uh, tossed them somewhere. Over there. . . ." She jerked a finger toward the corner.

He tracked down the ball of crumpled directions. "I've been known to file directions like that," he said with a soft laugh. He unfolded the paper and spread the directions out on the wrought-iron table. After studying them for several minutes, he whistled softly and shook his head.

"You weren't far wrong tossing these away. What a mess. Tell you what. I think I can figure out this puzzle." He crouched down and spread the directions on the floor. "Just have to be creative." He immediately began work.

Heather understood about getting sucked into the work.

While Bo began laying out the cage pieces in order, she retreated to the living room to unpack her boxes of books and art supplies.

"Would you mind if I turned on some music?"

"No, I like music," Bo replied, looking up.

"Classical okay?"

"Sure. Got to say, though, I enjoyed that Johnny Cash you had playing earlier."

"I can play that," she rushed to say.

"No, I like classical, too. Fact is, there's little music I don't like."

She smiled, pleased he didn't crumple his face with distaste. She slipped her phone into a speaker and teed up a medley of classical music. At the first few notes the birds burst into song, standing at the fronts of their cages, chests near bursting with passion. Bo looked up from the floor to watch them, then turned her way, a grin of surprised pleasure on his face.

Looking back, Heather would remember that as the moment she fell in love with Bo Stanton. But at the time she only felt a surge of inexpressible delight that this man shared her passion. He'd heard and thrilled to the incomparable joy of the birdsong, as she did.

After that, they settled into a companionable working mode. While she unpacked and sorted out her paints, brushes, and paper, she sometimes hurried to his side to hold the cage panels steady while he tightened the screws. She discovered that Bo could fill a silence. While they worked he talked on and on in a monologue, which suited her fine. He was very engaging and she didn't have to worry about carrying on her part of the conversation. Bo regaled her with the history of Isle of

Palms and Sullivan's Island, as well as some of its more color-ful natives.

"Did you know Olivia Rutledge?" she called out to him from the living room. "The woman who owned this house?"

"Sure. Cara's mother. Everybody knew Miss Lovie. She taught all us kids about the loggerheads. And let me tell you, she'd tan the hide of any boy fool enough to try to ride on the back of one." He paused, screwdriver in hand. "My daddy told me about the time back when he was in high school when he and some pals were walking the beach, probably drinking beer. All of a sudden they saw this turtle crawling back to sea. It was a big ol' mama. Not something you see every day. They were drunk and they began hassling that old girl, taking turns riding on her back. Then out of the dark comes Miss Lovie, running at them and shaking a broom. She swatted their be-hinds, I can tell you. Chased them clear away from that turtle. My daddy and his friends took off. Nope. No one messed with Miss Lovie." Bo wagged the screwdriver to make his point. "God broke the mold when He made her."

Heather hesitated, then asked in a nonchalant tone, "Is Cara like her?"

Bo paused, considering. "Hard to say. But no, I don't think she is."

"But . . ." Heather was confused. "She's a turtle lady, too."

"Yeah," Bo acknowledged. "And she's dedicated. Don't get me wrong. But . . ." Bo returned to screwing together the cage panels. "There was a genuine sweetness to Miss Lovie. I never heard her say a bad thing about anyone. She was a real lady."

The doorbell rang. "Be right back," Heather said as she

hurried to the front door. She swung open the door to find Cara carrying a bouquet of flowers. Her face was only slightly made up, blush, mascara, and lip gloss, but with her tanned skin that was all she needed. She was wearing skinny jeans that showed off her slim figure, a well-fitted navy blazer over a simple white cotton shirt, and polished boots. Her thick, glossy dark hair fell loose to her shoulders.

Heather thought of her father's comment when she spied the sizable pearls at the ears and neck. Cara looked polished, as if she might be on her way to work.

Heather tucked her long blond hair behind her ear, suddenly self-conscious in her rumpled shorts and flip-flop-clad feet.

"Good morning," Heather stuttered, caught off guard.

"Hi, there," Cara said. "I hope I'm not interrupting. I'm on my way to Charleston for a meeting and realized there was something I left in a closet. I'm terribly sorry." She raised the large bouquet of flowers in her hand. "I brought you a little something for your trouble."

"Come in," Heather blurted out, and swung the door wider. "There was no need for flowers. It's your house."

"It's yours for the summer," Cara corrected her. "Better put these right in water. It was hot in my car." She walked toward the kitchen, then stopped short, peering into the sunroom. "Bo? Is that you?"

"Hey, Cara," he called out from the floor where he was assembling a wall of one cage. Rising, he walked into the front room, wiping his hands on his jeans, and leaned forward to kiss her cheek. "Nice to see you."

Heather registered their closeness.

"And you," Cara replied, smiling. To Heather she said, "I see you two have met."

Heather nodded, feeling awkward at having Bo in the house rather than outside working on the deck.

Bo obviously felt the same, clearing his throat as he shifted from foot to foot. "Hope you don't mind, boss, but I'm helping Heather put her birdcages together. I'll get back to the deck when I'm done."

"Of course I don't mind," Cara replied magnanimously. "That was very kind of you, Bo. I know how much Heather loves her birds. Go on, get back to it. I'm just stopping by."

With the same authority she'd shown the day before, Cara walked into the kitchen and headed straight for a specific cabinet. Heather followed meekly. Opening it, Cara pulled out a glass vase, then handed it to Heather. "Here you go. I left something in the back closet. Can I grab it?"

"Of course," Heather replied.

Cara headed down the hall with the ease of someone who knew the house like the back of her hand. Heather filled the vase with water and added the flowers, then set them on the table. When done, she followed Cara down the back hall, unsure what the correct, polite thing to do was in such a situation. She found Cara in one of the two back bedrooms. Cara had told her during the walk-through that this room had been her childhood bedroom. She'd redone it with creamy walls and bright, tangerine-colored bedding. Heather paused at the door. She didn't want to tag along like a puppy or make Cara feel like she was shadowing her in her own home.

"How did you sleep last night?" Cara asked over her shoulder as she rummaged through the closet.

"Not great at first," she admitted.

"What a shame. Did you open the windows like I suggested?"

Heather looked at her feet. "I, uh, tried. But I was pretty . . . jumpy at every bump in the night." She blushed when Cara laughed at her response. Heather couldn't imagine someone like Cara being afraid to leave the windows open. Heather turned and idly looked at the framed photographs hanging on the hallway wall. They were all from the early days of Isle of Palms. There was a sepia-toned photo of a big Ferris wheel near a low-roofed wooden hotel. Another of a trolley car parked at a depot. One of a narrow road leading into a maritime forest. What was most amazing to Heather was how bare the island was. There were very few buildings. Just lots of sand.

She came to a stop before a photograph of a lovely, fair-haired woman, tanned and smiling, with her arms around two young children. They were the same children painted in the portrait over the bed—one dark-haired girl and a towheaded boy. Heather leaned forward, squinting, and looked more closely at the woman in the photograph. She jerked back and covered her mouth with a gasp.

Cara came from the bedroom carrying a box. "Got it. Thanks." Then, seeing Heather's expression, she took a few steps closer and asked, "What's the matter?"

Heather pointed to the woman in the picture. "Who is that woman?"

"That's my mother. Lovie Rutledge."

Heather turned to Cara. "That's the woman from my dream," she stammered, her voice shaking.

Cara's face immediately sharpened with interest. "What dream?"

Heather licked her lips. She didn't want Cara to think she was crazy. She looked again at the photograph—at the woman in the photo. Her smiling face once again was both reassuring and comforting.

"Oh, it's nothing. I'm just being silly."

"No, I'd like to hear."

"Well," Heather began feeling embarrassed. "Last night. I had this dream. It . . . it was very real, you know the kind?" she asked, glancing at Cara. When Cara nodded, Heather continued, "A woman was in it. She was very kind. She made me feel welcome. Not so afraid." Heather put her hand to her forehead. "I remember her stroking my hair."

Cara suddenly seemed extremely interested. "She stroked your hair? The woman from the photograph?"

Heather nodded.

Cara looked at the photograph, and her face revealed an indescribable longing. "My mother used to stroke my hair when I couldn't sleep." She shrugged. "You probably just saw the photograph during the walk-through yesterday and it stuck in your subsconscious."

"Yes, I'm sure you're right, that must be it. She just seemed so real, and she smelled like jasmine." Heather looked at Cara. "It was so strong, it filled up the room."

Cara's face went very still. "That was my mother's scent."

Chapter Six

WHAT A DAY, Cara thought when she finally arrived back on the Isle of Palms. She felt hot and sticky in her work attire and couldn't wait to take a shower and relax. Maybe have a glass of wine to ease the tension after what she'd learned at the bank. Pulling into her driveway, she was surprised to see Brett's truck already parked. She glanced at the clock in her car. It was only two o'clock. He didn't usually get home until four or five, depending on the tour schedule. It was a beautiful May afternoon, sunny and without too much wind. There wasn't a cloud in the sky. She would have thought he'd be busy with the tour boats.

"Honey?" she called out upon entering the house. She set down her purse on the front table and removed her stifling blazer, rolling her shoulders with a satisfied moan.

Brett came around the corner from the kitchen. He was wearing his running pants and a T-shirt and carrying a bottle of Gatorade. His trim, muscular body looked fit and healthy.

"Hey, there you are," he said. "Where were you?"

"The bank," she said, dropping her blazer on the back of

a chair. "First I went to the beach house to check on Heather—"

"Oh, yeah," he interrupted in the manner that revealed he'd forgotten all about it. "How did meeting her go? I never had a minute to ask you yesterday. Is everything squared away?"

"Yeah," she replied absently. Yesterday seemed like ages ago after the busy day she'd had today.

Usually they sat together at dinner and discussed all that had happened in the day, sparing no details. But the night before had been a late night. Their tour services included catering for special events, and last night they'd catered a charity event on Goat Island. They'd hired extra staff for the large group, but still neither she nor Brett had had a moment to sit and catch their breath all evening. By the time they'd cleaned and packed up the supplies and arrived home, they were utterly exhausted and collapsed into bed without any of their usual conversing. Then it was the usual rise and shine early in the morning.

Cara ran her hands through her hair, giving her head a vigorous scratch as she crossed the room toward him.

"Heather's a very nice young woman, neat and tidy." She dropped her hands. "But a bit strange."

Brett propped himself against the counter. "Strange?" he asked with a mock face of horror. "I knew it was too good to be true."

"No, not weird strange," Cara said. "More quirky. She's shy. Really shy. In fact, she barely uttered a word. I don't know how we would have gotten through the ordeal if not for her father. David Wyatt's a really good man. Good-looking, too," she added. "Polished. Considerate. He adores his daughter, you can tell. Oh, Brett," she said as a new thought sprang to mind. "You should have seen Heather's eyes light up when she saw the sunroom. You'd have been so proud of all your work."

"Really?" Brett replied, a delighted smile stretching across his face. "That's nice."

Cara nodded. "It's going to make the perfect home for Heather's birds, which is a good thing. She seems to open up around them, really loves them. Very attached."

"How many birds are there?" he asked, unscrewing the top of his Gatorade.

"Not too many, thank heavens. Three. Oh, and this is interesting. She's spending the summer painting shorebirds for"—her eyes sparkled with amusement—"wait for it . . . postage stamps!"

Brett was bringing his drink to his lips, but his hand stilled midair. "You're kidding. Postage stamps?" He took a sip. "You know, I've always wondered how the government selected the images for those things."

"Apparently it's very competitive. They choose who to give the commission to from a pool of applicants. And she got it. Shy little Heather Wyatt. Rather cool, isn't it? I'll have to buy loads of them when they come out and tell everyone I know the artist."

"What does she look like?" Brett asked.

"She's very waiflike. Pale with long blond hair and big blue eyes. Luminous, really. She could be a model for *Faerie* magazine. Or *Vogue*," she added on further thought. "She's gorgeous in her own way. Different. Tiny-boned and slender.

Actually," Cara said with a chuckle, "she's rather like her canaries."

"People are often compared to their pets."

"Right. Except those birds are so spirited and curious. And Heather seems so reticent. Cautious." Cara shook her head and added in a wry tone, "I don't expect we'll have any trouble with wild parties with her, at least."

"Thank God."

Cara thought again of the young woman in the beach house, her lack of confidence, her youth, her vulnerability. She'd been trying to figure out who Heather reminded her of all day, and suddenly it struck her. When she'd moved home to the beach house ten years earlier, she'd discovered, to her dismay, that her mother had taken in a woman as a caretaker. The woman was young and blond, like Heather. "She reminds me of Toy when I first met her. Without the attitude." She smirked. "Or the heavy eyeliner."

"Our Toy?"

"Is there another? She has that same nervous reticence. And lack of confidence. For all her impressive artwork, I get the sense that Heather is still a young woman trying to find herself. Like Toy used to be."

"And *she* certainly blossomed."

Cara's face eased into a smile as she recalled the young woman she now considered both a friend and the daughter she'd never had. The beach house—and her mother—had worked its magic on Toy as it had on her.

Cara froze, remembering Heather's dream. Something about what she'd told Cara had raised the hairs on the back of her neck. Usually she second-guessed anything she considered the slightest bit woo-woo, but she couldn't deny what she'd felt.

"Heather told me the strangest thing today." She stood with her fingers tapping her crossed arms, lost in thought. "Very unsettling. It stuck with me."

"I'm all ears."

"Well," she said, warming to the story, "remember I told you I went back to see her this morning? I had to pick up some paperwork I'd left at the beach house. I brought her some flowers, to welcome her. Oh," she said by way of an aside, "Bo was there, by the way. He was helping her build birdcages."

"Birdcages? That wasn't on his to-do list."

Cara chuckled. "No. He's such a sweet guy. I'm sure he couldn't stand by and watch Heather struggle with them. They're enormous, by the way. Not your grandmother's birdcages."

"So, what happened?" Brett asked, bringing her back to the story.

"Oh, yes. Anyway, when I asked her how she'd slept, she pointed to the photograph of my mother on the wall in the back hall. You know the one with me and Palmer?"

Brett nodded.

"She asked me who it was, and when I told her, she said she'd had this vivid dream. I almost rolled my eyes—you know how I hate to hear people tell me about their dreams."

He laughed. "Yes, babe, I'm familiar."

"But I was polite and listened. Then she tells me that my mother was the woman in her dream! That she stroked Heather's hair." Cara's eyes widened. "That's what my mother used to do for me when I was sad or sick and had trouble sleeping."

"A lot of mothers do that."

"That's what I told her. But then she said . . ." Cara paused to rub the sudden chill she felt down her arms. "She said the room was filled with the scent of jasmine."

Brett pushed away from the counter. "Jasmine? That was your mother's scent."

Cara nodded.

Brett stepped close and put his hands on her arms and gently rubbed. "I can see this has you worked up."

Cara felt a flush of embarrassment. "I'm not the type of woman who gets worked up about dreams and all that voodoo."

"I didn't know there was a type."

"But I have to admit it was unnerving. You know, I've always felt my mother's presence in the beach house."

"That's only natural. It was her house. It's still filled with her things."

"True," Cara said doubtfully. "But it's more than that. I really feel her. But she's never come to me in a dream. I've certainly never smelled her perfume. So when Heather said she'd seen Mama in her dream, it just made me wonder. What if?" She looked at Brett beseechingly.

"And maybe you're a little jealous, too?"

"Jealous? Of what?"

"That your mother came to this new girl instead of you? Maybe that's what made you compare her to Toy. You used to be jealous of your mother's affection for her, too."

Cara felt a niggling of discomfort at the truth in that. She and her mother had had such a difficult relationship that when she'd returned home to mend fences, she had been incensed to find this arrogant, needy young woman taking her mother's time and attention away from her. Yes, Brett was right. She'd been jealous of Toy. And now . . . was she jealous that her mother had come to yet another lost young woman—instead of her?

Cara's practical side pushed the notion far back into the nether regions of her mind. She had other, more important issues to discuss with Brett today. She exhaled the last of her angst over the matter and slipped from Brett's arms.

"Anyway, what's up? You're home early," she called out to Brett as she entered the kitchen.

She always felt pleasure stepping into this room. She'd knocked out a wall and created a big kitchen space, outfitted with modern appliances and new tile. An island now separated the kitchen from the eating area and offered the kitchen the same grand views of the wetlands. As with the kitchen, she'd not only changed the house architecturally, but also had redone all the floors and light fixtures and had designed an efficient, sleek office space from the third bedroom. She'd poured so much of herself into this house, all her hopes and dreams as a bride. It was why she loved it, in some ways just as much as Primrose. While the ocean and beach had their own magnificence, as far as she was concerned, the real action with change of seasons, birds, and tides happened on the back side of the island.

Brett followed her into the kitchen. "I cut out. I was feeling off. Probably tired from last night. Robert was there and we weren't that busy, so I decided to come home for a run."

"Careful, old man," she said. "It's pretty hot out there today. You should start running in the evenings. I don't want you to get overheated."

He came closer to kiss her forehead. "My little mama hen." Then he swatted her behind. "And who're you calling an old man?"

She scoffed, slipping under his outstretched arm. She was already mentally preparing for the meaty discussion that was coming up. She opened the fridge and pulled out a can of flavored seltzer water. Flipping open the can, she turned to face him. Her face and tone were serious.

"Brett. We need to talk."

His face immediately grew equally sober. "Okay. About what?"

"About today. I went to the bank."

He took a drink from his bottle. "Oh, yeah?" he asked in a casual tone, but his eyes appeared hunted. "What did they have to say?"

Cara had promised herself she wasn't going to get into an argument with Brett about what she'd learned at the bank, but she could feel the anger and resentment she'd managed to quell during the car ride home bubble up again.

"Maybe we should sit down."

"Babe, I was about to go for a run." Brett looked longingly at the door.

Cara knew how much he hated to discuss finances. The subject of profits and losses always put him on edge. But she couldn't avoid this one.

"This is really important. It won't take long, but we have to discuss it. Now."

She went to sit on the leather sofa, then looked up at him expectantly.

Brett reluctantly followed and plopped down on the opposite side of the sofa with obvious pique and stretched his long arm along its back.

"So, what's this all about?"

Cara skewered him with a cool gaze. "Want to take a guess?"

He leaned back against the cushions and looked at the ceiling. When he lowered his head again, his face looked wan. "The boat," he said with a sigh. It wasn't really an answer but a statement of fact.

"The boat," she affirmed. "That enormous, ridiculous, going-to-drown-us-financially boat!" She felt her self-control slipping and struggled to rein in her frustration. "Brett, it's not good."

Brett's tanned face paled and his brows drew together. "Okay."

Cara licked her lips. "You recall that when you wanted to buy that new tour boat, we had to take out a home equity loan?"

Brett nodded warily.

"Well, the loan just adjusted upward."

"It *what?*" he asked, leaning forward. His eyes flashed, indignation mixed with confusion that the bank could do such a thing.

Cara swallowed an irritated sigh. For all that Brett was a very intelligent man, his knowledge of business and finance was virtually nonexistent. More because he didn't care to learn than that he lacked the ability to grasp concepts. When she'd married him, he'd been skating merrily along, happy to make enough money to get by and still be able to fish and surf and live the lifestyle he enjoyed. That was all well and good for a man in his twenties. A bit doubtful for a man in his thirties, but bordering on ridiculous for a man hitting forty. Yet Brett was an original. He took great pride in the tour boat company he'd established and felt honor-bound to educate children and adults about the wonder of the ocean. It was more than a job to him. It was a mission. And if it wasn't wildly profitable, so what?

She loved that about him. Admired him. Married him for it. Yet Cara was savvy enough to know that Brett was reaching the point when he had to begin being realistic about the issues that arose in the latter half of life. When they married and she'd taken over the business side of the tour company, she'd had to convince him he needed to be smart and plan health-care benefits, start setting money aside for his retirement—an ongoing battle for a man who still believed death was a long way off—and, for a time, to plan for children.

"Brett," she said, trying to keep exasperation out of her voice. They'd discussed this before. "It was an adjustable loan. Of course it was going to change. I just didn't realize how much." She licked her lips again and took a breath. "We went through the numbers." She waved her hand and reached for her drink.

Brett dropped his arm from the back of the sofa and sat straight. "Explain it to me in a nutshell."

She sat back and her eyes met his, flashing with emotion. "We're screwed."

He stared at her. "What do you mean, we're screwed?"

"I mean, I don't know how we can make the payments. On our current combined income, we can't. Simply put, Brett, that big luxury tour boat you bought is not bringing in the money projected when we took out the loan. In fact, it's essentially bleeding money. It's nothing but a huge financial drain. We have to find a source of money from somewhere to pay off the loan, or . . ."

"Or what?"

"What always happens when you don't pay your loan. The bank will come after your collateral. In this case—our house."

"Are you talking bankruptcy?"

She shrugged. "Possibly."

"Shit," he said, and fell back against the sofa. There was a moment of silence as they both absorbed the impact of that word. "I bought the boat for a steal," he said by way of self-defense. "Half its original value."

"A boat's not like a house, Brett. It doesn't go up in value over time. It sinks. No pun intended."

He nodded grimly. "Okay, then. I'll sell the boat."

Cara had already thought of this and discussed it with a maritime company. "We have to do that," she said in the same monotone that the loan officer had used with her when her own voice began to rise. "But it won't be enough. Just in the few years we've had it, it's taken a tremendous loss. What's that saying? The two happiest days of a boat owner's life are the day he buys his boat and the day he sells it."

Brett didn't laugh. His face was filled with regret. "I'm sorry, Cara. I really thought—I hoped—it was a good idea."

He sounded so dejected her heart lurched. She'd been dubious about the investment at the time but, when faced with

Brett's unwavering optimism, she'd relented, even though a part of her had known it was a poor business decision. And now they were both going to pay the price.

She scooted to his side of the sofa and put her hand on his thigh. "I know you did. You convinced me."

Brett smiled wryly. "Not really."

She laughed softly and shook her head. "Not really."

"So what do we do now?" he asked her.

She sighed and leaned back against the sofa. This part was the hardest. "That's what I spent the afternoon talking to the loan officer about. Basically, we have to make the payments, and to do that we have to come up with a new source of income, fast. We both know that the boat won't sell quickly—if it sells at all. So the next thing to consider is laying someone off."

"Who?" Brett asked, alarmed at the prospect. "We've already laid off everyone but me and Robert. We need two to crew a tour at bare minimum. We have interns working in the summer. And you—"

"I don't get paid," she finished for him. When they had purchased the boat, Cara had volunteered to give up her salary until the boat brought in some money. It never did.

Brett's smile was filled with love and compassion. "No."

Cara curled her legs up beneath her on the sofa. "We could sell the house."

Brett frowned and clasped his hands together. "Where would we live?"

"We could move into the beach house."

"But it's rented."

"Actually, being rented is not a problem. We'd just have to

find a place to rent until the beach house is free." She waited while he digested this. "This place should sell quickly, and for a good price. It's on deep water."

"Well, why sell this house? The beach house will fetch more money. And we don't live there. We wouldn't have to move."

"True." She looked at her hands. She'd known he'd fight to save this house. It was his home, after all. His name was on the deed. He'd lived in it for years. But not nearly as many years as she'd lived in her mother's house. "Brett, I've gone over and over this at the bank, and our options are limited. It's really very simple."

Cara held up her hand and began counting off. "One, we sell the boat." She rolled her eyes. "That's not likely to happen and, even if it does, it might not bring in enough money to dig us out of this rut. Two, we lay someone off. You just told me that can't happen. Three, I quit and get a decent-paying job. Or should I say, a job that pays anything." She paused and licked her lips. "At my age, that's not going to be easy, but it's possible. The downside? It might take too long to get a job that will pay me what we need for the loan. Four, we sell this house. Or five"—she paused—"we sell my beach house."

"I go for number five," Brett said automatically.

Cara tightened her arms around herself and stared at him with barely constrained anger. "Let me get this straight. You don't want to sell your house. You want me to sell *my* house, an heirloom from my deceased mother, to pay off the debt from *your* tour boat."

"Are you forgetting how we got caught in this financial bind in the first place?" Brett said brusquely.

Cara's eyes flashed. "Of course I'm not forgetting. I'll never forget. And it wasn't just your money we spent. It was all my savings, too. We both invested everything we had into those in vitro programs."

Her voice choked up as she recalled the endless hormone shots, the ice-cold metal tables, the doctors' furrowed brows as they gave her and Brett bad news, again and again, cycle after cycle. First hope, and then stubbornness, and finally denial had kept them coming back long after they should have stopped trying, and long after they could afford to. But the rainbow baby they'd so desperately longed for had never come. And when Cara had decided to turn toward adoption, she'd been shocked and dismayed when Brett—kind, caring Brett—hadn't followed.

He'd had reasons. He'd dreamed of having his own biological child—one that looked like a perfect combination of the two of them. He'd also wanted to enjoy a pregnancy with Cara, to hear the child's heartbeat, to watch the ultrasound excitedly as the doctor told them whether it was a boy or a girl. Finally, he was firm that he wouldn't feel the same way about an adopted child that he would about a biological child.

Cara had been devastated by her failure to give Brett that child. But Brett had never blamed her. Instead he'd descended into what she could only call an early midlife crisis. He was determined to make his mark in life. He went gung-ho for his scheme of expanding his business—buying the luxury tour boat. By that point, Cara was numb with depression and really didn't care one way or the other.

It felt like something had just sucked all the air out of the room. Cara rose from the sofa and paced to diffuse the whirlwind of emotions. The anger was gone, replaced by a pervasive anguish that she knew both of them kept deeply buried.

"I don't want to fight," she said wearily, worn out from the day's back-and-forth maneuvers at the bank to try to come to some sort of workable plan.

Brett's anger dissolved in an instant. He came to stand by her at the window and wrapped his arms around her. "I don't, either."

Despite their words, she still felt the residue of unresolved feelings. She stood stiffly in his arms, not daring to speak.

"We'll figure something out," he said reassuringly. "We always do."

"I know," Cara replied. But her tone belied her vote of confidence.

After a minute, when it became clear nothing more was going to be said, Brett dropped his arms and took a few steps back. "Okay, then. I'm off. I can still get that run in."

Cara nodded, lips tight. It was typical of Brett to run off from a difficult money discussion, especially when it started to get heated. Money and emotion were never a good combination. She knew he'd worry about it, in his own way at his own pace. If she stopped him now the argument would only escalate into something ugly. So she said nothing and let him go.

A moment later she heard the door close. Only then did she release the ragged sigh she'd been holding. She didn't know what she was going to do. She was still too angry to make plans. But she felt the weight of the world on her shoulders.

She strode into the kitchen and retrieved a wineglass. This she filled with red wine. She took a long swallow. Then another. Then, because she couldn't think of what else to do, she carried the glass and the bottle into the living room, turned on the television and plopped down on the sofa, tucking her legs beneath her. She didn't care what she watched. She merely needed a distraction. Something to calm her down before round two began when Brett came home.

That was what she was doing when the front doorbell rang a little later. She was watching some inane reality show about a hoarder. It was creepy to see how someone could hang on to so much worthless stuff. Rising to answer the door, she looked around the house as though checking to see she didn't have too much clutter.

She opened the door, and her breath caught in her throat. Two uniformed policemen stood on her threshold with somber expressions. She felt her heartbeat quicken.

"Good afternoon, officers. Can I help you?"

"Mrs. Beauchamps?"

"I'm Cara Rutledge, but, yes, I'm married to Brett Beauchamps."

One officer looked at the other. This one cleared his throat and seemed to have difficulty speaking. "Can we come in, please?"

"What's this about?"

"We have some news. Please, could we come in?"

Cara swallowed thickly and stepped aside, allowing the officers into her home. She was aware of the television noise in the background. The half-empty bottle of wine and the glass on the cocktail table.

The senior officer spoke again. "You should sit down." He indicated the sofa with his hand.

"I don't want to sit down. What's this about?" Cara replied in a terse voice.

The officer cleared his throat and assumed a face of regret. "I'm terribly sorry, Mrs. Beauchamps," he began, using her wrong name. "There's been an incident. Your husband collapsed on the street. Someone called an ambulance. Thankfully, that person also recognized him for an ID."

"Brett . . ." His name escaped her lips. "Is he all right? Which hospital did he go to?"

"The ambulance took him to MUSC."

Cara was already hurrying toward her purse.

"Ma'am," the second officer said, going to her side as she snatched up her purse. He touched her arm.

Cara wasn't listening. She was in a panic. All she could think of was getting to the hospital as fast as she could. To get to Brett. She needed to be at his side.

"Ma'am," the officer said again, louder this time.

Cara stopped and looked into his face. His eyes were downcast in sorrow, his skin pale with the news. With dreadful certainty, she knew what he was going to say. She began shaking her head. She didn't want to hear it.

"I'm sorry. Your husband, Mr. Beauchamps, had a heart attack. I'm sorry," he said again. "He didn't make it."

Chapter Seven

DISCOMBOBULATED. HEATHER LOVED words, especially those that sounded like what the word actually meant. She snorted and scratched her head as she woke slowly. Discombobulated was exactly how she felt. When she opened her eyes, it took her a few minutes to remember where she was. She was steamy, covered in a sheen of sweat from another night with all the windows shut and locked. Heather wondered how long it would take before she woke up and felt the beach house was home.

Sitting up, she looked around the bedroom. It was a pretty room, very Jamaican with white paint and dark wood. Lovie's room, once upon a time. Then Cara's. Two strong women. Heather hoped some of their strength would flow into her through some cosmic osmosis.

This morning, however, the room felt foreign—and it was a mess. Her clothes were still in suitcases, and boxes cluttered the floor. Her stomach was growling and she didn't have a clue what there was to eat for breakfast. She felt like a guest in her own house.

Out in the sunroom, her canaries were chirping, and she smiled. At last, something she recognized! Looking at the clock, she saw she'd overslept again. The poor birds were still under their covers. She heard their insistent, demanding chirps as *Wake up, sleepyhead! Where are you, you hopeless dawdler? Rise and shine!* One of the birds had even started singing under his cover, a slave to his hormones and eager to start his day.

"Coming, babies," she called out, whipping back the covers of the large, spacious cages that Bo had put together for her. "Pavarotti, look at you, all alert and sitting by your seed dish. Don't worry, fatty, I'll feed you." On to the next cage. "Good morning, sweet Poseidon! Hearing you sing made me feel at home. Thank you." In the third cage, Moutarde was chirping stridently. He didn't like being the last to be uncovered. "Such a fuss, Moutarde," she called out, removing his cover. "We're all a bit out of sorts this morning. But you don't have to complain. I'll feed you first, okay?"

Heather enjoyed her chatter with the birds. For her, the seemingly meaningless exchanges were very meaningful. Talking to her birds, especially living alone and with her anxiety keeping her from others, connected her to other living creatures. She didn't feel so alone in the world—or in this still strange house. Her canaries were her greatest allies. Her dear little friends that let her know in a thousand chirps each day that she was important to them. She was good enough. They cared for her unconditionally.

Her mother had once told her that a canary in the house sang away the blues. It was true. One couldn't be depressed when a canary sang in the room. Their music was all heart and joy. Throughout the day, no matter what room she was in, they'd connect with her through their song. Sometimes they sang so brilliantly that she had to stop what she was doing to listen, a smile on her face. At the day's end when the sun lowered, casting shadows and changing the blue sky to deep indigo, she'd talk to them again as she covered their cages. The birds were her touchstones that marked the beginning and end of each day. And here at the beach house, they were her constant companions on this journey from dependence to independence.

Now that the sun was shining she opened all the windows, allowing the fresh air to fill the room and finished feeding the birds. Then it was time to deal with her own hunger. Sunlight filled the small kitchen, and in the light she saw that she'd left the kitchen a mess as well. The counter was littered with her empty soup can, cups with dried, wrinkled tea bags in them, a wineglass with the last of her wine congealing in the bottom, and bread crumbs and jam. In the sink were dirty dishes. She wrinkled her nose at the fetid smell coming from the garbage.

"There's no maid for you in this house," she told herself with a rueful sigh. "Welcome to the real world." She rummaged through the cabinets to find soap and towels and quickly cleaned the kitchen, popping whole-grain bread into the toaster while she worked. Once the strong scent of coffee filled the room, she felt better. After a quick breakfast and final cleanup, Heather gathered up the garbage. Now, where should she put it?

The obvious place was outside somewhere. She opened the front door and stood a moment blinking in the bright sunlight. The island heat was rising already. The unforgiving sunlight revealed the age of the house, but she could see that it was lovingly maintained. Fresh paint on the trim, new screens on the porches, and big pots of big cherry-red geraniums. Bending, she touched the soil. Needed water, she reminded herself. The dunes beyond the house were covered with wild grasses and flowers; most she couldn't name. But she would start to sketch them and learn. On the ground she spotted the skittering prints of ghost crabs that led to their circular dens. A big spiderweb in the corner of the porch was covered with dew. There wasn't a garage or shed, so she looked under the front porch and found the bins along with a rusting bicycle, a few garden tools, beach chairs, deflated beach balls, and a bocce ball set half buried under sand. So much to do . . . so much to learn, she told herself as she tossed the garbage in the bin.

A nagging voice crept into her mind, telling her she didn't have what it took to live on her own. That she was setting herself up for failure. She wasn't strong or resourceful enough. She couldn't even walk outdoors without looking over her shoulder.

Heather closed the lid of the garbage bin with a firm slap and silenced the voice. Her therapist had told her that people with social anxiety often filtered out their own strengths by ignoring them or explaining them away. Instead they liked to tell themselves of their flaws and shortcomings, anything to make them feel inferior.

"Yes, I can," she said aloud, slapping dust from her hands.

She walked to the tilting, rusting black mailbox affixed to a wood post. It squeaked when she opened it. Peering in, she jumped back as a small black spider scurried out.

"It's just a spider," she said aloud, calming herself. "It's probably more afraid than you are." The spider was the only occupant of the mailbox. Not even junk mail. Closing the box, she looked down the street at the row of beach houses. It was a quiet back street with a mix of houses—some big and impressive, but many smaller cottages like the beach house she lived in. Some had cars in their driveways; others were hidden behind thick barriers of palm trees and overgrown shrubs. Not a person in sight. The reality that she didn't know anyone here except Cara and Bo loomed large in her mind.

Bo. . . . Where was he? She didn't see him around the deck. Was he working on another job? Or had her nervous prattle scared him off? She hoped not. She liked him. It was a novel feeling for her. Almost a crush. She tried not to think about him, but from time to time she'd see his face in her mind. Or if there was a noise outside, she'd peek out the window, hoping it was him. If she'd felt this way about a man five years ago, she wouldn't have been able to be in the same room with him. She would have darted behind a closed door and ignored his presence, even though he was kind. So just the fact that she had invited Bo inside and conversed with him, albeit clumsily, was a huge sign that her therapy was working and she was getting better. That was something positive, wasn't it?

Heather went back indoors with a lighter step and dove into the task of settling into the beach house. She began unpacking her suitcases and boxes, finding the right place for everything. It was soothing work. She folded a shirt or pants, then placed them in the drawer. Bras, underwear, tops in the dresser. Shoes, dresses, jackets in the closet. Makeup, brushes, cleanser and moisturizer, hair dryer in the bathroom. Each space claimed made her feel like a pioneer in the new territories, setting down stakes.

Once her clothing was unpacked, the top priority was setting up an office/studio. Her work with shorebirds was, after all, why she'd selected Isle of Palms to spend the summer. Heather chose the sunroom for its light, but also because it made her feel like she was outdoors. She spent so much of her time indoors in Charlotte that she longed to go out more, to feel the fresh air on her face, to explore new destinations. The sunroom was for her a magical place that was part inside, part out. A step in the right direction. She erected her easel where it would catch the best light, and moved a small bookshelf in from the living room to house those texts she'd brought with her from Charlotte. She took great pleasure in lining up her different pencils, getting them ready for the inspiration she hoped would come. Stacking her sketch paper and notebooks was akin to laying the bricks for the big project ahead.

Heather took an odd pleasure in doing the simple tasks. Accomplishing them silenced that negative voice in her ear and gave her a bit more confidence that she could actually make it living alone. Over a quick lunch of an egg salad sandwich, she opened her computer and did a few chores online. She checked her emails and found the garbage and recycling pickup dates.

In this manner the next several days continued. Heather took small steps to make the beach house her own. She felt very much alone, like an explorer in a new world as she prowled through all the drawers, snooped through closets and cabinets. She didn't discover much of interest, just the usual utilitarian items found in most rental houses. She rearranged a few pieces of furniture, laid her favorite comforter on the back of the sofa, and took great satisfaction adding some of her own personal items. On the mantel she placed a silver-framed photograph of her and her mother taken shortly before her death. They were laughing with such joy and life. There was another of the family together at the Grand Canyon. One of her grandparents. She placed her favorite books on the shelves, lit a scented candle. In an extravagant gesture, she ordered new linens online. When they arrived at the end of the week, she couldn't wait to put them on her bed. And after several days of checking an empty mailbox, she hooted with excitement when she received her first piece of mail. It was verification that she lived here.

None of the changes she'd made were dramatic. She was simply nesting. It was important that she noticed the changes, that they made her feel more at home. It was making a small statement that this was *her* house—at least for the summer. Declaring to the world—and most important, herself—that Heather Wyatt was beginning a new chapter in her life.

At the end of her first week living alone Heather stood at the sliding doors of the sunroom staring out at the evening sky. She had just closed and locked them, as she had every night since her arrival. Not exactly the courageous behavior of a woman breaking old habits, she thought.

Bo had not returned to work this week. She missed seeing his warm smile, hearing his cheery "Hello!" and his conversation. The job wasn't done. Heather wondered when he'd return . . . if he'd return.

Out in the great sky, a full moon provided a breathtaking trail of rippling light along the ocean, a direct path to the stars. Heather was filled with a sudden, overwhelming sense of yearning. The moon, the stars, the sea, life . . . they were calling to her. She felt the pull at her heart.

She felt the coolness of the glass as she placed her hand against the windowpane. It was a solid thing, transparent, but one that kept her looking at the world outside from her safe haven indoors. Her fear kept her as caged as her canaries. The glass windows were no different from their metal bars.

MEMORIAL DAY CAME and went. A swarm of people had descended on the island, horns honking, clogging the roads and filling the beaches. Heather watched them from behind her window. Countless brightly colored towels spread out on the sand, families gathered under large umbrellas, young mothers hovered over young children building sand castles, people bobbed and splashed in the surf. Even though it was real life, watching it from behind glass had the same effect as if she were watching it all on television.

May was over and tomorrow June began. Heather felt a keen sense of urgency. After all, she'd come to Isle of Palms to sketch live shorebirds in their natural habitat. She couldn't delay her commission any longer. Creating a small postage stamp was a long, intense process. Developing it easily took two to three years from application to when the Postmaster General approved the final art. As they'd told her when she was awarded the commission: "Work small but think big!"

She'd submitted her proposal to the Postal Service a year earlier. Her proposal had passed the first set of rigorous reviews, a feat she'd never dared hope to achieve. The committee was highly selective and chose from a wide scope of both ideas and artists. Once the subject was approved, extensive verification by the committee had to be performed on each detail of a stamp's design. The production procedures were complex. Now Heather was beginning the creative phase. For each stamp she'd create a series of sketches and drawings to develop the design. Working with the art director, she'd explore different approaches to the topic. It was a mountainous task that involved many hours of work. She had to complete dozens of sketches of select shorebirds in different settings, then send them for review. The committee would select four to six, and from these she would create paintings for the judges. Out of these, only one or two would be selected for national stamps.

It was a great deal of work for not a lot of money. Nor recognition. Most people didn't know who the artists were behind the stamps. But the dollar amount didn't figure into her decision. Where else would her work enjoy an audience of millions of people throughout the United States and around the world? To see her art on someone's letter in the post—that was priceless.

Filled with resolve, Heather sat at the glass-topped iron table she'd converted to her work desk and pulled out all her previous research on shorebirds of the East Coast. Another artist had been assigned the task of shorebirds of the Pacific coast. Narrowing the scope to the Eastern Seaboard still left her with a large number of species that frequented the shore-line. From this list she'd selected birds from the most-endangered and most-threatened lists.

Soon Heather was enveloped in her work. She created a large tri-fold poster board to which she could add her photo-graphs and sketches. Then she pinned up her list of the Ten Most Wanted Birds to discover on the beach.

1. Piping plover
2. Long-billed curlew
3. Wilson's plover
4. American oystercatcher
5. Red knot
6. Least tern
7. Sanderling
8. Ruddy turnstone
9. Sandpiper
10. ?

Number ten was going to be a gut choice, she decided. A shorebird she fell in love with that demanded she paint it. Leaving the element of surprise in the process kept her open to new ideas as she worked. Especially in nature, Heather found she had to trust her instincts as much as, or more than, her intellect.

Her first job was the not inconsiderable task of actually getting outside. How many of her fellow artists had to deal with that challenge? *Doesn't matter,* she told herself, focusing. All that mattered was that she couldn't procrastinate any lon-ger. No excuses. She tapped her pencil against her lips. Per-haps if she went out to the beach at dawn? When there were few people walking about? That would be a good way to start. And she had to start somewhere.

Decision made, Heather fetched her backpack and laid it out on the table. Tomorrow she would rise with the sun and venture out before the crowds arrived. It would be a first foray to get a feel for the landscape and scout out where the shorebirds hung out. She packed only a few things—her binoculars, notebooks and sketch pad, and drawing pencils. The zipper hummed in the hush of the room. It bolstered her courage.

Chapter Eight

T HE FOLLOWING MORNING Heather awoke to music playing on her phone. The room was filled with the soft, pewter-gray light of predawn. She threw back the sheet and, rising, felt the usual sweltering heat of a closed-up room.

Today was a day for positive thinking and new initiatives. She quickly dressed in the clothes she'd laid out the night before: lightweight khaki-colored nylon fishing pants and shirt, her typical uniform when she did research. She hurried to the dimly lit sunroom, needing to draw a moment of strength from her precious companions before venturing out of doors. Her canaries were still one-legged puffballs on their perches. They jerked their heads up, startled, and began chirping as though to say, *Why are you up before the sun?*

"Sorry, sleepyheads," she crooned to the birds. "I'll be back to feed you soon." She slipped into her sandals, grabbed her backpack, and, resolutely ignoring the roiling sensation in her stomach, stepped outside.

Dawn by the ocean was a world fresh and new. Lifting her face, Heather breathed deep the moist air. A hush hovered over the land. Feeling the birth of adventure in her heart, she hoisted the backpack onto her shoulder and climbed from the side of the as-yet-unfinished deck to the ground.

She followed the narrow, winding beach path that cut through the dunes. The sand was cool and damp with dew. In and around the plants along the dunes she saw the narrow scratches of ghost crab trails. Suddenly the path opened up, and she stood before the vast vista of sea and sky as dawn broke around her. Great shafts of rosy light spread across the gray sky. The beach below, washed clean by the tide, shimmered in the pearly tints of the sunrise. Here and there she spotted horseshoe crabs dotting the beach, waiting for the next tide. This thrilled her because she knew that these creatures—twice as ancient as the dinosaurs—were laying eggs. And these nutrient-rich eggs were a feast to migrating shorebirds.

To her left a long swath of beach led to the pier miles away. From the maps she'd studied, that would be Front Beach, where shopping, hotels, and restaurants clustered. To her right, the beach curved where it met Breach Inlet, a no-swimming area of turbulent water; just across was the northern end of Sullivan's Island. This was where she'd read shorebirds were more likely to gather. Only one way to find out, she thought. Heather adjusted her backpack and took off to the right. As she walked, the pink light of dawn spread out to stain the entire sky and shimmer on the moist sand below. It was so beautiful it felt unearthly—almost like a fairy tale.

She smiled as a small group of sandpipers ran across the beach in their comical, stiff-legged gait, searching for their morning meal of crustaceans and insects. She pulled binoculars and a notebook from her backpack. Looking more closely at the birds, she made out the yellow legs and dark, ruddy brown coloring and corrected herself: "Least sandpipers." Lowering the binoculars, she put a check mark next to the name and noted where she'd spotted them. Heather paused, chewing the end of her pencil. She *thought* that was correct— but truth was, sandpipers were hard to distinguish from other "peeps" in the genus *Calidris*. There might have been a couple of semipalmated sandpipers in the mix. She tucked the binoculars back in her backpack, knowing she'd have to return to photograph them to capture the distinguishing marks that could be frustrating for casual bird-watchers.

During the spring and fall, shorebirds migrated in large numbers along the Carolina coast. Birdlife on the beaches was a sight to behold. Many of the shorebirds were just passing through. These beaches were important way stations for migrating birds, and they were hungry after traveling thousands of miles. Other birds stayed for the summer to nest and raise chicks, then left again in the fall. Still others made the Carolina beaches their winter homes.

Heather stopped short, listening, her heart pounding with excitement. Near the inlet she spotted numerous shorebirds poking in the sand and skittering from point to point, creating a cacophony of sound that, to her, sounded like a song of welcome. She stopped a fair distance away so as not to disturb them as they foraged for food. This was what she'd come for!

She sat on the cool sand and pulled the binoculars from her backpack. Resting her elbows on her knees, she peered at the birds she'd spent hours researching up to now only in books. In the brightening light she recognized royal terns, least terns, black skimmers, oystercatchers, and plovers, taking care to check off the species on her list. She felt elated when she spotted the endangered red knots that came to feast on the horseshoe crab eggs. Heather lowered her binoculars, grinning from ear to ear. It was so much more vivid and compelling to see them alive in their habitat, and it was the first time Heather could recall feeling real, unbridled joy in quite a while.

She had only meant to stay a short while, but she hadn't expected to see a cornucopia of shorebirds. So many on her list . . . She pulled out her sketchbook and began to draw. To create an authentic rendition, she had to observe a bird's interaction with its own and other species, its hunting pattern and diet, and how it ate, built its nest, raised its young, found shelter. She'd come to the right place. She'd concentrate on the chunky medium-size red knots today, high on her list of endangered shorebirds. They'd be moving on soon. There would be ample time for her to observe, photograph, and sketch other birds she needed for the stamps.

Her hand moved quickly over the paper as she drew the red knots. She was lost in concentration when she heard an excited bark, loud and gruff, coming from behind her. Heather jerked her head up to see a brown Labrador charging right for her—and the birds. Heather leaped to her feet and spread out her arms to chase the dog away.

"Stop!" she shouted, waving her arms madly. "Get out of here! Go away!"

The dog didn't even slow down. It simply detoured around

her and headed straight for the birds, still barking enthusiastically. Heather turned, mouth agape with shock, to watch the entire group of shorebirds scattering in the wind. The dog barked after them, tail wagging, having a good ol' time.

Heather stood staring at the now-empty shoreline with her arms limp at her sides, breath ragged and all earlier sense of peace as dispersed as the birds fluttering in the sky. And things had been going so well! Against her will, she felt the hot prick of tears behind her eyes, and angrily brushed them away.

A woman in a pink jogging outfit trotted closer with an angry scowl on her face. She was twice Heather's age and size, with an air of entitlement.

"What's your problem?" the woman shouted at her.

Heather turned, perplexed, toward the angry woman. She couldn't respond.

"It's no-leash time on the beach!" the woman shouted, clearly irritated that her dog had been perceived as misbehaving.

Heather felt her insides tighten as her fists clenched at her sides. Her mouth worked but no words would come out. She wanted to tell this woman that it wasn't the leash that was a problem; it was the fact that her dog was chasing the birds to begin with. It wasn't cute when a dog—or a child—scattered a flock of birds on the beach. One seemingly fun moment could spell disaster for shorebird families. Especially the migrating birds; forcing them to fly or run caused them to use up valuable energy for their journey. But Heather couldn't explain any of this to the woman, her breath still evading her. She could only clutch her sketchbook to her chest and point to the birds squawking and circling in the sky, hoping she would understand.

"What?" the woman demanded.

Heather wanted to run away. Even a year ago, she probably would have. But she'd come so far to run away now. She gathered her courage and finally squeaked out, "Your dog is chasing the birds!"

The woman looked at the birds, and then turned back. "So what? That's what dogs do!"

Heather felt as she had in high school when classmates had taunted her and she couldn't say a word back. She just stood there, offering no resistance, wishing she could just disappear, hoping she wouldn't throw up.

The woman walked closer and started thrusting her finger at her as she made her point. "It's people like you who ruin vacations. Busybody! I paid three thousand dollars for a week here and I'm following the rules."

Heather was trembling, but she felt the need to stand up for herself. This woman didn't understand. She had to explain, not just for herself but for the birds.

"The birds . . . they're feeding."

The woman glared at her. "And?"

Heather took a deep breath. It was very difficult to form words. "It's not good for them to chase them."

"Godiva is just playing. She does this every morning. It's none of your business." Her eyes narrowed. "I've never seen you around here before—where do you live? Are you even supposed to be on this beach? What's your name?"

Heather just stared at her mutely.

After another few moments, the woman scowled once more, then waved her hand in rude dismissal and turned her back, shutting down any further discussion. But to Heather's relief, she at last called the dog to her side. Thankfully, the Labrador obediently returned. She watched the insufferable woman jog off, her dog trotting faithfully at her side.

Heather was so shaken by the confrontation she felt light-headed, a sure sign a panic attack was about to happen. She couldn't prevent it, but she could try to manage it. She stared out at the calm ocean and took deep breaths. "Take it easy," she told herself. "You aren't in any real danger. It's just symptoms of panic."

She clenched her fists and sat down on the sand, willing herself to pay attention. "I accept that I'm feeling afraid at this moment. But it's only a feeling. I accept it won't kill me. This feeling is the worst that will happen. I just need to ride it out."

Heather remained in the same spot and continued talking to herself in a calm, placating voice. It was like counting to ten when she was mad. More and more of the shorebirds returned to cluster along the gulley and at the lapping shoreline. The waves rolled in and out in a regular pattern, and Heather matched her breathing to their ebb and flow. Gradually she felt her body relax and the panic attack subside.

Then it was gone. Heather felt drained but oddly triumphant. This was her first panic attack in a long while, and she'd used her tools to get through it. Still, what a loser she was. She still stood there like a mute, unable to respond. Her pencils and notebook lay scattered on the sand. She went to fetch them and stuffed everything into her backpack. She just wanted to go back to the beach house.

As she reached for her things, she spotted a small stone in the sand. It was a small oval pebble with a streak of black running across it—but there was a thumb-size indentation in the middle. Heather picked up the stone and held it in her hand. She lay the stone against her fingers and let her thumb slide back and forth in the depression. The movement was oddly comforting. She'd heard of similar stones used for self-soothing exercises—a worry stone, they were called. They had origins in many cultures but she'd never tried one. Rubbing her thumb across the stone did, indeed, give her comfort. Almost intuitive.

Heather put the stone in her pocket. She would bring out the worry stone when she felt anxious. It would serve to remind her that she had the strength within to overcome a panic attack, as she did today.

The sun was up and more people were walking the beach. She passed groups of women walking and talking at a fast clip. More dogs were running loose near their owners. Young men were setting out rented chairs and umbrellas. She'd been out longer than she'd planned. She could feel the heat of the sun through her clothes. Up ahead she spied a group of about fifteen people clustered near the dunes. Heather couldn't deal with more people, especially not after that earlier confrontation. She lowered her gaze and headed closer to the shoreline.

Then she saw the tracks. At first she thought they were tire tracks, but they went all the way across the beach to the dunes where the group of people clustered. One of them was the woman in the pink jogging suit with her dog. Heather swallowed her groan of annoyance, but she was pleased at least to see that the naughty Labrador had her leash on. Then she noticed that three of the women in the group were wearing pale green turtle team T-shirts. She squinted, trying to spot Cara, but she wasn't there. Curious, Heather drew closer.

One middle-aged woman with very short brown hair wearing a turtle team shirt stood in the center of what looked to Heather like a small crater in the sand. She guessed this was where the turtle had laid her eggs, as it was the center of focus. All the others gathered around to watch. The woman's knees were bent as if she were doing the pliés that Heather had learned as a young girl in ballet school. In her hands was a long yellow probe stick. Time after time the woman carefully slid the metal probe into the sand. Each time Heather could sense the collective intake of breath from all the onlookers. She'd made at least a dozen holes in the sand when suddenly the metal stick slipped deeper. Immediately the woman dropped the probe and went to her hands and knees to begin digging. Everyone took a step closer, craning their necks to watch.

After several minutes of anxious waiting, the team member lifted her arm in triumph. In her hand was a single white egg, the size of a Ping-Pong ball.

"We've got eggs!" she called out.

"It's the first nest of the season!" another member exclaimed.

There were hugs of shared triumph and exclamations of how this was going to be the best year ever for South Carolina nests. It was decided that the nest was above the tide line so it would not be moved. A second woman in a turtle team shirt began covering the nest back up with sand. Heather's attention was drawn to the large shell she used to dig. It cupped perfectly in her palm. Stepping closer, she watched as the team constructed a triangle of orange tape on wooden sticks and affixed an orange sign to mark the nest as federally protected. When that was done, the group of onlookers began to disperse.

Heather had turned to leave as well when she heard Cara's name mentioned. She hesitated and, looking over her shoulder, saw that the turtle team was still clustered at the nest, talking.

"I still can't believe it," one woman said. "Such a shock. Poor Brett."

"Poor Cara! She's devastated."

"Talk about shock. I thought she looked like Jackie at JFK's funeral. That vacant stare."

"I don't imagine it's sunk in yet. It was so sudden."

"He was too young. It's just too sad."

"Has anyone seen Cara since the funeral?"

"I dropped off some food, but I didn't see her. Emmi answered the door. She's the only one Cara wants to see now."

"And me," the oldest woman in the group corrected.

Heather recognized the woman as her neighbor, the deeply tanned gardener with the bright white hair.

"Well, of course she'll see *you*," the woman hastily corrected herself. "Flo, she'll always see you. You're like a second mother to her."

"And I worry about her like a mother," Flo said sadly.

"Cara's strong," the woman offered in a comforting voice.

"On the outside," Flo said. "On the inside, she's tender. When her mama died, she was prepared for it and could grieve properly. But this . . ." Flo shook her head. "How does anyone prepare for news like that? He was too young."

"Someone should stay with her."

"Well, of course someone's been staying with her," Flo retorted. "Emmi's been there since Brett died. But Cara wants her to leave. And you know Cara. She'll get what she wants. I reckon there's nothing more we can do other than keep bringing her food and checking in on her. She just needs time."

Heather turned away, stunned by what she'd just heard. Cara's husband had died? She couldn't believe it. She'd just seen her a week ago! It was no wonder she hadn't heard from her since.

"Can I help you?"

Heather turned swiftly at the voice. It was her neighbor, the woman with the white hair. The team members had packed up their gear and were heading out en masse.

"Oh. No, thanks," she replied nervously. "I was just passing by and saw all the excitement, thought I'd stay and watch."

"Your first turtle nest?"

"Yes."

"You're lucky to be here today. First nest of the season," the woman said with pride. "Yes, sir, the season's begun. And about damn time, too. Folly Beach already has two nests." She wiped sand from her hand and offered it to Heather. "Hi, I'm Florence Prescott. One of the turtle team. Everyone just calls me Flo."

Flo had to be about eighty years of age. Deep lines coursed through her leathery, tanned face, but one's gaze was drawn to her eyes, blue and bright as a summer sky.

"I'm Heather," she said with a swift smile. "Actually, I believe we're neighbors. I'm renting the beach house next to yours. For the summer."

Flo's face lit up. "So you're the young woman who's moved into Lovie's house? Well," she said with pleasure as her eyes scrutinized Heather's face, "I was hoping I'd meet you. Haven't seen you puttering about outside. I would've brought you a pie to welcome you, but"—she shook her head—"it's been a difficult week."

Heather paused then asked, "I, uh . . . I didn't mean to listen in, but . . . but did I hear y'all say Cara's husband died? Cara Rutledge?"

Flo's smile fell and she suddenly looked her age. "Yes. Lord, but that's sad news."

Heather lowered her head, feeling again the swift sadness the news brought. "Oh, I'm so sorry."

"We all are. We're still in shock, really."

"What happened?"

The old woman shook her head sorrowfully. "A heart attack. He was out jogging and suddenly collapsed. Right in the street. He was dead before they reached the hospital. He couldn't have gone too far. Someone in his neighborhood saw him fall down and ran out and called nine-one-one. The ambulance got there right quick, but . . ." Her voice trailed off. "They said he didn't suffer. That's something, I suppose."

"Was he older than Cara?"

"No, same age. Just turned fifty. Cut off in his prime, he was."

It was always sad to hear of a death, but the passing of someone so young seemed all the more tragic. "I-I'd like to send her something. Flowers or . . ." She shrugged. "Would that be all right?"

"I'm sure it would be," Flo replied kindly. She looked over her shoulder, noting that all the other members of the team had left.

Heather smiled quickly, liking the older woman immensely. Kindness exuded from every pore, supported rather than dispelled by her forthright manner. Heather got the feeling that with Florence Prescott, one always knew where one stood.

"You headed back?" Flo asked Heather.

"Uh, yes," she replied, flustered by the sudden question.

"I'll walk with you, if you don't mind. We're headed to the same place."

Heather took a breath and began talking to herself, listing reasons not to be anxious. She was meeting her neighbor. A nice woman she could call if she needed help or a cup of sugar.

As they began to walk, Flo spoke again. "I just have to ask. Do you have birds? When I've been out in my garden this past week, I could have sworn I heard the loveliest birdsong. I swanny, it's like a chorus from heaven."

A short laugh escaped Heather. She always felt relief talking about her canaries, a subject she knew so much about. "Yes, that would be my canaries."

"Canaries! I should've known. Well, I'll be. I haven't seen a canary in"—she tossed up her hands—"I can't remember how long."

"I have three."

"I'll have to come by and see them," Flo said. "With all

this sad news, I could stand to hear some birdsong to cheer me up."

Heather's heart started racing at the thought of Flo just dropping by. "I—"

"Now, come along, dear," Flo interrupted, striding off down the sand at a fast pace and leaving Heather nothing to do but follow in the older woman's wake.

Chapter Nine

HEATHER HEARD THE sound of hammering as she and Flo neared the beach house. Coming up the beach path, she recognized the broad shoulders of Bo Stanton as he bent over the new stairs of the deck. She was surprised to see Bo back at work, since she hadn't seen him since her first day at Primrose Cottage.

He straightened when he saw the two of them approach. Removing his work gloves, he wiped the faint sheen of sweat from his face with his forearm.

"Hey there," he called out.

"Hi," Heather responded shyly. She stared wide-eyed for a moment, trying to think of something to say. "You're back."

She cringed inside. *You're back?* Why had she said that? It sounded critical. *Idiot!*

"Sure. I'm back," Bo replied good-naturedly. "I'm not done, am I?" He turned to face Flo. "Morning, Miss Flo."

"Bo! What are you doing here?" asked Flo, clearly pleased to see him.

"Working on the new deck. Brett hired me to finish it

three weeks ago and, well . . ." He gave a slight shrug, his face suddenly filled with emotion. "I just wish he could see it when it's all done."

Flo patted his arm and sighed. "It's all so horribly sad, I know. How sweet of you to honor his memory by finishing a project so close to his own heart. He loved Miss Lovie, you know. By the way, Cara appreciated all you did to help with the funeral. Getting all the rental furniture and dishes picked up and put out, and the tent . . . We all did."

Bo bowed his head. "Of course. It was an honor to be asked to be an honorary pallbearer. You know, Brett was a mentor to me. We worked on a lot of projects together, and he taught me so much."

Heather suddenly understood where Bo had been the past week. His helping out friends in need spoke a lot to who he was as a man.

Bo said, "I still can't believe he's gone."

"Life goes on," Flo said, reaching up to give his shoulder a slight shake of encouragement. Her hand was large, her fingers slightly bent with age. "One of the hard-won wisdoms of old age."

Heather was eager to avoid any further conversation. She was exhausted from the confrontation with the dog lady and would only make more inane comments if she stayed. She started to shuffle off toward the house, mumbling something about needing to check on the canaries. Her surreptitious retreat was cut short.

"What in heaven's name is being delivered?" Flo suddenly asked, pointing toward the road.

Heather turned her head to see a large delivery truck pulling a long trailer attempting a sharp turn into the narrow driveway of the beach house.

"I wonder what that could be," Heather mused. It looked like the truck was going to hit the small loquat tree on the way in. She held her breath as the big front hood cleared the tree by mere inches. The truck emitted a roar and rolled up the drive, spitting gravel. On the trailer was a bright and shiny silver golf cart.

"Looks like you've got a delivery," said Bo, stepping closer.

She stared at the truck. "There must be some mistake. That's not for me."

"Too bad," Flo said with a shake of her head. "Those things sure do come in handy on an island like this. Always wanted one for the turtle team. Not that we can drive it on the beaches, of course. Still, I always wondered if we could get a permit for one of those four-wheelers."

The truck stilled and a man in a brown uniform jumped from the cab and approached them carrying a clipboard. He looked hot and tired as he flipped through the pages. Nearing the small group, he looked up and searched their faces.

"Which one of you is Heather Wyatt?"

"I am," she replied, surprised that he'd called her name.

"Got your golf cart here. Sorry it's a bit late. We've been backlogged for delivery. Just sign here and tell me where you want it."

"Wait," Heather said, confused, not accepting the clipboard. "I-I didn't order a golf cart."

The deliveryman appeared concerned that she wasn't expecting it. He referred back to his papers. "Says here it was ordered by a Mr. and Mrs. David Wyatt for Miss Heather Wyatt at this address."

Heather flashed back in her mind to her father's telling her that he and Natalie had sent her a gift. "It sure isn't a Crock-Pot," she muttered to herself with a light laugh.

"No, ma'am," the deliveryman said, all business. "And it's not really a golf cart, either. It's one of them street-legal carts. It's got all the bells and whistles."

Heather flushed. She hadn't intended for him to hear. "It's very nice," she blurted out.

"Let me get it down and I'll show you. Where you want it?"

"Uh . . . ." Heather quickly glanced around, and pointed near the porch. "Somewhere over there, I guess."

"Lucky you!" Flo exclaimed, sidling closer. "Isn't it cute? I'll let you take me for a spin, what do you say?"

Heather couldn't say anything. She was speechless. She hadn't asked for the golf cart. She didn't even want it. Bo came forward to help the deliveryman ease the cart off the transom. The man drove it with ease right up to the side of the house. It wasn't large; it could hold two people in the front and two facing the back. He handed her a thick packet of papers, then began walking her around the cart, pointing out all the features. Heather was silent and tried to keep up as the deliveryman raced through the explanations. She got that there was a windshield and wipers, electric lights and turn signals. But she was unsure what he'd said about the batteries. It all was very overwhelming.

After she'd signed the papers, the deliveryman managed to extricate his truck from the driveway and drove off in a hurry.

Heather turned back to see Flo standing with her arms crossed, grinning, apparently finding the whole experience very entertaining.

"I best be off, too. Have fun with your new toy, dear," Flo called to Heather with a wave, and headed through her fence gate toward home. "Don't be a stranger, hear?"

Bo waved to Flo, then turned to look at Heather. Suddenly aware that she was alone with him, she felt that dreaded awkwardness that left her tongue-tied. He appeared equally unsure. He slipped his hands into his back pockets and she thought he wanted to say something, but he only waved and told her, "I'll be out back." He turned to leave.

Heather stood for a moment staring at the golf cart with the heavy feeling that she was collapsing into a sinkhole. The panic attack had walloped her self-confidence, and now something as straightforward as a golf cart was overwhelming. The straw that was bending—if not breaking—the proverbial camel's back.

"Heather?"

She startled and turned to find Bo at her side. His eyes searched her face, and he seemed to read all the emotions she was feeling.

"I was wondering," he began, and scratched behind his ear to appear casual. "Do you know how to run one of these things?"

She looked helplessly at the golf cart. "No," she admitted. "Not a clue. Do you?"

"A golf cart? Sure. What's to know? It's a piece of cake."

"Really?" she asked, with a flicker of hope.

"I'll show you." He approached the cart. "Hop in."

Heather walked to the passenger side and started to climb in.

"Oh, no, you get in behind the wheel," he told her. "You're the driver."

Heather felt a sudden panic. "But . . . I've never driven one before."

"And that's what I'm going to teach you," Bo said in a tone that implied it was all very simple. Not giving her a chance to back out, he pointed to where the ignition key was still in its proper place, then climbed into the passenger side of the cart. "Come on, we're wasting daylight!"

Heather stood there flummoxed for a moment, then gathered her resolve: she would just have to be brave enough to master the art of golf carts. She climbed behind the wheel, very aware that Bo sat only inches away.

"Okay, I'm ready," she said, gripping the wheel.

Bo looked at her sideways, his eyes crinkling in what appeared to be amusement. "It's supposed to be fun, not torture."

"I-I get nervous behind the wheel. I d-don't like to drive," she managed to explain.

"You do have a license, though, right?" he asked in a half-joking manner.

Heather nodded. "Yes. But it's been a while."

"It'll come back to you," Bo said confidently. "Driving a golf cart is way easier than driving a car, anyway." He clapped his hands together to drum up enthusiasm. "See that key? Fire her up."

She did. When she stepped on the gas the cart lurched, and she braked hard. They both jerked forward.

"I'm sorry!" she blurted out, and flushed. She couldn't even get into gear. She must look like the biggest loser on the planet.

"At least we know the seat belts work."

She turned to see Bo smiling, and immediately they both laughed.

"Let's try that again," Bo said.

With that, he began teaching her the rudimentary skills of driving a golf cart. Even with a street-legal one, it was pretty easy to learn. He didn't rush her and gave her ample time to ask questions. She felt more relaxed after they did the requisite backward and forward moves till she got a feel for it.

"Let's take her out for a real spin," Bo said.

Heather felt a sudden shiver of anxiety at the prospect of driving in the street. She'd need to venture out for supplies for herself eventually—FreshDirect hadn't quite made it to the barrier island. Yet her heart began pounding as if on command, and all she wanted to do was park the cart and go inside and hide.

"I'm pretty tired," she said. "I think I'll just park it and try again tomorrow. Besides, I don't want to take up any more of your time."

"Hey, no problem." Bo slid from the cart with ease. The cart was sitting beside the porch. He went to look under the porch at the wide-open space provided by the raised house.

"You know," he said, "I could clear all this crap out of here, lay some gravel, and it would make a perfect parking spot for that golf cart."

Heather's face lit up. "Really? Will it fit under there?"

"Yep. Once I get all the grass out. I remember Miss Lovie used to park her VW bug under here. So that golf cart will fit, no problem."

"I saw Cara driving a gold VW. Was that it?"

"Yep. 'The Gold Bug,' it's called. From that story by Edgar Allan Poe. Everyone knew when they saw that gold bug drive by it was Miss Lovie. All us kids used to go wild for it. Cara's got a new model, but she drives it just like her mama did."

"I'll help you clean that space out. And buy the gravel. Of course," she quickly added, not wanting him to feel she would expect Cara to pay for it. "Cara has enough on her mind. I don't want to bother her with this. You don't think she'll mind?"

"Mind? She'll be thrilled. She's always complaining about Brett never throwing things out." Bo's face suddenly went still when he realized what he'd just said. He added sadly, "It's hard to remember that Brett isn't still alive. I expect him to drive up here any minute and check on how things are going on the deck."

She looked at his averted face, his long forehead, the way his blond hair fell over it in tousled waves, as free and relaxed as the man himself. She thought how Bo always seemed so ready to help her, not just because he'd been hired by Brett to finish the deck. That had nothing to do with *her*. Rather, and this was hard for her to believe, Bo seemed to genuinely enjoy her company. She wasn't imagining the way he looked at her with a spark of attraction in his eyes. It was very flattering, especially since she was discovering that the feeling was mutual.

How awkward could it be to go for a ride with him? They'd set off, remark lamely on the weather and the scenery they passed. He'd be sure to fill the dead air with interesting comments about what was happening on the island. They'd chat, they'd laugh. It was no big deal. Just friends. Then she sighed, not wanting to stick Bo into the friend zone.

"You know what," Heather said gathering her courage. "I was actually hoping to get something to send to Cara. Is there a flower shop on the island?" She shrugged. "Or candy?"

Bo shook his head. "Not on the island. Though you could get flowers at the grocer. We could drop them off on the way back. She lives right close to the grocery store."

"Drop them off? Oh, no, I don't think that's a good idea," Heather said, backtracking. "I heard Flo saying that Cara wasn't up to seeing anyone. I'm sure she wouldn't want me just stopping by."

"Emmi's there," Bo said all-knowingly.

"Who's Emmi?"

"Her best friend. They've been friends since they were both in diapers. Her family used to have one of the old cottages on the island near here, but they up and sold it a while back. Now Emmi lives with Flo."

"Emmi's my neighbor?" Heather remembered the woman she'd seen through the window. "Does she by any chance have red hair?"

"That'll be her. She's a fiery personality, too. I swear, I can't figure out how she and Flo can live together."

"Are they . . ." Heather paused. "Together?"

Bo looked at her as if she'd grown another head. "Like a couple?" He laughed and shook his head. "If you knew their personalities, you'd see why I laughed. No, Emmi moved in after her divorce. I reckon they're more like mother and daughter. Flo's been the maiden aunt for both Emmi and Cara all their lives. I reckon she'll take you under her wing next."

Heather thought she might like being taken under Flo's wing.

"Anyway, Emmi's accepting all offerings for Cara. It won't be a problem. We'll just drop them off and go."

"I suppose I have to get comfortable driving the golf cart, and I don't feel quite ready to go it alone." She laughed in a self-deprecating way. "I don't even know how to get there."

His eyes gleamed with pleasure. "It's actually a little tricky crossing Palm Boulevard to the store," he said. "Golf carts aren't allowed to drive on Palm. Are you ready to go now?"

She reached back and patted her backpack and gave him as confident a smile as she could muster. "Sure. Why not?"

Heather felt a little light-headed as she walked toward the golf cart. She wasn't sure what he was thinking. She wasn't sure what *she* was thinking. She climbed behind the wheel of the golf cart and held her breath as he climbed in beside her. His arm brushed against hers as he turned the ignition to start.

"Let's go."

~~~~

HEATHER WAS DRIVING slower than a Sunday afternoon. Bo glanced at her for the hundredth time as she drove the golf cart at a painstakingly slow fifteen miles per hour. He'd tell her the cart could go as fast as twenty-five, but he didn't want the journey to end any sooner. Bo was glad that he was wearing his sunglasses. He didn't want her to see how much he was enjoying himself. The wind gently tousled her long blond hair, and she was smiling.

"You're getting the feel of it," he said. "Do you like it?"

She nodded and looked at him for a moment, her face aglow. When she smiled at him like that, he felt sucker-punched.

"I do," she said with gusto. "I like feeling closer to the outdoors than in a car. I feel more a part of the island. You know? And the golf cart feels less threatening than a car."

Bo propped one arm up to rest along the roof and let the breeze blow back his hair as they drove along Ocean Boulevard.

"This is what we call Front Beach," he told her.

"I know," she said, slowing as they entered the busy section of the island. "I read about it in the guidebook."

"Well, hell," he drawled. "That's my job, to show you around."

Heather laughed. He loved to hear her laugh. She always had such a serious expression. Almost fearful or worried. It gave him pleasure to see it changed to a smile. She had the prettiest smile. . . .

Bo pointed out a local shop that had a live parrot inside where she could buy a hermit crab, Coconut Joe's for eating lunch while viewing the beach, and the mural by Gretta Kruesi that displayed magnificent sea turtles and dolphins. Heather appreciated seeing art proudly portrayed on civic buildings. It might not have been the official beginning of summer on the calendar, but here on the island it certainly was. Everywhere people meandered on the walkways in beachwear, soaking up the sun, laughing and talking, buying souvenirs, licking ice-cream cones.

Bo carefully guided her along the route beside Palm Boulevard, through the parking lot to the one crosswalk where it was safe for a golf cart to cross four lanes of traffic to the grocery store.

Suddenly nervous, Heather clenched the steering wheel. "Maybe you better cross."

"No, you're doing good. You have to do it someday. Might as well be a baptism by fire. Just take your time and wait for a break in traffic."

"I-I didn't realize how many people crowded onto the island in the summer."

"Yeah. You don't want to leave the island between four and six on weekend afternoons. Okay . . . all clear!"

She pressed the pedal, and successfully maneuvered the cart across the lanes of traffic into the parking lot.

She laid her head against her hands on the steering wheel. "Oh, my God."

"Good job," he told her and placed a hand on her back. "I told you you could do it."

She turned her head against her hands and her expressive blue eyes met his. He was suddenly aware he was touching her and smiled back.

"Thanks," she said in a soft voice. "For having faith."

Now his stomach clenched as her vulnerability struck him again. He unbuckled his seat belt. "Let's go shopping."

Heather and Bo got a cart and walked together through the aisles to the flowers. Heather bent to inspect a few bouquets, a frown on her face.

"These all look pretty tired," she said with a worried brow.

"Cara brought me the most beautiful flowers. She has such good taste. I just can't give her blue and pink carnations."

"Cara's not uppity. It's the thought that counts."

She looked around the store, eyes scanning the signs and shelves. "Maybe some food is the right thing after all. Though I'm sure it's like coals to Newcastle."

"What's that mean?"

"Coals to Newcastle? Well, Newcastle was a coal-mining town. It means bringing something to someone who doesn't need it."

"My daddy used to say it's like bringing water to the sea."

She laughed softly. "That's better here." She began walking toward the deli section. "I think lasagna for one seems unbearably depressing."

"How about cheese?" he asked. "Everyone likes cheese."

Heather's eyes brightened. "Bo, that's brilliant. Perfect!"

He was pleased, but didn't say anything. He watched as she carefully picked out a selection of cheeses without even looking at the prices, filling her basket. And most of them were from France. He wondered just how much money her family had. Not just anyone could rent a beach house on Isle of Palms for the entire summer, or give a fancy, street-legal golf cart as a surprise gift just because. He wondered in that moment if her father would like him.

~~~~~~

CARA AND BRETT'S home was a hidden gem on the river side of Isle of Palms. It was quite small, no bigger, Heather thought, than the beach house. But it was very stylish, as she expected based on what she'd seen of Cara thus far. She drove the cart between two gray brick posts with black carriage lamps, and past an enormous live oak that dominated the front and practically hid the house from street view. Like the beach house, this one was freshly painted and tidy, with cheery red geraniums at the front door. It did not appear to be a house of mourning.

"Should we just leave it on the front porch?" Heather asked.

Bo shook his head. "Let's knock. Emmi's there. That's her car."

The knocker was a polished brass anchor. She gave it three good raps and waited. Soon the door swung open, revealing a woman with red hair loosely pulled away from her face. She was dressed in a pale green tunic top and black leggings with flip-flops, a paper towel in her hands. Her face broke into a huge grin when she spotted Bo.

"Well, hey, Bo!" she exclaimed.

"Nice to see you, Miss Emmi." He looked at Heather. "This is Heather Wyatt, the lady who's renting the beach house from Cara. She heard about Brett and wanted to bring something over." He raised the bags weighing down his hands.

Even though Emmi's green eyes had shaded circles of fatigue beneath them, Heather felt the force of them studying her. "So that makes you my new neighbor. Nice to meet you, Heather. I've always liked that name. Maybe because I'm Scottish and anything to do with heather . . ." She let a slight shrug finish the sentence. "Do you want to come in?"

"I don't want to intrude," Heather answered quickly. "I just wanted to bring something by for Cara. I was so sorry to hear about . . . Brett. I'm sorry not to have been at the funeral, but I didn't know." Even as she said it, Heather felt her cheeks burn. What would she have been doing at the funeral anyway? It was a dumb thing to say.

But Emmi seemed touched by her words. "How could you? You only just got here. It was a very nice service. People came from all over and spoke so highly of him. I never saw so many people." She paused in reflection, then shook her head, coming back. "He will be deeply missed."

"I didn't have the opportunity to meet him," Heather said.

"Right, you'd just arrived. I think that's what's so hard for Cara. There was no warning, it all happened so quickly. Cara's not receiving visitors," she added apologetically. "But can I offer you something to drink?"

"No, really," Heather said, stepping back. "We just wanted to drop this off. It's some cheeses and fruit. I thought that way she could nibble on them whenever she wants. Nothing to heat up." She glanced quickly up at Bo, a signal that it was time to leave. "Thank you, Emmi."

"Nice to see you again, Miss Emmi," Bo said. "Give Cara my love."

"I'll tell her you were here." Emmi looked at Heather. "Both of you. I'll come by and say a proper hello when things settle down here. Thank you again for coming by. I know it will mean a lot to Cara."

Bo was lost in his own thoughts and uncharacteristically silent on the way back. The reality of Cara's loss lay like a heavy pall around them. Though they hadn't seen Cara, the grief permeating the house was palpable.

Driving along on the bouncy golf cart, Heather let her senses take in her surroundings in an effort to lift her now-dismal mood. It was early afternoon on a sunny day. The air smelled of salt and jasmine. The temperature was balmy—in the eighties and not too humid. It was perfect beach weather. They passed young couples tugging wagons filled with toys and children, an older couple holding hands, a few teenage girls in bikinis brazenly strolling in the street, a large dog dragging his walker—all holding colorful towels, all heading for the sea.

Despite the sadness of death, life went on, Heather thought. She pushed a shock of hair from her face in the breeze. She had to remind herself of that every day, find strength, even courage, in that knowledge. When her mother had passed, she'd thought she'd never get past her grief. Guilt was a terrible burden to bear. But she was slowly learning to do just that. Just one week here had opened the window to what was possible. As the beach house that was fast starting to feel like home came into view, she prayed now for Cara. She had to learn this painful lesson. And quickly. If you let it, grief could swallow you whole.

Chapter Ten

N O MATTER HOW prepared she thought she was for death, Cara couldn't have anticipated the depths of the loss she felt.

Her grief was all-encompassing. With her mother's passing, Cara had felt sorrow, of course. She still missed her mother deeply. But Brett's death was akin to dying herself. Her world had ended. She grieved her past, present, and future.

She'd lost her faith in God: Cara couldn't pray to a being that would take her husband away. She'd planned the funeral in a daze. She was confused, disoriented, flooded with waves of guilt and anger. A funeral was nothing they'd ever talked about. Funerals were something they'd plan much later in their lives. When they were older. They were still young, or so they'd thought. Yet now, in the space of two weeks, Cara felt very, very old.

Cara lay on her bed with her arm covering her eyes, even though no light pierced the darkness save for what leaked through the slits of the closed drapes. She felt lifeless. No energy, no desire to rise out of bed. All she wanted to do was sleep and hide from everyone. She grew aware of the sound of knocking on her bedroom door.

The knocking continued, more insistent. "Cara?"

"Go away, Emmi. Please." Her voice was low and rusty.

"It's not just Emmi. I'm here, too. Open up, darlin'."

That was Flo's voice. Dear Flo . . . But still, Cara couldn't bear to talk to anyone.

"I'm sleeping."

"You've been sleeping day and night for two weeks." The door pushed open. Cara removed her arm from her eyes and peered over, squinting in the dim light. She saw Flo leading the charge with Emmi right behind her.

Cara groaned and put her arm back over her head. "I have a terrible headache."

"No, you don't," Flo said as if she were speaking to a recalcitrant child. She sat on the mattress beside Cara while Emmi went to open the drapes. Immediately the room was drenched in sunlight. She reached out and, taking Cara's hand, moved her arm from her eyes. Cara resisted, but Flo was firm. She continued holding Cara's hand in a motherly manner, peering into her face.

Cara reluctantly opened her eyes.

Flo smiled and squeezed her hand encouragingly. "Hello, precious," she said with great warmth.

"Hello," Cara replied despondently.

Flo spoke in her typical matter-of-fact style. "We're worried about you."

"I'm fine."

"We don't think you are fine," Flo replied. "You're not

leaving your room, barely eating—honey, it's just not healthy."

"So?"

"So, we've come to help you," Flo replied in a cajoling tone.

"Look, I appreciate what you're trying to do," Cara said, pulling back her hand and clasping both arms across her chest, turning her face to the wall. "But I've been through the five stages of grief, okay? And now I'm tired and just want to rest."

"Honey," Flo persisted, not one to be pushed aside, "grief doesn't come in five neat stages. You're bouncing around all of them like a pinball and landing squarely in the depression zone at the end of each one. You forget I was once a social worker and I know about this stuff. You also forget that I was with your mother when she was in this very same state after Russell Bennett died."

Cara turned her head back to search Flo's face. She'd never heard this before. "Mama?"

"Yes, Lovie. She'd locked herself in her room, inconsolable, as you are now. She'd lost the love of her life, as you have. That kind of grief is dangerous. It can destroy you, if you let it." Flo squared her shoulders. "I didn't let it destroy your mama, and I'm sure as hell not going to let it destroy you."

Tears filled Cara's eyes and she reached up to wipe them away, surprised that she had any tears left to shed.

Flo cleared her throat, moved by emotion. "Now," she said firmly, bolstering her resolve, "Emmi and I know you don't want to see anyone right now, and that's okay. You're entitled. Grief doesn't have a timeline. You take all the time you need. But you have to take care of yourself while you grieve. Frankly,

Cara, you need to bathe. Give us a chance to change these sheets."

"No!" Cara exclaimed, panicked, as she curled on her side. She spread her palm against the sheets on Brett's side of the bed and rubbed them caressingly. "I can still smell him," she choked out.

"Oh, Cara," Emmi said in a broken voice.

"I'm not asking you to get rid of his things," Flo said. "But we are going to help you take a nice bath. Wash your hair. Tidy up some in here. You'll feel better."

"I don't want to feel better. I don't deserve to feel better," Cara said brokenly.

"Now, why would you say such a thing?" Flo asked.

Cara squeezed her eyes shut in agony, remembering again, as she had been remembering over and over since Brett's death. "We fought," she began haltingly. "On the day he died. We fought."

Flo exchanged glances with Emmi. After a pause, she asked Cara, "Do you want to tell us about it?"

Cara did. "I came home from the bank and he was already home. He'd come home early from work. He said something about feeling strange. I wish I could remember his words," she said, rubbing her forehead with her fist. "Why didn't he go to the doctor then?" She shifted her head on the pillow to look at Flo beseechingly. "Why didn't I listen?"

"I don't know. Maybe because we all say things like that from time to time. No one pays it much mind."

Cara heard the words, let them digest. "There was a problem with the loan for the boat. The bank . . . well . . ." She stopped with a defeated sigh. She didn't want to talk about the boat or the loan. That all meant nothing, less than nothing, to her now. "We argued," she continued, piecing the memory together. "I told him that it was his fault we were in trouble with the bank. Because of his buying the boat and all. One thing led to another." She paused. "I told him I wasn't happy." She swallowed hard, wishing she could take back those words. She felt the air suck out from her lungs.

"Cara?" Emmi said.

"I was a fool. I had *him*!" Cara cried. "All I needed for happiness. Why did I say that?"

"Because you're human," Flo said in a weary tone. "Because you didn't know it was the last you'd see of him. You thought you had time."

Her face crumpled. "I did." After a few moments, she wiped her face and sniffed. "But we patched it up at the end," she said, more to herself. Hearing herself tell the story aloud helped her to think it through clearly. "He said we'd make it work out. How we always made it work."

"That's good," Emmi said encouragingly. "See? That's not fighting."

Cara shook her head. "But I was still mad at him. I held it inside, like I always do," she added with a heavy dose of self-recrimination. She could see Brett again in her mind, his gray T-shirt and jogging pants. He'd caught her gaze before he left and smiled. She saw again his eyes, so blue and hopeful . . . trusting . . . confirming that all was well between them. But she hadn't smiled back. She was still annoyed.

"He went out for a run. I heard the door close and . . ." She slammed her hand to her mouth as tears sprang to her eyes. "I didn't say good-bye," she burst out on a sob, covering her face with her hands.

Cara completely broke down. She had named her greatest grief. If she could go back in time and change one thing, she'd go to that single moment. She'd run into his arms and tell him, "Yes, I believe all will be well because we're together. I love you."

But that moment had passed. She'd not said good-bye, and the guilt of having withheld her farewell would curse her forever. Cara wailed openmouthed, howling, and feeling no need to hide her emotions with her dearest friends. Flo and Emmi put their arms around her as she wept, keeping her safe as she released a torrent of feelings—fear, guilt, unspeakable sorrow.

She didn't know how long she cried, but in time the heaving sobs dissipated to a tremulous sighing. Her face was wet with tears that she wiped away on the bedsheets. But she felt spent, willing to do as her friends asked. Emmi quietly rose and went to the bath. Soon Cara heard the water running full force. Together Emmi and Flo guided Cara to the bathroom and helped her remove her pajamas, unbuttoning her top, guiding her feet from the pants—left foot, right foot. She felt tended to like a child, and it was surreal and soothing. The scent of lavender wafted through the room, otherworldly and calming. Next she stepped into the tub—left foot, right foot. It was hot but not scalding. She slowly eased into the steaming, scented water. While Flo changed her bedsheets, Emmi washed her hair, chattering about something of little importance. Cara closed her eyes and relished the feeling of Emmi's strong fingers massaging her head. It felt like she was slowly awakening from a long, heavy sleep. She stepped into a thirsty towel, and let Emmi dry and comb her hair. Then Cara brushed her teeth and slipped into clean clothes.

They gathered again on the sofa in the living room with cups of hot tea. Emmi put out a plate of cookies that no one touched, but it seemed proper to have them there, just in case.

Cara sat with her fingers wrapped around the warm mug and looked around the room. Her house was clean and tidy, thanks to Emmi. Her eyes searched out every corner. Everything was just as it had been the day Brett left the house. His bicycle was still parked by the front door. His gym jacket hung on a hook by the door, his wallet and keys in the sweetgrass basket on the front table. It was all unchanged. Normal.

"I expect to see him walk into the house any minute," Cara said quietly, feeling another wave of anguish.

"You'll feel that for some time," Flo said.

"How long?"

"It's different for everyone."

"I can't go on feeling like this much longer."

"Like how?" asked Emmi.

"Like I'm going crazy. Sometimes I lie in bed and wonder if all this is really the dream and if I wake up he'll still be here." She paused. "How was the funeral?" she asked them, feeling in a daze. "I barely remember it."

"It was just beautiful," Emmi assured her. "Everyone came."

"And his ashes? Where . . . ?" The one thing Cara and Brett had spoken of once over too many bottles of red wine was that he wanted to be cremated. "Ashes to ashes," he'd pronounced, clinking his glass against Cara's when she'd agreed she wanted cremation as well.

Flo patted her hand. "They're waiting for you to decide what you want to do."

Cara licked her lips. "What I want to do," she repeated softly. "You know, one of the things we talked about that—that last day was how I didn't know what I wanted to do. For a job. Seems so silly now." She laughed shortly. "Now I don't have any idea of what to do for anything. For my life. I don't know what to do with myself. All I can seem to manage is to lie in bed."

"What do you want to do?" asked Flo.

She chuckled without humor. "That was what Brett asked me. I didn't have a clue then, and I have even less of one today."

"You're grieving, Cara," Flo told her. "Don't be so hard on yourself. Grief can make you question your goals and purpose. How you want to spend your life."

"A life without Brett . . ."

"Well, you could make an appearance at the office," Emmi suggested.

Cara looked at her. "Are you serious?"

"It would give you a purpose." Emmi shifted closer. "Robert's been by a few times. To check on you, of course," she quickly added. "But also to let you know the summer season is taking off and he can't manage the tours and the office alone. He sounded desperate. He was wondering if he could hire another captain."

"I don't know," she said dully.

Emmi took a deep breath. "If you could just tell him it's okay."

Cara shrugged. "It's okay."

"I'll let him know. See? That wasn't so hard, was it?"

Cara didn't think it was hard because she hadn't made a real decision. She was just going along with things, saying yes at the appropriate places. In the back of her mind was the niggling thought that she really shouldn't take on another employee. There was that mess with the bank to muddle through. But all that seemed so deep in a fog she couldn't see it clearly.

"Also, Cara," Emmi continued, "I'm afraid I must go back to my job, honey. I've run through all my vacation time."

"Oh, Em, you used your vacation days to babysit me?" Cara was horrified.

Emmi saw her distress and was quick to wave it away, rolling her eyes. "I had a blast."

Cara released a short laugh. Emmi was always good at cheering anyone up. "I'll find a way to make it up to you. I don't know what I'd have done without you."

"Frankly, Cara, neither do I. That's why we're having this little talk. Honey, your grief will take a long time to heal. We're not trying to tell you to move on or any such fool thing. In time—a few months, maybe—you'll find you're able to resume usual activities. You'll be able to remember Brett without feeling that intense pain."

"Never," Cara said with a brusque shake of her head.

Flo nodded vehemently. "Trust me, my dear, you will. In time. But for right now we must be practical. Frankly, you really must climb out of bed. Emmi won't be here to prepare your meals, so you must do it for yourself. I know it's going to be hard. But there's a freezer full of food, and people are still dropping things off." She pointed a finger. "And when people offer help, accept it."

"I can't. I don't care."

Flo sighed. "Honey, the first week we understood you not wanting to get out of bed. Even the second week. Now, I'm not saying you should go back to work, or go out shopping. But if you can't manage to take care of yourself, then maybe it's time to get some help."

"You mean a therapist? Or a maid?"

"Someone you can talk to."

"I don't need a therapist." Cara brushed away the suggestion.

"We'll see," Flo replied, unfazed.

"We'll be by often," interjected Emmi, hoping to help. "You won't be alone. In fact, I can just keep staying here."

"No, you can't," Flo reminded her. "Your grandchildren are arriving this week."

Emmi's face contorted with conflict.

"I'll be fine," Cara said, though she didn't really believe the words.

"Good, now, that's the spirit!" Flo set her mug on the table and, with some effort, rose to her feet.

Cara realized with a pang of worry how old Flo was getting. Her once indefatigable hardiness was gone. Her spirit was still strong, but her body had weakened—she was thinner, frailer, slightly stooped. Cara leaped to her feet and came to Flo's side.

"Thank you," she said, and wrapped her arms around

Flo. "Thank you for being there for me." Flo hugged her back, and once again Cara felt like a young girl with the woman who had been a second mother to her all her life. Flashes of summers past when she'd go running to Flo's house next door to play cards or for art lessons with Miranda, Flo's seemingly exotic mother, who always had sweet tea and sugar cookies waiting.

Cara reached out to Emmi and reeled her in. "You, too, of course."

She looked at her two friends' faces. They both looked pale and tired. New lines coursed through their faces, as she was certain they did through hers. Grief was a harsh taskmaster. They'd been there for her since she'd called them in hysterical desperation after the police had delivered the news. The policemen had been very considerate. One had stayed with her until Flo had rushed over. Emmi had met them at the hospital and stayed by her side ever since. These two women were more than her friends. They were her family.

"I'll try," she told them. She looked around the house, feeling anew the pain of memories. "But I don't know how I'll manage when everywhere I look I see him."

Flo kissed her cheek. "Maybe you should do what your mama did."

Cara, needing desperately to hear about her mother now, leaned forward. "What was that?"

"She cut loose and returned to the only place that ever truly felt like home to her. The beach house."

Chapter Eleven

Bo had made up for lost time over the last few days, working long hours to finish the deck. Heather's canaries loved the sound of the buzzing saw and sang enthusiastic arias to accompany the hum and whistle of Bo's assorted power tools. So much so, in fact, that Heather had had to move her work from the sunroom to the kitchen table to concentrate. It didn't hurt that, from this vantage point, she could watch Bo as he worked.

She could tell he took pride in his work by his careful precision as he set the railings into place, the way he sanded the wood until he was satisfied. He was methodical in applying the deck stain, his arms swinging back and forth in a steady, unhurried rhythm with the brush. She couldn't prevent herself from picking up her pencil and sketching the way his arm muscles moved and his back shifted, the expression of intense concentration—narrowing brows, lips slightly protruding. This afternoon he'd applied the last stroke of stain, sealed up the cans, and begun cleaning up the work area and loading up his truck.

Heather loathed that the home improvement project was coming to an end. No more deck building meant no more Bo. Heather found she'd gotten quite used to his presence every day, and she was none too much looking forward to losing it— put simply, Bo made her feel less alone.

It had been such a wonderful week! One that she couldn't have imagined just a month or two ago. The stars had aligned somehow, and everything had seemed to fall into place. She'd started this week with a renewed burst of energy, going out to the beach every morning at dawn to photograph the birds. When she returned home, she'd poured herself into the process of sketching from the photographs to the backbeat of Bo's hammering outdoors. She'd focused first on the red knots. She'd been so lucky to find a few stragglers of this endangered shorebird still on Isle of Palms. Yearly these master navigators flew more than eighteen thousand miles round-trip between their wintering and breeding grounds. And to think she'd caught a few on her first day out! She'd drawn dozens of sketches of their chunky, long-winged bodies, their short yellowish legs and thin black bills. Sketches and photographs were taped to the walls and windows of the sunroom, along with profiles that described her selected shorebirds. A large map of the South Carolina coast was hung on the wall, and red pins marked where the different shorebirds that she spotted were, and green pins were where there were reported sightings.

Heather loved to see evidence of her ideas come alive around her. Her workroom energized her now. It was where she spent most of her time. She was pleased with the week's work. Yet, looking at her sketches today, she saw with chagrin that most of them were really of Bo Stanton. With an exasperated sigh, she pushed the sketches back with frustration. *What am I doing?* she asked herself, putting her face in her palms. *I have serious work to do.* Her attraction to Bo was becoming nothing short of an obsession. She thought about him too much. She'd even dreamed about him.

Since their golf cart ride, there had been an undeniable shift in their relationship. Bo was much more attentive than someone who merely came to work on the deck each morning. Whenever he paused to come inside for ice, he would linger, talking about anything and everything. She loved every minute and listened, utterly engaged. No doubt urging him on with their flirtation. Now she lowered her hands and expelled a gusty sigh of frustration. All this was clearly distracting her from her work, and that was unacceptable for someone like Heather. She looked again at the sketches of Bo, then in a rush gathered them up and placed them in a file folder. She was falling behind schedule. She could feel the pressure mounting, and rubbed the spot that ached at her breastbone.

"Enough," she said, and dropped her hands. Work was the only thing that would help her get through the anxiety that was building in her chest. "Red knots," she said aloud, pulling out fresh sketching paper. She methodically smoothed it with her palms, then picked up her pencil and focused on the photos of the birds clustered at the shoreline. She studied the rusty, reddish color of the feathers, how some stood straight as though staring out to sea with their dark, bright eyes. Some were bent at an angle, digging their sharp beaks into the moist morning sand for a meal of small snails, bivalves, or, if they were lucky, horseshoe crab eggs. She began to draw.

Some time later, she heard a knock on the front door. Glancing at her watch, she saw that an hour had passed already. Reluctantly, Heather rose and hurried to the front door, her mind still occupied by her work. Opening it, she was surprised to see Bo. Carrying a bouquet of yellow tulips, no less.

"Come in," she exclaimed, near giddy despite herself at seeing him, and opened the door wide.

Bo passed her, and she felt again the fluttering in her stomach. She smoothed back her hair, which was slipping from its clasp, ran her hands nervously over her slim-cut jeans.

"I ran out to grab something to eat and I saw these," he told her, and handed her the tulips. "Their color reminded me of your hair."

Heather couldn't stop the flush of pleasure that bloomed on her cheeks. "Thank you," she said, and brought the bouquet to her nose. "This is so . . . unexpected. They're beautiful." She didn't think any man but her father had ever brought her flowers before.

"Well," he began with a grin of pleasure, "I came to tell you I'm finished. The deck is all done."

"It's beautiful. Great job," she said, feeling unusually tongue-tied again with him. The job over, there was a new tension between them. What would happen next?

"I wouldn't go out there for a few days yet. Give the stain time to dry. The weather should hold for the next few days. Then I'll swing by and deliver the chairs. Brett started painting them, but he never got to finish. I can start that tomorrow and come by with them when I'm done," he added with a smile.

"I'd like that," she said, clinging to the chance to see him again.

Then his expression changed as an idea came to mind. "You know what'd be real nice?"

Heather shook her head.

"You ought to invite Cara to come on over to take a look, now that it's all done. It'd be a way to get her out of her house. Flo was around the other day and told me Cara still hasn't come out, not since the funeral. It'd do her good."

It wasn't the invitation she'd hoped for, but Heather was both oddly relieved and touched by his concern for Cara. Thoughtfulness came so easily for him. In truth, she should have thought of it herself.

"That's a great idea. I will. And I'll invite Emmi, and Flo, of course. Flo will have a hissy fit if I don't." Her nervous laugh followed. She sidled a glance at Bo. "You'd come, of course."

"Of course! Wild horses couldn't keep me away. I'm proud of that deck; it's the last project I worked on with Brett. It really means something." He looked at his feet. "And I'd like to have an excuse to come back and see you," he added quietly.

Heather stared back at him, her anxiety spiking. Her sudden speechlessness didn't seem to bother Bo in the slightest.

"Say, I have a friend who's the chef at a restaurant on the island. The Long Island Café. It's real good. I'm talking about the best fish on the islands. All local, too. I was wondering if you'd like to come out with me. We could go there for dinner."

She swallowed hard. "When?"

"How's tonight?"

She felt her throat clutch. She wanted to go. Very much.

But just the idea of going on a date was sending her anxiety spinning out of control. She couldn't breathe. She felt light-headed. In a moment she'd be sweating as if she were running a marathon. Excuses rallied in her brain—she had nothing to wear, she had to wash her hair. *Oh, stop being such a baby,* she scolded herself. After all, it was only dinner at a local restaurant at the end of a long day. They were friends. It was the equivalent of going out for coffee. And if she was being honest, the steady diet of organic soups and salads-for-one with only the canaries for company was beginning to wear on her.

"So?" he asked. "Do you want to go?"

The negative voice in her mind screamed, *You can't do this! No way. You'd have nothing to talk about. You'll just be nervous, scared. He'll only reject you. Of course he will.*

"I'd love to . . ." The negative thoughts raced through her head, magnifying her fear. ". . . but I can't," she said in a rush.

"Oh."

"I have to get sketches turned in and—and I'm behind schedule. I don't dare take time off."

"You've got to eat," he argued with a convincing smile. "I'll bring you right back. Promise."

She shook her head. She couldn't look at him.

"How about tomorrow night?"

She took a deep breath, afraid she'd burst into tears. "I'm sorry. I can't."

He ran his hand through his hair. "Okay, then," he said in a different tone. Almost a monotone. "Well . . . I best be off."

Heather glanced at him. Bo's face was pinched and his eyes narrowed; he was clearly disappointed, perhaps even hurt.

She moved to open the door and stood aside to let him pass. She tried to smile, but he wasn't looking.

"Thanks again for the flowers."

Bo didn't reply. She watched as he walked down the stairs, counting each one as she felt the thuds reverberating in her heart.

CARA LEFT THE lights on throughout the night. She couldn't face the darkness. When she'd awakened in the middle of the night, her arm was stretched out on Brett's side of the bed. For those first few seconds of wakefulness she wondered where he was. For those brief, stolen seconds he was still alive in her mind. She tried to hang on to the moment between sleep and wakefulness, clinging to it with desperation, especially emerging from a dream in which he'd been so alive she could feel him, touch him, smell him. Yet the longer she waited, the more heartbreaking it was to face the truth. *He is gone.*

So she kept the lights on. She found if she woke quickly and could see the empty bed, the pain was more a dull ache when she realized, *He is gone.*

Each morning when the sun was bright in the sky, Cara rose. As she'd promised Emmi and Flo, Cara showered, brushed her teeth, her hair. It was all very mechanical. She didn't think about what she put on. Pants, a bra, top, flip-flops. Nothing seemed to fit anymore. Her clothes hung shapelessly from her frame.

It seemed to take more effort to do the smallest things. Everything made her so very tired. Her mind drifted; she'd walk into a room and find herself standing there, staring into space, having forgotten what she'd come for. She was never hungry. She ate mostly because she'd promised Emmi that she would. She went to the fridge and found it jam-packed with Tupperware and foil-covered dishes. She opened one marked CHICKEN KIEV on the foil cover and, looking in, gagged. It had gone bad. She tossed the entire dish into the trash. She went through a few more, sniffing suspiciously, and, when in doubt, tossed those, too. She reached for a white baker's box. Inside she found a mother lode of pastries and cookies. She pulled out a thick, chocolaty oatmeal square and began eating it mindlessly as she tossed one of the tiny cups into the coffee machine. Chocolate was one flavor that reminded her she was still alive.

She licked her fingers, tasting the dark chocolate sweetness, smelling the coffee brewing, then reached for another bar, feeling a sudden insatiable hunger. Outside, the fronds of the palm trees waved gently in the breeze. White clouds floated in a blue sky and boaters were racing along Hamlin Creek. She could hear their whoops of excitement. It was a sunny summer day. Brett would have a lot of tourists out on the boat, she thought.

She stopped herself and put fingers to her forehead. "Must stop doing that," she said aloud. It was a month since he'd died. Thirty days today. She had to stop thinking he was coming back.

She'd read so much about the grieving process over the past month. Devoured articles on the Internet, ordered books. All of them were clear that there was no timeline for grief. They were specific about symptoms of grief—the sensations of choking, shortness of breath, feelings of emptiness, endless crying. But nothing warned her that when she wasn't experiencing those symptoms of anguish, all that was left was a sense of meaninglessness. A great, vast gray space of nothingness. Limbo.

She tried to rally, pulling together her power of cognitive thought. She'd promised her lawyer and accountant that she would gather the important papers they needed by tomorrow. She ran her hand through her hair. She'd always done the bills and financial planning, so she knew where those papers were. But where did Brett keep his personal papers? He'd always been creative in his filing. When she'd first met him years ago, he'd taken money from his customers for the tour-boat ride and simply put it into an old, dented metal box. No record, no receipt. Why hadn't they shared with one another where they kept their important papers?

She set aside the coffee and cookies and began prowling through the house, considering likely places Brett might put his papers. His closet was a good start. She opened the door and was met with an overwhelming surge of scents—sandalwood and cologne with a hint of the salt water Brett had perpetually carried on his person from his time spent out at sea. It sent her reeling and tears burst from her eyes. She brought her palms to her face. After she collected herself, she pulled back the hair that had fallen into her face. It was damp with her tears.

It was painful to go through his closet, but she soldiered on, she had to, or she'd curl up in his bathrobe and sleep. On the top shelf she found an old Nike shoebox. She stepped off the stool and opening it, she couldn't believe what was in it. There was the deed to the house, along with an old Nikon camera, a collection of keys, some coins, and a picture of a young blond woman with a Farrah Fawcett hairstyle.

"In the shoebox," she said with disbelief. She had to laugh.

She climbed out of the closet and sat on their bed with the box in her lap. Forgetting the deed, Cara picked up the photo. She was a pretty girl, young with peachy skin and a radiant smile. Staring at it, she felt no jealousy, just a morbid curiosity. This had to be Ashley, the young woman Brett had once been in love with. The young woman who had died in that terrible motorcycle accident. Brett had been driving. It wasn't his fault, but that didn't matter to him. The incident had scarred him deeply and left him changed. The thought that they were together again in heaven popped into her head. She shook it away. Though it stung to see he'd kept her photograph, she told herself that it was only right. Ashley had been an important person in his life. She set the picture back in the box.

She carried the box to his office. His was an old desk that had once belonged to his father—a crackled leather top, missing handles. He'd loved it. Scattered among the tall tilting piles of papers on top of his desk she found receipts, gum wrappers, lottery tickets, index cards filled with to-do lists. She ran her finger over his distinctive bold printing. She collected his blank checks and checkbook from the middle drawer and a file marked *Insurance* far back in the bottom desk drawer. His life insurance was what she needed most, and she sighed with relief and sat in the chair and began reading the policy.

Her blood chilled. She reread it.

It couldn't be true. She covered her open mouth with her palm. Brett hadn't kept up with his payments. He'd let the policy lapse.

"Oh, Brett," she breathed out on a long sigh, feeling a rush of dismay. She slipped down into the chair, a deep heaviness in her heart. She felt in shock again and rested her forehead against her fingers. Then she slowly shook her head in disbelief. Brett wasn't good with money. He wasn't one to think of planning for a future. But allowing a life insurance policy to lapse was one of the worst financial decisions possible. The policy could have been a lifeline for her, now that he was gone. A way to ensure his wife was taken care of, her future preserved—or the reverse, if she had been the first to go. But it was lost. Gone up in the ether, despite all the payments they'd made.

They'd been having difficulties financially, but why hadn't he come to her if he couldn't make the payments? She would have begged, borrowed, or stolen to front the cost. What was he thinking?

Cara rubbed her eyes. He must have been that sure that neither of them would die young. That they had time to take care of their future. Cara could feel the tongues of financial ruin licking at her heels. She quelled the sudden panic and straightened her shoulders. No time for self pity. She had to be sensible now. *Think!* she told herself. She was never one to gloss over a problem. She preferred to deal with it head-on.

She felt cold, whether from anger or fear she didn't know. Maybe a little of both. She set the shoebox and insurance policy on the dining table, then went to fetch the box of cookies and a second cup of coffee. Next she carried the large laundry basket filled to the brim with mail to the table as well. Emmi had been collecting it in the basket for her to plow through when she was ready. It was shocking to see how much mail could accumulate in a month's time. Well, ready or not, Cara had to deal with it.

First she sorted the mail into three piles: bills, personal, and junk. The junk pile went straight into a recycling bag. She sifted through the personal letters, checking return addresses. Most of them were cards or letters of sympathy that she saved to read later. The bill pile was alarmingly high. She'd missed her credit card payments, but she thought she could probably get the overdue charges eliminated when she explained the situation. Her heart skipped a beat, however, when she saw the thick file from the hospital. She'd been given the file when she left the day Brett had died, but she'd never read anything in it. With trepidation, she slowly studied one page, then the next, one after another. Most of them were medical insurance forms with instructions for how to fill them out. Her hand stilled when she saw the medical report. The Emergency Department Physician's Record had been filled out by hand.

Brett Beauchamps was received for triage at 3:40 p.m. There was no pulse. The physician noted: Cardiac arrest. Massive. DOA. Pronounced 3:53 p.m.

DOA. Dead on arrival. No chance for survival.

She sat motionless for quite a while, trying to digest the information. When the doorbell rang, she jumped. Reading this report, the doorbell was too eerily a reenactment of *that* day.

The doorbell rang again.

Just go away, she thought. Strangers at the door were only bad news. She couldn't talk to anyone, especially not right now. She'd been spoiled by having Emmi here to cover for her, telling everyone to go away. The doorbell rang again. But

Emmi wasn't here now, she told herself. She'd promised to try to live a "normal" life.

The doorbell rang again, this time followed swiftly by three strong knocks.

Cara reluctantly set down the mail and went to the door. Peeking out the window, she saw it was Robert, Brett's cocaptain at the tour business. With unexpected joy, she swung open the door.

"Robert! I'm so glad to see you."

Robert was short, wiry, and deeply tanned. His short blond hair was spiky, stiff from the salt and sun. She hadn't seen him since the funeral, and it did her heart good to see the man who had been like a brother to Brett. They'd been colleagues and friends since he'd started Coastal Ecotour.

They hugged, feeling each other's grief in the gesture. She'd needed a hug just then. Badly.

"Come in," Cara said, ushering him inside the house.

Robert's eyes appeared clouded with concern as he looked at her. "Are you all right?"

"Me?" she asked, surprised he'd ask such a thing. "No, of course not. But I'm managing."

"I thought Emmi was here with you."

"She was, but she's gone home now. She has her own life, and, like I said, I'm managing."

He gave her a doubtful look. "Are you eating?"

She went to the table and lifted the box of cookies. "I am. Can I offer you one? A cup of coffee?"

Robert shook his head and walked closer. He appeared uncomfortable, even nervous. "No, thanks, I don't have a lot of time." He jerked his thumb toward the door. "I have to get back to the boat. The new guy, Phillip, is a good enough captain, but he's young. He has a lot to learn. But he's willing to work for less, which is a good thing, eh? I don't want to leave him alone too long. We've been slammed."

"That's good to hear. What about the *Caretta Caretta*?" she asked, referring to the luxury boat.

Robert made a face and shook his head. "Sorry. It's slow. No takers there, I'm afraid."

Cara was afraid, too. She and Robert both knew that the boat was an albatross around the tour business's neck. "So then, Robert. Is this a social call? Or business?"

"Business, I'm afraid."

Cara indicated a seat and they both sat at the table.

"I hate to bother you with this," Robert began apologetically. "Brett used to handle this sort of thing."

Cara didn't know what he was talking about. "Handle what?"

"Payroll. It's, uh, due today."

"Oh! My God, of course," Cara said in a rush. "You're right. Brett used to hand me the forms, I'd write the check, and he'd give it to you. I've completely lost track of time. I'm so sorry."

"Nothing to be sorry about, Cara. You've had other things on your mind. I hate to bother you about it, but Phillip is new and all. Don't want him to think there's any problem, with Brett gone. You know what I mean." Robert handed her the invoices. "It's all there. My amount's the same, of course. Phillip is getting a starting salary. Like I said, I think he'll fit in just fine. We also have a new intern starting Monday, unpaid, college credit, which is ideal for us right now. You don't have to worry, Cara. I got things covered. You and Brett created a well-oiled machine; all I have to do is my part to keep it running."

Cara was touched by Robert's willingness to step up and help keep things going. "Thanks, Robert. I know he'd be proud of the way you've taken over. Wait here a moment, would you? I'll get the checkbook. Oh"—she spun on her heel, remembering—"do you have the receipts from last month?"

"Yes, ma'am. Right here," Robert said, handing her the bank envelope. "It should all be in order. It was a busy month. Boat was full most every time."

Cara strode across the room to her office. She sat at her desk and pulled out the business's checkbook. Her hands were shaking and she felt suddenly light-headed; her heart began pounding. Things were already beginning to slide. She needed to stay on top of them. Take over at the dock. Except she didn't want to deal with the business or the banks or the mail. She wanted to crawl back into bed, put the covers over her head, and go back to sleep forever.

She cleared her throat and straightened in her chair. But of course she couldn't do that, she told herself firmly. She flipped open the business checkbook with crisp movements. She added the receipt amount to her balance. A shiver ran through her. With the increase for the home equity loan payment due, her balance was dangerously low. Chewing her lip, she wrote a check for Robert and one for Phillip. The tour business was doing very well this season, she noted with relief. That was something.

Cara tried to smile as she strode from the office and handed the two checks to Robert.

"Robert," she said hesitatingly. "Could you please not cash the check until next week?" She saw his eyes widen. "I know this is unusual, but these are unusual times. I have to go to the bank and make a few changes. I just need a little time. Would that be possible?"

"For me, no problem. I'll check with Phillip. But I should think all is good." He paused. "Cara, is everything okay?"

"I don't know," she told him. She felt he deserved her complete honesty.

Robert's face clouded. "Okay," he replied. Then, "You'll let me know what develops? I care a great deal about the business, you know. Brett and I, we built it together."

"I know. And I will."

After she thanked him again for his good work and patience, he left.

Cara returned to her cup of coffee and took a sip, frowning upon discovering it had gone cold. She was exhausted. To the left was her bedroom. Its cool darkness called to her. Before her, the tabletop was cluttered with papers. Duty won out. Cara sat back in her chair and tore open the two bank envelopes. The first was a friendly reminder that her payment on the loan was due. The second informed her that the payment was late and she'd incurred an interest charge.

"Right," she said aloud. Grabbing a large pastry, Cara rose and went to collect her phone from the bedside stand. Wiping crumbs from her fingers on her pants, she first called her brother.

"Palmer?"

"Hey, Sister. How are you holding up?"

"I need to talk to you. Can you come by?"

His voice lowered with concern. "I'll make a point of it."

After hanging up with him, she found the number of her lawyer. John Denning was the son of her mother's lawyer, Bobby Lee. He was bright and well educated, with all of his father's southern gentlemanly qualities, and in her opinion was quite worthy of taking over his father's firm after Bobby retired. She dialed his number, the line that went directly to him.

"John Denning here." His voice held a thick southern drawl, yet he still sounded busy.

"John? It's Cara Rutledge."

"Cara!" She heard the warmth seep into his voice, as she'd expected. "Hello. How are you faring?" he asked with concern.

"Not very well, I'm afraid. I have a problem and must come see you. Things are in a terrible mess. I went in search of the important papers you requested and discovered that Brett let our life insurance policy lapse."

There was a brief pause. "To be clear, did he miss a payment or did the policy lapse entirely?"

"It lapsed," she informed him. "Some time ago."

"I see." His voice was a monotone.

"Also, the adjustable home equity loan rate for the boat has gone up. I'm late in making that payment as well. Frankly, John, I don't know how I'm going to continue to pay them."

Another pause. She imagined him reaching for his schedule, grabbing a pen. "Can you come in tomorrow?"

"Yes," she replied with relief. "What time?"

"Two o'clock okay?"

"I'll be there."

Chapter Twelve

D AYS FLEW BY, one after another. Each morning Heather awoke with the sun. She was determined to stick to her new schedule. She'd read somewhere about the positive power of new habits. Also about how exercise released endorphins in the brain, chemicals that improved mood and relaxation, so she'd decided to work that into her daily routine. She vowed to fight her anxiety with everything she had. To overcome her fears.

Her work was progressing well. She'd driven her golf cart to the far northern point of the island and far south on Sullivan's Island to observe and sketch the birds that clustered there. She always brought her camera on her forays, and more and more often her spotting scope. Some days she sat for hours spying on those shorebirds that would remain on Isle of Palms and Sullivan's Island for the summer—plovers, sandpipers, oystercatchers. As well as the seabirds that most people readily recognized—pelicans, gulls, and terns.

No matter how busy she kept herself, or how many miles she walked, each morning she missed Bo. She missed his easy smile, his conversation, and his presence. She missed *him*. The little beach house had a sense of silence with him gone that felt like loneliness. One morning she'd come back from the beach to find the freshly painted chairs on the deck. Four pristine, empty white rockers. That he'd dropped them off and not waited for her to return delivered a pain she felt she'd deserved.

Of course Bo had felt rejected. He'd asked her out, and she'd refused. There were a million reasons to say yes, but only one for saying no. Her anxiety. At that moment she'd felt utterly overwhelmed. She needed some space and time to think. And that meant being alone. But how could she let him know that the problem was with *her*, not with him? That despite her anxiety, she didn't want to be alone any longer. That she missed him.

Striding along the beach this morning Heather lifted her hands to her hair, clutched it tight and gave a little scream of frustration. She hated being this way! She had to stop letting her anxiety rule her life. Her hands formed fists at her sides as she picked up her pace. If her heart rate went up, it would be for a damn good reason, she told herself.

This morning she'd veered away from Breach Inlet and instead headed north toward the pier. She wanted to scope out a new area. The waves rolled in at a lazy pace, lapping the shore. The beach was smooth and as yet untrammeled. Beyond the dunes, the walls of pastel-colored mansions were dark. The sunrise was reflected in the plate-glass windows.

She'd walked at a brisk pace more than two miles when, closer to the pier, she spied an odd, unmoving mass on the beach. It was too big for a horseshoe crab. Maybe a piece of driftwood? Or . . . She paused. A sea turtle? She stopped and took a look around. There was no one else nearby. No dogs, thank heavens. She walked toward it, lifting her hand over her sunglasses and squinting into the sunlight. A few yards away, she stopped again. The mass was a brown pelican!

It looked fully grown, though she knew the brown pelican was the smallest of the seven pelican species. She walked slowly, so as not to startle the bird. Even when she drew near, it didn't fly off. Its lovely yellow-and-white head lifted up a bit to regard her approach, revealing its long, gorgeous, chestnut-brown-and-white neck. Then it subsided again, as if the bird was too tired to hold it up. The long beak lowered to rest on the sand. It was a mournful sight.

"Poor baby," she muttered softly. Clearly the bird was sick or injured. She kept a distance, not wanting to startle it. What to do? She pulled her cell phone from her backpack and looked up who to call for a bird emergency. Finding a listing for the Center for Birds of Prey, she punched in the number.

In short order, a woman answered and got her location.

"Can you wait with the bird until someone from the center arrives?"

"Yes. I won't leave its side."

"Thank you. It won't be long. Oh, and don't try to lift it. The beak can be quite snappy. It's got a pointed hook at the end. Keep onlookers away, if you can. It needs to stay put. If the pelican gets into the water, we won't be able to catch it."

"I'll do my best."

The pelican had grown nervous with the chatter and tried to rise and walk away.

"Oh, don't do that, baby," Heather crooned.

The bird didn't walk very far. Weakened, it sat again, tucking in its wings. One wing drooped lower.

Heather sat on the sand and pulled her backpack around to withdraw her sketch pad. She scoped out the area, relieved that no one was walking close by. Out on the ocean a healthier pelican sat on the waves, rising and falling gracefully. Was it a mate? she wondered. The injured bird didn't appear disturbed as long as she sat at a distance, so she used the opportunity to sketch it. Early bird artists, like the great Audubon, had worked from stuffed birds. Modern artists had the advantage of photographs, and she used her binoculars and spotting scope, too. But nothing compared to the up-close and personal study of a bird in its natural habitat.

Her hand moved swiftly across the page capturing the color variations, the shape of its eyes. Especially the eyes. The eyes were blue, which meant the bird was in breeding season. Her canaries' eyes were dull and slitted when they were ill, their usual brightness dimmed. Looking at the pelican's eyes, she saw the same listlessness. Every angle reflected illness.

Heather had always thought the pelican was an elegant bird, with its long neck and the distinctive pouch that made it unique in the bird world. If she dared mention a favorite bird, it would be the pelican.

Heather didn't have to wait long for the bird center's emissary. Within half an hour she saw a man approaching her from the beach path. He looked professional, wearing long pants and a brown T-shirt and carrying an animal carrier. She put her sketchbook into her backpack and rose to greet him. As he drew nearer, Heather recognized the long gait, the broad shoulders, the shaggy blond hair. Her breath caught in her throat and she felt her heart rate take off. As happy as she was to see him, she also felt a cold dread at the prospect of their first awkwardness after what she'd come to call "the dinner debacle."

Bo walked at a steady pace toward her and the bird, then stopped cold. He stared for a moment, then began walking again. As he drew near, his face registered surprise and even happiness at seeing her.

"'Of all the gin joints in all the towns in all the world, she walks into mine.'"

Heather was delighted with the quote and relieved at his humor. It broke that first awkwardness, despite the fact that Rick and Ilsa's romance was doomed.

"*Casablanca*'s one of my favorite movies." She smirked and returned another quote. "'I've heard a lot of stories in my time. They went along with the sound of a tinny piano playing in a parlor downstairs.'"

Bo raised his brows. "I'm impressed."

"I know a lot more than that," she admitted. "Like I said, it's a favorite, and I'm kind of a nerd about old movies so . . ." She let it go, a bit embarrassed at her intimation that she spent so many of her evenings alone, watching old movies. "But," she said with import, "considering all the stories I've heard you tell, I don't remember you ever telling me that you're a rescue worker for the birds of prey center."

"I didn't?"

"You didn't."

He shrugged. Then his expression changed and his eyes cooled. Suddenly he was the professional. "I guess it never came up." Bo set the large animal carrier on the sand as his gaze turned to the pelican. "You the one who called it in?"

Heather nodded, noticing his tone had a new edge to it. She took his lead and straightened, then spoke to him as if he were a stranger, a professional who'd come to help. "I was walking along the shore to the pier when I saw the bird just sitting there on the beach. Not moving."

Bo went directly to the bird, all business now. "We've got a brown pelican," he said aloud as he wrote on a clipboard.

"Do we have white pelicans here?" she asked. She'd never seen them listed on the range maps for shorebirds.

"Yes, but not many. Though numbers are increasing. Mostly we have brown pelicans in South Carolina. He paused. "Has it moved?"

"Very little. It tried to walk when I was talking on the phone. Tottered is more like it. Then it collapsed. I think it's either sick or injured."

Bo stopped writing and glanced at her with a hint of mockery in his smile. "Do ya think?"

Heather flinched. He wasn't making this easier. "Actually," she said, irked, "while I was sketching, I noticed its left wing was held lower."

Bo lowered to inspect the wing. "There's the problem," Bo said, waving her closer and pointing. A large fishhook was visible piercing the wing, and the fishing line was wrapped around it. "What a mess. It's good we caught this early. It's embedded deep. I don't dare try to cut the line off. Nope, it's got to go in." Bo walked back to his supplies and pulled a towel out of the crate.

"Heather, you walk around on the ocean side of the bird.

I'm going to catch it. If it starts heading toward the water, ward it off. If it goes into the ocean we've lost it. Okay?"

"Okay," Heather replied, though she couldn't imagine the pelican going far. It could barely walk. Still, she hurried to the shoreline and held out her arms at the ready.

She watched as Bo slowly approached the pelican. As she'd expected, the poor bird didn't move. In one swift movement, Bo wrapped the towel around the pelican and, bending at the waist, scooped it up into his arms. Heather came closer to see if there was anything she could do to help. She could see the bird's dark webbed feet dangling from beneath Bo's arms.

"Could you keep the people away?" he asked as he hefted the bird toward the carrier.

Looking over her shoulder, Heather saw two women approaching. They were in jogging gear and, seeing the commotion, trotted closer. Heather's eyes widened. Her last experience keeping a woman away hadn't ended well. But she wasn't going to back down in front of Bo. Heather licked her lips and hurried across the sand at an angle, cutting them off.

"Hi," she began with a smile. She pushed on. "Sorry, but could you wait here? The pelican is injured and very nervous. He's putting it into the carrier."

"Of course," one of the women replied. "He's a professional?"

"Yes."

"That poor bird. Can I take a picture?"

Heather was relieved at their willingness to cooperate. "Of course." She waited by the women while Bo put the docile pelican into the carrier. Then she thanked the women and hurried back to his side.

"What happens next?"

"I take it to the birds of prey center."

"Of course."

Heather watched as he put a towel over the carrier and gathered his backpack, zipping it and sliding it onto his back. His movements were slow and deliberate. Then he turned to face her, a final gesture.

"Thanks for calling it in."

"Do you need any help? I can carry your backpack."

"I got it. Thanks." He bent and picked up the bird carrier.

Heather walked beside him as he carried the bird to his truck. He put the carrier in the back and secured it. Heather hung around, feeling like an awkward teenager, wondering how to ask if she could go with him.

Bo slammed the gate closed and slapped the sand from his hands. He looked up and appeared almost surprised that Heather was still there.

"Do you need a ride home?" he asked.

She shook her head. "Uh, no, thanks."

After an awkward pause he said in a professional manner, "Okay. I better get going."

"Bo?" she blurted out.

He looked at her. His face gave away nothing.

"Would it be out of line for me to—to go with you? To the center?"

"You want to come along?"

"Yes! *I really* want to come. I promise I'll stay out of your way."

"It's a long drive. I don't know when I'll be done."

"I don't care."

Bo considered this. He nodded once. "Then hop in."

On the forty-five-minute drive to the center, Heather sat in the passenger seat of his truck looking out at the view as they whizzed past, desperately trying to make a few comments about the scenery or the weather. They were inane, but she didn't have to facilitate brilliant conversation, she told herself. She just had to engage. This wasn't a date, after all. It was just two people riding together to rescue a pelican. She was dressed comfortably in her nylon fishing pants and shirt. Not in some tight dress with high heels. It helped her feel emotionally comfortable.

"Have you been a volunteer long?" she asked Bo.

"Eight years," he replied. "It's hard work, but I love it. Love being out with the birds." He paused. "Mostly the Center for Birds of Prey has raptors—eagles, hawks, falcons, owls. They're a lot different than shorebirds." He glanced at her. "And those sweet little canaries you've got." His gaze returned to the road. "They're *wild*. Fierce. They might be injured, but their MO is to get you. That's why we wear leather gloves and gear. And we don't name them. The goal is to release them, and they need to have the predator instinct to survive in the wild. So we've got to be careful not to habituate them. But they'll take a chunk out of you if you're not careful." His hands tapped the wheel. "Yes, they will."

"So why volunteer with shorebirds?"

"I love raptors, don't get me wrong. But being a surfer, my heart's with shorebirds. My first rescue was a pelican. A fledgling that wasn't making it. The birds of prey center started taking in shorebirds after they signed on for oil-spill disaster relief. So I volunteered for transport. I know how to catch them and bring them in."

He drove a few minutes, then added, "You know, in some ways shorebirds are like canaries."

Heather turned her head to study his profile. His long forehead, straight nose. A gentle face that came together so pleasingly. But from this angle she couldn't see his eyes. Oh, God, she loved his blue eyes.

"How so?" she asked.

"Well, shorebirds tell us about the health of our oceans because they eat the local fish. If they're sick, that warns us about what's happening out there. Kind of like canaries in coal mines."

"I never thought of it like that. It makes sense. So?" she asked, curious. "How are the shorebirds doing?"

He made a face. "Not good. Shorebird populations have shrunk on average by an estimated seventy percent across North America since 1973. Experts are worried that without action, some might go extinct."

Heather felt a sense of dread. And it was personal. All those magnificent birds she'd been photographing and sketching . . . "I didn't realize the drop in population was so massive."

"Most people don't. It's especially bad for those birds that migrate thousands of miles." He turned his head, his eyes gleaming. "See, they make these epic round-trip journeys each year, some flying farther than the distance to the moon over the course of their lifetimes. Imagine that." He paused, then glanced at her again. "Those big issues are for the experts. I figure the rest of us can either sit back and moan, or do something. It's the old *act locally* thing." He shrugged lightly. "So I rescue shorebirds."

"Light one candle," Heather said, quoting from the Bible verse.

He smiled, appreciating that she understood. "Yeah, something like that."

"What about pelicans?" she asked. "They rebounded from the pesticide pollution of the sixties. Wasn't that a success story?"

"It was. But now plastic and abandoned fishing line, like the one that got this poor guy, is threatening not only pelicans but dolphins and turtles and all marine life. At some point in a pelican's life, in Florida, eighty percent will become entangled either in an active line or in discarded line thrown thoughtlessly into the sea."

Heather was shocked the statistic was so high and couldn't respond.

They drove for a while in silence, but this time it didn't feel uncomfortable. Heather leaned back and stretched out her legs. She glanced again at him. He was so handsome. His cheeks bore stubble and she hoped he wasn't growing a beard. Today she'd seen yet another side of Bo. He never failed to surprise her. His humor, his breadth of knowledge, his endless capacity for kindness. She usually felt very shy with men, but Bo made her feel like she'd known him forever.

Perhaps he kept surprising her, she pondered, because she was limiting him in her mind. Sabotaging him so that she wouldn't fall in love with him. That was a frustrating part of her mixed-up self-defense system of social avoidance. And yet Bo had persevered. He had become, with no apparent effort or goal, a part of her life. And if she'd learned nothing else the past week, she'd learned that when he was not in it, she was lonely.

Bo had talked about habituation, how at the center they didn't want raptors to become accustomed to humans so that they would remain wild. By contrast, her therapist had helped Heather work out a plan to habituate herself to her new surroundings. To seek out small challenges that would raise her anxiety levels without triggering a full-scale panic.

For step one of her plan, she'd started walking the beach for short spurts of time, gradually getting used to the area, seeking out reassuring markers. Day by day she'd added more time until now she was out for hours. She'd succeeded with that step.

The second step was to fight her social avoidance with low-risk opportunities. Basically, to talk to nice people one-on-one. Bo had been an answer to a prayer. He worked around the house every day, so it was low-risk. And he was exceedingly friendly, a great storyteller, and easy to talk to. Mission accomplished.

Step three was to speak with someone she'd be potentially interested in dating. Right from the start, Heather had felt an attraction to Bo. Seeing him, she understood what women meant when they talked about having butterflies in their stomachs. Not from anxiety, oh, no. This was a very different kind of fluttering. With most other men, if she was even remotely interested, she'd start self-sabotaging and clamming up, unable to do more than blurt out inane responses. It had been—and still was—humiliating. But with Bo . . . even if her nervousness made her comments less than brilliant, she'd kept up her side of the conversation, not slipping into long silences. She'd even enjoyed the conversations, more than she could have imagined.

The problem had come when Bo asked her for a date. What would seem like a harmless and casual date to most people felt daunting to people with anxiety. She'd backed off, come up with excuses. And in the process threatened a relationship that meant a great deal to her.

Heather slid another glance at Bo as he drove. Her heart melted just looking at him. She had a huge crush, there was no denying it. If she wanted to salvage any hope of a relationship, the moment was now. She had to let Bo know about her anxiety symptoms. If she didn't, she'd wait and wait and wait and only grow more anxious and stand to lose any chance with him. What was the worst he could do? she asked herself. The answer came quickly. He'd walk away. But he'd do that anyway if she didn't explain. She clasped her hands in her lap, squeezing tight.

"Hey, Bo?" she said in a soft voice. He didn't hear her. Heather cleared her throat and started again. "Bo?"

He swung his gaze from the road. "Yeah?"

She looked at her hands. *Tell him now, while he's driving. While you still have the nerve.* "I . . . I wanted to talk to you about . . . about when you asked me to dinner." Heather looked up quickly to see that though his eyes were on the road, his face had grown taut. She knew he was listening. "I want to explain . . . to try to explain why I didn't go out with you."

He swung his head from the road to look at her again, amazement in his eyes. "Okay."

She willed herself to say the words, to not back down now. She clutched her hands together and unconsciously began wringing them in her lap.

"You see, I have what's called social anxiety. My mama used to call me shy, but it's much more than that. I had a hard time through high school, but after graduation my mother's car accident made everything spiral downhill."

"You were in a car accident?"

"Yeah," she answered in a soft voice. "I was in pretty bad shape. My mother died in that accident."

"I'm so sorry."

She heard the shock in his voice. She had to force herself to continue. "Over time my body healed, but my anxiety symptoms were so much worse. No one could say I was shy anymore. I had a breakdown. I felt nervous and tense all the time. I wouldn't leave the house. I wouldn't look people in the eyes."

She paused to glance at him again, to gauge his reaction. His face was unreadable, his eyes on the road. Worry nagged at her: What did he think of her? Did he think she was bat crazy? She wanted him to say something, but he remained quiet. Listening. The silence dragged on, each second excruciating. Heather gathered herself together and pressed on.

"Anyway, I've been in therapy since then. And I take medication. I've been working very hard so I wouldn't be stuck like that forever. And I've made progress," she said, her tone more positive. "I still don't like going to parties and I hate small talk. I get nervous in new situations and find it hard to go out alone to new places. And"—she laughed lightly—"I'm guessing you figured out I get very anxious during conversations. I'm even nervous talking to you right now."

"Why?" He turned his head to look at her. "It's just me."

"I'm not always nervous talking to you," she hurried to add. "Actually, you're one of the few people I'm not nervous to talk with. I enjoy talking with you." She paused. "A lot."

"But you're nervous now?" he asked gently.

"Yes. Because I'm trying to explain what's going on in my head, and it's embarrassing." She felt blood rush to her face. "It's not something I usually share with anyone. But I care about you and I want you to understand what I'm experiencing. So you'll understand that the night you invited me to dinner, I wanted to go."

He looked at her, and his eyes were bright, but he didn't speak.

"All my old fears flew up in my head again. I wanted to go." She threw up her hands. "It sucks having anxiety. It's not you. It's *me*." She felt tears threaten and knew she had to finish quickly. "Please don't be frustrated, and try to understand. If you'll be patient with me, and maybe even ask again someday . . ." Her voice cracked and she took a deep breath, then looked up at him.

Bo turned his head from the wheel and she saw in his eyes the same glow that she witnessed in the sunrise—fiery, ablaze with hope. He reached across the seat and grabbed her hand from her lap and held it.

"I'll ask you every night, if you like," Bo said. "Till you say yes."

She felt dangerously emotional, afraid of tears. "Okay."

He squeezed her hand.

As Bo turned the truck into the entrance of the Center for Birds of Prey, Heather felt a tremendous relief. The pelican wasn't the only creature being saved that day, she thought.

Chapter Thirteen

T HE FOG ROLLED in, thick as a wet blanket. Even though it was late afternoon, the sun was blocked by clouds. The behemoth cargo ship coming into Charleston Harbor bellowed out its mournful foghorn again and again as it made its slow journey to port.

Cara sat on her sofa staring blankly at the television set, unaware and uncaring of whatever midday court drama was playing out on the small screen. She felt frozen with fear after her visits with her lawyer and accountant. Unable to think beyond the fact that she was, for the first time in her life, feeling utterly helpless. She didn't know what to do.

This feeling was foreign to Cara. She was accustomed to confrontation, even enjoyed going toe-to-toe with adversaries. She'd learned from the best, after all. Her father had been a mean son of a bitch who tolerated no disobedience, especially from what he considered the weaker sex. Theirs had always been a turbulent relationship of glares and threats, shouts, and a volleying, circular pattern of his demands and her refusals. It had been only a matter of time until their headstrong relationship came to a crisis. Cara had persevered. Her motto was that what didn't kill her only made her stronger. She'd moved to Chicago and landed a low-paying starting position in an advertising agency. It was the perfect fit for the creative, bright, and hungry young woman. While her colleagues on the bottom rung of the corporate ladder went out for drinks after work, Cara had gone to night school. She was like a dog with a bone, not letting go of her goals. For seven long years she'd persisted, finally getting her college degree in communications as she slowly rose up several rungs on that ladder. She'd impressed her seniors with her drive and intelligence. When she was finally offered the job of junior marketing executive, she'd been ready to soar.

She'd moved up fast after that, taking no prisoners. She had the reputation of being tough but fair. She'd tolerated few errors and no fools. If anyone confronted her, she chopped them off at the knees.

And then came the mass layoffs. It was a hard time for a lot of people—Cara among them. She and the other high-level execs were unceremoniously walked out of the offices of Leo Burnett by an armed guard. A humiliating experience that had sparked a midlife crisis. At forty years of age, Cara felt her life come to a screeching halt. She'd given up everything for her career, mainlining work, and the abrupt collapse sent her running home to her mother—back to Charleston.

That was when she'd discovered her mother was dying, and Cara had dug deep and found the strength and courage not only to start again, but also to help her mother. In retrospect, she could see that thinking of another person had made her open up and heal herself. She had been happier that summer than she'd ever dreamed possible. That summer Cara had found her softer, sensitive side, and wasn't afraid to let go of her control and fall in love. Brett had come to her like a ray of sunshine to a piece of ice. He'd melted her resistance, and she'd blossomed under his warmth.

Now he was gone, and with him all that they'd worked for together for the past ten years. Cara didn't know if she had the strength to rally a third time in her life. She felt empty. Nothing left to give. So she sat, staring vacantly at the television hour after hour, not even registering what program was on. Her mind was blank.

When the doorbell rang, she winced. Why did people persist in bothering her? She ducked so no one could see her from the window. "Go away, go away," she mumbled with clenched fists. It rang again.

After several moments, the knocker on the door banged insistently.

"Go away!" Cara shouted.

More knocking.

"Please!" she shouted louder, then put her face in her hands.

"I hear you say *please*, sister mine. But I'm still not going away. You gave me a key, remember? The knocking was just a courtesy."

Cara moved her arm from her head and lifted her head toward the door. "Palmer?"

She heard a key clicking in the lock, and the door opened. Her brother stood holding the door handle, uncharacteristically sheepish. "Can I come in?"

Cara looked at him in surprise. She knew she must look a

fright. Her mouth was dry; she was probably dehydrated. She couldn't remember the last time she'd eaten—could it have been since those pastries?—and she certainly hadn't expected Palmer to walk into her house today. But seeing him, his face scrunched up in worry, made her glad he'd come. He'd been around a lot in the days immediately following the funeral, but had seemed uncertain how to help his sister through her grief, and had appeared almost relieved to leave her to the careful, tender ministrations of Flo and Emmi.

Until now.

"Of course," she said in a hoarse voice, pushing herself up to her feet. "I-I wasn't expecting to see anybody today."

"Good. Because I'm not anybody. I'm your brother!" He stormed in then in his usual blustery manner. "Why the hell is it so dark in here?" He strode to the windows and with brash movements pushed open the curtains and flipped open the shutters.

"Oh, don't do that," Cara said, squinting in the flood of light drenching the room. "And don't look at me. I'm a mess." Self-consciously, her hand went to her hair.

"You asked me to come by."

She paused, hearing a voice behind him, and groaned inwardly. "Is that Julia?" Julia had also hung around in the days after the funeral, but her presence had always made Cara feel ill at ease, as if she had to put on a mask of competency in the face of her put-together, well-heeled sister-in-law. Cara had heaved a sigh of gratitude when Julia had left to get back to her day-to-day routine. Not that she didn't like Julia. In doses. But every hair was always in place with her. She didn't feel like being judged this morning.

"Yes, she came with me. The children wanted to come, but we told them next time. We didn't want to come down on you like a ton of bricks."

"Cara, my poor sweet girl, how have you been holding up?" Julia crooned, rushing in behind Palmer. She was impeccably dressed in a blue chambray linen dress with bold strands of blue and white coral around her neck. Julia's blond hair was neatly cropped around her ears in an elegant, sleek style.

"Hi, Julia," Cara said in a dull voice.

Julia hurried to wrap one arm around Cara, cupping her face with her other hand. "Just look at you! You're so thin. It's shocking. Why, you're just withering away. Well, don't you worry. We're here and we are going to take care of you and get you fixed right up. Aren't we, Palmer?"

Cara couldn't respond to the force of Julia's concern, even felt tears come to her eyes.

Julia stared her down appraisingly. "I'll just bet you haven't eaten yet today."

Cara shook her head, embarrassed, but she didn't have the presence of mind to lie.

"I thought not. Tell you what we're going to do. Palmer, you sit and chat with your sister a minute while I go fix her up something to eat." She looked to her husband. "Well, go on!"

Palmer approached his sister as Julia vanished into the kitchen, and they shared a commiserating glance. He chortled and indicated the sofa.

"Come on, we might as well just go along with her plan. I find it's easier that way. Sit down, Cara, and tell me how you are. I mean, *really* are. Because I've got to tell you. You look like you've been washed, spun, and hung up to dry." He sat down with a soft thud and patted the seat beside him.

Cara came to sit beside her brother and, without speaking a word, leaned into him, resting her head on his shoulder. Palmer, caught unawares, sat stiff in surprise, his hands still in the air. This was so uncharacteristic of Cara. After a moment his face softened, and he rested his hand on her back, stroking her shoulder.

"I remember the last time you came crying to me," he said in a gentle voice. "You couldn't have been more than six or seven. You wanted to play ball with us boys and we didn't want you on our team. The boys said some mean things to you."

Cara sniffed. "They told me my hair was a rat's nest."

She heard his laugh deep in his chest. "Well, it was! Kind of like it is now."

Cara choked out a laugh. It was true, and only he could tell her. "I was mostly mad that they wouldn't let me play. Because I was a girl."

"Yeah, I know. I felt bad about that."

"You got in a fight for me."

"I wasn't a very good fighter. They beat me up, if I recall. Some hero."

"You were my hero."

He paused and swallowed thickly. "I'm sorry if I fell off that pedestal you sometimes put me on."

"Look at me, brother mine. None of us are perfect. I'm lying prostrate on the floor."

"Now, honey, you were knocked down, good and hard. There's no denying it. But you'll get up again. When you're ready. You always do."

"I don't know. Maybe not this time." Cara straightened and wiped her eyes with her hands. Palmer dipped into his pocket and pulled out a pressed handkerchief. He had always maintained the old-world ways of Charleston. Cara blew her nose gratefully and twisted the delicate linen in her hands, then folded it into a smaller and smaller square as she forced herself to find the words to tell Palmer what had happened.

"It's more than just Brett being gone," she confessed. "My life is a mess." She looked up at him. It was her style to be blunt when necessary, and there was no sugarcoating this. "I'm in serious financial trouble."

His blue eyes sharpened. "Oh?"

Cara quickly brought her brother up to speed on her financial situation, sparing no details.

"In a word, I'm broke," she finished helplessly.

"I had no idea," Palmer said in a hushed voice. He shook his head. "I loved Brett like a brother. But right now, I'd like to kick his butt."

Cara chuckled, glad he could freely voice his feelings with her. "Yeah, but we both know he wasn't the best at finances. But it's done, and now I have to move forward. Palmer, I'm not angry. I'm scared."

"What are you going to do with the business?"

Cara set her mouth in a firm line, the way she used to when she needed to ream out a wayward employee at the ad agency or bring an account back into line. "I have to sell it."

"Is Robert interested?"

"I think he is, yes. Whether he can come up with the money, I don't know. I only know I can't keep it going. And honestly, I don't want to. The ecotour business was Brett's passion, not mine. Selling it might not even be enough." She gestured vaguely around her. "I might need to let the house go, too."

Palmer looked mildly alarmed at that. "But if you sell this house, where will you move?"

"I'm still working that out. Palmer," she said, raising her eyes from the handkerchief she was still twisting in her hands to meet his gaze. "I need your advice. John said I'm going to have to sell something to pay back the loan. Right away. How long will it take for this house to sell?"

Palmer considered the question, then shrugged. "I don't have a crystal ball. But we're smack in the summer season and, you've got the advantage of having a modest-size house on a deepwater lot. There are only so many of those around. I'd be surprised if it didn't go quick. In fact, I may know of someone who's been looking for just such a place. He might just jump on it."

"Then would you put it up for sale? Just get me the best price you can as fast as you can."

"Sure I will, but let's just talk this through a minute. This is your home. The one you lived in with Brett. You can sell the beach house, too, you know."

"I could, but I can't do anything until Heather moves out. And I'm not sure I want to sell it. You know how I feel about Primrose. Palmer, I simply cannot live here because I'm surrounded by memories. This was Brett's house." She paused. "I . . . I think I might want to live in the beach house for a while. It's my home. I need to feel safe."

"Sure, honey, I can understand that."

"So, you'll take care of it for me?"

"Of course. And of course there'll be no commission."

"Thank you." It was heartfelt.

He seemed taken aback by her gratitude. "Honey, of course I wouldn't charge you commission. You're my sister!"

"That's not what I was thanking you for."

"No? For what, then?"

She shrugged. "For understanding. And for not badgering me to sell Mama's house like you did earlier this spring."

"Don't thank me yet. I haven't sold either of them yet. Like I always say, you never know."

Cara sighed, pressing her palms together. "Time's the one thing I don't have right now. Mortgages are due, payroll has to be met." She turned to him. "I hate to ask you, and I wouldn't except I'm desperate, but . . ." She swallowed. "Could you float me a loan? Just until I figure out what to do? John and I worked out a realistic financial plan, but as you said, we can't control how long it will take for this house to sell, for the business to sell, and for me to find somewhere else I can afford to live."

Palmer's face grew troubled and he rubbed his jaw in thought. "Cara, I'd love to be able to lend you money. I would. But truth be told, I'm pressed for cash. Remember that deal I told you about? It's in the works, and I've had to invest heavily. I just don't have it to give at the moment. I'm sorry." He paused. "Why don't you come stay with me and Julia and the kids for a while? Just until you sell the house and get your feet back under you. It'll be no trouble at all. We'd be delighted to have you."

Cara hadn't expected that. In the back of her mind, her brother was always in the wings, ready and willing to bail her out. Now all she had was the prospect of living with him and his family—which, while she appreciated the spirit in which it was intended, wasn't something she even wanted to think about.

"That's the kindest offer. Really. And I appreciate it. But . . ." Cara's façade of control broke. She hated the tears that sprang with a sudden urgency ever since Brett's death. A scent, a comment, a memory—anything could set her off.

Palmer reached for her hand. "You've done a lot in a short time. More than most of us could do in the best of times. And you had to do it all in the worst of times. You're exhausted. You try to be so strong, Cara. Always did." He leaned back. "Now, I admire it, sure. But damn it, sometimes you just have to let us help you out."

"Then help me sell this place. I need that the most."

"Consider it done."

She released a heavy sigh and patted his hand by way of thanks. "As for the rest . . . I'm a big girl. I can figure out where I'll go from here."

"Cara!" Julia called from the kitchen in a voice that was iron coated with syrup. "Bring your sweet self in here for some lunch. Hurry now, you don't want it to get cold. You, too, Palmer. Come on, now, hear?"

Palmer looked at Cara, and suddenly they were both children again being called to dinner by their mother. Cara leaned into her brother again as they both broke out in laughter. It had been so long that she'd forgotten how healing a good laugh could be.

Part Three

HEALING

Barbara J. Bergwerf

SEMIPALMATED SANDPIPER

These birds are small and stocky with short necks, moderately long bills, dark gray-brown plumage, and lightly marked chests. The name "semipalmated" refers to slight webbing between the toes. Important because of their large numbers, they are long-distance migrants who nest in arctic tundra and winter in South America. Often called "peeps," they are frequently seen chasing waves on their short legs as they feed.

Conservation status: *High Concern*

Part Three

HEALING

Chapter Fourteen

BO PULLED INTO the parking lot on the northern end of Sullivan's Island by the bridge. He grabbed his Ducks Unlimited ball cap and slapped it on his head. Then he met Heather's gaze. Her blue eyes sparkled with excitement. "Let's go!"

Bo jumped from the truck and came around the back to open her door, but Heather had already climbed out. He spotted her standing at the border of the parking lot, one hand holding on to her straw hat, the other over her eyes as she peered out over Breach Inlet. She appeared more relaxed and confident than ever before, as though she'd set down a heavy burden and was free of its weight. She looked sporty in her jean shorts, tennis shoes, and white T-shirt. Her blond hair was pulled back in a ponytail.

Bo leaned against the gate of his truck and stared at the vision of Heather against the blue sea and sky. He couldn't take his eyes off her. Truth was, he'd been smitten from the first moment he saw her dancing to Johnny Cash. Who wouldn't be? She was gorgeous. But seeing her sitting on the floor struggling with the pieces of the birdcages had cinched it. He was caught—hook, line, and sinker.

He still couldn't believe he'd been lucky enough to land a job where he could see her every day. He'd never won anything—not a contest or the lottery. But meeting Heather felt like he'd won the jackpot. He'd known lots of other pretty women. But all of them were just that—pretty. There was no substance. No passion. No *there* there. The better he got to know Heather, the more he saw how much more there was to her than her physical beauty. She was shy, that was obvious. And vulnerable. But she had real depth. He'd seen the sharp intelligence behind those brilliant blue eyes. The class in her demeanor. Her anxiety could make her clumsy socially, which might've turned off some guys. But it brought out the chivalry in him, learned at his daddy's knee. He'd been rebuffed by some of the other girls he'd dated when he tried to open a door or order for them both on a date, as if his manners some- how belittled their power. Those dates usually were one-offs. But with Heather . . . He smiled. Bo found her shyness be- guiling, her slanted glances flirtatious. Each bloom of a blush on her pale cheek bowled him over. It just made him want to do more for her.

Every morning on the drive over to the beach house, he had prepared what story he'd tell her that day. He'd knock on the screen door and she'd let him in with a tentative hello, but he could tell she'd been waiting for him. He could smell the coffee brewing, and he'd listen for what music she'd selected to play that morning. It clued him in to her mood. Then, while he sipped his coffee, he'd talk to her and she'd feed her canaries. He loved watching her with her birds. She moved like a dancer from cage to cage, cooing to them and singing out their names: Moutarde, Poseidon, Pavarotti. And they responded, singing their hearts out to her in return.

He smiled, thinking of Heather and her music. She was surrounded by song. She might have anxiety and spend much of her time alone and indoors—but had he ever met someone so alive? He could tell her mood by the music that was playing—opera when she was soaring, classical when she was drawing, country music when she was cooking or puttering about, Bruno Mars when cleaning the house.

He'd sung to Heather, too, in his own way, with his stories. He'd dug deep for every and any snippet of folklore and history, some amusing story, just so he could buy more time with her. So he could see the look of wonder spread across her face as she forgot her reservations and fell under the spell of the tale he was weaving. Heather's beautiful face, her luminous blue eyes, could conceal nothing. He was challenged to coax a smile or a laugh out of her. Each one felt like a gift because they were so infrequent and difficult to come by.

So when she'd refused to go out to dinner with him, he'd been crushed. He'd felt like a fool. To his mind, when she'd shown him the door on his last day working on the deck and told him good-bye, she was telling him she'd found him entertaining and now she was done, thank you very much. It had hurt. Bad. Just remembering that moment, he felt again the ache in the pit of his stomach.

He'd stayed away. With the job done, there was no reason for him to return. It was a miserable week. Then, on an ordinary day, he'd answered the call from the birds of prey center and there she was, hovering close to the injured pelican, looking at him with an expression every bit as fragile as the hurt bird. He'd put up his guard. Yet somehow she'd found the courage to explain to him why she'd refused his invitation. She'd humbled herself to be honest about her anxiety, and in response, he was humbled by her trust in him.

And here they were. Together again. Like peas and carrots, his grandmother would say. And as before, they didn't feel any awkwardness with each other. Bo felt a surge of happiness that tasted as fresh and full of hope as the early-morning air. With energy he reached in and hoisted the cooler from the back of the truck, then tossed a blanket over his shoulder.

"Hey, pretty lady!" he called out. "Stop gawking like a tourist and grab the rods. We going to fish or not?"

Heather turned and, upon seeing him, her smile brightened her face to rival the sunny sky. She hurried over to his side.

"I was watching a line of pelicans flying overhead in formation. They remind me of bombardiers on patrol. Made me wonder, how's our wounded pelican?"

"They think it turned the corner and is going to make it. For a couple of days it wouldn't eat, now it won't stop eating." He chuckled. "Apparently they've got to do physical therapy on its injured wing. To keep it mobile. If a bird can't fly, it can't survive."

"Can we see him?"

"Sure, I'll take you up again and we can check on the little fella." He paused to look up as another three pelicans flew overhead in V formation. "I'm always glad when they pull through. Lots of them don't. The ones we find injured we can bring in and hopefully help. Most of them, though, we don't see, and they just die out there." He glanced back at her and smiled. "Right, then. Let's grab the gear."

Heather reached far into the back of the truck to the rods, offering him a pretty view of her rounded backside. He felt a stirring and looked out at the churning waters of the inlet.

"Got 'em," she called out triumphantly.

Hefting the heavy cooler, he jerked his chin toward the beach. "Great. Follow me."

Bo led her down the slope to the small stretch of beach from the Hunley Bridge to a rocky edge. It was not a pretty beach. The bits of sand were patchy and rocky, and no swimming was allowed due to the deathly currents in Breach Inlet. This made it a good place to fish.

"Look, Bo," Heather said as they reached the beach. "The tide's out and there's so much sand. You could walk to Isle of Palms."

"Don't ever try it," he warned, setting down the cooler with a thud. "See that?" He pointed to the large NO SWIMMING sign. "That's for real. No fooling around. Every year some tourists who don't understand the tides see all the sand and try to walk across, or just see how far out they can go. Few things scare me more than driving over the bridge and seeing some nice family out there, looking for seashells. Naïve. They don't have a clue how fast and furious the tide can rush back in. It's a force of nature. And then there's the guy who comes to fish and just wants to go in the water a little bit to cool off. He never intends to go swimming. Just a toe in . . ." Bo shook his head. "People have stood in the shallows, and damn if the sand didn't give way and they got caught in the currents. Folks use to call it Breach Inlet Quicksand. And that doesn't even cover the sharks."

"Sharks?"

Bo looked at her with his brows raised. "Honey, you do know there are sharks in the ocean?"

Heather blushed. "Of course. I'm not stupid. But they're out there, right?" she said, pointing far out to sea. "Not close in." She grimaced. "Not a lot of them, anyway?"

"They're all over. I can't even count how many I've bumped into when I've been out surfing." Bo gestured toward the inlet. "But they really love it in Breach Inlet. It's a favorite feeding place for sharks. In fact, the largest shark I ever saw was right down there." He pointed to the shoreline. "It had to be twelve feet long. I was just standing there fishing and it swam right by me, so close I could've touched it. Course, I'm not that kind of fool." He laughed. "Dolphins love it here, too, for the same reasons. Mama dolphins like to bring their young here to teach them how to hunt. It's a feeding ground in there, with currents as crazy as a pot of boiling soup, and blood-thirsty sharks to boot—nope, no one should try to swim in Breach Inlet." He cocked his head and winked. "But it makes for great fishing."

He looked up at the sky to see large gray clouds gathered over the northwest, but the sky above the ocean where they stood was still blue with white clouds, and the wind was light.

"I don't like the looks of those clouds. Let's get started before they move any closer." He bent to pick up the cooler again with a grunt. "Just a little farther," he said, leading the way to a far corner of the beach where rocks gathered at the base of the slope. He set the cooler down while she spread out the blanket, anchoring it with the cooler and rocks. They gathered the gear and began hooking the bait.

"This here's shrimp. It's still alive. We want them dancing on the line. Live bait is the ticket." He held back a smile, observing Heather's intense concentration as she watched him demonstrate how to place the hook through the tail of the shrimp. "Do you think you can do it?" he asked.

She reached out to touch it tentatively. Her long fingers inched closer and at last barely touched the tip of the shrimp's fan tail; when it twitched, she yelped and jumped back. Bo laughed, but not too loudly.

Heather laughed at herself, a blush staining her cheeks. "Maybe I should watch you awhile first?"

"Your rod, ma'am."

Heather accepted the fishing rod from Bo without squeamishness. She held it in front of her with a determined gleam in her eye.

After he baited his own rod, he reached out and took her hand. He was pleased she didn't resist. Her hand felt slim and small in his. "Careful, now. These rocks can be slippery. On some of these I've paid the price of admission." He guided her up the rocks to reach a small flat bit of sand, a perfect perch for fishing. "This is my secret spot."

"Secret, huh?" she teased. "Every car that crosses the bridge can see us."

"Yeah, but they aren't looking at us. And even if they were, they can't see we're standing on sand. Besides, from where they're looking, they think we're just fools standing on the rocks looking for dolphins. Which, by the way . . ." He pointed toward the bridge.

Heather squealed with joy when she spotted the pair of dolphins arcing in the water under the bridge. The dorsal fins eased in and out of the water with enviable grace, heading their way.

"They're so lovely," she breathed, peering out over the water. "I've never seen a dolphin before. It's so incredible to watch them."

Bo loved watching her expressions shift, revealing her extreme pleasure in the simplest things. He doubted he'd ever tire of watching her face.

"I still can't believe no one's ever taken you fishing," he marveled. "How could a person reach twenty-six years of age and not know how to fish?"

"Easy," she replied. "I never knew anyone who fishes."

"Your father?"

Heather shook her head. "Nope."

"Well, thank God I came along."

She slanted him a gaze, smiling a little before glancing away. "Exactly."

HEATHER COULDN'T BELIEVE she was flirting so outrageously with Bo today. She felt that they'd crossed some line yesterday when she'd told him about her anxiety. Knowing that he understood and clearly still wanted to be with her helped her lower the steel wall she tended to raise at the first triggers of fear. There was a new freedom between them, hard to put into words. Perhaps playful, definitely flirtatious. Whatever the word, the mood was definitely reaching a new level.

Bo let her watch him cast a few times, to give her a sense of the movement. He was as fluid with his motions here as he was working with wood. As an artist, she appreciated how everything he did had a sense of elegance to it. His movements were controlled yet graceful. Her fingers itched to sketch the way his muscles tightened as he cast far out into the sea. Then his tanned forearms grew taut as he reeled the line back in. Over and over, in an intricate dance. He savored the practice, she could tell from the expression on his face. When he turned to face her again, she startled, wildly wondering if he could tell she was watching him rather than the rod and line. There was something in his smile that told her he knew.

"So what are you fishing for?"

"Whiting. Spots. Croakers. Maybe pompano. I like to use live bait for them. If I was alone and it was low tide like this, I'd go wander among the rocks and hunt for flounder."

"You can catch flounder here?"

"Can I?" He made a mock harrumph. "Honey, they call me the Flounder Whisperer. I work bait around the rock groins moving from groin to groin with light tackle, a five-gallon bucket, a cast net, a floating bait bucket, and a small nylon tackle bag. I wear old tennis shoes, though like I said, I've had my share of cuts and bruises on those rocks. Along here I can slide the flounder up on the sand, no landing net needed. I caught a twenty-six-inch flounder last summer," he added proudly.

"I have a lot to learn," she admitted. "I don't know one fish from another."

"You'll learn. Ready to try?"

"Absolutely."

Bo stepped closer to her and set down his rod. Moving slowly, as if he were approaching a skittish animal, he stepped behind her, and his long arms slid around her to take hold of the rod.

Heather smelled his pine soap, and when his body touched hers she felt his warmth and his power. She closed her eyes a moment to still the fluttering she felt. She turned her head to look up, but couldn't see his face. "Am I holding the rod right?"

Bo's face lowered closer to hers as he reached out to shift her hand into the correct position, adjusting her grip slightly, his fingers pressing lightly against hers. She swallowed thickly and felt warmth in parts of her body that made her light-headed. She'd never been so physically attracted to any man before. He was saying something about a bale, but she couldn't understand any of it for the pounding of her heart. When he stepped back, she felt a rush of cooler air and gulped, shaking away the fog in her brain. She had to pay attention.

"It's like throwing a baseball," he was saying, moving his arm back in a pitching motion. "You just put your finger on the line like I showed you, and then release it." He stretched his arm far out and moved his index finger. "Got it?"

"Could you show me again where to put my finger?" she asked, feeling silly for having to ask again.

Bo moved closer, but this time he didn't wrap his arms

around her. It might've been better for the purpose of the lesson, though she would have preferred it if he did.

"Your index finger is what we call the trigger finger. You grab the line with it. Like that, see?"

Heather nodded, determined to get it right.

Bo moved behind her again, and she closed her eyes as another surge of sensations raced through her.

"Pull back your arm; bring it back, that's right. Now out it goes."

She cast the rod with a sharp push, but nothing happened.

"The line didn't go out," she said, disappointed.

Bo laughed and shook his head. "You have to lift your finger from the line. That's why it's called the trigger finger. Don't be afraid, Heather. Let 'er rip."

Heather licked her lips and tried again. She brought her arm back and, once she cast the rod forward, lifted her finger and saw the bait soar out over the water to land with a satisfying splash.

"I did it!" She felt triumphant.

"Yes, you did. Now reel her in," he said encouragingly, stepping closer and showing her how to do it properly. "Do it a few times. You'll get better with practice. And lookee there"—he pointed to the water—"there's a nice red drum just taunting you."

She cast again and reeled in, honing her technique. Heather wasn't the type of person who would take things on by half measures. She was purpose-driven. She couldn't just linger in a tub of hot water and soak; she scrubbed up and out she went. When she went to the beach, she had her sketchbook in hand. Fishing would give her another reason to go to the water, she thought, pleased at the prospect. It was a sport she could practice and improve in. Better yet, perhaps she could begin sketching fish, and who knew? If her instincts proved correct, she might submit a proposal for fish stamps as well. Heather felt the tingling sense of knowing that she always got when inspiration struck.

Bo let out a whoop. Turning, Heather saw the rod bowed sharply, and the reel's drag began to scream. Bo spread out his legs and braced himself for the powerful run as the fish muscled toward the rocks.

"You got one!" Heather clapped her hands and laughed with a child's awe and wonder as he reeled the fish in. He began walking down the rocks to the shoreline. She followed, watching, mouth agape as the large, glistening silvery-blue fish emerged from the water, flopping at the end of the line. Bo declared it a nice-size bluefish and bent to grab it. Heather drew near, feeling sorry for the fish yet excited that he'd caught it. Holding the fish firmly with one hand, Bo removed the hook. As he did so, a pelican flew so near Heather heard the flapping of its large wings. She watched as the big bird landed on the rocks a few feet away, adjusted its wings, then stared at them with an air of expectancy.

"Hey, look who showed up," Bo exclaimed, looking over his shoulder at the pelican. "Right on time."

"You know this pelican?"

"Sure. That's Pete. Pete the pelican. That's what I call him, anyway. He shows up whenever I catch a fish. Pelicans are opportunistic, you know. Then again, a lot of birds are. I once saw a pelican catch a fish and some gull came to sit on its head. Well, when the pelican opened its bill to drain out the water, the gull stole the fish right from under him."

Heather laughed, delighting once again in one of Bo's stories.

"Not that this old bird steals from me," Bo assured her. "Petey and I, we've worked out a deal. I throw him a couple of fish I don't want, and he leaves the fish I do want alone." He turned back toward the pelican and tossed him the bluefish. "Ain't that right, Petey?"

The pelican stretched out its wings and neck and in an impressive display caught the fish in its beak. It jauntily flipped the fish into the air and caught it again, letting it slide in headfirst.

Heather laughed.

"We've got to be sure to keep our hooks and line away from ol' Pete," Bo said with a grin.

She eyed Pete and thought how wonderful it was to see a strong, healthy pelican after the injured bird they'd rescued.

She watched Bo as he cast again into the water. He was so at ease in the outdoors. A lowcountry man at home with the sea, sky, and land in equal measures. With every movement he exuded confidence, skilled and sure in his element. He was so different from any man she'd known before. The young men she'd dated spent their free time watching sports on television or playing video games. She'd spent a lifetime with her hand against the glass and looking out from her gilded cage. Bo had lured her outdoors as surely as he'd lured the fish with his bait. Bo could be her guide, opening up a whole new world for her.

Bo looked over and caught her staring. He smirked and put down his rod.

"Okay, break's over," he said, coming toward her. "Time for you to catch one."

Chapter Fifteen

HEATHER AND BO had enjoyed the morning together, each catching several fish that Bo promised would make for good eating. Satisfied with their catch, they'd stretched out on the blanket to eat the picnic Heather had packed. Suddenly a cool gust of wind, tasting of rain, had them grabbing for their paper cups.

Dark clouds were moving in with a gusty wind, the storm seeming to approach ever closer, just as Bo had predicted. Heather saw whitecaps forming on tips of the choppy, turbulent water of Breach Inlet. Pete had already flown off, having eaten his fill, to find a safe place to weather the coming storm. "I don't like the look of those clouds." Bo frowned at the sky. "We'd better pack it up," he said with a tone of regret. "When those fronts start picking up the speed, it's a race to the ocean." He sprang to his feet. He took one large, final bite, then set down his sandwich. Wiping his hands on his pants, he climbed up the rocks to the sandy plateau where he began collecting and packing up the fishing gear.

Heather set to work gathering the partially eaten

sandwiches—lean grilled chicken with homemade pesto on rye—and the cut fruit and homemade cookies she'd prepared, sorry that their time was cut short. She'd included a bottle of white wine that was chilling nicely in the cooler, but they hadn't opened it. Bo had informed her that alcohol wasn't allowed on the beach. Another strong gust of wind whipped a paper napkin from her hand and sent it twirling toward the sky. She leaped after it, chasing it down the beach, finally stomping her foot on it just before it reached the water.

She lifted it high in the air to show Bo, waving it back and forth. Looking up, she felt the first raindrop splatter on her face.

"Oh-oh!" she called out. "Rain's coming!"

The warning was too little, too late. Instantly more raindrops fell, fat and cold, that left imprints on the sand. There was no time to lose. She dashed back up to toss the remaining food into the cooler. The sprinkle was quickly turning into a steady, pattering rain.

"Hurry!" she called to Bo. She was just gathering the woolen blanket when the sky opened up—a sudden downpour of crashing, pelting drops that left her drenched in seconds, gasping from the shock of icy water. There was no point in trying to outrun it. Her clothing clung to her skin and her hair was plastered to her head. She stood, arms out, blinking in the deluge, and looked over to Bo. He was standing equally still on the plateau staring at her, an inscrutable look on his wet face. Looking down, Heather realized her soaked shirt didn't leave much to the imagination. The outline of her breasts and nipples poked out from beneath, as though the shirt wasn't even there. She flushed, feeling exposed. But looking back at Bo, she saw he'd already looked away and was making his way toward her in long strides, carrying the rods and bucket of fish.

"Head for the truck!" he shouted over the downpour. In one smooth swoop Bo reached down to pick up the cooler by the handle and walked off. Heather gathered the now soggy, heavy wool blanket and trotted after him. He tossed everything into the back of the truck, then reached out to take the blanket from her and threw that in as well.

"Hop in!" he called, his voice muffled by the sound of raindrops pelting the ground.

She scurried to her side and climbed into the cab, slamming the door shut behind her. The rain pounded the roof of the truck in a staccato beat, but inside they sat still, panting, in the sudden warmth. Heather felt like a drowned rat. Water dripped from her hair, down her face, to pool in her seat and on the floor of the truck. She swiped water from her face, then looked at Bo. He was doing the same thing. When they locked gazes, suddenly they both started laughing. For no reason they could articulate, the more they laughed, the funnier the situation became. They laughed till their sides ached. Heather couldn't tell where the laughter tears stopped and the dripping rain began.

"I guess we should've left with Pete," he said as they calmed down, still smiling and wiping his eyes.

"Do ya think?" she asked, using his own words as a tease.

That started another round of laughter that lasted several minutes, until finally subsiding into giggles, then hiccups, then comfortable silence once more. Heather felt like her face would split in two from how wide she was smiling; when was the last time she'd laughed like that?

"Let's head home." Bo fired up the engine, and soon the wipers were slapping water from the windshield. Over the ocean lightning flashed, a classic thunderbolt straight from the gods. They looked at each other once again, and the jolt of electricity when Heather's eyes met Bo's had nothing to do with the weather. A different storm was brewing, and Heather knew they both could feel it. Thunder rolled, closer now. Bo molded his hand over the gearshift and pushed it into first. As they pulled out of the parking lot and moved forward across the bridge, Heather looked out at the swirling, tempestuous water of Breach Inlet.

She suddenly realized with the force of a lightning bolt that here she was in a car during a storm again. Only this time, she wasn't experiencing a panic attack. She released a small smile as she felt a sense of awe. This was a powerful sign she was learning to live with worry. And she wondered, glancing over at the man at the wheel, how much of this change was because of him.

THE BEACH HOUSE was dimly lit when Heather opened the front door. The storm still rallied and thunder rolled, showing no signs of dissipating in its fury, but the house was dry and warm. Once inside, they stood for a moment in the hall, water coursing from their hair and clothes to puddle on the floor.

"Wait here," Heather said, and she rushed to her bathroom to grab two big bath towels. She ran back, almost slipping on the floor, to hand one to him. Their eyes were full of laughter as they both vigorously ran the towels over their bodies.

"There's a bathroom at the end of the hall," she told him, and clicked on the lights. "You'll find more towels in there." Feeling the hostess, she started toward the hall. "I'll see if I can find you a spare robe in one of the closets."

Bo grabbed her arm. "Don't worry about me. I'll look around. You take care of yourself." He then dashed off, creating a dripping trail down the hall.

She smiled, liking his concern for her, and hurried across the living room to her bedroom, also dripping water across the floor. Closing the bedroom door behind her, she began to strip off her clothing. Soon she was naked, feeling vaguely illicit at being so while alone in the house with a man, and not entirely hating that feeling, even as it unsettled her deeply, made her blush in places she didn't even know could do so. At twenty-six, she was still a virgin and had never been naked with a man. Her anxiety disorder had always found a way to end any relationship before it reached that point. She both treasured her virginity and was embarrassed about it. Based on everything she'd read in magazines and online, being her age and never having had sex made her an anomaly. Someone weird. Or, at the very least, she thought trying to be kinder to herself, someone afraid to date.

She went to the bathroom and hung her wet clothes on a hook to drip into the bathtub. Then she slipped into her white terry robe, tied the belt, and dried her hair with a towel, taking her time. Should she get dressed? she wondered. Or go out in her robe? What kind of signal would that send? The current between them in the truck had been so real. The tension had grown stronger the closer they got to the beach house. And when they stepped into the house, so dark and empty, the aura of expectation was as thick as any pheromone. She still felt the tingling in her body.

She wasn't totally naïve. She'd dated men before . . . a few, anyway. They'd kissed and more, but she'd always been able to stop when she wanted to. She was shy, yes, but in control of her reactions. But Lord help her, none of them had ever made her feel the way Bo did. She'd never fully understood the power of desire. This wasn't a girlish infatuation, or even a twenty-six-year-old's curiosity about sex. This was a woman's need. Heather wanted to feel Bo's lips on hers. His hands on her body. To see where their passion might lead them. It was both a frightening and an empowering physical reaction to the man. And her desire made her feel even more vulnerable.

Removing the towel from her hair, she stared at her reflection. She wasn't wearing makeup, but her face had gained some color from the morning spent fishing. Faint freckles peppered her nose and upper cheeks, giving her a natural, fresh appearance. Her hair was tousled . . . sexy? Heather shook off the thought. She picked up her brush and slowly eased out the tangles as she worked through her thoughts, her feelings. When her hair was straight and smooth, she headed back out to Bo.

He was already in the living room, looking at photographs on the mantel. He was wearing a ratty old navy terry robe that was clearly a few sizes too small for him. The sleeves stopped halfway up his forearms and the hem ended well above his knees.

She put her hand to her mouth but couldn't stop her laugh at the sight in front of her. But she had to admit that she'd never been so attracted to anyone in her life, miniature robe and all.

~~~

BO LOOKED UP when he heard a noise and turned to see Heather walking into the room wearing only a bathrobe, her hair combed away from her face and just begging his fingers to run through it. She took his breath away. He thought of her naked beneath her robe, and it made him feel suddenly nervous. He wanted her too much.

She drew nearer, a teasing smile easing across her face. "Nice robe."

"Hey, at least there are no flowers or lace," he retorted, his easy tone belying the roiling chain of thoughts racing through his brain.

Another short laugh escaped her. "Where'd you find it?"

"In the back bedroom."

"That used to be her brother's room. But that was forever ago."

"Coulda been. This robe looks like it's been there forever."

For the first time that day, he sensed nervousness between them. A sexual tension that was both unnerving and exciting.

"Would you like me to open up that bottle of wine now?" he asked after a loaded pause.

"Oh. Yes, that would be lovely," she replied eagerly, curling her toes. "I'll get the glasses."

He tightened the belt on his robe and went to the hall to fetch the wine from the cooler. From the corner of his eye he watched her quickly tiptoe through the room in her bare feet to the small kitchen. By the time he joined her there, she'd already pulled out the glasses. He filled them and offered one to her, and they headed for the sunroom, drawn by the loud rumbling of thunder to watch the storm. "It's really coming down," he said, going to stand in front of the window.

The sky was dark, making the afternoon feel like night. Lightning bolts pierced the sky in an impressive display over the ocean. Palm trees shook their fronds in the fury of the storm, tapping the glass. In their cages, the canaries hunkered down and were uncharacteristically quiet.

"It's chilly in here," she said.

Bo reached out and put his arm around her shoulders and drew her closer. "Better?"

"A bit," she replied, shifting closer to him. She lifted one bare foot. "But the floor is still cold."

"Do you have any firewood?"

Heather's brow furrowed. "Um, I think there's some in the fireplace. It's been set since I arrived, but I've never used it."

"What better time than a storm?" He stretched out a hand. "Come on."

Together they returned to the living room, where he handed her his wineglass and bent to inspect the fireplace. Logs were neatly stacked and there was a basket with tinder by the hearth. He reached far in and, craning his neck, checked the flue. He shifted the lever to open it, then stood up, clapping the soot from his hands.

"That ought to do it. If I can find a match. Aha! There!" he exclaimed, finding long matches beside the tinder. He hunkered over the wood, and soon sparks lit. He blew onto the wood, watching it glow, and before long there was the crackling sound of flickering flames.

Heather went to the chintz sofa and sat, curling her legs under her like a cat. She sipped her wine, looking at him over the rim of her glass. Bo stood close to the fire, slowly wiping his hands on the robe while he looked at her and thought she had no idea how sexy she was. If she were a cat, her tail would be twitching now.

"There are some board games in that bureau next to you. Why don't you pick one out and we can play."

He was amused, but was careful not to laugh. *A board game,* he thought as he nodded. Here they were, naked under their robes, a fire burning . . . he hadn't expected to be playing a board game. Bo bent to open the bureau and found a stack of old cardboard-boxed games that looked like they'd been there for decades. They probably had, he thought, going through the titles. Monopoly, Risk, Battleship, Yahtzee, Scrabble, and several gazillion-piece puzzles. He looked over his shoulder to see Heather perched on the sofa watching him, looking every inch a woman but with her inexperience shining in her expressive eyes.

This wasn't just any woman, he reminded himself. This was Heather. She was an enigma. As much a mystery to ponder as any puzzle in this bureau.

"Scrabble it is!" he announced, pulling out the board game.

She raised his glass to him. "Good choice!"

He joined her on the sofa, sinking into the ancient down cushions. The opening of her robe had fallen wider, exposing more of her slender chest and just a hint of a rounded breast. In a flash he saw again the vision of her standing in the rain, her breasts visible through the thin cotton, her nipples taut. Again he felt a rush of desire and wished his wine were something stronger, like good bourbon. He turned to the game and opened the box on the coffee table.

"Feeling warmer now?" he asked her.

"Mmm," she replied softly, almost like a purr. "I get cold easily. Always have. My father used to say it was because I needed more meat on my bones."

"I was looking at the photographs on the mantel. You look a lot like your mother. Small, like her."

"Yes," she said softly. She set down her wineglass and began gathering the tiles into the pouch.

Bo spread out the board game. It was an old board, without all the newer fancy plastic borders for the letters.

"Are you an only child?"

Heather shook the pouch in her hand. The clicking noise was a counterpoint to the snapping of the fire. "I am. Most people think only children are terribly spoiled, but that's not true. I don't think I had any more toys than most children," she said with a slight tone of defense. "My parents didn't buy me things and expect me to entertain myself. That's what was so great about my childhood," she added.

He watched her eyes shine with her memories but remained silent, listening as she opened up.

"We did a lot together, my parents and me. My mother knew I was shy and she refused to let me stay inside alone. So if we went hiking or swimming, we'd do it together. Or when we went to Europe, we'd plan the museums and places we wanted to go to together, study the history, and talk about it at dinner." Heather paused and took a deep sip of her wine, suddenly suffused with emotion. "My mother was my best friend," she said quietly with a catch to her voice.

Bo kept silent, eyes on the game, allowing her time to continue.

"It was my fault she died."

Shaken, Bo swung his head from the game to study her face. "How?"

"I was at my high school graduation party. The only party I went to all year," she added with a snort of derision. "I drank the punch and got too drunk to drive home. So I called her to come pick me up." Heather swallowed hard and clasped her knees tightly. Outside the thunder clapped, and she jerked her head up toward the window. "It rained that night. Like today. One minute we were talking about the party. The next minute some SUV was hydroplaning right for us."

"My God, Heather." He wished he could do something, anything, to take away the pain he saw on her face and make it just a bit better, even if only for a few moments.

Heather released a long sigh and took a moment to compose herself. "That's why I don't drink much. If I hadn't been drinking that night, she would still be alive today."

"We all drank in high school. It's a rite of passage."

"We shouldn't."

"Maybe not. But don't blame yourself for that, Heather. You were a kid."

"Then who do I blame?"

"No one. It was raining. A car lost control. That's why they're called accidents. It doesn't make it any less tragic, but you can't blame yourself. She did what she felt was right. What any parent would have done in those circumstances."

Heather reached out to set the pouch of letters on the table and picked up her wineglass. She looked at the glass as if she could see the answer to her grief in its clear depths. "I felt as though I'd died, too," she practically whispered.

Bo took a long drink, then set his glass on the table. Then he reached over to take her glass and placed it gently beside his. Moving closer, he grasped both of her hands and gently tugged, drawing her up to her knees and closer to him even as he shifted, stretching his legs out and leaning back against the armrest. Heather slid toward him, half on the sofa and half against the length of him.

Heather rested her head against his chest, her hand over his heart.

Bo wrapped one arm around her shoulders and let his other hand smooth the hair back from her face, curling it around her ear, then tilted his head to place a kiss on her forehead.

"I'm an only child, too," he said in a low voice.

"Really?" she asked, lifting her head a bit to meet his eyes. "That surprises me. I guessed you came from a big family. All boys."

He laughed. "I wish. I always wanted to be part of a big family. My father . . ." He paused. The subject of his father was always complicated for him to delve into. "He and my mother married late. He used to say he never found the right woman till he met my mother, and while I'd like to believe that's true, I think he liked his freedom too much to give it up. You see, my daddy was a musician. Guitar player. Pretty good, I'm told. He traveled all the time, picking up jobs where he could. Bars and music venues, joining bands and playing for weddings. It was his life. But when he married my mama, he left his traveling days behind and only played the guitar for himself. My mother is a lot younger than my father, so I guess it's lucky that I came along at all."

"Do you look like her?" she asked.

"Some. My eyes, I think. But folks say I look like my dad." He paused to finish his wine and stretched his arm out to place the empty glass on the table. He wrapped his arm around her again, holding her tight against his chest.

"Where do they live now?" she asked.

His brows rose. "I like to believe my daddy's in heaven," he replied. "He sure was a hell-raiser during his lifetime, though."

Heather's mouth dropped open a bit, her face a mask of pain for the loss Bo had suffered. "Bo. I'm . . . I'm so sorry."

"I was only three when he died, so . . ." He shrugged. "I don't remember him. I inherited his looks, his guitar, and a box of music he wrote. My mother never remarried. So it's just me. One and done," he added, trying to make light of it.

Heather reached up to run her fingers along the edge of his robe. "I'm not surprised you're the son of an artist. Do you play an instrument?"

"Me? No. I love music, though." His gaze caught hers. "But I guess you know that."

Her cheeks turned the pretty pink he loved. Sometimes he flirted with her just to see it bloom on her face.

"Who taught you to work with wood?" she asked.

"That would be my uncle Thomas, my father's brother." Bo's face softened. "Uncle Tom. After my father died, Uncle

Tom kind of took me under his wing. He had three daughters, so I guess I was the son he always wanted. He sure was the father I needed. A gentler, wiser man never lived. He had a small furniture-building company in Mount Pleasant. He was the real artist. That man could change an ordinary piece of wood into something beautiful. Uncle Tom used to say my father had the musical talent in the family. There wasn't an instrument my daddy couldn't play. But Uncle Tom claimed he was a sculptor. That's how he saw creating furniture. A kind of art."

"Of course it's art. You're an artist, too."

Bo scoffed.

"You are! I've seen you work. Even the way you fish. Do you build furniture?"

"Not really. I worked with my uncle at his business for years but I never found the same pleasure in making chairs and tables that he did. And frankly, most of what we did to earn a living was repair work. He made the new legs or arms for chairs. Me? I helped him—but I also did a lot of gluing. But he taught me a lot. Mostly, Uncle Tom taught me how to care enough to do the job right. To take my time with my work. It comes down to respect for the wood. Wood is very grounding, part of Mother Earth. You don't hack it. It's kind of like fishing—you respect the fish, handle them humanely. You take care of the water they live in."

"I can see that."

"It was Uncle Tom who taught me to whittle. He carved wood into furniture. I don't carve anything so grand. I like to look at a piece of wood until I can see something in it—the way the grain moves, the shapes it has formed. Somewhere in the wood I see an image emerge that is crying to come out."

Heather sighed, entranced. "So," she said, leaning back to study his face, "you're a sculptor, too."

"That's a highbrow word for whittling."

"When I think of whittling, my mind turns to some old man sitting on a porch in a rocking chair, a knife in one hand, a piece of wood in the other."

Bo laughed at that. "Well." He ran his hand through his hair. "I wish I was as good as some of those old men," he said. He looked at the table. "We ought to get back to our game."

"No, don't stop. I want to hear more about your uncle Tom and your childhood. What happened to the business?"

"When Uncle Tom died, the business was sold."

"So you lost both of them."

"Yep," he said, closing off that sentiment. "Aunt Sara is a good woman. She asked if I wanted to try to keep it going, but you have to love it to do it, and, well, I didn't. The way I see it, his business died with him. So I started working construction. I was still working with wood, but bigger. I found I love houses. I love seeing the design and the myriad pieces coming together like some ultimate puzzle." He smiled and thought of his insight into Heather earlier. He looked down at her. She was listening intently, giving him her full attention.

"Did you go to college?"

"Nope. I guess my career education was more an apprenticeship."

"You know so much about so many things."

"I read a lot. Education doesn't only come in schools."

She blushed at underestimating him again.

He continued in an even voice. "I make a decent living. Can afford what I need and even a few things I just want. I don't aspire to make a lot of money."

"I hear a 'but' in there."

"But . . . someday I'd like to have my own business. Small but respectable, like Uncle Thomas's place. I like the small construction jobs. Cabinetry, especially. Bookcases. I really like to solve problems with the homeowner. You know, that weird corner no one knows what to do with, how to take advantage of a view, get more space in a kitchen, or trying to figure out where to put bookcases. It's problem solving, sure. But it's also a sense of symmetry. I guess I have some of my uncle's training inside of me still."

He ran his hand through his hair; drier now, it fell over his forehead in a tousled wave. "That's enough about me," he said, moving her legs so he could stand up. "My mouth is dry from all that yammering. I'm going to pour some more wine. Would you like some?"

Heather shook her head. Her hair was also dry and fell forward across her shoulder in a silken veil. "No, I'm good."

"Okay," he said, accepting it without question. Bo walked to the kitchen. When he carried his full glass of wine back into the living room, he found Heather sitting in front of the board game again. She'd set up the racks and passed out seven letters to each of them.

"I didn't peek," she said when he came to sit at the other end of the couch. "I promise."

Bo gave her a suspicious look. "Okay," he drawled.

They each spent a few minutes sorting their letters. He had a Z and a blank, but he couldn't think of a decent word.

Across from him, Heather was moving around tiles obviously wild with possibilities.

"What about you?" he asked. "How did you become an artist of stamps? Is there like a stamp school or something?"

She laughed, looking at her tiles. "Yes. It's a very small school."

"Ha-ha."

"Do you want to go first?"

"No, you go first. Please," he added with a groan while looking at his hopeless letters.

Heather set five tiles on the board to spell PEACE. "Not great, but I like the word."

She counted up the points while he studied the board. "Really," he said, thinking. "How does one become a creator of stamps?"

"There is no one way. Artists come in all shapes and sizes. I'd been accepted at SCAD—Savannah College of Art and Design. I was excited to go. But . . ." She sighed. "After the accident, I—well, I couldn't possibly go away to school. I couldn't go to school at all." She laughed shortly. "I guess you could call that my gap year."

She glanced at him, but Bo didn't see humor in that.

"But at home I drew all the time," she continued. "It was my obsession. My own personal therapy. I didn't go anywhere without a sketch pad and pencil. My father was impressed and encouraged me to study. Eventually, when I felt I could, I took a class at the University of North Carolina in Charlotte. I could commute, you see. Then in time I took more, and then still more until I got my degree in fine art."

Bo moved his tiles on the rack. "Did you date anyone in

particular?" He kept his eyes down but could feel her gaze on him.

"Yes," she replied. "Of course."

"Anyone special?"

"One boy, Noah," she said. "Or man, I should say. I've known him since we were little."

"Do you still see him?"

"I do. On occasion. Our first date was a setup. Our fathers are business partners. I'd liked Noah since I was a little girl so I didn't feel anxious around him."

"Did you love him?"

"I thought I did," she answered honestly. "But what did I know of love? He was more my best friend. I could talk with him without feeling nervous. You know how important that is for me," she said with a nervous giggle. "We tried dating on and off. But we both knew it was never going to work." She sighed. "He's still a good friend. I'm glad of that."

Bo didn't respond. He picked up his tiles and made a word. "ZAG," he said and began counting points.

"That's not a word," she argued.

"Sure it is. Zag as in zig zag."

"That's zigzag as in one word. Where's the zig?"

"It zagged."

She laughed and shook her head. "Oh, sure, why not?"

"So," he said, reaching for his wineglass, "where do you work?"

"I work freelance. Sort of like you. I submit proposals, and if the client likes my work, I get the job."

He raised his glass toward her. She picked hers up.

"Here's to being our own bosses."

They clinked glasses, smiling at each other over the rims.

The fire snapped and crackled, warming the small room. Outside the storm whistled at the windows and rain pattered on the rooftop. Thunder rolled in tympanic majesty, a rhythmic backbeat to the sensations growing in their bodies.

Bo felt he was getting all the signals from her, but he knew she was shy. He didn't want to rush her. He shifted so he could look at her expressive face to gauge her emotions. Despite anything she might say, he knew her face would reveal the truth.

"Heather?"

Heather lifted her eyes, and Bo lost his breath at what he saw there. Desire, yes. But also tenderness and apprehension.

She reached up to trace her fingers from his forehead past his eyes to his jaw. He clasped the hand and brought her fingertips to his mouth, kissing each one, never breaking his gaze.

Slowly, by degrees, Bo leaned forward. Her fingers slid from his cheek through his hair, still damp from the rain, to his neck. Then at last his lips were on hers, soft and trembling, tasting her sweetness. He moved his lips to her neck as his hands slowly slid down her body, gently untying the robe, placing his cool, smooth hand against Heather's skin, warm to the touch. His fingers traced a path upward, rounding the curves of her breasts. When his hands at last caressed her, he bent his head and took in her nipples. She sighed, reaching up to bury her face in his neck. He brought his head back to her mouth, and kissed her, longingly, thoroughly.

Heather drew back, catching her breath. He felt her palm against his chest. A subtle pressure. A signal to stop.

Breathing heavily, he held his mouth over hers and waited.

"I think . . ." she said. Then inched back. Cooler air rushed between them. Heather sat back; flustered, she closed her robe with shaky fingers. "I think it's my turn." She quickly glanced at him to gauge his reaction.

Bo cocked his head. He understood that she was saying she needed more time. He'd give her all the time she needed. But he needed a little time now to cool down. He cleared his throat and swiveled to examine the board.

"I think it is. While you think of a word, and I'll bet it will take a while with the word I left you, I'm going to scrounge around for something to eat. I'm starving." He rose and reached for his glass.

"Wait!" Heather plopped four tiles onto the board and made a word. "Let me help. I'm starved, too."

Bo looked over his shoulder to check out her word. "What the . . . ?" It was a big-pointer using six letters. "Are you some whiz-kid ringer?" he asked as she dragged him into the kitchen.

They talked and laughed as they rummaged through the cupboards, pulling out crackers, cookies, nuts, anything that appealed to them. "You like your health food, don't you?" he asked, looking at all the different items. He picked up a bag of cookies and began reading the ingredients. He scrunched up his face in doubt. "Are these even any good?"

"Delicious," she said, and took the bag from his hand.

From the fridge Heather grabbed more of the grilled chicken, fresh mozzarella, rye, and every condiment she had. "We'll have another picnic," she said, getting into it. "You bring out the nuts and crackers. I'll make a platter of cheese and meat and meet you out there. Oh! And turn on some music. My phone's by the door, and you know where the speakers are."

"I'll pick the tunes," he said, gathering up boxes and jars and carrying them out to the table. He was feeling good and rubbed his palms together as he scanned the room. "Mood," he said aloud. Bo added another log to the fire, stoked it a bit, and then went to the back bedroom where he'd left his phone. Scrolling through his playlist, he smiled when he found the perfect music. Back in the living room, he set his phone into the speakers, then crossed his arms to listen. Soon the sultry, smoky sound of John Coltrane's saxophone was playing "In a Sentimental Mood."

"Ooh, that's nice," Heather called out from the kitchen.

He smiled again. Dropping onto the sofa, he looked at the board game and laughed. It was clear their hearts were not in the game. He scooped up the tiles, about to toss them all back into the pouch, when he got an idea. Quickly he began searching in earnest for the right letters.

By the time Heather returned carrying a large tray, he was leaning back on the sofa, chewing one of the cookies, which actually had turned out to be pretty good. Lots of nuts. He tracked her movements as she walked across the room with the grace of a fawn. And like that rare moment when he'd spotted the underside of a female deer's tail, snowy white, he relished the flashes of creamy white thigh he saw as Heather's robe prettily split open as she walked. She set the tray within reach on the coffee table to reveal a platter of meat, cheeses, olives, capers, and nuts. She'd also brought bottled water for herself and the bottle of white for him.

He stretched out his arm and took her hand, then reeled

her in as neatly as he had the fish earlier that day. She fell into his lap, laughing nervously.

"That looks amazing," he said, and kissed her nose.

"Thank you, kind sir," she replied, then reached down to close her robe, which had begun to slip open.

"Now, I believe it's your turn."

"Oh, I already put down my letters."

"And I just put down mine."

"You did?" Heather turned to look at the board. On it she saw the letters spell out:

WILL YOU GO OUT WITH ME

Heather turned and, with a shy smile, reached for the pouch of letters. She dug through until she found the ones she was looking for. These she laid in place below his letters.

Bo read the word over her shoulder and grinned from ear to ear.

YES

She turned back slowly and slid her arms around his neck. Her face glowed in the firelight and her hair took on the luster of twenty-four-karat gold. Miles Davis was playing a slow tune on the horn as she lowered her head toward his. He caught the scent of her perfume . . . jasmine, he thought.

"Y-E-S," she spelled out. Then she leaned forward to place her lips on his.

"You win," he said, then kissed her again.

Chapter Sixteen

HEATHER HAD SLEPT like a log the night before, even with Bo sleeping in the guest room. She giggled, remembering his face as he looked over his shoulder on his way down the hall. Like a man condemned. He might not have slept so well, she thought, giggling again.

When she awoke, she wasn't covered in a sheen of perspiration. Rather, the room was deliciously cool and the air sweet. She breathed deep. And wait . . . She sniffed again. That wasn't flowers. That was coffee!

She followed the scent like a hound dog toward the kitchen, stopping when she caught sight of Bo standing at the sunroom window, a mug in his hand, staring out. He was wearing only his pants, allowing her a view of his beautiful back—broad-shouldered and tanned, narrowing at the waist. Her fingers twitched to sketch him. All the windows were open and, as Cara had promised, a refreshing breeze blew in from the ocean. Pavarotti and Poseidon were chirping questioningly, asking him for seed. But Moutarde was already at his top perch singing loudly.

"You're up!"

Bo swung around from his reverie. "I didn't want to wake you."

"The scent of coffee is like a bugle alarm to me." She lifted her nose. "And is that bacon?"

"I'm going to make you breakfast."

Heather came to join him at the window, slipping easily into his arms. "How'd you sleep last night?"

"In the twin bed?" he asked, tongue in cheek. "The mattress is lumpy. Must've been Palmer's from back in the day. But that wasn't what kept me awake all night." He set his mug on the table then bent to kiss her soundly, taking his time, letting his tongue roll around the insides of her mouth.

His lips tasted of coffee. Heather felt her knees grow weak and a soft sigh escaped her mouth when he finished.

"Does that give you an idea of the tortures I endured knowing you slept prettily in your bed clear on the other side of the house?"

She giggled as color rose to her cheeks.

"And if that wasn't bad enough, it was a steaming oven in here. Baby, why do you sleep with the windows closed at night? You're supposed to open them up."

She ducked her head. "I . . . I've been sleeping with them closed because I was afraid to keep them open."

"Don't be afraid," he said in a gentle tone. He lifted her chin. "Not anymore. I won't let anything happen to you. Take a deep breath. Smell that?"

Heather closed her eyes and sniffed. She caught a heavy floral scent on the breeze. "Honeysuckle."

"That's right. And hear that? That's the ocean, not traffic. It's heaven out there. Don't cut yourself off from it because you're afraid. Life's too precious to live in fear. Open the windows and let the breezes flow in."

She listened to his words and believed them. This was her life, the only one she had. She wouldn't let fear destroy her chances at happiness. This was the first morning since she'd arrived that she'd awoken without the pressing heat of a closed-up house. The air was fresh and inviting, sweet as a morning should be.

"I will."

"Good," he said, kissing her on the nose. "Now how about some breakfast?"

Heather stretched her arms high over her head. "Mmm, yes, please!"

Bo slipped his arms around her waist and drew her in for another kiss. "You shouldn't go stretching like that. The morning light reveals all your attributes. Especially in front of a man who didn't sleep a wink all night for thinking of you down the hall."

Heather laughed, a bit embarrassed. She'd had no idea he could see through her nightie. They went into the kitchen, where she saw bread waiting in the toaster, bacon sizzling on the skillet, eggs whipped in a bowl. She settled in to watch him make breakfast, feeling taken care of. Watching him flip the bacon with quick twists of the fork, then step over to the grits and give them a stir, she couldn't believe she was in her own life, not some romance novel.

So this is what it's like to be in love, she thought, and mentally hugged herself.

CARA WAS STUCK in traffic over the bridge from Charleston to the Isle of Palms. It was a parking lot. She pulled out her phone and texted Emmi: Stuck on the bridge. Coming!

It seemed like she was always running lately. She was the little Dutch boy, running from place to place trying to stem the flow of money. She had a lot of support from her brother and John Denning but everything was moving so fast. Hurry up and wait. Stop and go. Just like this damn summer traffic.

After waiting through three lights she finally made the turn onto Isle of Palms. A few blocks later she was pulling into her own driveway. Emmi's and Flo's cars were parked there, and she spotted both of them standing in the front yard studying the FOR SALE sign. The temperature hovered around ninety and no one in their right mind should be standing outside. She cast a grateful glance at the large oak tree that shaded the front property under its pendulous branches. Thank heavens for the shade, she thought.

"Sorry I'm late," Cara called as she hurried up the front walk. She was dressed all in black—skinny linen pants and a flowy top. Her arms were loaded down with large bags bulging with supplies from a moving company.

Emmi reached into the plastic box below the sign to take one of the brochures, then came running across the yard. Her green sparkly tunic top caught the light dappling through the leaves. Emmi's freckled face was always animated, especially when her expression involved her wide mouth. It was rounded in an O of shock. She grabbed one of the bags from Cara's arms.

"Open the door, honey. Once we get inside and out of this heat, you've got some explaining to do."

"Like what in heaven's name is a FOR SALE sign doing up in your yard?" demanded Flo, huffing as she caught up with them.

Cara paused to look out at the front yard, then pulled out the keys and opened the front door. "Come in."

Cara dropped the keys in the bowl on the front table and walked directly to the kitchen. She set the bags down with a sigh. Everything tired her out. It seemed she was always either exhausted or sleeping.

She heard Flo and Emmi talking in the other room and sighed again, knowing she was about to get reamed out by her friends. She pulled out three tall glasses from the cabinet, filled them with ice, and poured sweet tea. Then, to stall for more time, she cut lemon wedges and added them.

"Well, for the love of Mike," Flo called out. "What are you doing in there? Cooking dinner?"

Cara placed the glasses on a tray and carried them out.

"You don't have to wait on us," Emmi said.

"I'm not," Cara replied. "But after keeping you waiting outside in this heat, the least I could do is offer you a cool drink. It's only civilized."

The three friends gathered around the coffee table with their iced tea. Cara took a long drink, enjoying the cool sweetness flowing down her throat like rain on a desert.

"So." Emmi put her glass on a coaster. "Please explain to us what's going on."

"It all happened very fast," Cara began wearily. She explained about discovering Brett's lapsed insurance policy and the financial problems she was facing, sparing no details. "I had to be sure the life insurance had expired, so I went to see John Denning."

"Good man," Flo said in her forthright manner. "Like his daddy."

"He's an angel of mercy," Cara agreed. "He got me right in to see him. We went through everything—the insurance policy, the loans, the mortgages, the cost of continuing Brett's business. It's a mess, I'm afraid."

"Brett was never one for business," Flo said. "God rest his soul."

"He tried," Cara said in his defense. "And he had so many other gifts. That boat was his last dream. Unfortunately, it turned into a nightmare. After we got the boat loan, I suspect he stopped making the other payments to fund that one."

"Putting all his eggs in one basket, so to speak," said Flo.

"More like robbing Peter to pay Paul," Emmi piped in.

"I know, but nothing to be done about it now." Cara took a sip of her tea. The sweetness was already rushing through her bloodstream, reviving her.

"And?" Emmi prompted.

Cara set down her glass. "Once John assured me the insurance policy had indeed lapsed, there was nothing left for me to do but figure my way out of the whole mess. It was clear the fastest way to pay off the debt was to sell this house."

"But, Cara . . . selling your house?" Emmi said, reaching across the table to take her hand. "Do you really have to?"

Cara had gone over this heart-wrenching scenario a hundred times in the past few days, and always she came up with the same answer. "Yes, I do."

Everyone was silent for a moment, no one knowing what to say next.

"It could be worse," Cara said with a light laugh that held no humor. "I won't go bankrupt. I'm lucky I have this house to sell to pay off the debts. It was Brett's debt and his house. Looking at it that way, he came out even." Cara looked around the room and said with a sigh, "Besides, I want to leave this house."

Emmi sat back in her chair. "You *want* to leave? Why?"

"Brett's everywhere here. Everywhere I turn I see something of his. This was his house when we got married. His dock, his boat. He loved it here, and I loved living here with him. We were happy. But with him gone . . ." Cara's voice caught, and she shook her head. "It's too hard. This life is over. I need to get out of here or I'll lose my mind with grief."

"Sure you do, darling," Flo said, her face crumpled in worry.

"But, Cara, I mean . . . are you sure you should be making big decisions like this so soon after Brett's . . . you know?"

"After Brett's death. It's okay, Emmi. I can say the word. I know he's gone. I feel his absence every minute of every day. And you're right. John said he doesn't advise a widow to make big decisions too soon after the death of her spouse as a rule, but in my case, he agreed I had no choice. And"—she sighed—"I already got an offer on the house."

"What?" asked Flo, stunned.

"Palmer knew someone who'd been looking for just such a spot. It's a one-in-a-million offer. They bid over the asking price. Cash. On the condition they can close quickly. In two weeks."

"You're kidding! So fast?" Emmi whistled, eyebrows high on her forehead. "Well, tell them you can't close till the end of summer!" she exclaimed with heat. "You shouldn't be rushed. You need time."

"No one's going to want to wait till the end of summer for a *summer* house, Em. Least of all this buyer. He's pushing to get in and enjoy the rest of the season. Can you blame him? It's a miracle offer."

"It's not a miracle. It's your deepwater dock," said Flo matter-of-factly.

Almost imperceptibly, Cara lifted her shoulders. "Well, I accepted the offer. I close in three weeks."

Stunned silence reigned as this news was digested.

Cara lifted her head to look out the window to where the dock stretched into Hamlin Creek. She could almost see Brett bending low and pulling up his crab pot, muscles rippling with the effort. The opposite bank was a thick wall of green trees and shrubs. Between the banks, the water appeared blue . . . calm . . . deceptively serene. Cara felt a tug of regret that she was leaving this view then turned away from the window. Cara knew better than to fall under its spell. Beneath the beautiful façade raged a dangerous current.

She straightened and spoke with more confidence. "Palmer's been a great help. He knows some people who are cheap who can put what I want to keep into storage. But I still have to sort and pack everything up. I'll pick out a few things of Brett's I want to keep, but everything else . . ." She paused. "I'm selling or giving it all away to charity. That's why I asked you to come here today." She took a deep, fortifying breath. "To help me go through his things. I can't do it alone."

"Of course we will," Flo said. "We're your friends. That's what friends do."

"Where will you go?" asked Emmi. She was clearly worried and trying to keep up. "Will you rent a place?"

"No. I really can't afford a summer rental. Palmer very kindly invited me to move in with him and his family until I'm on my feet again." She paused, then added on a wry note, "But I'd rather live outside in a tent than with my brother and Julia, bless their hearts."

Flo laughed heartily at this, having known Palmer since he was in britches.

"I've given this a lot of thought," Cara said, her voice wobbling. "I want to go home."

"To the beach house?" asked Emmi incredulously.

"Yes, of course the beach house," Cara replied. "It's like Flo said. The beach house is where my mother went to heal after Russell Bennett died. Right?"

Cara turned to Flo. The old woman said nothing, but her eyes filled with the sadness of memory. She nodded.

Cara felt again the reassurance of knowing she was, in a sense, following in her mother's footsteps. It gave her something to hang on to so she wouldn't drown in her sorrow.

"I'll feel her spirit there," she said, convincing herself as much as her friends. "I'll heal there. It won't be the first time I've found myself at that beach house." She summoned a lopsided smile and glanced at Flo for affirmation.

"No," Flo said in a tired voice.

"But . . ." Emmi gave Flo a worried look.

Cara looked at her testily, not wanting her decision challenged. "But what?"

"But it's rented."

Cara sniffed quickly, and then put on her business face. "Of course. I know that." She frowned and wiped away something on the table with brusque movements. "I'll talk to Heather. Once I explain that I need to move back into my own house, I'm sure she'll let me break the rental agreement. She's a nice girl, and she can move back home. I don't think she was too happy to be here in the first place."

Flo's face appeared troubled. "I don't think we're talking about the same girl, honey. I saw her the other day, and she's blooming, just like my roses. She's happy here, out walking every morning sketching those shorebirds. And she's in love."

Cara swung her head around. "She's in love? With who?"

"Bo," Flo said with a big grin. "And you never saw a man so smitten."

"Bo?" Cara was stunned.

"Why not? He's a very good-looking young man with a noble heart. Not unlike Brett at that age."

Somehow that comparison rankled. "Regardless," Cara said belligerently, "it's my house, and I need to move back in." She frowned and looked out the window again. "I have to go to the beach house. I have to find some way to start over. Just like Mama."

Chapter Seventeen

THREE WEEKS PASSED in a blur and Cara was running on empty. She'd been pushing herself to get the house sold, her belongings crammed into storage and emptied in time to meet the new buyer's aggressive close date. She'd had countless meetings with Robert and the bank to initiate the paperwork for the sale of the ecotour business. And with the sale of the house, to settle the equity loan. Thanks to John Denning and Palmer, the pieces were all beginning to fall into place. There was still much to do, more time would have to pass before papers were signed, but she had hope she'd come out on the other side still standing on her feet. Barely. On the upside, being busy kept her from constantly thinking of Brett and wallowing in self pity. On the downside, she was exhausted and heading for a crash.

Cara's felt the thin veneer of her mask crack when she pulled into the gravel driveway of the beach house. The yellow cottage with the Charleston green shutters, the screened front porch, the wide staircase, the lovely disarray of natural plants along the dunes . . . nothing had changed about this sweet place since her childhood. She'd returned here once before, broken. Now here she was again, life-weary and inconsolable, and she wondered if this simple little house could work its magic again. She had nowhere else to go but home, she thought, gathering her resolve. She had to remain strong a little longer. She had to get back home. In her heart she knew this was where she was supposed to be.

She had meant to park the Gold Bug in its usual spot but saw Bo's truck parked there. She squeezed in behind him and rolled up the windows. She took a moment to collect her wits. A dull ache pressed in the right side of her head and she groaned at what she knew was the onset of a migraine. She'd not had one in years but she'd awoken with the aura of flickering lights and felt light-headed. She wasn't shocked, what with all the stress of making important, life-changing financial decisions at a time she should be left to quietly licking her wounds.

She opened the door, grabbed her purse, and stepped out into the July heat. The bright sunlight exacerbated her budding headache, and she groped for her sunglasses. Slamming the door, she noticed the golf cart parked under the porch. She walked closer and saw that it was one of those fancy new street-legal carts, and already there were Center for Birds of Prey, Island Turtle Team, and Protect Your Local Shorebirds stickers on the back window. It occurred to her that Heather appeared to be settling in more than she'd suspected.

Worry creased her brow, but undaunted she walked the familiar path to her front door. Standing there, she thought it was improper of her not to have called in advance. But she was here, so there was nothing left for her to do but knock. Taking a breath, she raised her hand and did just that.

~~~~~~

THE DOORBELL SOUNDED, followed by a quick knock on the front door.

Bo looked at Heather. She shrugged and shook her head to indicate she had no idea who it might be.

The knock sounded again, louder and more insistent.

"Coming!" Heather called, wishing she had dressed. She and Bo had gone together to the beach at dawn, as they did often in the past few weeks. They'd returned, showered and only just sat down for breakfast. Running her hand through her unbrushed hair, she opened the door a crack and peered out.

The last person she expected to see was Cara Rutledge. She was dressed in a black shift dress that looked two sizes too big for her, her dark hair pulled severely back in a clasp that only made her face appear more gaunt. Heather hadn't seen Cara since the day after she'd arrived. She must've lost ten pounds since then, Heather thought. At least. She was a shadow of the vibrant, confident woman who'd welcomed her to the beach house.

"Cara?"

Cara presented a tired smile. "Good morning, Heather. I tried to call. Do you have a minute?" She lifted a white baker's box. "I brought pastries." Cara looked at her robe and down to her bare feet.

"Uh, sure. Come in," Heather stammered, and stepped aside. Closing the door, she turned to see Bo emerge from the kitchen in his pants but no shirt and barefoot. He stopped short, and his smile slipped to reveal his surprise when he saw Cara.

"Hello, Bo," Cara said, her eyes wide with surprise. "I didn't expect to see you here. I thought the deck was done."

"Yeah, it is," he replied as he reached up to scratch behind his ear.

When Cara's gaze met Heather's again, there was no doubt she knew what was going on behind this closed door.

Heather looked up as Bo approached and they shared a commiserating glance. What to say? A million excuses as to why Bo would be here, half dressed, filled her mind, but one was more lame than the next. Her training in etiquette kicked in.

"We, uh, we were just sitting down for breakfast. Won't you join us? I'll open up these pastries."

"Oh, no. I'm sorry. I didn't mean to interrupt your breakfast." Cara looked up at the hall clock. It was nearly ten o'clock. "At this hour."

Heather cringed and turned to Bo. He gave her a knowing half smile as though to say, *Who cares?*

"Look, I'll come back," Cara said abruptly. "I came to talk to Heather about something important, but . . ." She appeared lost for words and pressed two fingers to her temple.

"No problem," Bo said. "I have to take off. You two have your powwow."

Heather looked up at him, uncertain what to do next. Bo winked at her from behind Cara and gave her an encouraging thumbs-up as he left the room.

"Maybe I will have that cup of coffee, then," Cara said with a quick smile. "It smells so good."

"Be right back," said Heather. "You know where to sit."

Heather hurried to the kitchen, where she found Bo gulping down a few spoonfuls of grits from the pot.

"You don't have to leave."

"Yes, I do," he replied, then reached out to grab a piece of bacon and stuff it in his mouth. He spoke as he chewed. "It has to be important if she got up and came all the way over here to talk to you. The woman's been in hiding since the funeral." He gulped down some coffee. Putting his mug down on the counter, he added, "It wouldn't be kind to send her away."

"You're right." Heather chewed her lip. "I wonder what she wants to talk about? I hope my father paid the rent."

"Only one way to find out." Bo plucked more bacon from the platter, slapped it between two pieces of toast, and gave her a quick kiss. "I'll grab my things and get out of here. I'll call you later."

Heather paled and reached out to touch his arm, staying his progress. "You promise. Okay?"

Bo's eyes kindled as he took a step back to her. He lowered his head to touch her lips.

She tasted bacon and kissed him back, fiercely.

"You know I will. Now, you best go back in there with Cara's coffee. And," he added, patting her bottom, "eat your breakfast, too."

"Bo," she said, worrying her lip, "what do I say? What do you think would bring Cara over here, unannounced, so early?"

"First, it's not that early. And who knows? Don't worry," he said and met her gaze.

Bo stepped into the living room, and she heard him exchange a few words with Cara. Heather took the opportunity to hurry on tiptoe across the room; they paused to look at her, but Bo kept up the brief conversation. In the bedroom Heather threw off her robe and grabbed a sundress from her closet. She slipped it over her head, going commando, and stepped into her flip-flops. Dashing into the bathroom, she raked her hair with her fingers and pulled it back into a clasp. That was as good as it was going to get.

Pausing at the door to take a calming breath, she entered the room to see that Bo had left and Cara was standing by the birds in the sunroom making soft whistling noises.

"I'll get our coffee," Heather called and hurried back into the kitchen. Taking a breath to calm her nerves, she poured mugs of coffee, added cream. With a last longing look at the grits, she reentered the living room.

Cara strode across the room and sat on the chintz sofa. She gracefully accepted the mug of coffee. Heather noticed how thin Cara's arms were. "Are you sure you won't have some breakfast? We could open the pastries."

Cara shook her head. "No, thank you. Please, help yourself. I hope you like them. I didn't know what you liked."

Heather opened the box and breathed in the mouthwatering scent of a dozen freshly baked pastries. She picked up a scone, more for politeness's sake than hunger. Her stomach was tied up in knots. She bit into it, tasting the sweet cinnamon flavor, then set it on a napkin on the table. Oh . . . she should've brought out plates, she thought. Brushing away a few flakes from her dress she asked, "Are you sure you don't want any?"

Cara only smiled and shook her head.

Heather felt a renewed worry for Cara. She wondered how long it had been since she had eaten a decent meal.

They each sipped from their mugs; looking over the rim, Heather felt all the relaxation and contentment she'd felt earlier dissipate. Once again she felt her shoulder muscles tighten and her stomach clench in anxiety as she worried over what Cara had come to talk to her about. It took all her willpower not to shake her foot. When the mugs were both placed on the table, there followed an awkward silence.

Cara looked out at the ocean. "It's a beautiful morning."

"Yes, it is."

"I hope you've been comfortable here."

"Yes, very."

Cara folded her hands in her lap. She paused, then looking up again asked, "Would it be terrible for you to consider breaking the lease and leaving early?"

Heather's brows rose and her mouth opened in a silent gasp. "*Leave early?* But—but why?"

"It's complicated," Cara replied in a reserved manner. "My circumstances have changed, as you know. I'm consolidating my holdings. So I have to move back into my house. *This* house," she emphasized to be clear.

"But what about your house?"

"As I said, I'm consolidating. Or, simply put, that house is sold."

Heather took a moment to speak. "But I have a lease until September."

"I realize that. That's why I've come to talk to you. To ask you to break the lease. You'll get back your deposit, of course."

"Where would I go?"

Cara lifted her shoulders slightly. "Why, you could go home," she replied evenly. "I believe you weren't completely happy to have left there in the first place? That your father was the one who thought it was a good idea. Now you have an excuse to return. Isn't that what you'd like?"

"No," Heather blurted out. "No, it's not what I'd like." This came out with more heat than she'd intended.

Cara's smile had slipped and her brows were gathered. "I see," she said carefully. She lifted her chin while brushing away a piece of lint on her skirt. "Then I'm really very sorry. But I need to return here. It's my home. I have my reasons."

Heather only looked at her.

"So, I have to ask you to leave. Would the end of the month be all right with you?"

Heather felt her heart rate zoom and the early signs of a panic attack flood her senses. She rose abruptly to her feet.

"Excuse me." Her hands were clenched at her sides as she walked quickly from the room into the kitchen. She bent over the counter and stood for a moment with her eyes squeezed tight, breathing deeply and swallowing away her nausea. *Why did Bo have to go?* She needed him here with her. To talk to and figure out what to do. *How can I argue with Cara? She's so calm and superior, and here I am, having a panic attack in the kitchen, trying not to throw up.*

Her inner critic was shouting at her: *You're not up to winning this argument. You won't be able to get a word out. Why take the chance if it's going to blow up in your face anyway? Someone like Cara wouldn't be telling you that if she hadn't checked with her lawyers.*

Heather pushed away from the counter and began pacing the floor, opening and closing her fists rapidly as her mind went through her options. Cara seemed so sure in her knowledge that she could effectively break the lease. But could she? Part of Heather felt powerless against someone like Cara. She was the landlady. She owned the house. But something was off. What rights did Heather actually have? She saw her phone on the kitchen counter and, thanking her stars, grabbed it. Immediately she started to call her dad. He'd always come to her rescue.

Then her hand stilled. *No,* she told herself. *No, no, no! Ya feel like vomiting? Afraid you might have a panic attack? Sweating profusely from every orifice of your body? Well, nobody has to know unless you want them to! You can't cower in here. You don't need your daddy to defend you. You don't need Bo. This is* your *house.* Your *life. It's up to you. You have to put on your big-girl pants and deal with this yourself.*

She looked down at her phone and went to Google. She typed in can a landlord break a lease. She quickly had legal information at her fingertips. She read through several sites, and when she finished the third she lowered her hand and felt her heart rate slowing. She set the phone back on the counter, her fingertips tapping on it as she thought. According to what she'd read, Cara could not simply kick her out. She'd done nothing to break the renter's agreement, so Cara had no grounds. Heather released a smile that felt like hope.

Now all she had to do was go back in there and stand up for her rights. She felt a flutter sweep over her. That, of course, was her biggest obstacle. She thought of Bo's parting words: "Don't worry." *You've got this.*

She closed her eyes again and pictured Bo's face. A series of images flashed through her mind. His knowing grin when he knew she could do something—drive the golf cart, catch a fish, talk to Cara. Bo rejected her belief that she wasn't good enough. He showed her in meaningful ways that she was worthy of his love. Did she love him enough to believe him?

Knowing she was valuable and worthwhile—that she was good enough—was a new feeling for her. But—and this made Heather catch her breath—she instinctively felt it was true. She just needed the confidence. Shutting out the negative voice, she tried to think of reasons she would succeed.

She had proved she was successful when she put her effort into something. She was intelligent, capable. She ran her own small business. She could at the very least have a conversation about the subject and not just cower in the corner and do what she was told. Even if her confidence faltered again in the future, for now, she had to take the first step.

She saw the worry stone on the windowsill by the pot of basil, where she had put it. She picked it up and, holding it tight, walked back into the living room.

Cara was still sitting on the sofa, one elbow on the armrest and her head bent against her palm, eyes closed. She straightened when she heard Heather walk into the room.

"There you are," Cara said with a pained smile. "I thought for a moment you'd abandoned me in a fit of fury."

Heather walked back to her chair and sat down. She set her hands in her lap, the worry stone in one, crossed her legs, and straightened her shoulders. "I wasn't angry," she said, squeezing her hands together. "I was upset. I needed to collect my thoughts."

"And?"

"And . . ." She took a breath. "Cara, you are mistaken. You can't break the lease."

Cara shifted her weight on the sofa. "I own this house. It's *my* house. I can do what I want."

Heather heard the wavering emotion in Cara's voice and suddenly realized that Cara hadn't checked with her lawyer about this. She couldn't have. She'd just given herself away. Heather lifted her chin a notch.

"I just checked my rights," Heather said. "I Googled it. That's what I was doing in the kitchen. And I know that though you own this house, you can't just kick me out."

"I'm not trying to kick you out. I'm giving you an option to break your lease."

"And if I don't want to?"

"Why go that route?" Cara said with weariness entering her voice. "This needn't be unpleasant."

Heather's words came bubbling out. "Cara, I need to stay! I love it here. And my work is going so well. If I left now, it would stop my progress cold. Don't you see? It's not the money. I can't afford the break in time. I have to work while the birds are here. And the committee has deadlines for my sketches."

Cara dropped her hand and looked up. Her eyes were dull and she squinted slightly, as if she was in pain. "Couldn't you find someplace else to rent on the island?"

"Couldn't you?"

Cara rubbed her palms together, as if trying to control her emotions. "For me . . ." She stopped and looked away. Then she said resolutely, "There is no other place."

Heather looked at Cara and suddenly saw not her landlady but a widow. She was pale and gaunt and holding on to her composure by a slender string. Heather gentled her combative tone. Being on terra firma, she could find empathy for Cara.

"There are specific reasons for which you can evict me," Heather explained, "such as having a pet without permission. Or doing damage to the house. Or not paying rent. I truly doubt my father has missed a rent payment. My father has a team of lawyers, and they made sure we had permission from you for me to have the three canaries. And you signed it. Take a look around," she added in a softer tone. "I love this house and I've enjoyed taking care of it."

She waited to see if Cara would respond. Cara merely stared at her with a blank face. It wasn't encouraging. So Heather squeezed the worry stone in her hand and pressed on. She didn't feel especially anxious when she was stating facts. The emotional part was harder to say.

"As I said, my father has a team of lawyers. So, unless you have a reason, Cara, you can't evict me. My lease runs until September first."

Cara brought two fingers to her right temple and began making small circles. She mumbled something softly.

Heather leaned forward but couldn't catch it. "I'm sorry. What?"

"I need to come back," she said softly.

Heather felt her emotions spill over. "It's only until September. I'll go home then. Surely—"

"I need to come home now!" Cara cried out, rising to her feet. She paced back and forth, then went to the window and looked out, clutching the curtain in a tight fist.

Heather sat back in her chair, stunned by the outburst.

"I can't wait until September!" Cara's tone rose to a wailing plea as her shoulders slumped. She swung around, and Heather could see that tears flooded Cara's eyes. "Please, Heather." She had lost all control. Her face looked lost, tortured. "I have to come home. Let me come home. Please . . ."

Heather was undone as Cara collapsed back onto the sofa and her palms went to her face.

Only one thing mattered at that moment. Heather couldn't watch Cara, another woman, a widow, in such pain without helping her. She hurried to the sofa and placed her hand on Cara's shoulder. She felt it shake in sobs beneath her palm.

"It's all right," she said in the same crooning voice in which she sang to her birds. "It's all right." What could she do to help? she wondered. She felt boxed in, trapped between what was good for her and what was good for Cara.

"I need my mother," Cara choked out. She leaned against Heather. "I miss my mother."

Heather slipped her arm around Cara's shoulders and felt the frailty and the sharp bone. With those words, Cara had won her argument. No legal points, no strong-arming, not even her superior attitude when she'd walked in. Cara hurt, she was broken, and she missed her mother. This Heather could relate to at the most intimate level.

"I understand," Heather said. "I miss my mother, too."

Heather sighed and rising, walked to the window and stared out. Silver cirrus clouds streaked the blue sky hinting at the rain that was forecast. She hoped the incoming rain would break the record-breaking heat streak. "Cara," she said, turning back toward her. "Why don't you move in with me? There's enough room for both of us. We could both live here. It'd only be for the rest of the summer. Then, come September, I'll leave. As planned."

Cara turned on the sofa to face her with a look of disbelief. Her face was blotchy from crying, and she wiped her cheeks with her palms. "You'd do that?"

Heather nodded, a weak smile on her face. "Why not?"

"You hardly know me."

"I know you need to be here and so do I. If the tables were turned, would you share your home with me?"

Cara sucked in her breath. "I would."

"It's the only possible solution. I can't leave. So what do you say?"

"I don't know what to say. I come here and threaten to evict you. Quite wrong of me. I apologize."

Heather didn't reply.

"And now you want to live with me?" She paused. "Why?"

"Because I miss my mother, too."

Cara blinked heavily twice, comprehending the magnitude of that statement. Then she sighed, and a small smile eased across her face. It was more than the smile of relief. Certainly not the smile of victory. When Heather looked into her eyes, she saw a depth of gratitude in the dark brown. The message pulsating there went from one woman to another and stirred instincts that ran very deep. Perhaps right to her X chromo-some.

"All right, then," Cara said with a slight smile. "Let's give it a try." She held out her hand.

"For the summer," Heather said taking it.

"For the summer," Cara echoed. Then, with a squeeze, she added, "Thank you."

Chapter Eighteen

T HE RAIN RETURNED, and it suited Cara's mood. The beach house was quiet. Rain pattered in a steady, gentle pace. She heard the *tap-tap-tap* on the rooftop. Even without looking out at the night, she knew a heavy fog had settled in. Out in the harbor she heard the low bellowing of a foghorn as some huge container ship navigated its way either into or out of the harbor, she couldn't tell. The horn sounded to her like the melancholy wail of a lost soul.

Cara brought her arm up over her eyes, moist with tears. Another two weeks had passed. She couldn't believe she was back in her childhood room where she'd spent those summers at Primrose. History was repeating itself. She snorted. It felt like some sort of cosmic joke.

Heather had offered her the choice of sleeping in the master bedroom, but Cara wouldn't hear of it. She would move back into her mother's bedroom in September, after Heather left. The least she could do after Heather's generous offer to share the house was to allow her to stay put.

Heather couldn't have been more welcoming, bless her

heart. For Cara's arrival this afternoon, she had freshened the sheets, set out fresh towels, and filled a sweetgrass basket with dark chocolates, nuts, dried fruit, and bottled water for her room. Tonight for dinner Heather had prepared poached salmon with asparagus, boiled potatoes and parsley, with fresh fruit and cream for dessert. It was a lovely spread, but the aura of yet another brewing migraine had nauseated Cara. She'd nibbled some but couldn't swallow much. With apologies, she'd retired early to her bed. She didn't miss Heather's expression of relief. She was a sweet girl and she was trying so hard. The thought that her mother would have loved Heather made her laugh.

Over dinner, Heather had shared that she still had an occasional visit from Cara's mother in her dreams. And, on occasion, she'd catch the scent of jasmine in the house. Cara brought her shaking fingers to her throbbing forehead. Once again her mother was doting on the young waif who needed guidance. Just as she had with Toy Sooner when Cara had first returned home to this very beach house.

Cara turned to her side and tucked her hands under her pillow. "Mama," she whispered fervently, clutching the pillow as hot tears streamed down her cheeks. "Why are you ignoring me when I need you, too?"

A foghorn sounded again, and soon after a low echo of thunder rumbled, closer this time. It sounded like a wail. Cara pushed herself up on her elbows and scanned the shadowed room.

"Mama," she said louder, hoping she was being heard. "Are you here?" She waited, ear cocked and listening to the night for some sign that her mother was here with her. The rain pattered, the wind gusted, but that was all. She knew that if anyone heard her talking to a possible ghost they'd howl with laughter. Strong, pragmatic Cara Rutledge had gone off her rocker. But she didn't care. She had to try. The heart could be demanding—especially when desperate.

~~~~~

CARA FELT FINGERTIPS at her forehead. Then a soothing coolness that eased her throbbing head. The touch was gentle. Caring. A feeling of comfort flooded her. Thunder rolled and the white noise of a steady downpour filled her ears. Opening her eyes a crack, she saw that the room had the dull coloring of a rainy morning. A short while later a slim figure entered the room carrying a tray. Her blond hair wreathed her head like a halo.

"Mama?" she said in a croaky voice.

"You're awake."

Cara reached up and found a cool washcloth on her forehead. It was Heather, she realized, waking further. Tugging it off, she asked Heather, "What time is it?"

"Almost eleven."

"So late."

"Who cares? It's a sleepy, rainy day. And you need your rest. Especially with your headache. How is it?"

"Better."

"But still there?"

Cara's answer was a muffled groan.

"I brought you something that might help." Heather balanced the tray on her hip while she moved the water glass, then set the tray on the bedside table. "Some fresh water to take your medicine, and a few pieces of dry rye toast, which should be okay for your tum. And my special morning drink. It's got some caffeine from maté, some maca powder, protein powder . . ." She trailed off. "Well, all sorts of good things. You need some bolstering." She picked up a blue ceramic mug with a turtle on it. "For you."

Cara looked at the steaming mug in Heather's hands suspiciously. Her furrowed brow must have given her away, because Heather laughed. "It's good, really. Creamy. Trust me, you'll love it."

Cara didn't know if she could take the heady brew. "My stomach . . ."

"Cara," Heather said, "I know where you are. I've been there. You've been through trauma. You're fragile. Let me help you through this. Believe me, when I was eighteen, I was a mess. As thin as you are now, and as emotionally depleted. The heart will take time to heal. But let's at least start with your body. Okay?" She held out the mug. "Today is the first day of the rest of your life."

"Oh, Lord," Cara said with another groan. She didn't think she could face Heather's determined cheerfulness. "If I drink it, will you stop with the platitudes?"

Heather laughed again. "I promise."

Cara hoisted herself to her elbows, grimacing when her head began throbbing anew. Any quick movements could be punishing. She licked her dry lips, then pushed herself up to a full sitting position. Her body ached and she felt weak. "I've turned into an old woman," she lamented.

Heather hurried to add a few pillows behind her back for support. "You're not old. You're sick."

Tru dat, she thought. The nausea had subsided. She was

surprised to find she was actually hungry. She could eat something. With a weak smile of gratitude she reached up and took the warm mug from Heather's hands. Peering inside, she saw it looked creamy, like a latte. Sniffing it, she caught the faint scent of chocolate. "Chocolate can be bad for my migraines."

"It's just a bit of raw cocoa. No sugar."

Bottoms up, she thought wryly, and brought the mug to her lips, taking a small sip.

"Oh. That's good."

"Don't sound so surprised," Heather said, clearly pleased with her response. "I drink it every morning. I call it my morning potion. I'll make it for you every day, too. Too much coffee isn't good for you, though I do love my coffee. And this is chock-full of superfoods. Now, just sit back and enjoy the quiet. You don't have to do anything today. Not a thing. I'll be working in my office. I mean, the sunroom," she quickly amended. "Just call me if you need anything."

Cara slanted her gaze. "Were you always such a mother hen?"

"Actually, yes," Heather replied. "After my mother died, I took care of my father. We had a lot of help, but I was the one who made sure his dinner was ready when he got home, that his shirts were cleaned." She laughed nervously. "Basically, a mother hen."

"Well, nurse, thank you for this," Cara said, raising the mug in salute. Heather held back her smile. She picked up the empty water glass and turned to leave, but stopped at the foot of the bed. Cara looked up from her mug to see the shyness return to Heather's expression.

"You're my first roommate," she said, looking at her hands. "I hope"—a blush stained her cheek as she looked up again—"I hope we'll be friends as well." She smiled tentatively and walked out.

Cara watched her leave, her muddled brain trying to make out who this young woman was. There was a kindness at her core. It revealed itself in everything she did. But Heather was nobody's fool, either. That was the part Cara hadn't expected. Heather had done a respectable job of turning the tables on Cara regarding the lease. And now she'd maneuvered her into committing to getting herself together a little bit, something even Emmi and Flo hadn't been able to accomplish. "Watch out for the quiet ones," Cara herself always used to say. Good Lord, she thought with chagrin. Next she'd be doing yoga.

Then she thought again.

When Heather had walked in, Cara had momentarily mistaken her for her mother. Heather was slight and blond, yes. But it was everything else, too. The cool cloth on Cara's head, the lowered shades, the special drink and dry toast. The offer to share the house. All these were gestures Lovie would have made.

Heather was a lot like Lovie. The notion gave Cara pause. Was that why Cara found her so intriguing? Beguiling, even?

She picked up the mug and smelled its strange but appetizing aroma. When Cara thought of herself, she thought of a woman who was smart, capable, practical. She'd always prized her toughness under pressure, her ability to confront, to go toe-to-toe with an adversary. To her mind, that defined power and strength for a woman in a man's world. Her specific battle arena was one of words, thus her display of wit and intelligence won points even if—especially if—it wounded another.

She snorted and shook her head with self-contempt. *Look how well that's been working out for you,* she told herself.

In the midst of all her mourning and heartache, Cara had turned fifty. In the end, it was just another day. She had reached that milestone with a whimper, not a roar. Perhaps it was appropriate, she thought. Instead of lamenting that she was getting older, it was time for her—at last—to grow up.

When she'd marched out of her parents' house at eighteen, she'd forged a life with a chip on her shoulder. She'd climbed the ladder ruthlessly. Got the corner office with a window, a good salary, a title—and it still wasn't enough. Not in that world. She'd thought she'd given up that lifestyle when she'd stayed on the island and married Brett. To an extent, she had. But in truth, a spark of that misplaced ambition still burned inside of her. Not being a boss in a business didn't stop a woman from being coldhearted and strategic in her personal life. How many women who'd never entered the corporate world could say they didn't wage battles at home?

Well, she'd had her "come to Jesus," as Mama would've said. Guilt was a terrible thing. Regret even worse. Since Brett's death, she wasn't guilt-ridden thinking she hadn't loved him enough. She knew without doubt that she'd given him all her love, freely and without reservation. He'd known that she loved him. However, the guilt that haunted her at night was how often she should've been more understanding. Kinder.

More careful with her words. More grateful for what she had. She recalled the conversation she and Brett had had earlier in the spring about her sense of inertia, how reaching the milestone of fifty was making Cara feel so unmoored and unsatisfied, in need of a passion to pursue. Hah! She longed for the days when not feeling professionally fulfilled was her greatest cause for upset.

At Brett's funeral, one person after another had spoken of his generosity, his kindness, how he'd always been there for a friend. How he had the right priorities and lived life fully. How he was the very definition of a lowcountry man.

Like Brett, Lovie had been an embodiment of all that was best about the South—exuding a lowcountry woman's gentility, natural grace, a vulnerability that opened her heart and tamped down her ego, empathy for others, generosity, and strong conviction of right and wrong. Like the graceful palm tree she treasured, Lovie bent in the harsh wind but did not break. At her funeral, someone had declared that Lovie had never said a bad word about anyone. Enough said.

What, she wondered, would people say about her when her time came? It was a daunting thought.

Cara swallowed hard and lowered her head, humbled by this self-reckoning. *Power isn't telling someone what to do*, she told herself. *Strength isn't having the upper hand. Nobility and grace are revealed in the manner in which love is given.*

She took another sip of Heather's magic potion, feeling the caffeine and whatever superfood ingredients were in it racing through her bloodstream. And, more, the kindness that Heather had shown in making it for her.

Damn, but it was good.

〜〜〜〜

IT WAS A glorious morning on the islands. The rain and storm of the past several days had cleared, taking with them the pressing humidity and the pesky bugs. At least for a short while. Heather reveled in these post-storm mornings, when the air smelled as green and moist as God's promise to Noah, when everything felt fresh and renewed.

Bo walked beside her on Sullivan's Island for her dawn patrol. He had heard her talk so often about sighting a flock of shorebirds on the beach at dawn that he wanted to see it for himself. Bo had proved to be one of those rare individuals who were as comfortable with silence as with conversation. They held hands as they walked along the deserted beach, bumping hips, each awestruck by the majesty of the brilliant sunrise over the ocean. The world was aflame with pink and gold.

"I see this almost every day," she said to Bo. She stopped and he stood beside her, slipping his arm around her waist as they stared out at a beauty that was indescribable and overwhelmed logic. "I never grow tired of it. I think everyone should take time, at least once a week, to catch a sunrise. Just to feel alive and that there's hope." She leaned into him. "I don't know how to explain it. There's something about that rosy light that silences the negative voices in my head and reaffirms that there is something good in me."

He pressed her closer. "There's so much good about you, Heather."

She felt the blanket of security she always did when he said such things. Looking up, she met his gaze.

They turned and continued walking. Heather picked up

an occasional seashell. Bo inspected each intriguingly shaped piece of driftwood, settling on one large chunk he declared held promise.

After tiptoeing around the house trying not to disturb Cara, Heather appreciated being back outside in the fresh air and searching for her birds. That's how she was beginning to feel about the shorebirds that clustered along both sides of Breach Inlet—as *her* birds. That was silly, of course. The birds belonged to nobody, and also to everyone. If more people understood that, she thought, the shorebirds' future would be protected.

Approaching beach entry point Station 22, Bo explained to her it was so named because it was a remnant from the time a trolley would drop visitors off at different stations. They found a large cluster of plovers and sandpipers—so many she couldn't count them. Bo set up the tripod for her scope while she spread out a towel behind it. Bo stretched out his long legs beside her.

Heather got comfortable in front of the tripod and put her sketch pad in her lap. She looked out over the beach and the water, then tilted her head to let the early-morning sun warm her face. She sighed contentedly.

"The light here is so beautiful and so different from the light in Charlotte. It reminds me of the light in Florence." She turned her head. "Have you ever been there?"

"To Florence? Sure, many times."

"Really?"

He laughed. "Sure. It's just an hour away."

Heather did a double take. "What?"

Bo laughed his low laugh. "I know you meant Florence,

Italy. Baby, I've never been to Europe. I don't even get to Florence, South Carolina, that often. Truth is, I've never been outside the South. Someday I'd like to travel. But frankly, I don't feel the urgency." He looked out at the sea. "Not when I live here."

She matched his outward gaze toward the Atlantic Ocean, calm today after the stormy weather. "It *is* beautiful here," she agreed. "Light helps define a place. Here the light has color. It changes throughout the day and it's unpredictable. I'd never grow tired of painting here."

"Glad to hear that."

She caught his meaning and dipped her head to look into her scope, not ready to think about what the future held for her—and for them—when summer ended, and with it her lease at Cara's.

In this moment, she had work to do.

There had to be twenty-five sandpipers out there. They walked steadily on their little legs, picking at the sand. A few were squabbling, spreading their wings, beaks open. She selected one feisty sandpiper in particular and, putting pencil to paper, began to set up her sketch. She became aware that Bo was watching her. She turned her head, a question in her eyes.

Bo grinned, a little sheepishly. "Sorry. Does it bother you if I watch?"

"A little. I'm not used to it."

"I'll stop."

"No, it's okay," she said quickly. "It's silly of me."

"How do you know where to begin?" he asked, looking at the blank paper.

"It depends on what kind of work I'm doing. When I'm out in the field using a tripod and a scope, first I just watch. I look at the angle of the body." She began to sketch as she talked. "What are the bird's posture, proportions, angles?" Her hand moved more quickly now over the paper. "The sandpiper has a plump body with balanced proportions. Now I'm getting a basic silhouette. Before getting to details, it's more of a road map. I draw it as lightly as possible. See?" she said, showing him her sketch. "You can barely see it on the paper. Just a ghost of an image. Then I'll take it back to the studio and add all the details. These little peeps have such personalities."

"I can see the bird taking shape already." Bo's tone was one of admiration.

"I've got a long way to go. What about you?" Heather asked, eager to deflect the attention from herself and her process. "You found that piece of wood. How do you begin?"

"Well," he said, scratching his jaw, "first I just look at the wood. I ponder it. Just that can take a long time. I don't put a knife to the wood until I see where I'm headed. I can't erase my mistakes. Whittling or sculpting is really a long series of decisions. When you make good ones, you have a product you like. When you make a bad one, you toss it and start again. And there are always lots of bad decisions. But the good ones are worth waiting for."

Then they both set to work. They worked in a companionable silence, Heather absorbed in her sketches and Bo contemplating the piece of wood he'd picked up. Yet wordlessly, Heather felt their bond grow from this shared experience. She'd never imagined how such simple pleasures could bring so many fulfillments. After about an hour, she set her charcoal pencil down with a gusty sigh. "I'm spent," she said. She glanced over at Bo's piece of driftwood and gasped. "Whittling" didn't do his work justice. Like magic, the lump of wood had somehow morphed into a dolphin.

"Oh, Bo!" she exclaimed. She'd had no idea he could create sculptures like that.

"It's just a little something," he said modestly.

"It's beautiful."

"I whittle wherever I am. If I have my pocketknife, I'm set." He lifted the dolphin higher, twisting it to the left and right. "The tricky part is knowing when to stop."

"You've inherited your uncle's talent with woodworking, for sure."

He raised a brow. "Do you think so?"

"Yes," she said with conviction. Every time she was with him, he revealed some new facet of himself. He truly had the soul of an artist. He found beauty in everything. Even her. "Somehow you found this dolphin hiding in that piece of driftwood and freed her."

He smiled and looked at her, unusually abashed for a man as confident as Bo. "Well, now . . ." He handed it to her. "It's for you."

"I'll treasure it forever," she said, letting her finger run along the rough wood from the rostrum to the tail fluke.

The day could not have been more perfect—yet something was niggling at Heather that she couldn't quite shake. "I was just thinking, we've had such a great morning . . . it's sad that Cara keeps herself cooped up inside. Coming from me, that's like the pot calling the kettle black. But perhaps because

I've been a shut-in so long, I'm sensitive to it. She's so different from how she was the first time I met her, at the beginning of the summer."

"She's still grieving."

"I know. But even Flo thinks she should be getting out more. And she was a social worker before she retired. And . . ." Heather drew circles in the sand. ". . . I talked to my therapist about Cara." Heather had maintained her weekly session with her therapist in Charlotte via phone over the summer.

"You did? What did she say?"

"We talked about the different phases of grief. After the first phase of mourning, one moves into a longer phase of intense psychological pain. Weeping. Guilt. Hopelessness, that sort of thing. When someone is grieving, it's easy for them to let go of their health. The way Cara's sleeping all the time, watching TV, not eating well, is not unusual."

Heather couldn't quite put her finger on why, but she felt a sense of responsibility and even protectiveness toward Cara. Maybe it was because Cara reminded Heather so much of herself after her mother's death, or maybe it was just a woman witnessing another woman in excruciating pain. Whatever the reason, Heather wanted—no, needed—to help.

"So I've been thinking. We have to try to lure her outdoors."

"Wait," Bo said, holding up his palm. "An agoraphobe is going to lure Cara outdoors?"

"I know, right?" Heather said with a self-deprecating laugh. "That's why I need your help."

He raised a brow. "Oh?"

"I have a plan."

"You can tell it to me over dinner," he said, scrambling to his feet.

"Dinner?"

He held out his hand and with a firm tug pulled Heather up, then put his arms around her waist and gently pulled her closer. "Yes. Tonight I'm taking you somewhere special."

Chapter Nineteen

THE EVENING ARRIVED slowly. For Heather, the day had felt as if she were driving through a long tunnel, sure that the end would never come. She'd dutifully sent off her first collection of sketches to her commissioning art director in the morning. Letting go of the carefully wrapped package had been an exhilarating moment of completion. She'd finished this portion of her deadline on schedule. She had stood at the counter and watched the clerk affix the tags and postage with pride and relief. Yet as soon as she'd stepped out of the shop door, she'd stood blinking in the heat of a July morning, steeped in quandary. What would she do now? She had to wait for the decision of the committee as to what shorebirds were approved before she moved forward. She'd become fixed in her routine, and abandoning her daily schedule was not something that worked well for someone like Heather.

So she'd spent the day doing everything she normally did, and during the block of time in the afternoon that she allotted for perfecting her sketches inside the house, she'd worked on some personal art instead, drawings of the expanse of beach and wide swath of blue sky visible from her sunroom. But throughout the day, in the back of Heather's mind was her date with Bo.

She wasn't nervous—they'd been together almost daily for weeks. He stopped by for coffee in the morning before heading off for a job, or they'd grab a bite at the Long Island Café on the island. Sometimes they'd just sit in the back deck rockers and listen to music while they read, talked, and looked out to sea. He was waiting for some signal from her before going further, she knew it. And tonight, when he was taking her out to celebrate the completion of her sketches, might just be the time to give him the green light.

Of course, she'd been battling her inner fears over the implications of tonight, which made the day seem even longer. The hours crawled, despite her carefully regimented schedule and blocked-off segments of time. As the afternoon grew late she soaked in a scented tub and let her tense muscles loosen. Closing her eyes, she brought to mind the feel of Bo's lips on hers, saw in her mind the extraordinary color of his blue eyes, so clear it was akin to looking at the sky on a sunny day.

Then, suddenly, it was time to get ready. She saw the light at the end of the tunnel.

Feeling giddy with anticipation, Heather took her time getting dressed. For the first time she put on the new lacy underwear she'd ordered, then polished her nails and dabbed her favorite perfume behind her ears. She agonized over choosing the right outfit and finally selected her white sundress, because he'd commented once how much he liked it, and high strappy heels. She brushed her hair out methodically, stroking the mother-of-pearl–handled comb through her waves until they shone like burnished gold. She let it hang long and straight down her shoulders. Finally, she slipped on pearls for her neck and ears.

When she walked into the living room, she found Cara sitting on the sofa reading. Cara looked up and closed the book.

"You look lovely," Cara said, her dark eyes lighting. "Bo's a lucky man."

Heather felt a great relief that Cara approved. She'd felt self-conscious stepping out for this date in front of a woman who had recently lost the love of her life. But Cara seemed truly excited for Heather, a spark entering her eyes that she hadn't seen since Cara had moved back in.

"I wanted to let you know," Cara said in a casual tone. "I'm spending the night at Emmi's. We're going to have a good old-fashioned girls' night watching movies, eating popcorn, giggling." Cara swirled her wine. "So I won't be here when you get home." She quickly took a sip of wine, her look inscrutable.

"Sounds like fun," Heather said, looking away. Cara's message was as subtle as a truck. She quickly changed the subject. "I couldn't decide on shoes," she said, lifting her leg to show off a very tall, very sexy heel. "Are these too high?"

"Depends. Where are you going?"

"I don't know. It's a surprise."

Cara's eyes flashed and her face shifted to an amused grin. "A surprise? Oh, Heather," she said with humor in her voice. "When a lowcountry man tells you he's taking you out on a surprise dinner date, you'd better wear flats. I remember the surprise dinner date that Brett took me on when we began dating. Let me just say he picked me up in a johnboat."

Heather laughed. "I could see Bo doing that."

Cara smiled again and her eyes reflected some personal memory. "And put mosquito spray everywhere!"

———～～～———

BO ARRIVED IN his truck a short while later, and as she opened the door Heather was intrigued to see he wore the classic dinner attire she'd come to associate with a lowcountry man—khaki pants and a blue blazer. He towered over her in her flats, and his astonishing, pale blue eyes seemed even livelier than normal.

"You're beautiful," he said simply, upon seeing her. "Are you ready?"

"Yes. Let me just grab my purse."

She went to the front table as Cara meandered by, holding a glass of wine in one hand.

"You clean up well," she said to Bo in a complimentary way.

He laughed lightly. "Special night."

"So I understand." She pointed her finger and said with mock gravity, "You treat our girl well."

"Yes, ma'am."

"Bye, Cara," Heather said with a private warning glance. Secretly she was glad Cara was coming out of her shell and up to teasing.

"Don't wait up," Bo added. Cara let out a little laugh and raised her wineglass in acknowledgment.

Once they were in the car, Heather asked, "Are you going to tell me where we're going?"

Bo backed out of the narrow gravel driveway and then, shifting gears, headed south toward Sullivan's Island. "You'll know soon enough."

"Is it a popular restaurant?" she asked.

"No, I wouldn't say that."

"Good," she said with a sigh of relief. "Going to a packed restaurant with lots of people would make me so nervous I might not appreciate what I'm eating." She glanced over at him. "And I want to enjoy every minute of our date."

He swung his head to glance at her, smiling. "That's the plan."

They drove over the Hunley Bridge. The sky was beginning to shift colors as the sun lowered. Breach Inlet shimmered below them in translucent lavender. The radio station Bo had turned on was playing country music, which suited Heather's mood, and, caught in the mood of mystery, neither of them spoke. They didn't travel far. Bo didn't turn to go over the bridge toward Charleston. Instead he turned right on Middle Street, staying on Sullivan's Island. They inched down Middle Street where the restaurants were jam-packed with summer visitors, past the fire station and the park. Heather sat up in her seat as they left the small business district and turned toward the back of the island. Where was he taking her? she wondered.

He turned again, off the paved road onto a dirt road that ran along the back of the island. The houses here were large, discreet, and mostly hidden by shrubs and trees. He turned into the driveway of one of them, toward a white clapboard house half hidden by an enormous live oak tree, its heavy boughs seemingly cradling the old house. "Where are we?" she asked.

"Sea Breeze." They rounded the circular driveway. Bo turned off the engine beside a small wooden garage, and the big truck shuddered to a stop. "My friend Taylor lives here with his wife and baby. They're out of town and said we could use the dock in the back. I wanted tonight to be special, and this is the best damn dock on the island," he added. He turned toward her, his eyes twinkling with the game. "That's your first clue. Now, stay put for a few minutes. I have to get a few things done first. Okay?"

"Okay." She watched him trot up the driveway and behind the house, her brain buzzing with questions. There was still light in the sky despite it being nearly eight o'clock. She let her gaze wander around the circular drive. The place had the handsome architecture and quiet dignity of old money, with a wide, welcoming front porch and curved front steps under gabled windows. To the right of the property stood a charming white cottage, the very picture of what a lowcountry cottage should look like. With the garage to the left of the home, Sea Breeze was more than a house. This was a compound.

Heather's eyes were wide with curiosity when she spotted Bo trotting back toward the truck. She smoothed her dress as he opened her door then lifted his hand to help her out. Everything felt more formal tonight. They were both on their best behavior. He tucked her arm in his and they'd begun walking toward the house when a voice called out.

"Bo Stanton? Is that you? Come on over here and introduce me to your young lady."

Heather's heart skipped a beat, and she swung her head to look over toward the cottage. There she saw an old woman sitting on the front porch in a white rocker. Her hand was in the air, and she waved them closer with an unmistakable air of authority.

Bo lowered his head and said softly, "I didn't expect this. But it's okay. You'll love her." Then he lifted his hand and called out, "Coming, Miss Marietta!" As they approached the cottage, Bo explained, "This is Mrs. Muir. She's Taylor's wife's grandmother and lives in the cottage now. This used to be her house." They walked up the stairs to the porch. Bo stepped closer to the old woman and kissed her cheek.

"Nice to see you, Miss Marietta. I hope we're not bothering you. Taylor and Harper said we could use the dock tonight."

"You're not bothering me in the least," Mrs. Muir said in the kindest manner. "Harper told me all about it. She said you're going to have dinner out there. How simply wonderful!" She brought her hands together, and looked at Heather. "And who is this lovely lady?"

Bo stepped aside and held out his arm to guide Heather closer. "Ma'am, this is my friend Heather Wyatt. From Charlotte."

Heather's heart was pounding in her chest, but her manners were ingrained. She held out her hand. "Nice to meet you, Mrs. Muir," she said in a soft voice. She forced herself to look Mrs. Muir in the eyes and she was glad she did. The old woman's pale blue eyes gleamed with welcome.

"Welcome to Sea Breeze," Mrs. Muir said. "I wish my granddaughters were here to meet you. They're close to your age." She turned to Bo. "Someday you'll have to bring Heather back and we'll have a dinner together. Won't that be fun?"

"I'll do that."

"But for tonight," Mrs. Muir said pointedly, "I'll say good night. I'm going inside and will retire early."

They bid the regal woman farewell, and as Bo led her back around the great house, Heather couldn't help but think that the world was conspiring to give her and Bo their privacy.

"Taylor and I met working together on house projects with his dad. That's how we became friends. Taylor's moved on to other business, but his daddy still owns his own construction company. We keep in touch."

Heather sucked in her breath when she saw the back of the house. It was even more beautiful than the front. The house was built to get the maximum view of the winding cove that stretched far out to the Intracoastal Waterway. From here she could see against the radiant colors of the sunset, the double arches of the Ravenel Bridge from Mount Pleasant to Charleston. In the soft light it looked like two great sailing masts, a perfect symbol for the historic port city.

Three decks led down to the long dock that stretched out over the winding water. As they descended the stairs in the lavender light, Heather caught sight of a covered dock aglow with the flickering of dozens of candles.

"Oh, Bo," she gasped, clutching his arm tighter. "It's breathtaking."

He patted her hand, pleased with her response, and guided her down the narrow wooden dock to where the night was shimmering with candlelight. Under the canopy he'd set up a table and two chairs. Instead of heavy damask linen, however, the table was covered in newspaper. She had to cover her mouth with her hand to hide her smile. On top were two small wooden mallets, a bottle of hot sauce, and a roll of paper towels.

"Come sit," he said, pulling out her chair. "It should be a magnificent sunset. I ordered it just for you."

He hurried to the cooler, where he pulled out two champagne glasses and a bottle. He returned to their table and she watched as he expertly teased out the cork. It emerged with a satisfying pop. She clapped her hands. Bo poured the wine and handed one flute to her and raised his.

"To all things great and small, especially postage stamps," he toasted, a twinkle in his eye.

Heather laughed and they clinked glasses as she met his gaze and sipped the cool, bubbly liquid. She was grateful for his support over the past weeks. It spoke loudly to the man he was. Bo was her biggest cheerleader. Knowing this made the wine taste especially sweet.

"Now you sit back and let me get dinner."

"I can help."

"I've got it all under control. Besides, I've seen how hard you've been working to make your deadline. Tonight you get to relax. Watch the sunset," he added, gesturing to the surreal explosion of sienna, purples, and gold in the sky beyond.

Bo removed his jacket and slung it over the back of his chair. Then he rolled up his sleeves and got busy being chef, waiter, and sommelier all at once. It was, indeed, a magical night. She leaned back and listened to the sound of water lapping the wood pilings, the moist breeze off the water caressing her cheeks. It smelled of salt and sea and crabs cooking. From somewhere out in the cove she heard a loud splash and wondered if a fish had jumped or if it was a dolphin.

While she sat and sipped champagne, Bo pulled crabs from the steamer, one by one, and set them on a wooden platter and carried it to the table. From a box he withdrew a long baguette wrapped in foil.

"Careful, they're hot," he warned. He made several more trips to the cooler for the salad, dressing, and lemons, back and forth until the table was overflowing with food. Last of all, he flicked on the music. The silence was filled with the soft crooning of Randy Travis. Heather caught her breath—she'd told Bo once that "Whisper My Name" was her favorite of all Randy Travis's songs, and that was the melody that washed over them now. Finally he took the seat across from her. He switched from champagne to beer and raised his can.

"Let's dig in!"

Heather sipped her wine, looking at the pile of steaming crabs uncertainly.

"What do I do?" she asked. "Is it like lobster?"

Bo put his beer on the table. "You're kidding me. You've never had steamed crabs before?"

She shook her head, wondering if he thought she was backward.

"You must've wondered why I had newspapers all over the table," he said with a laugh.

"Well, I just thought you were being creative."

He barked out another laugh. "Or cheap! No, honey, this is a classic lowcountry meal. I caught these crabs off this here dock earlier today. It's a delicacy and you're going to love it. I'll show you how it's done. See, first you pick out a crab."

He lifted one from the top and showed her a large crab with blue-tipped claws and a pale, creamy underside. "This here's what we call a Jimmy. That means it's a male. We can tell by the pointed markings on the underbelly. Kind of looks like—well, like the Washington Monument."

Heather smirked. "The spitting image. What do you call females?"

"A Sook. They have a rounded apron on the belly. Hold on. . . ." He poked through the pile of crabs, then pulled one out. "Here, this is a Sook." He flipped the crab over to reveal a rounded curve on the shell.

She looked at him, feeling very much the Sook to his Jimmy.

As the blaze in the sky faded, Bo taught Heather how to use the mallet to break the shells, how to dig with her fingers to find the sweetest, most succulent meat she'd ever tasted under the shoulders and in the claws. It was messy work and she was awkward at first, gingerly picking at the crabs, frequently glancing at Bo making sure she was doing it right. She worried she looked unladylike as she pounded the shells and ate the tender morsels with her hands. But Bo was ripping into the crabs with gusto and taking no notice. The Old Bay seasoning coated her fingers, flavoring every bite. It was pure heaven. It wasn't long before she was laughing when her splintered shells flew into the air and lifting the meat to her mouth with her fingers like a true lowcountry girl.

They talked long after the crabs were finished and cleared from the table. Past the last dregs of the champagne, until the stars shone and the moon took her place in the velvety sky. They talked until there were no more words to say. Yet their eyes continued to communicate a shared knowledge of an appetite not yet sated. Their hands entwined on the table, his thumb gently stroking her palm. Her skin thrummed with anticipation.

Bo stood and offered her his hand.

"Are we leaving?" she asked.

"No, ma'am," he said as he reeled her up into his arms. "We're dancing."

"I don't know how to dance," she said, feeling a flush of anxiety sweep over her.

"Everyone can dance. Come on, I've seen you dance when you think no one's looking."

Heather felt heat rush to her face as she slapped his arm. "You spied on me?"

"Not exactly. I just watched you through the window while I worked. Girl, you've got moves."

She blushed and turned her head toward the water, smiling, unable to step away because he held tight to her hand.

"Well, I've never slow-danced," she said.

"Relax," he said, drawing her into his arms. "There's nothing to learn. Just hold on and follow me. Like this . . ."

He slipped one hand around her waist and took her hand with the other. He brought it close to his chest, then lowered his cheek to hers. "See? It's easy. We sway in time to the music."

At first Heather felt like a marionette, stiffly following Bo's movements. Gradually she relaxed and caught the rhythm of the music. He'd selected slow songs by some of her favorite country singers—Blake Shelton, Brad Paisley, the Dixie Chicks. Their music filled the dark night. She was enveloped in love songs. The balmy breeze coming off the water ruffled her hair and lifted the skirt of her dress; Bo's hand gently caressed her back, his humming in her ear. He pulled her closer and she felt her body mold to his. They fit together perfectly. Hip to hip, they swayed. Left, right. Left, right. Easy and slow.

His lips lowered to begin a scorching trail across her neck, to her ear, then her mouth, their breaths mingling, the sweet taste of bubbly champagne mixing with the spices. Bo moved his head to gaze into her eyes. Still dancing, he sang the lyrics of the Randy Travis song close to her ear:

> *I'm gonna love you forever and ever*
> *Forever and ever, amen.*

Heather clung to Bo even tighter and felt the heat between them, felt the wine floating in her brain, felt she was living in a dream.

A new tension was spiraling between them. *I'm tipsy,* she thought, but this time she didn't fear it. There was nothing to fear. Not with him. She lifted her head off his shoulder and leaned back in his arms to look into his eyes. She reached up and gently traced a line from his temple over the sun-roughened planes of his face, gently trailing her nail along his bottom lip.

Bo's eyes sparked. "Let's go."

THE BEACH HOUSE was dark when they entered.

"Where's Cara?" Bo whispered. "Asleep?"

"She went next door for a sleepover."

Behind her she heard a soft, low laugh. "That was thoughtful of her."

Heather felt her cheeks flame with both titillation and

shyness. She'd never brought a man back to her place before. She'd lived at home, and though she had a suite of rooms, she'd never felt that she was truly alone. More than that, it had never felt like the right thing to do with any of the men she'd dated before.

Yet it felt so right for Bo to be here with her. He was the one for her; she knew that with every fiber of her being. Heather had always trusted her intuition, and she knew that Bo was someone she would love for the rest of her life.

"Do you want something to drink?" she asked, her sense of heightened anticipation triggering her innate hostess manners.

Bo turned her to face him and slid his arms around her, kissed her softly on the lips, silencing her inner critic. Their kiss deepened and she leaned into him, feeling her inhibitions slide away and dissolve in the rising heat of passion.

Still in her dreamlike trance, she let her hand slide down his arm to take his hand. This time Heather led the way, across the hardwood floors to her bedroom. The four-poster bed loomed large, full of promise and import. She raised her fingers to his shirt and began unbuttoning the buttons, one after the other, while he stood quiet, watching, his breaths coming short. His skin felt warm beneath his shirt as she reached up to his shoulders and let her palms glide across the broad, muscled expanse of them, sliding his shirt off his body.

Bo turned her around by her shoulders. She heard the hum of the zipper in the darkness, then felt his hands as they ran along her body, nudging the dress off until it fell in a pool at her feet. His hands moved smoothly, with experience, to unsnap her bra, and his hands reached around from behind, gently caressing her breasts.

He slowly turned her again to face him and lowered his head to kiss her lips, her cheeks, her eyes, her ears, until she felt her own breathing shorten and heard a soft sigh escape her lips. Leaning down, he gently kissed between her breasts and slowly let his tongue play with her nipples. Her hands dug into his back as she arched into him, filled with new sensations. Her hands moved to his pants, fumbling, as she undid the buttons and slid them down his trim hips.

He laid her back on her bed and they came together in what felt like slow motion, his body against hers, skin on skin. She closed her eyes and was awash in sensation. She felt his lips everywhere, searching, finding, bringing her pleasure she couldn't have imagined. She felt a tension growing deep in her body, luscious and demanding, coiling tighter and tighter.

"Heather."

She heard her name and drew herself back from somewhere far away to open her eyes. Bo was arched over her, his eyes burning as bright as fire.

"Are you sure?" he asked.

He knows, she thought. *He knows he'll be my first.* She'd expected to feel shy. Maybe even embarrassed. She was twenty-six and still a virgin. But she felt none of this. She desired him. She wanted Bo, only Bo, to be the first, and she was glad of him knowing it.

Heather parted her lips and drew his head to hers. Slowly, deliberately, her tongue traced the inner rim of his lips, moist and tremulous. Immediately his tongue probed in response, gently touching hers. A whimper rose in her throat, a final cry of surrender, and in a rush she wrapped her arms around him.

"Yes."

Bo kissed her hungrily, possessively, as he moved to blanket her with his body. Nothing was slow now. They came together like the rushing tide—resolute, turbulent, white-capped with passion. Heather buried her face in his neck, her mouth open. She heard his panting and, excited, matched it with her own, drowning in sensations as he moved against her. Her naïve, tender body finally found his rhythm and began to move with him in a dance lovelier, more nuanced, than the ones they'd danced before out on the dock. Faster they danced, keeping the rhythm, he and she together, nothing to fear, until with a final cry she relinquished, not with a whimper of defeat but with a soaring cry of triumph.

BO WOKE THE next morning to the sounds of birds chirping. The light coming in through the shutters reflected the blue-gray color of dawn. He pushed back the hair from his face and looked around the room, blinking, taking stock. Then, as he remembered the night before, a slow grin eased across his face. He let his hand drop to the opposite side of the big four-poster bed.

It was empty.

Where was she?

He tore the top sheet from the bed and wrapped it around his waist, then walked out of the bedroom into the dim front room. There was no light on in the kitchen, either, no scent of coffee brewing. A sense of dread filled his chest. Perhaps she was off somewhere regretting the events of the previous night, wishing it—he—had never happened. That thought nearly brought Bo to his knees. He'd never hurt Heather, never wanted to do anything that caused her distress. He ran his hand through his hair. Had he missed some sort of signal? Gone too fast, pushed too hard?

The faint sound of humming came from the sunroom. He swung his head around, and his breath caught.

Heather was perched on a stool in front of a large canvas, one knee bent with her foot propped on the rung, the other leg stretched out long for balance as she leaned forward, paintbrush in hand. She was wearing nothing but his shirt, rolled up at the sleeves, her long blond hair loosely collected at the nape of her neck. The silhouette of her slender body was visible in the morning light.

Later Bo would become aware that that was the precise moment he fell in love with Heather. She was all that was beautiful and radiant and right in the world. He could not imagine a day not waking up to her beside him. In his bed. In his home. In his life. With a primeval surge, he knew. *His.*

He crept up behind her and slid his arms under the shirttails, his hands locking around her bare waist. She startled and jumped with a high-pitched yelp, then laughed and leaned back into him. His hands moved up to caress her bare breasts as his lips burrowed into her neck. She arched against him with a soft moan. He turned her around on the stool to face him. Her blue eyes were bright with amusement, curiosity, and something Bo recognized as unmistakable lust and, yes, even more. Bo took the brush from her hand and let it fall onto the drop cloth below. Then he lifted his hands and gently smoothed the hair from her face so he could look into her expressive eyes. He had to tell her how he felt. When a man felt as strongly as he did, when he was so sure, he couldn't wait for a so-called perfect moment. That moment was now.

"Heather, I love you," he said.

Her eyes widened with surprise, then myriad emotions flickered: joy, exuberance, and, at last—and Bo gloried in the surety of this expression—love.

"I love you, too."

Chapter Twenty

READY OR NOT, here we come!"

Flo's voice boomed through the sunroom as she slid back the glass doors. It was a hot day in late July and all the windows were closed to let the air-conditioning do its work. Heather came from the kitchen, drying her hands on a towel. Flo's snowy white head was poking through the doors, her bright blue eyes searching the room. In her arms she carried a large brown box filled with goodies.

"Y'all are early! Welcome!"

"Early? You said six o'clock, didn't you?" Emmi said, closing the sliding glass door behind her with one hand, balancing a pie in the other. Emmi was wearing a lilac-print sundress and her hair was pulled back in a purple clasp. She even had lilac cloisonné earrings in her ears. Flo was dressed in bright red capris and a white linen shirt, large turtle earrings dangling from her lobes.

"Six thirty, but who's counting?" Heather replied with a light laugh, even though any company arriving—especially early—gave her a jolt of nervousness. *But this isn't company, these are friends*, she reminded herself sternly.

Immediately the canaries started chirping, excited by the sound of voices. Moutarde began singing first, as usual.

"I'm sorry you had to close up your doors and windows. I miss hearing your birds. They cheer me up," Flo said, walking across the room. Her head turned from left to right as she scanned the room, curious. She stopped in front of Heather and handed over the box, her bright eyes sweeping over her like searchlights. "Don't you look nice."

Heather looked down at her pink Lilly Pulitzer dress. "Thanks. It's cool on a hot night."

"Amen! It's hotter than Hades out there."

Emmi dabbed at her brow with a tissue. "Just walking from our house to yours worked up a sweat."

"I know," Heather said, accepting the box filled with offerings. "Even at dawn."

"Climate change," Flo declared in her matter-of-fact tone.

"Goodness, what all did you bring?" Heather asked, returning to the kitchen. Setting the box on the counter, she pulled out a loaf of Flo's homemade honey wheat bread, a jar of honey from her bees, two jars of her homemade strawberry jam, and two bottles of wine. She carried the wine out to the table. "You're spoiling us," she chided Flo.

"I've got to give it to someone. How much honey can a woman eat? Blueberries will be coming in soon. I'll bring you some jam from that, too. And don't worry—I won't put too much sugar in it. I know you don't like it."

Heather grinned, grateful. "You're too generous. That bread you brought last week was heaven. Thank you."

Flo lifted her hand. "No thanks necessary."

Emmi stepped forward with the pie. "This *I* made," she said with pride. "Flo's not the only one who can bake. When she lets me have a turn at the oven."

Heather took the pie and made a show of peeking under the aluminum foil. "It's beautiful. Thank you!"

"It's strawberry rhubarb. Made from scratch," she added, with a smug smile directed at Flo.

"If you're done talking about pies," Flo interjected. "I'm as dry as the desert. You wouldn't happen to have anything to drink?" She looked pointedly at the bottles of wine on the table.

"Bubble water or plain?" Heather asked, heading toward the kitchen.

Flo scrunched up her face. "It's after five o'clock. How about white or red?"

"Flo, give the girl a chance," Emmi scolded her.

Heather set the pie on the counter and paused, feeling her cheeks flame. Of course they wanted wine. What sort of hostess didn't offer wine instantly to her dinner guests? She poked her head out the kitchen entrance, smiling self-consciously. "I'm sorry. I'm not very practiced at being a hostess yet. Red or white?"

"Oh, you're just fine," Flo said with a wave of her hand. "Most people don't have to deal with an opinionated, brassy old woman for their first dinner party. But since you're asking . . ." She walked to the table and picked up a bottle. "I'll have some of this red I brought. I drink only red these days. Hear it's good for my heart. At my age, you've got to try everything."

"If you're pouring," Emmi chimed in. "I'll take white. Whatever you have that's chilled. The Chardonnay I brought isn't cold. Here, darlin', you might want to stick it in the fridge." She handed Heather the bottle of white as well.

Heather stuck her head in the well-stocked fridge and peered around. "All I have chilled is Pinot Grigio," she called out to Emmi.

"Even better. Need any help in there?"

"No, thanks," Heather responded. She poured, and carried the two glasses of wine out to her guests.

"Where's Cara?" asked Emmi, looking around. "Please say she's not in bed."

"She's fine. She's still getting ready," Heather replied. "She made the tabouli salad from scratch. It's delicious. She'll be out in a minute." She leaned in and spoke in a softer voice. "So we have a minute to chat."

Flo and Emmi gathered closer.

Heather pressed her palms together. "I don't know how to explain it."

"Explain what?" asked Emmi, leaning forward, brows knitted.

"I hope I'm not speaking out of turn."

"Of course not. We're her best friends. What?"

Heather took a breath and pushed on. "Sometimes I see her walking around the house . . . and her lips are moving. As if she's talking to someone."

Flo and Emmi exchanged a worried glance.

"Maybe she's talking to Brett," Emmi suggested. "You know, part of the mourning process." She looked to Flo for confirmation.

"It's not all that unusual," said Flo. "No big psychological meaning. When you're used to sharing your life with someone for years, it's only natural."

"Except," Heather continued. "I'm not sure it's Brett she's talking to. I hear her say 'Mama.' And almost every night she goes out to sit on the dune outside. She sits there for at least an hour. Just staring out."

"That dune right out there?" Flo asked, pointing out back. When Heather nodded, her eyes flashed in understanding. "That's Lovie's dune. Lovie used to sit out there, too. It's a long, sad story."

"Not just sad," interjected Emmi. "It's beautiful, too. Romantic."

"Maybe," conceded Flo.

"Tell me?" asked Heather.

Flo took a sip of wine. "Back when she was a young woman, Lovie fell in love. Problem was, the man she loved wasn't her husband. She ended it, as she had to back then. There wasn't any support for women back in the day, and for a woman of her position to get a divorce would've caused the biggest scandal. She wouldn't do that to her children. It near killed her, though. This beach house was her sanctuary. Her salvation, even. Then sometime later we learned that Russell, the man she was in love with, had died in a plane crash. He was flying along the beaches on a survey and his plane went down." She turned and pointed to the ocean. "Right out there."

"That *is* sad," said Heather, hanging on Flo's every word.

"Tragic is what it was. Anyway," she continued after a breath, "Lovie used to sit on that there dune and remember him. Talk to him, too, if I recall. It was her special place."

Heather understood all. "And that's why Cara's there. To talk to her mother."

"And to Brett," Emmi added.

Flo took a gulp of her wine. "Cara said you've had dreams of her mother? Lovie?"

Heather nodded. "Not often. A few."

"And you smelled her perfume?"

"I smell jasmine," Heather said. "But that could be coming from outside."

"Could," Flo agreed, then skewered Heather with a look. "But Cara thinks it's her mama. From all you say, I think she's trying to get in touch with Lovie." She pursed her lips in thought. "I wouldn't mention your dreams if you get any more. Leastwise, not till she feels better."

"Cara's going to be fine," Emmi said in a bolstering tone. "We'll get her back to her old self."

"Honey," Flo said sadly, "Cara's never going to be her old self. Her life has changed. But we'll help her be the Cara she's meant to be now."

"I hope our plan works," Heather said. She'd invited Flo and Emmi over under the ruse of a simple dinner party, but the three women intended to use the opportunity to lay out a plan they hoped Cara would approve of for getting her outside and back into her life.

"Of course it will work," Flo said sotto voce. "It's got to. I have to hand it to you, Heather. You came up with the idea of luring her out of the house with places and things she loves while the rest of us were just wringing our hands."

"It'll be fun for us, too," added Emmi. "Cara and I talk all the time about places we want to go, things we want to see, but we always seem to be too busy. This gives me a purpose."

"It's a shame we need a purpose just to have a nice time," Flo admitted. "Sad state of affairs."

"As long as we get her out," Emmi said. "Okay, I'm taking her to Bowens Island for dinner tomorrow night. She and Brett used to go there all the time back when—well, you know."

"That's real nice, dear," Flo said. "It'll bring back pleasant memories for her. Next week I'll take her to Middleton Place. She's been yammering for years about wanting to go back to see the gardens."

They looked at Heather expectantly.

"Cara told me she fell in love with Brett on Capers Island. It was their place. So Bo said he'd take us there in his boat."

Emmi's face softened. "Oh, what a good idea! Capers is so romantic. That was their first time out together, even before they started dating. Then later . . ." Emmi looked to the ceiling and laughed. "Unless, of course, you want to know where they really fell in love. You'd have to find Brett's secret hammock." She raised her brows knowingly. "It was where he took all his girlfriends, I heard. But I doubt even Cara could find it on her own. He was pretty closemouthed about that place."

"Don't listen to her. Capers is perfect," Flo said with an amused roll of her eyes.

"I wasn't sure if we should go on the ecotour boat," said Heather. "I thought that might hit a bit too close to home."

"Good decision," Emmi said.

"The point is that we take her to places that have good memories of time she spent with Brett. And just get her outside." Heather sighed. "It's so strange for me to see Cara holed up inside when that person is usually me."

"We won't let that happen," said Emmi, and raised her glass. "Here's to the plan."

"Wait a minute!" Heather exclaimed. "It's bad luck to toast if I don't have a glass." She ran to the kitchen and returned with a glass of white wine. The three women clinked glasses.

"Starting without me!" Cara's voice sang out as she entered the room.

Startled, the women swung around, each hoping Cara hadn't heard their discussion. She was wearing her black shift dress again, and it hung like a sack on her skinny body. But her hair was washed and hung down to her shoulders in a thick, luxurious mass. Her dark eyes glittered at seeing her friends gathered together, the first sign of real life Heather had seen in her since she'd moved back into Primrose.

Emmi and Flo took turns hugging Cara and exclaiming how wonderful she looked. Heather took the moment to slip into the kitchen and pour a glass of white wine for Cara. Returning, she basked in the sight of the three women, heads bent toward one another, talking away. The love and attachment they shared was obvious.

When Heather had gone to Emmi and Flo's house earlier in the week to ask for their help, the women had come on board with boundless enthusiasm. They'd sat on Flo's back porch overlooking the ocean and sipped sweet tea while they came up with ideas.

It was then that Emmi had shared how Cara had been her rock during her heartbreaking divorce from her husband and the subsequent sale of her family beach house. Flo told the story of how Cara had saved her from having to sell her family home by arranging for Emmi to come in and buy it with the money from her divorce settlement. Flo stayed on as a roommate. Sharing the house had meant neither of them had to live alone or leave the beach where they both had spent their lives. The three women had been lifelong friends and had been through thick and thin together. Cara had always been there for them. And it was crystal clear to Heather that both Emmi and Flo would go to the moon and back for Cara.

Heather stepped forward and offered Cara a glass of wine, happy to see her more animated among her friends. Cara's husky laugh was music to her ears. They pulled together to bring dinner to the table—Greek lamb, tabouli, and a green salad. They lit the candles, turned on music—Heather had selected Ingrid Michaelson for the evening—poured more wine, and settled in for some good old vintage girl talk.

It wasn't long before they came to their favorite topic—sea turtles.

"It's busy out there," Emmi said with a gusty sigh. "We're having one of our best seasons in ages, but we're having a hard time keeping up. And that's with a full team. Now you're gone and I don't know what we'll do when Tee goes to Thailand next month. We'll be down two team members just as the nests start to hatch." She looked to Cara.

Cara looked down at her plate.

Flo picked up the baton. "Well, I'm getting too old to run around to multiple nests in the morning, and my eyesight isn't good enough at night to help y'all much. The spirit is willing but the flesh is weak. Mornings with the new nests and nights with the hatching nests. . . ." Flo shook her head. "Cara," she said, looking Cara in the eyes. "I know it's still soon after Brett's passing, but coming outside to the beach, getting involved again—that'll be good for you. Take your mind off your grief and give you something positive to do. Not to mention"—her blue eyes shone with appeal—"we really need you out there."

Cara ran her hand through her hair, her face agonized. "I don't know if I'm ready."

"Sure you are. And I'll help. I'll keep doing the paperwork until you say so. Does that make a difference?"

Cara looked up at her friends. "Tee's leaving?"

Hearing her wavering, Emmi nodded vigorously. "For a month. And next to you, she's our eagle eye for finding the eggs. Please, Cara. The turtle team needs you."

"Oh, all right," Cara said with a defeated laugh. "I can't win against all of you."

Emmi squealed and leaped from her chair to hug Cara. "Honey, don't you know? Just by you saying yes, we all won."

Chapter Twenty-One

I T FELT GOOD to be back on the turtle team. Walking the beaches every morning, searching for turtle tracks, answering calls from the volunteers who had found tracks themselves, all gave Cara's life renewed purpose. At night when one of the nests hatched and more than a hundred tiny turtles emerged from the sand, flippers waving, tumbling one over the other as they poured out en masse in a race to the sea, she felt each one of the hatchlings was her baby. She'd shepherd the hatchlings until they met the surf, keeping them safe from predators. That was where her protection ended, where land ended and sea began. Once the hatchlings crossed that border, they entered a world where she could not follow.

The days became weeks and August continued the unyielding, unwavering procession of ninetysome-degree days that was a southern summer. And the bugs were back in town. Whether it was the unusually warm winter, the excessive spring rains, or the pressing humidity of this summer, Cara had never seen bigger or more aggressive skeeters.

The turtle team was hit hard by mosquitoes and the tiny,

invisible sand flies they called no-see-ums, especially as they patrolled the nests at night. Bottles of repellent were passed around continually. On especially buggy nights when the armadas of insects relentlessly swarmed, some of the team waved the white flag and retreated. Cara, however, was what Brett had laughingly called "unattractive" to mosquitoes. She didn't know why some people were magnets and swarmed by bugs, while others, like her, were left alone. There were lots of theories—who did or didn't eat bananas, who drank beer, what color clothing someone wore. No matter the reason for her immunity, she counted her blessings.

She still couldn't sleep well anyway, so she was happy to take on turtle midwife duty at the beach on nights when nests were due to hatch. And on the nights when there were no expectant nests to keep her occupied, Cara sat on Lovie's dune. On this night, with no nests to watch over, Cara brought her knees to her chest and wrapped her arms around them, resting her chin on them.

Oh, how she missed Brett. Especially at times like this when the balmy breeze was not windy enough to toss sand in her eyes but was blowy enough to keep the bugs at bay and rattle the straw-colored panicles of the sea oats. They sounded like castanets. On a night like this when the moon was full and shone majestically in a sky littered with stars, while pinpricks of light on the shore below seemed to mirror the stars, Cara could feel his presence.

It was near midnight, and from where she sat it seemed the world was asleep. The lights were out in the wall of mansions facing the sea. She whispered a thank-you to the people inside who heeded the "lights out for turtles" message. Sea turtles emerged from the sand and followed that natural light home to the sea. Out in the distance, the sky and sea blended together into an inky blackness. This was how it had been for thousands—millions—of years when the moon and the stars were the brightest lights on the horizon. Today, electricity had changed that ancient formula. The brightest lights were no longer over the sea but shone in the streets and houses, in the ambient light of cities far away. The hatchlings emerged from the sand and followed their primeval instincts to run to the brightest lights. And if that light was artificial, they inadvertently scrambled away from the sea, their home, to their certain deaths.

That was how she felt, she thought. She'd hatched into this new world of widowhood and wasn't sure where to turn now for her own personal source of light. Lost without bearings, scrambling madly toward some unseen goal. She no longer trusted her instincts. She didn't know how to be alone. She was afraid to be the solitary swimmer she'd once been. Brett had changed that in her. She needed the companionship of her friends more than ever.

Even Heather.

Especially Heather.

Cara stretched out her legs and leaned back on her arms, lifting a handful of cool sand and allowing it to run through her fingers. When she was in this sort of pensive mood, sitting on her mother's dune, Cara felt each gentle breeze against her face as a caress from Brett. Closing her eyes, she heard the rhythmic rush of the waves against the shoreline as Brett's beating heart. She wished she could have just one more conversation with him, to ask for his advice about what she should do now that he was gone.

I'm here, she heard whispered on the wind.

Cara closed her eyes, accepting the voice, believing in it. Her mother had told her she'd talked to Russell on this small bit of sand. Why couldn't she talk to Brett? Even if it was her imagination, it brought her comfort.

"What's my problem with Heather?"

Your problem?

"Yes. She's been so good to me. So kind and thoughtful. She makes me a special energy drink in the morning, prepares a healthy meal at night. Cleans the house. She's a worker bee, always attentive. What's holding me back from feeling close to her? Is it because she's young?"

No.

"Why?"

You know why.

Cara shook her head with a sigh. "I don't. . . ."

Who does she remind you of?

"No. Don't say it."

The wind blew, a whistling in her ear that sounded like laughter.

"Okay," Cara said begrudgingly, sweeping away a biting ant with a swipe of her palm. "She reminds me of my mother."

Yes, the wind answered.

"But I loved my mother. I miss her terribly. Especially now that you're gone. Why did you have to go?"

Only the muffled roar of the gentle waves sounded in the night.

"I miss her comforting words. Her guidance." The words were like pinpricks of pain in her heart.

She is guiding you.

"No, she isn't! She's ignoring me!" Cara squeezed the sand resting on her palm to form a fist. "She's guiding Heather."

You're jealous.

"No, I'm not," she fired back—but even as she said the words, she knew she was lying. She *was* jealous of Heather. Sweet, generous, gracious Heather.

Yes.

But why was she jealous of Heather? Cara struggled with the question. The woman had given her no cause. Cara knew it wasn't only because her mother visited Heather's dreams and not hers. Or that Heather smelled her mother's perfume when she was uneasy and Cara could not catch the scent, no matter how doggedly she wandered the house. Cara put her elbows on her knees and rested her chin in her palms as she stared out into the vast darkness. And Cara knew.

Yes.

Cara knew why she'd been jealous of Heather. Her delicate appearance was not what troubled Cara, or the fact that she resembled Lovie. And neither was her sweetness or youth or even her connection with her mother.

Cara was jealous of Heather's passion. It shone in her eyes and sang in her voice. Her passion was the music she loved and the way her spirit danced when she worked. How many mornings had Cara awakened to find Heather already gone, hiking the beach with her sketchbook and gear? How often had she come running back into the house, jumping with glee, shouting, "I saw a piping plover!" or some other shorebird? Heather couldn't wait to get to her studio to dive into her work with a zeal Cara could only imagine. Cara watched her hunched over her paper, her hand moving quickly, creating a stunningly beautiful rendition from nothing. A miracle. And now that she was painting the final four birds, how many hours did Heather spend sitting at the easel, paint dripping over her, forgetting to eat, an expression of focus lighted by moments of ecstasy on her face?

Cara was jealous that Heather had found such passion in her life. As her mother had discovered her passion—the sea turtles. Cara knew a great emptiness in her soul. This passion, this fervor, this excitement for living was what she was missing in her life. It was the reason she'd felt untethered and lost *before* Brett's death. Why turning fifty had loomed large as an obstacle rather than a milestone.

Passion was the wind in her sails. The source of her imagination. She smiled. The bubbles in her champagne. She missed feeling that excitement when she woke up in the morning, eager to get started on some project. She missed those moments while taking a walk when a great idea would burst forth from the fallow ground of her mind, one that she couldn't wait to work on. What had Van Gogh said? *I would rather die of passion than of boredom.*

Cara rose and stretched, feeling the lateness of the hour. A slight chill was in the air. She slapped the sand from her pants and took a final, sweeping gaze at the sea. Far out in the distance she saw the slim line of lights of a ship heading out to sea.

"Good night, Brett," she whispered into the night.

Only the wind answered, whistling softly in the tall sea oats surrounding her.

HEATHER FELT A dramatic difference in Cara since she'd returned to the turtle team. Her skin, no longer pale and drawn, now sported a suntan that matched her renewed vigor. And she'd gained a few pounds that rounded out the sharp edges of her contours.

The same could be said of Cara's attitude. Gone were the sulking and depression, replaced by, if not happiness in the traditional sense, an acceptance of the change in her life and a willingness to move forward. Not to say she wasn't still struggling. There were good days and bad, and Heather knew from the light footfalls outside her door at all hours that Cara still wasn't sleeping well. But it seemed that walking every day on the beach, having a sense of purpose, taking over again as the team leader, filled Cara's time so she was no longer curled up in bed dwelling only on her loss.

Best of all, Cara had warmed up to Heather. Something had shifted in Cara, a lowering of her guard, a tincture of time to build trust, and now they talked freely to each other, laughed at each other's comments and jokes. They prepared meals together, invited Emmi and Flo over to dine, and went to their house as well. The doors were always open between the women's houses.

Emmi and Flo continued to take Cara out to restaurants, the theater, art shows, and such, according to the three women's plan. But in these final weeks of August, Heather had to remain at home and work. Her September deadline for the four completed shorebird postage-stamp paintings was fast approaching. She'd struggled to find the right approach to best present the personality of the three birds selected by the committee—the red knot, the American oystercatcher, and the semipalmated sandpiper. Being ultimately so small, the art had to have a big impact. She'd cast away at least a dozen paintings as unsuitable. Cara argued with her that they were perfect. Flo, in her succinct manner, told her she was plumb crazy and they were great. Emmi was supportive. She loved them all.

It was precisely at such times that Heather had to trust her instincts. If she sensed something was off, hers was the only opinion that mattered. She was never shy when it came to her work.

Yet, as time was running out, she felt the pressure mount. She worked long hours, slept little, and ate less. There was no more time for dawn walks on the beach or studying birds in their natural habitat. She was strictly in production mode, and every stroke of her brush counted. It was taking its toll. She missed being out on the beach at dawn, seeing the sun rise over the water. It was very spiritual, akin to going to church. Sunny or rainy, foggy or clear, she loved whatever manner of light she captured in her art.

To make matters worse, Bo had taken an extended job on Dewees, a small island off Isle of Palms. It couldn't be helped, he'd told her. He'd reserved these few weeks in August every summer. He had several jobs scheduled, including a big one he was nervous about, and he couldn't cancel now. Bo had returned to Isle of Palms to see her three evenings in the past week but, like Heather, he was under deadline to finish the projects before the homeowners returned and had to spend most of his time working. Everything seemed to be coming to a close so swiftly; it felt like her world was spinning. Not the best feeling for a woman prone to anxiety.

"I brought you some lunch," Cara said as she entered the studio.

Heather reluctantly turned from her painting of the sandpiper to see Cara carrying in a tray. Her face was pink from a morning spent in the sun, on the beach with the turtle team. She was still wearing her ISLAND TURTLE TEAM shirt, this one yellow.

"Thanks. Can I eat it later? I'm almost done."

"Just don't forget to eat. It's tuna salad. You shouldn't let it sit out too long." She set the tray down on the table and leaned over Heather's shoulder to study the painting. "Oh, Heather, well done," Cara said with awe. "You've captured the personality of our dear little peeps."

Heather studied the painting critically. The semipalmated sandpiper was a lot of personality packed into a small, chunky body. In her painting she wanted to show the short legs in motion, the way most people recognized the peeps as they played tag with the sea. She sighed and set down her brush.

"I think this one's okay."

"Okay? It's your best one yet. I love it," Cara crooned.

As though on cue, Moutarde began singing at the sound of Cara's voice. His clarion voice reached new heights as he perched close to Cara, his throat bobbing with passion.

"I swear, that bird is in love with you," Heather said with a much-needed laugh.

"I have that effect on spicy males," Cara quipped, but she smiled as she spoke and turned to make soft whistling noises to the yellow canary. Hearing the fuss, the other two canaries joined in, and the entire room was suddenly filled with song.

Her concentration broken, Heather wiped her hands on her painter's cloth and reached for the sandwich. She'd skipped breakfast that morning, fueled only by her power drink, and now she was starving.

"I don't know what I'm going to do after you leave," Cara said with a note of sadness. "I'm so used to the birdsong. Not to mention you," she added with a smirk. "I may have to get myself a canary."

Heather slowly finished chewing a bite of tuna salad on toasted multigrain bread as a thought took root in her mind. She rarely acted on impulse. Yet something about this felt so right that she couldn't stop the words from spilling out. She wiped her mouth, then said, "Cara, would you like to keep Moutarde with you?"

Cara's face stilled and her eyes widened.

"Only if you really want him, of course," Heather hastened to add.

"I don't know what to say," Cara said, a bit breathless. She swallowed. "This might be the time to tell you I've never had a pet before."

"Never?" Heather asked, surprised. "Not even growing up? Not a dog or a cat? Not even a hamster?"

Cara shook her head. "My father forbade animals in the house, and my mother was only interested in wild animals outside. And then I was always working. . . ." She turned and bent closer to the birdcage and began making soft kissing noises. Moutarde jumped from perch to perch, cocking his head and flirting with Cara with his shiny black eyes, all the while offering his questioning chirp. Cara turned back to Heather.

"Are you serious?" she asked hesitatingly. "You'd really give him to me?"

For a moment, Heather regretted her offer. She loved Moutarde. He had the most personality of all her birds. He was the first to greet her in the morning and the last to bid her good night. Yet the thought of leaving Cara all alone in a quiet house was unbearable. She couldn't stand to think that Cara would slip back into the abyss of loneliness. At least with Moutarde, she would have something to look after and care for, and in return Moutarde would fill her days with joyful song. She loved Moutarde—but she loved Cara more.

She nodded resolutely. "Yes."

"Oh, Heather. I'd love to keep him. You're sure?"

"I'm sure. He'd be brokenhearted to leave you anyway." Heather's face fell. "As will I."

Cara came to hug Heather. "Thank you," she said close to her ear. "This means more than I can ever tell you." When she stepped back, Cara said, "Do you have to leave, Heather? You know you can stay here."

Heather sighed. As the August days had worn on and the commission deadline drew ever closer, she'd become more and more aware that her time on Isle of Palms and at Primrose was all too swiftly drawing toward its end. "Cara, you know I'd love to. But I really need to go home. My father expects me, and he's already been so generous that I don't want to disappoint him. But I admit it's going to be very hard to leave. I can't even think about it or I'll break down in tears. I love it here." Her gaze swept the room. "I love this house."

Cara nodded and cocked her head to the side as though

contemplating something, then tucked a dark lock of hair behind her ear. "Do you still have dreams of my mother?"

Heather was startled by the question. She had been warned by Flo not to mention her dreams to Cara, but in truth, she hadn't had any more. She hadn't realized it until this moment.

"No," she replied honestly. Then she added, "I guess she knows I don't need her anymore."

"And the scent?"

Heather shook her head. "Whenever I smell jasmine, it's *you*."

Cara laughed self-consciously, acknowledging that she'd begun wearing her mother's scent.

"But Lovie is still here," Heather said in a serious tone, looking around as though she expected to see a ghost. "I feel her presence in every nook and cranny of this beach house. It's a calming presence. Serene. Like looking at a bouquet of fresh flowers." She hesitated, then asked Cara, "Do you?"

Cara's face grew solemn. "I do," she replied in a soft voice filled with quiet conviction.

Heather looked at her watch. "Look at the time. I'd better get cleaned up. Natalie should be here very soon."

Cara was immediately protective. "Are you okay having your stepmother visit?"

"Please. Don't call her my stepmother," Heather said with a feigned shudder. "She'll never be any kind of mother to me." She scowled. "But I have to be polite. She *is* married to my father."

Cara asked, her face half averted, "Why is she coming here? Alone?"

"My father is on a business trip and I suspect she's making an effort. I could hardly say no. She's not staying here, thank God. I don't think I could've handled that. For that matter, I doubt she could, either. She has never really liked me. Nor I her," she admitted honestly. Heather unconsciously began to wring her hands. "We aren't exactly on the best of terms," she added with a nervous laugh. "She let me know she has a hotel reservation in Charleston. I'm sure the city will be much more to her liking than the island."

Cara looked at Heather's clenched hands. "You don't have to do this alone. I know it's hard for you. I can hang around if you like. Be the obnoxious roommate."

Heather laughed at the very idea of Cara playing the obnoxious roommate. "You can tell I'm nervous?"

"Honey, you're coiled like a wire about to spring."

It was true. Heather felt her heart pounding just at the thought of having to chat with Natalie one-on-one. Cara's offer was certainly tempting—having her there would make things easier. She would be able to fill in the awkward moments skillfully. A voice in her head told Heather to accept the offer. There was no way she would be able to deal with Natalie alone without doing something stupid or collapsing into her nice-girl mode and agreeing with everything she said. But a newfound strength emerged and quieted the negative voice. She hesitated. Then she said something she'd never thought she'd say.

"Thanks. But I can handle it."

Cara lifted her brows and smiled approvingly. "All right, then." She turned and crooned to Moutarde with renewed spirit: "Oh, you sweet boy. I'm going to spoil you rotten."

Heather smiled as she faced her painting and looked at the bright eyes of the sandpiper on her canvas. This had been a summer of discovery. While her caged birds had shown her how to sing, outdoors the wild birds had revealed to her what it meant to be free. Heather felt a sense of knowing wash over her. One that left her skin tingling, her blood racing, her heart pumping with certitude.

Chapter Twenty-Two

HEATHER SHOWERED, PUT on a freshly ironed Lilly dress that she knew would please Natalie, and carefully applied some makeup despite the challenge her shaky hands posed. She sprayed herself with scent and, after a final approving glance in the mirror, went to the kitchen to set out a plate of fruit and cheese. Natalie didn't eat "anything white," as she put it, so most crackers were not acceptable to her diet. She was driving from Charlotte and had announced she would arrive in time to take Heather to dinner, so Heather figured she would just set out a small aperitif in case Natalie expected some pre-dinner drinks and conversation.

"Don't cook," Natalie had instructed on the phone. "Let me take you out. Pick out the best restaurant on the island."

Heather sat on the sofa reading a paperback romance to distract her while she waited, but the next half hour was exhausting as she tried to silence the critical voice in her head telling her this was going to be awful, that it was a mistake to let Natalie come. With every excruciating minute that passed, she felt her anxiety growing.

Natalie had told her five o'clock, and at precisely that hour the doorbell rang. Heather almost jumped out of her skin. She took a belly breath, then walked to the front door with smooth, even strides.

Heather fixed her smile as she opened the door. "Hello, Natalie."

Natalie was a beautiful woman in her late thirties. Her blond hair was trimmed in a severely chic haircut that accentuated her sharp cheekbones and slightly tilted blue eyes. Her dress, unlike Heather's shift, was expertly cut to reveal her toned and tanned body.

"Hello, Heather," Natalie replied with equal politeness.

Heather led Natalie into the living room where she had iced sweet tea and her platter of fruit and cheese waiting. Natalie followed her in, her head turning from side to side as she perused the house. She stepped into the sunroom where Heather's paintings and sketches covered the walls and were stacked beside the desk. Natalie walked past them all, pausing in front of the birds. They chirped questioningly as they always did when a person stood close.

"I see you still have your birds," Natalie said with a tight smile.

"Of course. Where else would they be?" Heather indicated the sofa, determined not to let Natalie's smarmy tone get under her skin. "Won't you sit down?"

Natalie returned to the living room and lowered herself gracefully into one of the two side chairs, primly crossing her ankles.

Heather offered her the platter. "Cheese and fruit?"

"We have dinner reservations at six, don't we?"

Heather colored faintly and set the platter back on the table. "Yes. At the Long Island Café. Very close by."

"I'll just have some tea."

Heather felt she couldn't do anything right as she hurried to pour. She handed Natalie a tall glass with a napkin.

"You're looking well," Natalie said. "You have great color."

"I've been on the beach nearly every morning doing my research."

Natalie took a sip of the tea. "How is your stamp project coming along?"

"Very well, thank you. I'm heading into the final stage. I'm almost finished painting the final four birds. Then I deliver them to the art director. She takes them to the committee, and I await their decision."

"And then you'll be famous, won't you?"

"Hardly," she said modestly. "No one ever knows the name of the person who created the stamp. But I will be proud, yes." She hated how nervous and false her laugh sounded.

"Now, don't be shy," Natalie said patronizingly. "Surely this accomplishment will open doors for you?" she pressed. "Present opportunities for your career?"

Heather smiled briefly. "Well, yes. Maybe. . . ."

Natalie put her glass on a coaster on the table. Moved it an inch to the right. When she straightened, she placed her hands in her lap. "Are you still planning on returning to Charlotte at the end of the month?"

"Yes, of course."

"But aren't you happy here? You seem to be doing quite

well living on your own. Your father mentions how proud of you he is all the time. We both are." She gave her a quick smile.

"Well, thank you," Heather replied, not quite sure what else to say. "Yes, I've been happy here. But my lease is up, so—"

"Would you like to extend it?" Natalie interrupted. "I've talked to your father, and he agreed that if you felt you needed—or wanted—more time, that could be arranged." She paused.

"Okay," Heather said slowly, unclear on where this was going but feeling like she was missing something. "How long do you two lovebirds want me out of your hair?"

Natalie didn't smile. "Indefinitely."

Heather knitted her brows. "What are you saying?"

Natalie straightened in her chair and looked at Heather with resolve.

"You're my family now. I only want what's best for you. I hope you know that," she began in a manner that sounded as if she had rehearsed the lines. "But I also want the best for your father. My husband," she added with import. "We've just begun our life together." She shifted her weight, her first sign of discomfort. "And if you come back, well . . . it'll change everything. You don't want to spoil your father's newfound happiness, now, do you?"

The question slammed into her. Heather felt her throat closing up and her heart began pounding while her brain screamed, *Run away!* "I, uh . . ." she stammered.

Natalie pushed on, taking advantage of Heather's frozen state. "I've spent my life focused on my career. And I'm proud that I've built a successful clothing business. I didn't expect to fall in love. But I did. I didn't think I ever wanted to marry. But . . ." She looked away for a moment and her face softened. When she turned back, she leaned forward in her chair, pressing her palms together as she made her point. "Heather, I love your father. Very much."

Heather snorted in an unladylike manner.

Natalie's eyes narrowed and she leaned back in her chair. Her lips thinned. "I know you think I only married him for his money. Frankly, when he first asked me out, that might have been true. But I fell in love with David, whether you can believe that or not. And your father fell in love with me." She spread out her palms as though to say, *There it is.*

Heather stared at her.

"Look, I know I have a lot to learn about being married. I may not be the kind of woman your mother was. The perfect homemaker," she said with a hint of disdain. "I know she was a very special woman. And that you miss her." She paused. "I'm not trying to take her place. To be honest, I never wanted children." She shifted her weight and said pointedly, "We're both grown women, only a few years apart. I'd love to have a relationship with you. But I didn't sign up for a daughter. And I'm sure you didn't sign up for a new mommy."

Heather was shocked. Insulted. "Who do you think you are?"

"I'm your father's wife."

An uncomfortable impasse followed. Heather sat numbly wringing her hands, looking out the window. How could she respond to that? Wife trumped daughter every time.

"Heather," Natalie said, drawing Heather's attention back. "I didn't come to argue. I'm not known for candy-coating my words," she added with a hint of pride. "Here's what I've come all this way to say. I know you're a good girl. Smart, talented. And your father's a good man. He loves you. He would never do anything to hurt you. I'm not the evil stepmother. But it's not good for us as a couple if you come back. So I'm asking you. You can move back to Charlotte if you'd like. But don't move back into our home."

"If I came home . . . I wouldn't bother you." She hated the squeak in her voice. Her inner voice shouted, *Why did you say that? It makes you sound weak. Like a little girl.*

Natalie looked at her as she would a child. "You know you're not the easiest person to live with."

"What?" Heather said on a gasp.

"You never leave the house! You're always there. How are we supposed to live our lives as husband and wife if you're always hanging around watching us? Or worse, competing with me for his attention. Heather, think. It isn't a good scenario for either of us. Surely you can't want that either."

Heather was truly shocked. She hadn't seen this coming. She was ashamed to be seen as an inconvenient adult child who still lived at home. Mortified to be in this position. Angry at her father for putting her in this position. Lurking in the back of her mind was the kernel of truth in what Natalie had said. After all, she *was* a grown woman living with her father.

She had no words. All Heather could do was nod, silently agreeing with her.

Natalie released a sigh of relief, then smiled. "Good. That's settled, then. I knew we could work things out between us. Just us girls." She sat forward and clapped her hands together. "Now we can start figuring out where you're going to live."

Heather glared at her.

"Well," Natalie said, looking at her watch. "We should get going if we're going to make our reservation."

Heather rose to her feet. "Excuse me, please." She felt light-headed and feared if she didn't leave the room she'd faint. Wouldn't that be the perfect swan song for this debacle? It took all her studied composure to hold her chin high and her back straight as she walked into her bedroom and softly closed the door. She leaned against it for a moment to catch her breath. Tears threatened to choke her and she swallowed them down, trying desperately not to cry. Not to be the little girl she'd just been accused of embodying.

Then she fell onto her bed and let the tears flow.

That was when she smelled the scent of jasmine surrounding her.

~~~~~

CARA STOOD BEHIND her bedroom door, seething. She'd heard every word of the conversation. Or rather, every word that Natalie uttered. Heather had barely made a peep, poor thing.

Cara strode to her mirror with purpose. She brushed her glossy dark hair, pulling it back into a severe chignon. Then she applied some fresh red lipstick. Her black shift dress was simple, but in such times, simplicity spoke of class. She checked her reflection in the mirror: her dark eyes glittered. This was the look she wanted.

"Hello," Cara said in an imperious tone as she strode into the room. "I'm Cara Rutledge. I own this beach house. You must be Heather's stepmother."

Cara was pleased to see the woman visibly cringe at the word *stepmother*.

Natalie quickly rose and moved forward to take Cara's extended hand. "Hello, I'm Natalie Wyatt. I didn't know Heather had company."

Cara let that slide. Natalie obviously didn't know that she'd moved back into the beach house. She smiled inwardly, realizing that Heather must be pocketing the rent that Cara was paying her. *Smart girl,* she thought admiringly.

"Are you one of the Charleston Rutledges?" Natalie asked.

Cara offered an indulgent smile. "Of course."

Natalie seemed impressed. "Such a wonderful family."

Cara only tilted her head and smiled politely. She was not going to make this easy on the woman. "You've only recently married David Wyatt, isn't that so?"

"Yes. We were married in May."

"Congratulations."

"Thank you."

"Where did you go on your honeymoon?"

"We took a short trip to Montreal. David loves the city," she added almost apologetically, as though making excuses for the lack of international glamour in their honeymoon destination. "We plan to take a more extended trip in the winter. To Australia."

"That should be exciting."

"I've always wanted to go there. David just didn't want to

do anything extravagant right off the bat, give me a chance to get settled into our new life."

"And Heather, of course. For her to get settled into her new life."

"Of course," Natalie said with a tempered smile. "He's such a sweet man."

"Yes," Cara agreed. "I only met David briefly, but even in that short time it was clear to me that he's a good man. A family man, devoted to his daughter."

Natalie's face shifted. She looked as if she'd just tasted the lemon in her tea. "He is."

"And she to him."

"Yes."

Cara let a short silence follow. "I couldn't help but overhear your conversation with Heather."

Natalie straightened her shoulders. "Yes, well, I thought it went quite well," she said stiffly.

"Did David know that you were coming to talk to Heather today?"

"He's in Europe," she replied vaguely, studiously avoiding the question.

"Ah, I see," Cara said. "I take that as a no." She paused. "I didn't think so. I can't imagine what he'd think of your suggestion to Heather that she not return home." She emphasized the word *home*.

Natalie narrowed her perfectly made-up eyes and gave Cara a hard look. "I don't see where this is any business of yours."

"Heather is my dear friend," Cara said in a steely tone. "Everything that concerns her is my business."

"I disagree," Natalie said. "This is a family matter, but, more important, it was two adult women coming to an agreement over something that has nothing to do with you." She turned and went to grab her purse. "And I don't intend to continue this conversation with you."

"I don't have much more to say," Cara said. She caught Natalie's gaze and held it—a move she'd used often at executive meetings at Leo Burnett. "I don't believe in candy-coating my words, either. We both know David Wyatt would be very upset if he was to learn what you did and said here today." She was satisfied to see unease spark in Natalie's blue eyes. "Don't worry. I'm not going to be the one to tell him. But I suggest that you do. So he'll understand why his daughter is not returning to Charlotte at the end of the month."

Natalie's face reflected her confusion. "I don't understand."

"I happen to agree with you that Heather should not go back to live in your house. It would clearly be a toxic environment, what with you being there. Heather's made tremendous progress this summer, and I would be very sad to see her slide backward."

Cara went to the front door. "Now, why don't you run along?" she said neutrally. "I'll make up some excuse for Heather. I trust she'll be relieved to see that you've left." She opened the door and Natalie walked slowly through, clearly perplexed as to what had just transpired. Natalie turned around at the threshold as if about to speak, but Cara cut her off. "Bye-bye, now," she said with a false smile, and promptly shut the door in the younger woman's face.

HEATHER HEARD A gentle knocking on her door. She groaned inwardly, inhaling deeply and fanning her face, hoping she didn't look like she'd been crying. She'd left Natalie sitting alone out there for too long. She couldn't bear to sit through dinner with her. It was time for her to get up, wipe her face, and have it out with her "stepmother."

"Heather?"

Heather shifted to her back, confused. That was Cara's voice. "Come in."

Cara stepped into the room. She looked very chic with her hair pulled back and bright red lips. Heather smoothed her own hair back from her face and pushed up into a sitting position.

"I know. I should get up," she said despondently.

"No, it's all right. She left."

Heather swung her head up. "She left?"

Cara appeared a bit nervous. "Yes. I hope you don't mind, but I couldn't help overhearing your conversation. And, well . . ."

"What did you do?" Heather asked, alert.

Cara shrugged. "I asked her if your father knew what she'd said to you. It was obvious he did not."

"Of course he didn't," Heather said. "You didn't threaten to tell him?"

"Not exactly. I suggested *she* tell him. Because you weren't going back home to that toxic environment. Then I asked her to leave." She looked warily at Heather, gauging her reaction.

"Why did you do that?" Heather asked, incredulous.

"Because you're my friend. And no one talks to my friend like that."

Heather saw the fierce loyalty in Cara's eyes, and a thousand thoughts flew through her mind. She'd lain there thinking of all the things she wanted to tell Natalie. Some of them real zingers. And now she wouldn't have the chance.

She cringed. But would she really have said them? Or would she have caved, as she always did with Natalie? Of course she would have. She always ran from confrontation. She liked to think she would have stuck up for herself in the end—but now she would never know. She felt like such a loser. Why couldn't she be more like Cara? Cara had stood up for her as a friend. And Heather loved her for it. That alone was almost worth all this drama. And the sense of relief that Natalie was gone and she wouldn't have to go out to dinner with her was so acute she nearly sagged back into her pillows.

She looked at Cara, suddenly feeling very tired. "Okay," she said.

Cara sighed with relief. "Okay," she repeated. She smiled at her. Then, lifting her head, she sniffed the air and looked quickly around the room. "Is that jasmine?" She looked at Heather with attention. "Are you wearing my mother's scent?"

Heather shook her head and released a small, knowing smile.

Cara's eyes widened, and she gasped with understanding. "I smell it, too!" she said with joy. "At last!"

Chapter Twenty-Three

THE STRUCTURE ROSE among the trees looking like it was part of them. Gazing at it, Bo felt his chest swell. He had never felt prouder of anything he'd made.

The tree house was a small space, only one room, nestled among the strong branches and foliage of neighboring trees. He'd built in bookshelves, nooks and crannies. Electricity, of course. The wooden walkway from the house's deck to the tree house was very Swiss Family Robinson. The small space was meant to be an office for the homeowner. Bo thought if it was his, he'd put a bed in there and dream of jungles.

It was the first tree house he'd built. He'd designed it with his friend, an architect, more than a year earlier. He spent months tweaking the plan, taking his time, until the owner was satisfied. Then he'd gathered a crew of builders he knew were up to the task. Getting the materials to the island required special handling. Finally, after a year of prep and planning, the whole team had come together. The project had been more fun than he'd expected: when it was time to finally construct the tree house, every single guy on his team was excited to see it take shape, as giddy as though they were young boys again watching their dream fortress materialize.

The first person he wanted to show the tree house to was Heather. In the span of one summer, she'd quickly become the most important person in his world. When he'd described the project—and his fears about it—she'd listened quietly, as was her style. Then she'd looked at him and said, "You're afraid because this isn't just another job. This project represents what you really want to do. It's creative. It's art. And it's important. If you succeed"—she smiled—"you've proved what you're capable of, not just to the world, but to yourself. Failing would crush that dream. I have faith in you. But you need to have faith in yourself. This is *your* baby. Own it."

And now it was done. He looked at his watch. She'd arrive on Dewees soon. He didn't want to be late to pick up Heather at the ferry. God, he'd missed her. The more time they spent together, the more he discovered they had in common. Music, art, humor, quiet times, dawns, sunsets, being outdoors. They were like two sides of one coin.

He loved her. He didn't question that. She was his best friend. She cared about his day, lifted his spirits when he was down, and celebrated his accomplishments. And she was always so grateful for anything he did, great or small, to show her how much he loved her, which let him know that she loved him, too.

Her loving him made him want to be a better man. To be worthy of her. He looked again at the tree house. He had to admit, it was nothing short of spectacular.

A knock on the front door of the main house drew his

attention. He hurried through the rooms and swung wide the door. A small blond woman wearing a crisp white shirt with DEWEES ISLAND embroidered on the pocket smiled warmly at him.

"Judy!" Bo said with surprise. Judy Fairchild was the island's mayor. She oversaw just about everything that happened on the small island, especially construction. She looked perky and cute and was easy to work with, but looks could be deceiving. She was sweet, but she was also as smart as a whip. Nothing slipped past her, whether it was about construction, sewers, or wildlife. The woman was a walking encyclopedia. She mixed it up with the guys, but always knew when to bring down the hammer. And he respected her for it. She was likely coming to take another look at the tree house, make certain it didn't violate any island codes. Luckily, Bo had been careful and precise.

Judy walked into the house and looked around, no doubt making sure he was keeping everything tidy. She felt a personal responsibility to the owners to check their property when they were out of town. Especially when work was being done.

"I expect you want another look at the tree house?"

"Actually, not this time," Judy said. "There's something else I'd like to discuss with you, if you have a minute."

"Why, sure, of course." He glanced at the clock, but saw he still had a good forty-five minutes before the ferry arrived.

Judy went to sit in one of the dozen chairs positioned around the long wood table. The dining room had large windows that offered tremendous views of the small lake outside. Bo spent most nights sitting on the screened deck just outside, staring at the birds as the sun set. Naturally, the sight always made him think of Heather.

He brought two glasses of water to the table and took a seat beside Judy. They exchanged a few words about the tree house. She checked on the schedule for equipment and trash removal by barge. Then she leaned forward and folded her hands on the table.

"You know everyone on Dewees thinks very highly of you."

Bo's brows rose. "Thank you."

"You're the number one request we get whenever a homeowner needs work done. That's impressive. We have a select list of names, and unless it's an emergency, most homeowners say they'll wait for you."

"I'm grateful for the opportunity," he replied modestly.

"You're good," Judy continued. "And dependable, honest. And you're the best carpenter I've ever worked with."

"You make me blush."

She laughed. "I'm not blowing smoke," she said with a wry grin. "It's just the simple truth. So . . ." She punctuated her statement by spreading her palms out on the table. "There's an opening for the island maintenance manager. It's a full-time job with full benefits. And it includes the caretaker's cottage. You'd be working directly under me. The board discussed it, and the decision was unanimous. We'd like to offer the position to you."

Myriad emotions rushed through Bo at this unexpected offer—surprise, but also pride, excitement, uncertainty.

His face eased into a grin. "I'm honored. Thank you."

Judy's eyes sparkled with pleasure. She reached into her

bag and pulled out an envelope. She set it on the table. "This is the formal offer. Read it. Think about it. Then call me." She put her fingertips on the envelope and slid it across the table to him.

With that Judy stood up. Bo jumped to his feet, almost tipping over his chair. He walked her to the door. Judy turned and offered her hand. When he took it, she gave it a firm shake and looked him square in the eyes.

"Bo. I hope you say yes."

~~~~

HEATHER HAD NEVER been on a ferry before. She waited at the Dewees Marina on Isle of Palms with six or seven other men and women until the captain signaled it was time to board. Most of the others knew the drill. They gathered their parcels, children, and dogs, most of them dragging carts filled with groceries, luggage, and purchases made in town. There were no shops of any kind on Dewees and these folks were prepared. Heather towed her small suitcase behind her down the well-worn wooden dock. Bo had been doing carpentry for several of the houses on the island. He still had another week's worth of work lined up after today. When he'd called to invite her to visit, she'd wondered if he'd heard the dejection in her voice. She didn't want to tell him about Natalie's visit on the phone or in a text. She felt at a loss about what she would do come September. The one person she wanted to talk to about it was Bo. With him she could open up and let her true feelings flow, good and bad, and not worry about being judged.

So she'd packed a bag and was on her way to a small island a ferry's ride away. She couldn't stay longer than a night, as she had to get back to painting her shorebirds with the September deadline looming. But for today, she was on vacation.

The captain stepped off the boat, waved his arm, and called, "All aboard!" Heather joined the queue of people, kids, and pets. Once on the boat she secured her luggage and signed in with the steward. The atmosphere was friendly. Everyone seemed to know one another. She heard exclamations of "Welcome back!" and "My, look how much you've grown!" directed at the children. There were plenty of seats in the airy space below, but she didn't want any of the friendly chatter directed toward her, so she climbed up to the top deck. Here only two other older girls sat shoulder to shoulder, ignoring the view and tapping their phones. The sun shone on her face and the morning air was ripe with the scents of salty sea and fish. Once everyone was seated, the captain started the big engines; they churned the water as the ferry slowly backed out of the dock, rocking gently. They slowly motored out of the no-wake zone. Heather leaned against the metal railing and played tourist, gawking at the scenery. On the right were huge houses with long docks, each with boats at moor. She looked at them, wondering who lived there, what they were like. Pelicans roosted on the jute-covered pilings. On the left was Isle of Palms Marina, which housed boats ranging from huge yachts to fifteen-footers to Jet Skis.

Once they were on the open water, the captain opened up the throttle and they sped through the Intracoastal Waterway. White-capped waves created wide wakes that rippled far across the expanse of blue water. Heather grabbed her hat and smiled, despite the melancholy that persisted. On either side of the ferry was a panoramic view of lush green landscape, wide blue water with snaking creeks that meandered through acres of sea grass, and everywhere were birds—flocked on shorelines, flying overhead, wading in creeks. Heather let go of her self-doubt and guilt at taking a bit of time off and simply enjoyed the luxury of time cruising the water. Yet she still felt her fingers twitch for a piece of charcoal to sketch the birds she was observing.

One simply had to see the lowcountry by water, she decided. It was the best way to experience the magnificence of the landscape and the wildlife. But it was more than that. During the journey across the water, she felt all the stress and anguish that she'd been holding in since Natalie's visit slide away, and she opened up her frame of mind. She spotted a pair of buoyant dolphins chasing the boat's wake, as though to punctuate her realization.

Fifteen minutes later she spied the white beaches of Dewees Island and, closer, the island's dock. The captain reduced speed and neatly maneuvered the ferry into the dock. The moment he cut the engines, the passengers rose en masse, grabbed their carts, bid farewell to friends, and disembarked.

She stepped off the boat and right away heard Bo calling her name. A jolt of excitement and anticipation coursed through her. Searching the small group of people waiting, she spotted the one man taller than the rest, his long, lanky form clad in faded brown shorts and a T-shirt. He lifted his arm in a wave, and she noticed he was carrying a dozen yellow roses. Her heart did a flip as she waved back, then made her way up the ramp, dragging her small overnight case.

It had been only two weeks since they'd been together, but it felt like much longer. Her attraction for him redoubled as she took in his handsome features and sky-blue eyes. Absence did indeed make the heart grow fonder, she thought.

He swooped in to wrap her in a hug. "I thought you'd never get here," he murmured as he held her close.

Tears threatened. "I missed you. I have so much to tell you."

"Me, too," he said, and kissed her. Then, stepping back, he grinned and said, "Later." He took her bag and extended his arm. "Your chariot awaits."

Bo led her to one in a long row of golf carts parked along the dock's walkway. Cars were not allowed on the environmentally concerned island, so everyone got around by golf cart, bicycle, or on foot. He lifted her suitcase into the back and smiled with eagerness, like a boy about to show off his favorite secret place.

"Do you come to the island during the rest of the year?" she asked as he fired up the cart.

"Yeah," he replied as he looked over his shoulder, backing out of the space. "I've been doing work for the homeowners here for more than five years. I come back and forth a lot, but every once in a while I get a bigger project that keeps me on the island for a couple of weeks, like the tree house." He swung around, his eyes gleaming. "I can't wait to show it to you."

"It's done?"

"Yep. I'm pretty proud of it." His eyes sparkled before he put on his sunglasses.

As they pulled away from the parking area, Heather looked at all the carts. "Now I know why you're so familiar with golf carts," she teased as she put her own sunglasses on.

Bo acted as Heather's guide to Dewees, pointing out the nature center and post office as they drove away from the dock. They bumped along crushed-shell roads under the lofty shade of trees. Heather was enchanted by the wild green landscape. Everywhere she looked there was something else to see. On one side of the road creeks meandered through lush cordgrass where egrets and a great blue heron were wading. Beyond was a glimmering lagoon where a large alligator sat sunning on a floating dock. Butterflies fluttered in the shrubs and songbirds darted from tree to tree. She felt she was in some sort of sanctuary. A safe haven not only for the wildlife, but for humans, too. Dewees made Isle of Palms look about as coastal as Charlotte.

Then, in a moment of clarity, she realized what was so different. Why she immediately felt so comfortable and at ease on Dewees—she didn't see any other people.

"Bo, where is everyone?"

"They're here. Somewhere. There aren't many people on Dewees. It's a private island, and the people who come here like seclusion. That's why you don't see houses from the road. They're all set far back in the trees. You're meant to feel like you're alone. And the community is committed to the environment. You saw that there are no stores or restaurants of any kind."

"Yes. But isn't that difficult? To get food, or go out to dinner or a movie?"

"It's a different way of life. People here know how to make it work. It takes a bit of planning. And there's the ferry—it goes back and forth on the hour. But for folks who live here, it's worth the effort. Dewees has its own pump and treated drinking water system and a state-of-the-art waste facility. Best of all, more than ninety percent of the island will remain wild."

Heather looked around at the great expanse of water, trees, and sky and felt at home. "I didn't know such a place existed."

Bo took her on a loop around the island, continuing to point out sights as they drove, then turned into a driveway half hidden from the road by a thicket of trees. A tall, dark wood house loomed, large but discreetly nestled in the trees.

"This is where I'm staying," he told her. He drove the cart up the wooden ramp to park under the raised house.

"It's gorgeous," she said, stepping out.

"You ain't seen nothing yet." He grabbed the suitcase from the back of the cart and stretched out his hand. "Come on."

The inside of the house, like the outside, was decorated in a cool palette of browns and grays. The furniture was wooden, modern, and sparse. There were a few paintings, modern as well, and very good. Clearly the owner wanted to create the sense of camping in the woods. She could see Bo living in such a place. It was a lot like him—spare, simple, hidden depths. They moved quickly through the house. It seemed Bo had his own agenda he was eager to get to. He led her to the screened porch. "This is it," he said excitedly, opening the screen door.

Heather gasped. Connected to the main house by a walk-way was a small, tidy turret hidden in the trees. It was both fanciful and solid. Something out of a storybook she'd read as a child. This incredible creation, she knew, revealed the heart and soul of Bo Stanton. Art, form, imagination—it had it all. She could picture him sitting on this porch for hours, staring at the trees, studying the depths and shadows, waiting to see the shape of the house emerge in his imagination.

"Oh, Bo," she said with a soft sigh. "It's like a dream I once had come true."

He slipped his arm over her shoulders and looked at the house with pride. "I had a lot of help," he replied with typical modesty, kissing Heather softly on the tip of her nose. "Let me give you the tour."

They traversed the walkway together, and Heather was relieved to find it as sturdy and strong as any deck. Once inside the octagonal walls of the tree house she felt like a hobbit. An intricately carved desk stood in the middle surrounded by bookshelves and windows. A single rope light hung from the wall over the desk. It was the fantasy *room of one's own.*

"I'd put a bed in here," Bo said.

"No," Heather said on a breath. "I'd paint in here."

After the tour they returned to the main house and made their way to the master bedroom, planning to change into their swimwear. It was another magnificent room. The tall windows had wooden shades, all lowered to steep the room in tea-colored light. The ceiling was dramatically pitched over a large teak bed intricately carved in a design that resembled monkeys. Crisp white linens dressed the bed, which was topped with lots of large white pillows. It was a room meant for relaxation—sleep, talk, reading, making love.

Heather finished removing her bra and, looking up, saw Bo standing across from her. He was naked, and it was clear that he wanted her. Looking into his eyes, she slid her panties down her legs and kicked them aside. It was just the two of them. The room was shaded and cool. Their bodies were warm. She felt she was in some dream world, deep in the jungle. Without speaking Bo reached out, beckoning her. Without hesitation, she stepped into his arms.

~~~~~

SO MUCH FOR PLANS, Bo thought ruefully. Neither of them wanted to leave the comfort of each other's arms and the great teak bed. He cradled Heather's head on his shoulder and traced his fingers along her silky hair.

Their passion spent, Heather's mood had clearly shifted. Her smile disappeared, replaced by an expression of sadness. She curled up beside him, her fingers holding tight. Bo pulled her into the crook of his arm and held her close.

"Baby, what's the matter?" he asked.

In a broken voice, she told him about her stepmother's visit. She left nothing out. Bo felt his anger rising, and fisted his hands when he heard Natalie's insults. But what disturbed him the most—actually hurt his heart—was hearing the defeat in Heather's voice.

"I couldn't stand up to her," she told him. "I wanted to, but I was afraid. All my words got stuck in my throat. I couldn't push them out."

Bo brought his finger to her lips. "It's all right. She broadsided you. You didn't see it coming."

"I didn't!" she cried with heat.

"So don't beat yourself up. She had four hours to plan what she was going to say to you. You had ten seconds."

Heather shuddered, releasing a long sigh. "You're right. I didn't think of that. I still can't believe she drove all that way here to tell me something she could have told me on the phone. At least if she'd done that, I'd have had the pleasure of hanging up on her."

A sigh rumbled in Bo's chest. He met people like Natalie all the time in his line of work. Entitled, seemingly fierce. Empty shells, he thought. All their energy went to buying more things. Any creative kernel they had was buried in all that stuff. So when they saw someone like Heather—all heart and passion and vision—they felt threatened. In their hearts, the Natalies of the world knew they couldn't compete with the Heathers of the world. They were not even in the same league. So they attacked.

He held Heather tighter. "I imagine she wanted to be sure she got her way. When your father left, she saw her opening. She figured she had to come meet you face-to-face for that."

"Maybe," Heather agreed, playing with the hairs on his chest. "But I hate that she could make me squirm. I thought I'd gotten past that." Her voice wavered. "To tell you the truth, I think what hurt the most was that there was some truth in what Natalie said. After all, I *am* a grown woman living with my father." She paused and her voice hushed. "It always hurts the most when it is true."

She was consoled by his gentle squeeze. "She doesn't want me to live with them—no, what was the phrase she used? 'You're not the easiest person to live with.' That was more than insulting. It was so hurtful."

He felt his anger surge again and made a dismissive gesture. "Forget her. She's obviously never lived with you."

"Thank you, honey." Heather laughed. "But neither have you."

"Well, as for that, I'm glad she came," Bo said.

Heather raised her head. "What?"

"Hell, baby, I don't want you to go back to Charlotte. You know that. It just took something like this to convince you that Charlotte isn't where you belong anymore."

She laid her head back against his chest. "But now I have to figure out what to do next," she said quietly. "Where to go."

Bo was silent. Then he turned onto his side, resting on his elbow so he could look down at her face. "Do you remember the night we first made love?" His voice was tender.

Heather's cheeks bloomed and she averted her gaze. "Of course," she mumbled.

"I'll never forget it," he said. "I told you then I'd always be there for you."

"I remember," she said, and reached up to draw his head down to her lips. Their kiss was soft, searching.

"Do you like it here?" he asked her when they finally broke apart.

"In bed with you?" she asked with a light laugh. "Yes. . . ."

He chuckled and shook his head. "I'm serious. I mean here. On Dewees Island."

"I've only just arrived. It's very remote. Isolated—which I like."

"So you like it?" he prompted.

She delivered a suspicious gaze. "I'm shy with strangers and love animals. For someone like me, it's a paradise. Why do you keep asking?"

He couldn't contain his grin. He stroked the hair from her face, wanting to catch her reaction. "Well . . . do you think you could live here?"

Her eyes sharpened and her fine brows drew together in thought. "I . . . I don't know. I might. Everything feels right here. The natural environment. The birds, of course. The philosophy." She worried her bottom lip, then said, "It feels like I belong here, in a sense. As if I've come home."

Her answer was more than he'd hoped for. He kissed her softly on the lips. "I hoped you'd feel that way," he said. He took a breath and said with a resigned smile, "Because I just got offered a job here."

Heather's lips parted as she sucked in a surprised breath. "A job?"

Bo shifted to sit cross-legged on the mattress. "Yeah. The Dewees Island board offered me a full-time job. As head of island maintenance," he explained, no longer able to hold back his excitement. "It's a really solid job. I beat out a lot of other great contractors. And I'd get a house! Well, they don't give it to me, of course, but it's mine to live in while I'm the manager. I'd take care of the island's property. But I'd be free to continue to do my private work when time allowed."

"That's—that's amazing," Heather stuttered, her face looking stunned. She brought herself up to a sitting position and wrapped the sheet across her breasts. Pushing back her hair from her face, she asked, "Are you sure *you* want to live here?"

Bo nodded with conviction. "I love it here. I always have. I just never thought I'd be able to afford to live here. It's everything I love most about a place. Beautiful surroundings and people who are committed to caring for them."

"Then you should take the job."

He grinned, appreciating her support. He expected no less from her. "I intend to."

She smiled then, and in her eyes he saw her pride in him. He felt a tightness in his stomach as he took her hands. "Move in with me."

Her smile slipped. "Move in with you? Here?"

"Yes, here," he said with a teasing smile. When she hesitated, he pushed on. "You aren't going to return to Charlotte. Your lease is up soon. You don't know where to go. It's an answer to your problem, isn't it? Move in with me."

She looked down and shook her head slightly. "I don't want to move in with you just because I don't have anywhere else to go."

"That's not the only reason I asked," he said. "You know that, I hope. I want you to move in with me because I love you. We might fight over how we squeeze the toothpaste tube, but we get along pretty well. It makes sense."

She didn't look convinced. "I don't know. It all feels too easy."

"Who says it has to be hard?"

She didn't respond.

"Do you love me?"

She nodded. "Yes, you know I do."

"I love you. That's all we need to know. The rest"—he shrugged—"we'll take day by day."

She still didn't say anything. He felt sucker-punched all of a sudden. "Heather, what's the matter?"

She seemed to be weighing her words carefully. "It's just . . . there's a lot to consider."

"Like what?"

"Well . . . it's all happening so fast. I thought I was going home."

"But you're not."

She looked out the window, her face clouded with indecision. "I want to talk to my father," she said in a soft voice.

"Your *father*?"

"I don't know if he'd understand my moving in with you."

"Heather, you're twenty-six years old. I don't think he'd be shocked."

"I don't want to upset him."

Bo was feeling frustrated now, blocked at every turn. "I didn't ask your father to move in with me," he said, trying to keep his voice calm. "I asked you."

Heather made a tsk-ing noise of frustration and shook her head. "You don't understand."

"You're right. I don't. Explain it to me." His voice was sharper than he'd intended.

"I'm not sure I understand myself!" she cried. "I'm overwhelmed. Stop pushing me, okay?"

Bo took a deep breath. He was scaring her, and she was retreating into her shell like a frightened turtle. Heather had a hard time with change. He had to remember her reaction to his first date offer. Her inner voices were probably screaming at her right now.

"I'm sorry, Heather," he said, making an effort to soften his tone. "Just . . . just tell me what's going on, and we'll figure it out together."

She took several deep breaths, calming herself down. "I'm sorry, too. I-I don't feel myself right now." She reached out for his hand and he took hers. "I'm not saying no," she ventured to explain. At last she looked up, and he saw the tears in her eyes. "If I say I might not be ready for us to move in together, you won't take it as another rejection? You won't get angry? Because I'm not saying no. I'm saying I don't know."

He swallowed his disappointment. "I understand that."

"I just need time to think about it."

He breathed out a long sigh. "That's fair." He played a moment with her fingers. "But promise me something."

"Okay."

"Promise me that whatever decision you make, you'll do it for you." He looked up to catch her gaze. "I know you, Heather Wyatt. You always try to make everyone else happy. Your father, Cara, Me," he admitted. "Without giving thought to what you really want."

She bit her lip and nodded.

He had to admit he was disappointed. He'd expected her to jump up and down with excitement at the prospect of living here with him. It had seemed a dream come true for both of them, and he'd thought she would be overjoyed at the timing, take it as a sign that it was the right thing for them to do. But when did Heather ever do the expected?

She looked forlorn sitting across from him draped in the white sheet. He stretched his long arms across the bed to clasp her waist and slide her into his lap. She slid her arms around his shoulders and nestled her head into his neck.

"Don't worry," he said. "Whatever you decide, I still love you, Heather Wyatt."

~~~~~

THE FOLLOWING MORNING they rose early to catch the first ferry. They were both quiet, even subdued. The previous night they'd feasted on shrimp that Bo had caught off the dock, then returned to the great teak bed and made love again. Heather lay in Bo's arms and they'd talked for hours about so many different topics. But they each were careful not to bring up again the one subject at the forefront of their minds. They'd fallen asleep as the sun lowered and risen with it at dawn.

The island's winged inhabitants were awake. The dawn chorus was raucous as unseen birds sang to one another as the sun broke the darkness. Already humidity moistened the air, hinting at the scorcher the day would become. They rode in silence on the trip to the ferry, bumping along the rutted road. Heather held the cart's frame to steady herself as she looked out at the waterway speckled with white ibis, willets, and other wading birds searching for their morning meal. As they rounded a bend in the road, Heather's eyes widened and her heart rose in her throat.

"Bo, stop!" she shouted, and almost leaped from the golf cart.

He veered to the side embankment and parked. Heather stepped gingerly through the tall grass.

The small lake mirrored the dawn, awash in its rosy hues. A faint fog hovered above the stillness, shrouding the scene with an otherworldly aura. Among the grasses were wading birds. One group was taller than the rest, walking on long red legs in a regal procession. Pastel pink and crimson, their feathers were the color of the dawn. Heather brought her fingers to her mouth to silence her gasps of delight.

"Roseate spoonbills!"

Bo came up behind her and put his hand on her shoulder. "I thought they were flamingos."

"A lot of people think that. But look at that spoonbill and you'll never make that mistake again. They're usually found in Florida." She sighed and said with awe, "And yet . . . here they are."

Bo tapped her shoulder. "We have to go if we're going to catch the ferry."

"I don't want to leave," Heather groaned.

"Hey, that can be arranged."

Glancing up at him, she saw the hope on his face. She turned to take one last look at the almost magical sight of pink birds standing against a background of summer green. As she watched, one roseate spoonbill stretched out its wings and seemingly stepped across the water and took flight. Heather put her hand to her heart as the long wings angled, giving the bird the appearance of a pink arrow piercing the gray-blue sky.

Chapter Twenty-Four

HEATHER RETURNED TO the beach house from Dewees with a renewed sense of urgency to complete her final painting. As predicted, the morning had heated up and was now downright steamy. Yet she felt rested after her mini break, freed from the shackles of Natalie's imposed doubts. Although she had a new worry to contend with now—Bo's request that they move in together, and what she planned to do about it.

The beach house was blissfully cool upon entering, and from the sunroom she heard her canaries singing. Pulling the key from the lock, she swiftly closed the door behind her, eager to see them. Last night was her first away since she'd arrived in May—it felt like ages ago. It filled her with pleasure that, crossing the threshold of Primrose Cottage, she felt as though she'd truly come home.

"You're back!" Cara called, stepping out from the kitchen, smiling with obvious pleasure. Cara was dressed in uniform. Her ISLAND TURTLE TEAM shirt, this one aqua, still had bits of sand and moisture. "I didn't expect you for hours."

"We both had to work. And that sure wasn't going to happen with us together," she explained, blushing. "He's just finished the tree house, and cleanup must be done before he begins his next project."

"A *tree house*?"

"Not just any tree house." Heather launched into an exuberant description of Bo's masterpiece, sharing photos from her phone, feeling pride at Cara's impressed expression.

"He sure is talented, our Bo," Cara remarked, returning to the kitchen. "And so are you. You two make a great couple. Hey, listen, I'm parched. Just finished moving what we think is our last nest of the season. I made a batch of sweet tea. Want some?"

"Love some."

"I made some raisin pecan toast, too. It's organic whole wheat," she added, and Heather smiled, knowing that extra bit of information was for her benefit.

They poured sweet tea into tall glasses filled with ice and carried them along with a plate of toast to the table.

"I know you were gone just a short while but somehow you look better than when you left," Cara observed.

Heather laughed and picked up a piece of toast. It was still warm with melted butter dripping down its sides. "I feel better," she acknowledged. "I needed to get away. It's amazing how a little distance can give so much perspective. Sometimes a day can feel so much longer."

"Sometimes a day can feel like forever."

Heather skipped a beat. "Agreed." She bit into her toast.

"I'm worried about Moutarde," Cara said. "When I went to feed them this morning, I found feathers everywhere. In fact, all the birds seem to be losing their feathers. Is it something I did?"

"Lord, no. It's normal. They're molting."

Cara's eyes widened. "Molting?"

"That's when they replace all of their feathers. Some two thousand of them. It's normal. All birds molt. Imagine wearing the same suit of clothes all year—it would get pretty worn. The canaries have been molting for a few weeks and will continue till fall. You just haven't noticed because I'm such a good roommate and tidy up after my pets. Don't look alarmed," Heather soothed with a light laugh. "I'll write you a list of instructions before I leave. I have some books on caring for birds I can give you, too."

Cara screwed up her face. "You're still planning on leaving, then?"

"September first is around the corner. I don't know where I'm going yet, but I've got to go somewhere. Time for me to shed my feathers and move on, too."

"Please tell me you aren't going to Charlotte."

Heather looked at her glass, considering her answer. "I'm not going back home, that's certain. But I haven't ruled anything out." She looked up and suddenly was very glad to have Cara as her friend. She needed someone to talk to now. A girlfriend to whom she could spill all the details and her private thoughts.

She leaned closer to Cara. "I've got to tell you—Bo just got offered the most wonderful job on Dewees. He'll be the new maintenance manager."

Cara leaned back in her chair, her mouth open. "That's news!"

"And it comes with a caretaker's cottage on the island."

"Really! Amazing. I'm so happy for him." She paused. "But how do you feel about that?"

"There's the ferry, of course. And he has his own boat."

"Oh, true, true."

"And, well . . . he asked me to move in with him."

Cara's expression shifted from joy to wide-eyed concern. "Move in with him?"

Heather nodded. "It's an option."

Cara shook her head decisively. "It's too easy."

Heather frowned, remembering that she'd said the exact same thing when Bo had presented the idea, but somehow coming out of Cara's mouth it sounded wrong. She took a long swallow of her tea. "It could work."

"Someday, maybe. Not now."

Heather found Cara's conviction mildly irritating. "Why not now?"

"You haven't known him that long, for starters."

"We've been inseparable since June, Cara. That's a long time."

"Is it? For someone, shall we say, unaccustomed to dating . . . maybe it does seem like a long time. But beyond that, you've only just moved out of your father's house. This was your first foray into living on your own. Why rush into another living situation where you're being taken care of? Isn't that what Natalie said that made you so upset?"

"I haven't been taken care of. I've been living on my own all summer," Heather countered.

"Your father is paying your rent. I don't mean to sound harsh, but let's call it what it is."

Heather quietly fumed.

Cara pressed on. "You've come so far this summer. Don't you want to be independent? You don't need to be in another position where you're being forced into making a decision, much less a commitment." Cara paused, then said, "My father was a cruel man. He didn't like strong women and he scorned their opinions. When I was young, I thought my mother was weak. But she was determined to keep the beach house and did, despite the fierce pressure my father, and later Palmer, exerted to take it away. Because of the household I grew up in, I was equally determined never to lose control over my destiny. I never depended on a man to provide for me. I swore no man would ever lord over me. Heather, this is your time to see what's really out there. You're going to regret it if you don't."

Heather shook her head lightly. "Cara, you forget. I love him. I'm not being forced into a decision. He made an offer and I'm thinking it over. It doesn't have to be forever. Maybe just for right now."

"If you do really love him, you should take your time and not rush it. The relationship needs time to grow. I'm sorry, but what you think love is sounds an awful lot like a summer romance. Real love takes time. And y'all just aren't there yet." Her eyes glittered with intent. "Here's what you need to do. . . ."

Heather sat back in her seat, silent. She felt like she was being presented with one of Cara's marketing pitches.

"Move in with me for real! Here's why. One, you like it here. Two, the rent will be affordable." She winked. "Three, you have a great roommate who cares about you. Four, I really want you to stay. I need you, too. We do pretty well together, don't we? You have your workroom all set up, and the birds love it here. You're settled. If it ain't broke, don't fix it."

Heather felt the power of her persuasion. Cara made it all sound so simple. So logical. Yet something didn't sit right in her gut. Her instincts tingled.

"And you can continue to see Bo as much as you wish," Cara concluded. "After all, he has the boat, right?" She smiled and lifted her glass as though in a toast.

Heather picked up her glass and looked at it, clenched in her hand, the ice cold against her palm. She felt frozen. "That all sounds really nice," she said in a soft voice.

"I think it will be great," Cara said with enthusiasm.

"Uh, listen, I'd better get to work," Heather said. She rose to her feet, shaking. "That final painting has to be in the mail by Friday."

"Sure. Good luck with that." Cara pushed back from the table as well and squeezed Heather around the shoulders, oblivious. "I'll make dinner! Seared ahi tuna and a grapefruit salad sound good to you? I'm so excited."

With a smile still frozen on her face, Heather turned and walked away.

~~~

HEATHER PUT ONE foot in front of the other making it halfway across the living room when she heard her canaries chirping. The molting season was a time birds were weakened, lethargic and quiet. So it was a special treat to hear the sweet sounds. She changed course and went to stand by the three large cages. Her presence delighted the little birds. They jumped from perch to perch, tilting their heads to look at her with their shiny eyes. Moutarde was deepest in the molt. A few long wing feathers lay at the bottom of his cage. Pavarotti's feathers were scruffy, as if he'd been in a fight and lost. The tiny pinfeathers on Poseidon's head made him look like he'd been given a buzz cut. Below the cages feathers littered the floor like snowflakes. The old feathers were being cast off, making room for the new.

"What a shaggy group we are," she said to them with a gentle smile. She went to get a bag of flaxseeds and went from cage to cage offering each bird a pinch. She sang softly and talked to them. Poseidon came to the end of his perch closest to her and chirped his questioning tone. Delighted to hear his voice, Heather stepped back and called his nickname: "Hey there, Posey. How are you feeling?" After three chirps, the little white bird let loose with a melodic song. It was softer than usual. A brief serenade, but rich with water notes.

Heather heard the song and felt a surge of joy. It was especially rare to hear a canary sing during the molt, and thus all the more special. *Oh, little bird*, she thought. *You have no idea how much I needed to hear your song today.*

Inspired, or possibly not to be outdone, Moutarde and Pavarotti came to their top perches and began to sing as well.

Heather closed her eyes and listened to the soft music. The melody soothed her and transported her mind to that place she went when she was tapping into her creativity. She knew this place well. It was where she went when she painted.

Where she got her best ideas. She couldn't force them. She had to mentally let go so her mind was open.

In the beautiful song of her canaries she heard a warning note. *Pay attention*, the notes told her. *Listen!* Not to Natalie or her father. Not to Cara. Not even to Bo. For once she had to listen to herself. She'd been asking all the wrong questions. What did everyone else want her to do? This was a turning point in her life. The question she had to ask herself was, what did *she* want to do? Bo's words came to mind: *Promise me that whatever decision you make, you'll do it for you.*

She looked again at her birds. They were quiet again, sitting on their perches, watching her in all their scraggy, molting adorableness. Waiting for her next move. Heather had been a caged bird for most of her life, her song muted by depression and anxiety. She had things she'd wanted to say, but always she'd said nothing. She never wanted to hurt anyone's feelings. But in the end, she hurt herself.

"I hear you," she said to her birds. "It time for me to shed all my insecurities and fears. Let them fall to the ground. It's time for me to find my voice and fly."

Heather knew what she had to do. She felt suddenly free, as though a great burden had been lifted from her shoulders. She hurried through the living room and stopped before the table where Cara sat working on papers.

Cara looked up from her papers. Her face was open and curious.

"Cara, I'm sorry to disappoint you, but I'm going to move in with Bo."

Cara's face registered surprise. She set down her pen. "But we just agreed—"

"No, we didn't agree. You told me what you wanted, and I listened."

Cara seemed to recover slightly. She pushed back her chair and stood up. "But, Heather," she said in a reasonable tone, "this is a terrible idea. You have to be sensible. Is it money? I know you don't want to take more money from your father. I applaud that. You don't have to pay next month's rent. I've got you covered. The last thing you should do is make your decision based on money."

"My decision has nothing to do with money. It couldn't be further from that. I'm making my decision based on love."

Cara sighed. "It's not that easy, Heather."

"Why does it have to be hard? Isn't love supposed to be easy? Cara," she said, her voice rich with emotion, "I love him. He loves me. What else do I need to know? You told me that one summer isn't long enough to know. You fell in love with Brett in one summer, and married him. I'm just moving in with Bo!"

Cara turned her head. When she spoke her voice was lowered. "What if it doesn't work out?"

Heather shrugged. "Then I move on. I still have my talent. My life. You're the one who told me not to live in fear. I'm listening to you. If I don't act on my instincts, then I'm afraid to act on what I know is right. And this is right. I feel it in my heart. In my soul. I know what to do."

Heather paused to look out the window. The palm tree was gently waving its bright green fronds against a brilliant blue sky. The ocean sparkled in the sunlight like diamonds. She turned to Cara again. "I've got to go."

"Now?" Cara asked, once more surprised.

Heather nodded. "I've got to tell Bo."

"You've only just got back!"

Heather couldn't stop the grin that spread from ear to ear. "I've been waiting my whole life to make my own decisions. Now I have—and I can't wait another minute."

She turned to leave, then spun around to face Cara who stood staring at her, eyes wide.

"Thank you," Heather said sincerely. "Thank you!" She turned again and flew back to her room to pack.

~~~~~~

CARA WAS DUMBFOUNDED. She strode toward Heather's room with long, purposeful strides. Their conversation was far from over. Cara had to convince Heather to stay at the beach house. She *needed* her to stay. She couldn't be left alone. She reached the bedroom door, lifted her fist—but couldn't bring herself to knock.

Of course she could say none of these things. All these reasons were because of what *Cara* wanted Heather to do, not what she truly felt was in Heather's best interest. She brought her palm to her head and pressed hard. Heather was right. She had to make the decision that was best for her. And Cara had to let her.

She turned away and walked back to her chair and slid down onto the wood. She folded her hands on the table and waited.

She didn't have to wait long. Heather opened the door to her room and emerged in a flurry of motion. Once again she dragged her travel bag behind her. The wheels made a whirring noise as she hastily crossed the floor toward the door.

"Heather, wait," Cara said, rising and going to meet Heather by the door.

Heather looked at her. She was wearing a glow of happiness. But her eyes were wary.

"Good luck," Cara said. She saw Heather's expression shift to relief, and in a rush the two friends hugged.

"Cara, I'll be back. I just have to go tell Bo," Heather murmured into her shoulder.

Cara nodded almost imperceptibly, but enough to let Heather know she understood and supported her. "Be happy, sweet friend."

Heather squeezed her tight. "I will."

Chapter Twenty-Five

THE FULL MOON illuminated the beach like an amphitheater. Smooth and glistening shells and bits of stone reflected the light, twinkling like earth stars. On the ocean, white ruffled waves stretched farther up the beach as the tide rose.

Cara sat on Lovie's dune and gazed out at the sea as she did most nights. Her head was filled with images and memories of the summer she had fallen in love with Brett, brought to the forefront of her mind from her earlier conversation with Heather. She smiled ruefully. It *had* been only one summer. . . . At that summer's end, Cara had known without a shadow of doubt that she loved Brett. She could not see her life without him. She hadn't thought twice about giving up her career in Chicago to stay in the lowcountry with him.

Who says it has to be hard?

She laughed to herself. Love wasn't hard, she thought. Losing love was.

Over the past month, her friends had taken her back to places that held happy memories of her and Brett. At first the memories had left her heartbroken. But time, that all powerful healer, had allowed her at last to remember Brett without the stabbing pain of bitterness, sorrow, or regret. Those feelings would return, she was sure of it. Grieving was a long process. She was grateful nonetheless for moments of serenity and, dare she say, joy, remembering the beautiful times they'd shared. She dreaded thinking what her life would have been like had she never met him, loved him, and spent the most memorable ten years of her life with him.

The evening breeze drifted across the beach. The long hot days of summer were ending, and all that was green would soon turn to gold. She drew letters in the sand with her finger: B-R-E-T-T.

Brett had been the great passion of her life. Loving him was unlike anything else she'd experienced before or since. Looking back, she saw their life together as a gift—a brief few years stolen from time. And now she had to accept that time was over. She would hold the memories of their love close for the rest of the days she was given. But for now, she had to move on. Heather, for all her youth and inexperience, had seen her path clearly and chosen to follow it. She was inspiring. Could Cara do any less?

She'd given the subject of what to do next a great deal of thought. She was fifty years old. Not young any longer, but certainly not old. As Brett had told her, she had twenty, thirty or more years left to live. In that time, she'd like once again to have something of her own. To do work she cared about. Not for success or money . . . Of course, she needed to find a way to earn dollars. And soon. But the pursuit of wealth would not inspire passion. If she was one of the very lucky, she would be passionate doing something she was paid to do, but would prioritize the passion above the dollar sign. Brett was the first example that came to mind. Heather was another. Neither of them got rich from their work, but they worked from morning till dusk and enjoyed the time spent in between. Life didn't get much better than that, did it?

Cara had loved her work in advertising, she realized. Developing ideas, writing copy, driving her ideas home to a boardroom full of clients. The flow of adrenaline, the thrill of the chase, rising to the challenge, deadlines, decisions—she missed all that. It was part of who she was—a part, she realized with sudden clarity, that she'd tried to squash for quite a long time.

She exhaled slowly. Ideas and thoughts began batting about in her head. New plans and possibilities . . . Suddenly Cara jerked her head up, her gaze narrowed on the water. It couldn't be, she thought, even as she leaned forward, squinting, alert. The dark shadow moving in the surf was large—much too large for a horseshoe crab. It could only be one thing. A loggerhead!

Cara remained stock-still on the dune; she didn't move a muscle as she watched the turtle inch her way out of the surf onto the beach. The loggerhead waited there, sniffing out the territory. If there were people walking on the beach, dogs, coyotes, any disturbance on the sand, Cara knew that the turtle would pivot and return to the safety of the sea. Coming ashore was an exercise in instinct and courage. The loggerhead had to leave the sea—her home where she was strong and graceful—and enter a foreign world on shore to labor awkwardly against gravity under the weight of her carapace. She would not risk the hard, plodding trek across the beach to the dunes to lay her nest unless her instincts gave her the green light.

Cara's first thought was of Heather. She'd told Cara several times how much she hoped to see a sea turtle. Catching one as it came ashore was a matter of luck. And God's good grace, as Lovie would have said. But Heather was gone to Dewees.

Cara didn't dare move lest she spook the turtle. The shadowy bulk moved forward. Her flippers stretched out to drag her body forward, and then she paused, catching her breath. Every few steps the turtle stopped again. She made good progress up the beach, inching her way straight to the base of Lovie's dune.

It can't be a coincidence that the turtle came tonight, to this dune, she thought with wonder. Cara smiled tremulously at the idea that the turtle had come right to her, as though predestined. *Thanks, Mama.*

This turtle was a big girl, a wise and experienced mother who'd been nesting on these beaches for many years. It being August, this wasn't her first nest of the season, either. It might even be her third or fourth. Likely her last. After tonight's labor, she'd return to the sea and a well-deserved rest.

The turtle began moving again. Cara could hear the flippers scraping the sand. Hidden behind the sea oats, she crouched and watched in awed silence as the turtle scooped up a flipper-full of sand, then another, again and again for almost an hour until she'd finished digging her nest. Then silence.

The moonlight lit up the night and Cara could readily see the majesty of this ancient ritual. She quietly slunk back from the front of the dune, then scooted around beachside to get closer. It was said that once a sea turtle began laying her eggs, she went into a kind of trance and was unlikely to stop until her last egg was laid. Cara found a spot far enough away not to distract the turtle, but close enough to see the white, leathery eggs fall into the nest. Her shell was dusted with sand and pocked by a few barnacles, trophies from thousands of miles of swimming.

She thought back to the first time she'd witnessed this event more than ten years earlier. It was a night much like this one, balmy with a bright moon. Lovie had been sitting on her dune and spotted the turtle coming ashore. She'd run to fetch Cara and bring her recalcitrant daughter out to the beach. Lovie had known then that Cara needed to see this.

And Cara believed her mother had somehow guided this turtle to her tonight because she knew her daughter needed to see it again. To be reminded of the continuity of life. That death followed life and life was renewed once again, over and over with the steadiness of the seasons. The memory of that night with her mother had been her touchstone through many difficult times since. Cara knew this night would, as well.

The turtle steadfastly laid egg after egg into the nest. While she labored, great streams of tears flowed from her eyes. Lovie had called them "a mother's tears." Cara had to take her word for it. She was not a mother. She never would be. She'd come to accept this.

But she was a woman. Her feminine intuition understood fully the turtle's sense of duty as she risked everything to lay her eggs. She identified with her maternal strength of purpose as she carefully, one flipper of sand after another, covered her nest, then flipped sand into the air to camouflage the next generation from predators. And when her nesting was finished, Cara comprehended the mother's regret as she turned away from her young, as all mothers would one day, to begin the long, lonely journey back to the sea, never to return.

Cara rose to her feet to walk a safe distance behind the turtle. The turtle stopped frequently, gulping air, exhausted from the arduous night. Determinedly she moved toward the sea, scraping the sand, dragging the burden of her shell. At last the turtle reached the first touch of salt water as the lapping waves slid up the sandy beach to greet her. She raised her head, sniffing the salty air. Above, the moon spread a golden path across the sea, as though guiding her home. She moved quicker now, with renewed energy.

The turtle never looked back. She plowed forward with fresh resolve into the first wave. The black water washed away the sand, revealing the glistening, burnished brown shell illuminated by the mother moon. With the next stroke of her great flippers, the turtle was swimming. In that instant she was transformed from a plodding burdened beast into a creature of grace. Buoyant and free from the drag of gravity, she swam farther out to sea, her head in the air. Cara watched, hands at her lips, tears in her eyes. One final breath, and the turtle slipped beneath the darkness of the sea.

Cara stopped at the water's edge. The sea was warm on her toes and swirled around her ankles. So inviting. But she dared go no farther. This was the sea turtle's home. Not hers. She stared out at the sea a little longer, hoping she might catch one more glimpse of the turtle. But she was gone.

Cara smiled then and felt a great rush of gratitude to her mother.

Mama, I see what you were trying to tell me, she thought. It was time for her to be more like the sea turtle she'd been named after. To be resilient in the face of tragedy. She had no more time to waste on self-pity. This was her journey across the sand. She was, like the sea turtle, once again a solitary swimmer.

She made her way back across the beach toward home. Overhead the stars winked. Cara had her eyes cast forward. She didn't see that, behind her, her footprints intermingled in the sand with the tracks of the great sea turtle until human and animal tread became one. A single ephemeral mark on the sand that couldn't be told apart at all.

Part Four

RELEASE

Barbara J. Bergwerf

BROWN PELICAN

Pelicans are sea birds and some of the largest and most easily recognized birds found on the East Coast of the United States. Brown pelicans are gray-brown birds with yellow heads and white necks, and characterized by their long bills with a unique underlying throat pouches. They feed by diving into the water from as high as sixty-five feet, but contrary to common belief they do not become blind from the impact. After nearly disappearing from North America in the 1960s and 1970s, brown pelicans made a comeback thanks to pesticide regulations.

Conservation status: *Least Concern *State wildlife action plan high priority*

Epilogue

SUMMER WAS OVER. In the lowcountry, children were once again ensconced in school, the sea turtles were off swimming in the ocean, and the new crop of fledglings had flown the nest and joined the adults on the great migration south. Throughout the lowcountry the skies were filled with flocks of birds.

For six brown pelicans, however, the journey was only about to begin.

Heather had joined Bo among the ranks of volunteers at the Center for Birds of Prey. Her commission on shorebirds was finished. Two of her paintings had been accepted and would someday grace Mr. and Mrs. Citizen's letters—American oystercatchers and semipalmated sandpipers. She'd submitted her proposal for wading birds and seabirds, and the response had been surprisingly enthusiastic—so much so, in fact, that she'd received word of her second commission! And the first bird she would paint was the brown pelican.

Heather was partial to the pelican. It was an elegant bird

with its oversized bill, and a masterful flier. Who didn't thrill to see squadrons fly above the water in formation? Or their stunning headfirst dives to catch fish? She and Bo had rescued dozens of pelicans in the short time she'd been a volunteer. Many of them were juveniles who'd never caught on how to fish. *Failure to thrive* was the diagnosis. Emaciated and caught in a downward spiral, many of them didn't make it, although the center did all they could for them. Only 30 percent of pelicans survived their first year. But the good news was that there were three here today that had.

She looked across the beach at the six large crates spread out in a straight line. A volunteer from the Center for Birds of Prey stood at each crate, waiting for the signal. Bo was one of them, framed by the shrubby maritime forest of Sullivan's Island and the brilliant September sky overhead. She smiled and waved. The sight of him still caused her heart to beat faster. The juveniles needed to be released to a flock of birds that would mentor them. Even the adults would have a better chance of survival if they joined a flock. Pelicans were exceedingly social, another reason she loved them.

Among the birds, three adults had been rescued from fishing gear entanglements—the only ones among many such birds brought in that had survived. Including the pelican Heather had rescued. That was the bird Bo was standing beside. Naturally they were partial to this pelican. There had been some iffy moments in his healing process. The fishing hook had dug deep. Pelican wings were difficult to heal, and their little guy had required a lot of physical therapy to stretch out his wings fully. Heather was worried whether he'd actually be able to fly today.

Heather waited near the water. She was part of the perimeter guard for the release. Higher up on the beach by the dunes, a small group had gathered to watch the release. Heather recognized some of them, and doing so gave her a strong sense of belonging. These were her neighbors, part of her new community. It was easy to spot Cara—taller than many of the other women, wearing a crisp white shirt and a red ball cap. Beside her were Emmi in green and Flo in a turtle team shirt, even though turtle season was done. She was talking to the charming older woman Heather had met that special night at the dock. Miss Marietta. Six or seven other men and women stood waiting. They'd been lucky enough to be walking the beach at the right time. Heather smiled and waved at them, especially the three children who stood, hands clasped at their chests and hopping up and down, excited to see the "big birds."

Prominent among them was her father. David had driven down from Charlotte after receiving her invitation to witness the release. Though they both knew he had come to check out Bo and see their cottage. He had come without Natalie.

She looked to Bo and her chest swelled at seeing him lift his hand and give her a thumbs-up sign. Nothing compared to the pride she felt in herself. She'd mastered her fears. She'd learned how to treat herself with kindness and compassion. And she believed she was worthy of being loved, just as she was. Bo proved that to her every day in many ways. She smiled broadly and returned the thumbs-up. Looking beyond, she saw Cara watching her, arms crossed and grinning, too.

Debbie, the center's medical director, looked out at the sky, her hand over her eyes. There wasn't a pelican in sight. They'd been waiting to spot even a small flock of pelicans for the release. There usually was a group along this beach, but not today. Debbie lifted her hands up, shrugging and mystified, as a murmur of worry spread among the volunteers that they'd have to scrub the release today.

Then Heather heard a steady, rumbling sound from the sea, *put-put-put* . . . She turned toward it and clapped her hands. A shrimp boat was slowly passing by on its way to Mount Pleasant, its nets lowered as it dragged the bottom of the ocean. Circling the boat, calling raucously, were dozens of gulls and pelicans looking for a free meal.

"We're on!" Debbie called out with enthusiasm. "Let them go!"

The children began jumping up and down, openly embodying the same excitement all the adults felt rippling through them. The six men and women volunteers bent to open the crates. Heather held her breath and watched.

One by one the six brown pelicans emerged from the crates. A couple leaped forward, flapping their wings, eager to be free. Others peeked out, their long bills protruding from the crates before they ventured out. The adults had long, gorgeous chestnut-and-white necks topped with white heads and pale yellow crowns. The juveniles were not as handsome in their brown-gray plumage, but, God willing, they'd survive to grow into their adult colors. All six were out now, walking across the beach in their gangly, awkward gait, flapping their wings, looking skyward. The shrimp boat was puttering on, moving beyond their beach.

"Go on," Heather whispered, her eye on the adult she'd

rescued. He was extending his wings beautifully. But the real test would be his taking flight. "You can do this," she urged.

As she watched, her bird suddenly called out and flapped his six-foot wingspan, picking up the pace of his gait. His excitement triggered the other birds; they, too, began to flap and run. With a few more powerful flaps, her pelican was the first to take off into the sky. Three more followed, and they climbed skyward as a group, heading out over the ocean. Everyone on the beach was cheering, Heather included. The final two, both juveniles, stared after them seemingly in wonder and confusion. Heather's heart sank. Would they have to rescue them again? Overhead the four pelicans circled. Seeing them, something clicked in the juveniles' heads, and in a rush they, too, took to the sky to join the others.

Now that the beach was clear, everyone hurried across the sand to stand at the shore, cheering them on. The pelicans flew across the sea in pursuit of the other pelicans circling the shrimp boat. Soon they became one with the flock, indistinguishable in the mass of flying dark bodies with sinuous necks gliding above the boat.

They've found their new flock, Heather thought with relief and joy. She felt Bo's arm slide around her waist and he pulled her closer as they watched the birds soar in the sky. She looked and their eyes met. He smiled slowly, knowingly, and lowered his lips to hers. Heather looked up to see her father watching with one brow raised over a half smile. Beyond him, clustered at the shoreline were Cara, Emmi, and Flo, smiling and clapping and cheering at the success of the release.

Heather smiled and thought, *And so have I.*

A SMALL GROUP clustered at the back of the Coastal Ecotour boat as it slowly crawled along the coast of Capers Island. Cara, dressed in pure white, stood flanked by Bo and Robert. Dawn was rising over an indigo sea, her majestic rose-and-gold raiment spreading its colored light through the radiant clouds.

Dawn had always been Brett's favorite time of the day. Looking at it now, Cara understood why. Breaking the dark shroud of night, the light was like a voice that sang out to the world with hope. *No more sorrow and regret! Take heart! A new day is beginning.*

Cara took a shuddering breath and looked down at the box in her hand, a small, nondescript container that carried Brett's ashes. He wasn't in this box, not really. She knew that. He was in the sea and the sky and on the shores of Capers Island. He was in each sunrise and sunset. He was the wind that caressed her cheeks, the moonlight that shone overhead. He was every star that twinkled down at her, watching from high in the celestial sky.

Still, he would want his ashes released in this place where once they had fallen in love. Cara could come here on days in the future when she needed to call her memories closer.

Tears threatened, and she held them at bay. She would not cry. She would be strong for her friends. Brett would expect nothing less from her. Clearing her throat, she turned to the small group she'd invited to share this private moment. Her gaze swept over the faces of her inner circle. Her family of blood and bonds. Her brother, Palmer, stood like a rock for her, her only living blood relative. He had one arm around

Julia's waist and a hand on her nephew Cooper's shoulder. Her niece, Linnea, who had somehow blossomed into a young woman overnight, stood beside Julia. Flo, Emmi, and Heather clustered shoulder to shoulder, flowers in hand. Toy and Ethan Legare stood beside them. Their daughter, Little Lovie, had been especially close to Brett and, being young, she couldn't stem the tears that flowed down her cheeks. Cara smiled at her reassuringly.

It was time. She turned to the boat's captain. Robert had purchased the ecotour business, and she knew Brett would be proud of the way he'd firmly taken hold of the reins. In a strong, clear baritone, Robert read the excerpt from the poem "At Dawn," by Alfred Noyes. Cara stepped to the railing and, listening to the words, taking them to heart, she opened the box. The ashes caught the breeze and scattered, whirling, spiraling, released far out into the great sea.

> *Are not the forest fringes wet with tears?*
> *Is not the voice of all regret*
> *Breaking out of the dark earth's heart?*
> *She too, she too, has loved and lost; and though*
> *She turned last night in disdain*
> *Away from the sunset-embers,*
> *From her soul she can never depart;*
> *She can never depart from her pain.*
> *Vainly she strives to forget;*
> *Beautiful in her woe,*
> *She awakes in the dawn and remembers.*

SPRING HAD RETURNED to Isle of Palms. The birds were returning to the island in force, singing raucously outside her windows, claiming territory, attracting mates, building nests. Wildflowers bloomed over the dunes, and green burst forth in the shrubs and trees and in the base of cordgrass waving in the waterways. The song of new life sang around her.

Cara felt the surge of new beginnings in her heart as she walked through the beach house a final time. Dressed in her city clothes, she had shifted her mind-set from the relaxed, easygoing pace of the islands to the crisp focus she'd need to conquer the challenges ahead. She'd been offered and accepted the position of PR director for the Tennessee Aquarium. She was uniquely qualified for the position and eager to implement all the new ideas and initiatives swirling in her mind. She felt alive again, a heady, eager sensation that she identified as passion.

The beach house was cool and dim, lit only by the rays of light sneaking through the slats of the plantation shutters. The dark pine floors gleamed with polish. Every piece of furniture, every pillow on every chair sat neatly at the ready. Everything was in its place. Cara paused before the fireplace. Her personal photos were packed away, but over the mantel Heather's painting of the sandpipers seemed to capture the few rays of sunshine to glimmer. Cara smiled as she always did when looking at it. Heather's talent had managed to capture the amusing personality of the little speckled birds, their legs a frenzy of motion as they played tag with the surf. Heather had given the painting to Cara as a gift, knowing how much she loved it.

Almost on cue, Moutarde began chirping. Her pet must've sensed her pensive mood, she thought. She admitted to feeling unsure, even afraid of what lay ahead. She was leaving her home, her friends, the lifestyle she'd carved out for herself, to begin again in a new city. Chattanooga was far from the sea, located high in the mountains. What, she wondered, would her life be like away from the gentle roar of the surf, the far-reaching beaches, the feel of the hot sun on her face? What would the dawn look like rising over the peaks of mountains rather than the vast expanse of sea and sky?

The doorbell rang, followed by three sharp knocks. Cara shook off her doubts and with long strides went to the sunroom to collect the small bird travel carrier. She murmured words of reassurance to Moutarde as she hurried to the front door.

"Are you ready, Moutarde?" she crooned. "Remember the song of the sea and sing it for me. Every day. Won't you?"

She couldn't tarry or she'd miss her plane. Grabbing her purse, she opened wide the door and blinked in the blinding light of a powerful spring sun.

"We'd better get a move on," said Palmer. His face was flushed from the exertion of loading her luggage into the trunk of his Mercedes.

"Hold this, please." She handed Palmer the carrier, then turned to lock the door. She heard the click. The sound resonated and in that instant a thousand memories—all of them happy—surged through her mind. A breeze scented with jasmine whisked past. Cara breathed deep and placed her palm against the wood of the door.

"Good-bye, Mama," she whispered, knowing she was heard.

Cara turned and took the bird carrier back into her arms. She lifted the house keys in the air. "Take good care of it."

Palmer caught the keys neatly in his palm. He flipped them once in the air. "You sure you don't want me to sell it?" His eyes shone with amusement, but also hope.

Cara stepped back to take a final look at the beach house nestled in the dunes. Primroses bloomed across the dunes, the same pale yellow as the house. This charming cottage with the wide front porch carried all her hopes, dreams, and memories. It had been her home—her sanctuary for all of her life. It had been a healing place for her, for her mother, for Toy and Heather. And someday, this very special house might heal the heart of another woman who was buffeted by life's harsh winds. This little beach house that had once belonged to her mother now belonged to *her*.

"Not a chance," she said to Palmer.

Cara walked to the mailbox at the end of the drive. She pulled a few envelopes from her purse, a few final bills that had to be paid before she left. She paused. It still gave her a thrill whenever she saw Heather's stamps. They'd turned out so well; everyone remarked on how beautiful they were. She smiled and ran her finger over the stamp on the *Save the Date* return card for Heather and Bo's wedding. She wouldn't miss it for the world. She popped the letters in the mailbox, lifted the red metal flag, then walked without delay to the white Mercedes. She climbed onto the creamy leather seat and settled the bird carrier in her lap. Everything was done. She was on her way.

The sound of hammering caught her attention. Turning her head, she looked out the window and watched as Palmer finished putting the sign up in front of the house.

BEACH HOUSE
FOR RENT

Palmer climbed in beside her and boosted the air-conditioning.

"Ready?" he asked.

Cara nodded, her eyes still on the little yellow beach house. As he pulled away, she took one final, lingering look.

"I'll be seeing you," she whispered.

Acknowledgments

WITH EACH BOOK I am fortunate to work with brilliant people who share their knowledge willingly, even enthusiastically. We all believe shared information is shared power. For *Beach House for Rent* I want to especially thank Felicia Sanders of the South Carolina Department of Natural Resources, for an education on shorebirds, seabirds, and wading birds, as well as for sharing her passion for them. Also thanks to Al Segars and Sally Murphy for guidance over many years.

At the Avian Conservation Center in Awendaw, South Carolina, miracles happen every day. Heartfelt thanks to Debbie Mauney, Kori Cotteleer, and especially to my dear friend Mary Pringle, who took me along to rescue pelicans.

I'm indebted to Steve Baptiste and Linda Marshall, canary breeders extraordinaire. Thank you for an education on canaries, for my five canaries whose songs brighten my every day, and for your friendship. I share your passion for these joyful singers.

I am blessed to have an amazingly talented editor who stands shoulder to shoulder with me during the writing process. Lauren McKenna—there are not enough words to thank you. Thanks as well to Elana Cohen and my copy editor Joel Hetherington. I am also blessed to have a stellar team at Gallery Books. Heartfelt thanks to my fabulous publishers Jennifer Bergstrom and Louise Burke, to Liz Psaltis, Jennifer Long, Jean Anne Rose, Angela Januzzi, Diane Velasquez, and Lisa Litwack.

My home team makes every book and every day I work with them a joy. Thanks for being my best cheerleaders and brilliant backup: Angela May, Kathie Bennett, Susan Zurenda, Meg Walker, Abby Dunne, and Lisa Minnick.

I cannot thank enough two amazing nature photographers (and dear friends) who provided me with photographs of birds for my research and inspiration. To Barbara J. Bergwerf and Judy Drew Fairchild, whose photographs grace my book, and to Barb's magic at creating the "stamps" in the book. Thanks to Judy, as well, for providing me the chance to stay at the magical place called Dewees Island.

A special nod to Shane Zeigler at the Barrier Island Ecotour on Isle of Palms. My scenario with Brett's Coastal Ecotour is strictly fictional but the character's devotion to guiding visitors to the joys of the lowcountry is inspired by Shane. The Barrier Island Ecotour business is thriving and I highly recommend that you take a trip.

The character of Bo Stanton was inspired by my friend Bo Stallings of Isle of Palms. He's a true lowcountry gentleman and I couldn't have written the fishing scene without his guidance. Thank you, Bo!

The name for my character Heather came from the winning bid for a worthy horse rescue group, HERD, in Tryon,

North Carolina. A joyous thank-you to Cindy Boyle and to Katherine Bellisimo for their donation that spawned the naming of two characters! The character Heather and her story are completely fiction, yet Heather Freeman inspired my character's gentle grace, intelligence, and passion for animals.

I'm fortunate to have writing friends who help the ideas flow, read and critique the pages, and keep me going. Much love and thanks to Patti Callahan Henry, Gretta Kruesi, Leah Greenberg, and Linda Plunkett.

As always, my final words go to Markus. Truly, I could not have written this book without you.

Beach House
for Rent

Mary Alice
Monroe

*T*HIS READING GROUP *guide for* Beach House for Rent *includes an introduction, discussion questions, and ideas for enhancing your book club. The suggested questions are intended to help your reading group find new and interesting angles and topics for your discussion. We hope that these ideas will enrich your conversation and increase your enjoyment of the book.*

Beach House for Rent

Mary Alice Monroe

Introduction

Two women of different generations are bound together one summer by a very special beach house.

Since returning to Isle of Palms ten years ago, Cara Rutledge, 50, has settled into a quiet, slower-paced life with Brett, her husband. She finds comfort living close to the beloved home she inherited from her mother—the same home she rents out for the summer to 26-year-old Heather Wyatt.

Heather is an artist who travels to Isle of Palms to paint shorebirds commissioned by the US Postal Service. Since her mother's death years earlier, Heather's anxiety has kept her indoors at her father's home. But living alone on the island, going out to the beach every day in search of shorebirds, feeling the ocean waves at her feet, the sun on her face—and meeting a gentle young man working on the beach house—chip away at her fears and open her up to new possibilities.

As the summer progresses, these two women's paths suddenly collide, presenting challenges and opportunities that will change not only the course of their summer, but the rest of their lives.

Discussion Questions

1. In the first two chapters, we learn of Cara's young adulthood—particularly, of her troubled past with her family and her late-in-life reconciliation with her mother. Can you relate to Cara's experiences? Is it ever too late to reconcile with someone after years of absence?

2. Heather's anxiety makes her resistant to change. How do you react to changes that occur in your life? Do you understand Heather's trepidation to move to Isle of Palms for the summer? Is her father's insistence that Heather move out an example of tough love?

3. Turning fifty is a milestone that stirs up lots of emotions for Cara. She's searching for the passion that she feels is missing in her life—and which she sees in Heather. After years of putting aside her dreams, she doubts whether she can find it again. Discuss how her infertility struggles and working for Brett's business prevented her from exploring her own career interests. Is Cara experiencing a midlife

crisis? Has a milestone birthday or event ever made you re-assess your plans? How important is it to continue pursuing your passions amid the challenges of our daily lives?

4. Heather is very attached to her canaries. She says her mother's pet canary "saved her" after her mother passed (p. 71). Discuss how animals can offer stability and love to their owners in times of need. Do you have any pets that help you through changes in your life?

5. Heather claims she felt the presence of Cara's mother, Olivia Rutledge, on her first night at the beach house. Do you believe this could happen? What do you make of Cara's reaction? Is she jealous, as Brett suggested, or does her response run deeper?

6. Cara's connection to her mother is closely tied to her involvement with sea turtles. Discuss the impact of the pivotal scene on the beach when Cara witnesses the mother sea turtle come ashore.

7. "Her fear kept her as caged as her canaries. The glass windows were no different than their metal bars" (p. 128). Describe Heather's struggles with anxiety. How does it affect her? What steps does she take to overcome her fears? Do you suffer from anxiety or know someone who does? How do you, or they, handle it?

8. Mary Alice Monroe often writes about the disconnect many people feel with nature. Heather is cut off from na-

ture by her anxiety. Is this fear of going outdoors to experience nature or the wild common today? Discuss the metaphor of Heather's mental cage and whether you think many people are also trapped indoors or are shut-ins.

9. Primrose Cottage (the beach house) is beloved by both women, but for different reasons. What does the house symbolize to each of them? Do you have a place that represents something special to you, too? How does the beach house setting influence the course of events in the novel?

10. Trauma and grief are major themes in this novel. Consider Cara's and Heather's experiences with death. How did they each come to terms with their loss? Discuss the methods they use to help each other. Do they ever come to a place of healing?

11. Navigating a romantic relationship is anxious territory for Heather. How does her anxiety interfere with developing any relationship? Discuss how common the negative voices in our heads are when we feel vulnerable or faced with confrontation. Do you have a worry stone?

12. The novel is rich with descriptions of nature and its healing powers. Heather quickly becomes enchanted by the island's beauty after settling into her new beach rental: "Suddenly the path opened up, and she stood before the vast vista of sea and sky as dawn broke around her. Great shafts of rosy light spread across the gray sky.

The beach below, washed clean by the tide, shimmered in the pearly tints of the sunrise" (p. 134). How is nature a source of strength for Heather, or to other characters in the novel? Is there a particular scene or passage that stood out for you? Does nature play a role in your life?

13. Discuss the structure of the novel. Cara's and Heather's stories approached the themes of grief, anxiety, and passion from different viewpoints, allowing varying perspectives of age and experience. What parts of their past helped you better understand their present selves? Who did you relate to more?

14. Cara believes that when she moved back to Isle of Palms ten years ago to care for her mother "she could see that thinking of another person made her open up and heal herself" (p. 210). Acknowledging this, how can Cara heal herself once more? Is moving back to the beach house the best way to mend her grief? Do you think her plan is inconsiderate to Heather? What would you do if you were Cara? What do you make of the two women's resolution?

15. *Beach House for Rent* is set against the backdrop of shorebirds. Monroe introduces readers to different species and the threats they face. When you go to your favorite beach, how will this novel influence your appreciation as well as your actions? Discuss the birds in your area. How many species can you name? How can you help protect them?

Enhance Your Book Club

1. Incorporate art into your next book club meeting! If you live near an ocean or park, go with your book club members to paint or draw some of nature's treasures. You could also venture to a Paint and Sip class for a more organized (and instructional) group activity.

2. Visit Isle of Palms! The wonder and peaceful beauty of this southern beach destination comes to life through the pages of *Beach House for Rent*. Plan a summer vacation with your family or friends to explore the island's exquisite beaches and charming town.

3. Read *The Summer Girls*, the first book in Mary Alice Monroe's Lowcountry Summer series, for your next book club meeting. And to find more books by Mary Alice Monroe, visit http://maryalicemonroe.com/.

4. *Beach House for Rent* can be read alone, but it is also the fourth book in the Beach House series. To go back and

read more of the Rutledge family of Charleston read Mary Alice Monroe's *The Beach House*, *Beach House Memories*, and *Swimming Lessons*.

5. *Beach House for Rent* offers a glimpse into the life of someone struggling with social anxiety. What have you learned about social anxiety from reading the novel? Discuss with your book club. To learn more about anxiety, visit the Anxiety and Depression Association of America's website at https://www.adaa.org/.